THE
ANATOMY
of GHOSTS

THE
ANATOMY
of GHOSTS

ANDREW TAYLOR

HYPERION
· · · · ·
NEW YORK

Copyright © 2011 Lydmouth Ltd.

Library of Congress Cataloging-in-Publication Data has been applied for.

ISBN 978-1-4013-0287-0

Hyperion books are available for special promotions and premiums.
For details contact the HarperCollins Special Markets Department
in the New York office at 212-207-7528, fax 212-207-7222,
or e-mail spsales@harpercollins.com.

Book design by K. Minster

FIRST EDITION

10 9 8 7 6 5 4 3 2 1

SUSTAINABLE FORESTRY INITIATIVE   Certified Fiber Sourcing   www.sfiprogram.org

THIS LABEL APPLIES TO TEXT STOCK

We try to produce the most beautiful books possible, and we are also
extremely concerned about the impact of our manufacturing process
on the forests of the world and the environment as a whole. Accordingly,
we have made sure that all of the paper we use has been certified as
coming from forests that are managed to ensure the
protection of the people and wildlife dependent upon them.

In memory of Don

"It is wonderful that five thousand years have now
elapsed since the creation of the world, and still it is
undecided whether or not there has ever been an
instance of the spirit of any person appearing after death.
All argument is against it, but all belief is for it."

Dr. Johnson, 31 March 1778
(Boswell's LIFE OF JOHNSON)

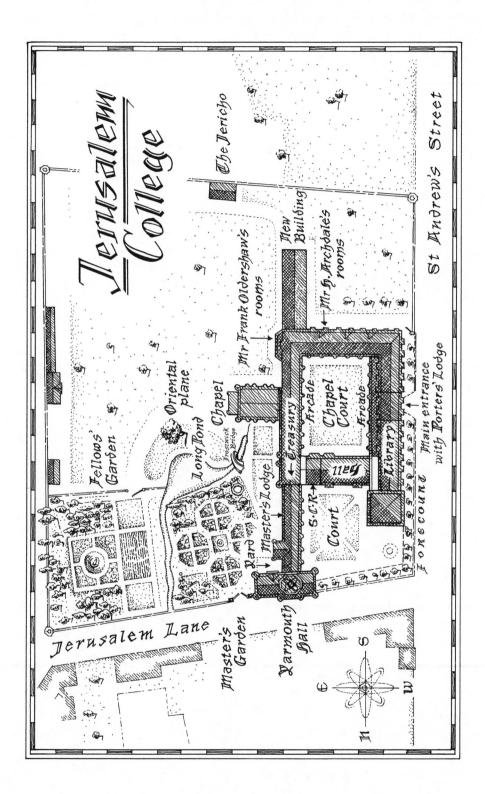

The Principal Persons Alive at the Commencement of the Narrative

AUGUSTUS, footboy to Mr. Whichcote

HARRY ARCHDALE, an undergraduate at Jerusalem College, Cambridge

BEN, servant to Dr. Carbury

THE REV. DR. CARBURY, Master of Jerusalem College, Cambridge

ELINOR CARBURY, his wife

LAWRENCE CROSS, steward to Lady Anne Oldershaw

DORCAS, maid to Mrs. Phear

ELIZABETH FARMER, wife of Ned Farmer

NED FARMER, a bookseller, of London

JOHN HOLDSWORTH, a bookseller, of London;
  the husband of Maria and the father of Georgie, both deceased

DR. JERMYN, a physician of Barnwell, near Cambridge

MEPAL, head porter at Jerusalem College, Cambridge

MULGRAVE, a species of servant, Cambridge

NORCROSS, a man in the employ of Dr. Jermyn

LADY ANNE OLDERSHAW, the widow of the Bishop of Rosington

FRANK OLDERSHAW, her son, an undergraduate at Jerusalem College, Cambridge

MRS. PHEAR, the widow of a clergyman, of Cambridge

THE REV. MR. RICHARDSON, fellow of Jerusalem College, Cambridge

TOBIAS SORESBY, a poor undergraduate of Jerusalem College, Cambridge

SUSAN, maidservant to Mrs. Carbury

TOM TURDMAN, properly known as John Floyd,
  a night-soil man of Cambridge

PHILIP WHICHCOTE, of Lambourne House, Cambridge

SYLVIA WHICHCOTE, his wife

Prologue

SHE WAS NOT ALONE. She would never be alone. And the key was in her hand.

Cambridge was a foreign city. The nocturnal miasma from the Fens oozed over the sleeping town. The streets lay under a fog of darkness so dense it was almost palpable to the fingertips. She had never been out at night without at least a servant to light her way, and never so late as this.

But I am not alone.

The ground underfoot was treacherous. Twice she tripped and nearly fell. If only she had proper shoes. As she crossed the bridge by Magdalene, she skidded on a patch of ice: her legs flew away from her and she sprawled, whimpering, on the stone pavement. Her cloak bunched around her shoulders. The cold seeped into her skin through the thin material of her gown.

But she still had the key. And she was not alone. In a moment, she was up and running.

There was neither moon nor stars. The few Corporation streetlamps were weak and fitful. Occasionally she crossed a wedge of brighter light thrown by a lantern over an archway or college entrance, and that was even worse, because she felt that all the world might see her as she fled.

She slowed to a walk as she passed the shuttered windows of a coffee house. A hand appeared from the shadows and snatched at her sleeve, tugging her towards the darkened entry. She slashed the key towards her attacker. It snagged on something soft and yielding. A squeal, and she was free.

She ran on. She had a stitch in her side. Her breath tore at her lungs, and blood raged in her ears.

At last there was Jerusalem Lane. She plunged across the roadway, stumbling in and out of a rut and then twisting her ankle on the edge of the gutter.

She stood by the gate, gasping for air. Her hand shook so much that she could not find the lock. She drew in a long, shuddering breath and tried again and then again. Metal whispered on metal as the key slid home. She twisted the key and the bolt scraped free of the jamb.

She pushed the gate. It swung away from her, into the garden.

THE
ANATOMY
of GHOSTS

I

LATE IN THE EVENING OF THURSDAY, 16 February 1786, the Last Supper was nearing its end. The new Apostle had taken the oaths, signed the membership book and swallowed the contents of the sacred glass presented by the late Morton Frostwick, to the accompaniment of whoops, cheers and catcalls. Now it was time for the toasts that preceded the grand climax of the ceremony.

"No heeltaps, gentlemen," Jesus commanded from the head of the table. "All rise. I give you His Majesty the King."

The Apostles shuffled to their feet, many with difficulty. Four chairs fell over and someone knocked a bottle off the table.

Jesus raised his glass. "The King, God bless him."

"The King, God bless him," bellowed a chorus of voices in return, for the Apostles prided themselves on their patriotism and their attachment to the throne. Each man drained his glass in one. "God bless him!" repeated St. Matthew at the far end of table, and his passionate exhortation ended in a hiccup.

Jesus and the Apostles sat down and the buzz of conversation resumed. The tall, long room was brightly lit with candles. A shifting pall of smoke hung above the table. A great fire blazed in the hearth beneath the marble chimneypiece. The curtains were drawn. The mirrors between the windows caught the flames, the sparkle of silver and crystal, and the glitter of the buttons on the gentlemen's coats. All the Apostles wore the same livery—a bright green coat lined with buck silk and adorned with prominent gilt buttons down the front and on the cuffs.

"How long do I wait?" said the young man at the right hand of Jesus.

"Be patient, Frank. All in good time." Jesus raised his voice. "Recharge your glasses, gentlemen."

He poured wine into his neighbor's glass and his own. He watched the other men obeying him like sheep.

"One more toast," he murmured in Frank's ear. "Then we have the ceremony. And then the sacrifice."

"Pray tell me," Frank said, resting his elbow on the table and turning towards Jesus. "Does Mrs. Whichcote know I am to be sanctified tonight?"

"Why do you ask?"

Frank's face had grown very red. "I—I merely wondered. Since I am to spend the night here, I thought perhaps she must know."

"She does not," Jesus said. "She knows nothing. And you must tell her nothing. This is men's business."

"Yes, of course. I should not have asked." Frank's elbow slipped and he would have toppled from his chair if Jesus had not steadied him. "A thousand apologies. But you're a lucky dog, you know, she's so very lovely—oh damnation, pray do not take it amiss, Philip, I should not have said that."

"I was not listening." Jesus stood up, ignoring Frank's desire to continue apologizing. "Gentlemen, it is time for another toast. All rise. I give you damnation to the Great Whore of Babylon, his foulness of Rome, Pius VI, and may he rot in hell for all eternity along with his fellow Papists."

The Apostles drained their glasses and burst into applause. The toast was traditional, and dated back to the earliest days of the Holy Ghost Club. Jesus had no personal animosity towards Papists. In fact his own mother had been raised in the Roman Catholic Church, though she had laid aside her religion at the time of her marriage and adopted her husband's, as a good wife should.

He waited until the clapping and cheering had subsided. "Be seated, gentlemen."

Chairs scraped on polished boards. St. James sat down but caught only the edge of his chair, which sent him sprawling on the floor. St. John rushed behind the screen at the far end of the room and could be heard being violently sick. St. Thomas turned aside from the company, unbuttoned and urinated into one of the commodes placed conveniently nearby.

There was a faint tapping on the door behind Jesus's chair. Only Jesus heard it. He stood up and opened the door a few inches. The footboy was outside, candle in hand, and his eyes large with fear.

"What?" Jesus demanded.

"If it please your honor, the lady below would be obliged if she might have a private word."

Jesus shut the door in the boy's face. Smiling, he sauntered back to the table and rested his arm along the back of St. Peter's chair on the left of his own. He bent down and spoke into St. Peter's ear. "I shall be back directly—I must make sure that all is ready. Let them toast their inamoratas if they grow impatient."

"Is it time?" Frank said. "Is it time?"

"Nearly," Jesus said. "Believe me, it will be worth the wait."

He straightened up. St. Andrew asked Frank a question about the merits of water spaniels as gundogs, a temporary but effective distraction. Jesus left the room, closing the mahogany door behind him. The air was at once much cooler. He was on a square landing lit by two candles burning on a bracket next to a small uncurtained window. For a moment he put his head close to the glass and rubbed a circle in the condensation. It was too dark to make out much, but at the far end of the garden a lamp glimmered above the side door of Lambourne House.

He walked quickly downstairs. The pavilion stood at the bottom of the garden. Its plan was straightforward—the great room above filled the whole of the first floor; the stairs at one end linked it to a lobby on the ground floor, where there were two doors. One door led outside to the garden, the other to a narrow hall running the length of the building and giving access to the covered terrace beside the river and to several small rooms. The footboy, who had the absurd name of Augustus, was sitting on a bench in the lobby. He sprang to his feet and bowed. At a nod from Jesus, he opened the door to the hall. Jesus passed him without a word and closed the door in his face.

Candles in pairs burned on brackets along the walls, creating globes of light in the gloom. Jesus tapped on the second door along, and it opened from within.

Mrs. Phear drew him inside. She stood on tiptoe and murmured in his ear, "The little weakling has failed us."

The chamber was small and painted white like a cell. But it was snug enough because a coal fire glowed in the grate, the curtains were drawn and the shutters closed. The room was furnished simply with a little bed hung with white curtains, a table and two chairs. On the table stood a bottle of wine, another of cordial, two glasses and a bowl of nuts. On the mantelshelf was a candle, which provided the only light in the room apart from the fire.

"Failed?" Jesus said.

"Look for yourself." Mrs. Phear wore a nun's habit with a black wimple that framed and obscured her face. "Take the light."

Jesus picked up the candle and went to the bed. The curtains were tied back. A girl lay on her back with her fair hair lying loose on the pillow. White cords attached her wrists and ankles to the four bedposts. She was dressed in a white nightgown with a loose neck. She must have been beautiful in life, he thought, the sort of girl you felt you could crush into a million fragments if you squeezed her hard enough.

He bent closer. She was young—perhaps thirteen or fourteen. Her skin was naturally very pale but her cheeks were red, almost purple. Her eyes were open and her lips widely parted. He held the candle nearer. There was froth on the lips, and a trickle of vomit at the corner of her mouth. Her eyes protruded from their sockets.

"God damn it."

"It is such a waste," Mrs. Phear said. "And I believe she was really a virgin, too."

"The little bitch. Was ever anything so unlucky? What happened?"

The woman shrugged. "I made her ready for him. I went up to the house for more candles, and she asked me to put a nut or two in her mouth before I went. And when I came back she was as you see her. She's still warm."

Jesus straightened up, though his eyes lingered on the girl's face. "It's as if someone smothered her." He looked quickly around the room.

"I locked the door behind me," Mrs. Phear said in a flat voice. "She choked on a nut, that's all. The footboy was in the lobby all the time and saw no one. Is he trustworthy?"

"He's nothing but a child. He heard nothing?"

"The walls are thick."

Candle in hand, Jesus moved about the room. Mrs. Phear waited, with hands folded and eyes cast down.

He pointed at the ceiling, to the great room above. "I cannot afford to disappoint Frank Oldershaw. Not him of all people."

"I suppose he would not take the girl like that?"

"What? Dead?" He stared at Mrs. Phear.

"I told you, she's still warm."

"Of course he would not."

"But would he notice?"

"Dear God, ma'am, yes—I think he would. He's not so far gone. Besides, that's where the sport of it is for them, the struggle. Believe me, that's what they brag about afterwards in their cups. That and the blood on the sheet."

"Are you sure it cannot be contrived?"

Jesus shook his head. "Not the struggle. And not with her face like that. I tell you, it would not answer."

Mrs. Phear kneaded the hem of her cloak. "So do you tell him he must wait?"

"He's mad for it, ma'am. He's not used to being crossed. We cannot cool his ardor with a Barnwell drab even if we could lay our hands on one at this time. When can you find me another such as this?"

"In a month or so, perhaps. Even then it would not be easy. Not so soon after this."

Jesus said, "He's worth more than the others put together. But I cannot tell him she's dead. I must say that she was terrified at the prospect before her, and stole away in the night."

"There's another difficulty," Mrs. Phear said. "What do we do with—with that?"

Jesus turned and looked back at the white body on the white bed. Suddenly time accelerated. Event stumbled after event in a disorderly rush. He heard a raised voice outside and footsteps. The door handle turned. He tried to reach the door, to hold it shut, but the bed and the dead girl were in his way. Mrs. Phear whirled towards the sound with surprising speed but her skirt snagged on the corner of the table and the door was already opening before she had freed herself.

Frank Oldershaw was swaying on the threshold. His face was red and his waistcoat was unbuttoned. "Ah, there you are, Philip," he said. "I am on fire, I tell you, I cannot wait another moment." He caught sight of Mrs. Phear and her unexpected presence made him falter. But he was too drunk to stop altogether and the last few words tumbled from his mouth in a dying whisper. "And where have you hidden my sweet little virgin?"

This body was found in Jerusalem on the morning of Friday, 17 February. The sun had not quite risen. The college gardens were filled with a gray half-light, which made it possible to distinguish the broad outlines of things, but not their details. It was very quiet.

The man who discovered the corpse was called John Floyd. But he was known to everybody—sometimes even to his wife—as Tom Turdman. He was as brown as his name, and a finder of unwanted trifles, discarded memories and excreted secrets.

Jerusalem occupied eight or nine acres of ground. The college was surrounded on three sides by a high brick wall upon a medieval base of rubble and dressed stone, and on the fourth side by the principal buildings. The walls were topped with rows of spikes. Behind the chapel, the Long Pond stretched in a curve towards the southeast. It was fed by a stream that the friars had culverted under the walls long ago, before Jerusalem was even thought of. On the far side of the pond were the Fellows' Garden and the Master's Garden. Most of the town lay some way off on the other side of the irregular huddle of college buildings.

The only sounds were the clack of Tom's overshoes, wooden pattens, and the trundling of the iron-rimmed wheels of his barrow on the flagged path. He visited four colleges: Sidney Sussex, Christ's, Jerusalem and Emmanuel. He preferred to work in winter because he was paid by volume, not by the hour, and the smell obliged him to visit more frequently in the summer. He worked for a retired corn chandler whom the undergraduates called the merchant of shit. His employer derived a modest income from selling scholarly manure to farmers and gardeners.

This morning Tom was now so cold that he could hardly feel his hands. He had just emptied the Master's privy, never a pleasant task, and wheeled his barrow along the flagged path at the back of the Master's Lodge, which was unexpectedly productive. The path led to a gate, which the head porter, Mr. Mepal, had just unlocked for him, and then over the Long Pond by way of an intricately constructed wooden bridge. The barrow wheels rumbled like muffled thunder on the wooden planks. He turned left towards the little boghouse the bedmakers used, which was modestly tucked away on the far side of the college gardens.

The path ran close to the pond in the shadow of a great tree. In the greater gloom under the branches, Tom slipped on a patch of ice. He fell, measuring his length on the stones. The barrow toppled on to the frosty grass and discharged at least half of its stinking cargo on the bank. The shovel, which had been balanced on top, slithered into the water.

Panting with cold, he righted the trolley. He would have to clear as much as he could of the filth, and hope against hope that rain would wash the rest away before anyone noticed it. But the shovel was somewhere in the pond, and he could do nothing without it. Surely the water near the bank could not be very deep? He took off his brown coat and rolled the sleeves of his shirt above his thin, pointed elbows. He was about to plunge his hand into the water when he saw a large, dark object floating among the shards of thin ice a yard or two from the bank.

At first he thought a sheet or a shirt had fallen into the pond, for the east wind had blown strongly during the last few days, often coming in savage gusts. The following instant he thought of a more interesting idea—namely, that the floating thing was a cloak or gown discarded by a reveller during some drunken prank the previous evening. He had retrieved caps and gowns from cesspits on several occasions and either restored them to their owners or sold them to a dealer in secondhand academic dress.

Tom Turdman thrust his right arm into the freezing water. He whimpered as the cold hit him. To his relief, his fingers closed around the shaft of the shovel. All this time his mind was partly distracted by the risk of Mepal's vengeful anger if he discovered what had happened, a risk that grew with every minute's delay.

The sky was becoming paler. But the goddamned tree blocked so much of the light. He straightened up and stared at the thing in the water. If it was a cloak or gown, it held the possibility of substantial profit.

He held the shovel in his other hand and leaned low over the pond. He stretched his arm towards the thing that lay just beneath the swaying surface. Water seeped over the lip of one of the pattens and trickled into the cracked shoe beneath. He tried to hook the shadow with the shovel, but it danced away. He leaned out a little farther. The patten slipped in the mud.

With a shriek, Tom Turdman fell forward. The cold hit him like an iron bar. He opened his mouth to scream and swallowed pond water. His feet flailed, seeking the bottom. Weeds curled around his ankles. He could not breathe. He flung out his arms. He was now desperate to keep afloat, desperate to find a handhold. As he began to sink again, the fingers of his right hand closed around a bundle of rotting twigs, each of them with something unyielding at its core. At the same moment his feet sank into mud, and the mud seemed to receive him in its embrace and draw him deeper and deeper into it.

He did not know that he was screaming. By that time, Tom Turdman was beyond thinking, almost beyond feeling. But long before he discovered what he was holding, he knew that there was nothing living in whatever curled around his fingers. He knew that what he touched was dead.

2

ANOTHER TOWN, and another stretch of water.
What John Holdsworth remembered most about the
house by the Thames was the light. Pale and shimmering, it filled
the rooms overlooking the river throughout the day. It was a fifth
element poised somewhere between air, water and pale fire.

Georgie used to say it was ghost water, not light at all, and sometimes he believed he saw apparitions swaying and flickering on the
walls. Once he roused the household with his screams, crying that
a drowned lighterman from nearby Goat Stairs had come to drag
him down to the bottom of the river. Later Holdsworth thought the
drowned man had been a portent of what was to come, a prelude of
sorts, for drowning ran like a watery thread through the whole sad
affair.

In November 1785, Georgie slipped on a patch of ice when he was
playing by Goat Stairs. As he struggled to right himself, he tripped
over a rope attached to a bollard. Maria, his mother, saw the whole
thing happen, saw the boy tumbling off the wharf. One moment he
was there, a vigorous, shrieking little boy. The next moment he was
gone.

The tide was high and he fell into the water, striking his head
against the side of a coal barge. It was possible that it was the blow
to the head that killed him. But the weather was rough that day.
The heavily laden barge was rocking and heaving against the side

of the wharf, and it was at least ten minutes before they got him out of the water. So it was not easy to say precisely how he died. His body had been ground between wharf and barge. It had sustained terrible injuries. But just possibly Georgie might have drowned before that. There was no way of knowing for sure.

Holdsworth preferred to think that his son had died at once, that the fall itself had killed him, perhaps with one of the blows to the head. He knew nothing of what had happened until it was over, until they came to fetch him from the shop in Leadenhall Street. He felt a guilty and intolerable gratitude that he had at least been spared the sight of his son falling to his death.

After that, nothing went right. How could it? Maria was unreachable in her grief. She refused to put up a headstone, saying that it would not be right, for Georgie could not be wholly dead. She spent most of her time praying in the house or beside the little mound in the burial ground. She gave what money she had to a woman who claimed to be able to see ghosts. The woman said she saw Georgie, that she talked to him, that he was happy and that he sent his love to his mama. She said that Georgie was now playing with lambs and with other children in a great green sunlit meadow, and the air was filled with the music of the heavenly choir.

Item by item, Maria sold her rings, most of her dresses and the better pieces of furniture. She fed the woman with more money. In return the woman told her over and over again that Georgie thought of his mama all the time, and sent her caresses and fond words, and that soon they would be together and God would never let them be parted again.

Sometimes Holdsworth did not know whether he was grieving for Georgie or angry with Maria. The two emotions were fused. He would have been within his rights to forbid his wife to see the woman, and to beat her if she disobeyed him. He had not the heart for it. He felt guilty enough already, for he had failed to save his son. Maria told him that Georgie had sent his love to Papa and said they would soon be together with the angels in God's heaven. Holdsworth swore at her, and she did not tell him anything else.

Holdsworth poured his anger into writing a little book that examined stories of ghosts, past and present, drawn from modern and classical authors. It was better than hitting Maria. He began with the story of Georgie's ghost, anonymously of course, and described how Georgie's mother believed it because she needed to, and how a wicked woman had taken cruel advantage of her credulity and her grief. His theme was that stories of the dead revisiting the living could not be taken at face value. Some of them, he wrote, were nothing more than childish superstitions that only children and uneducated women were likely to credit. Others were misunderstandings and delusions, perpetrated in good faith, but now increasingly explicable as natural science revealed more and more of the truth about God's universe. He conceded that some ghost stories had a useful moral or religious effect on the minds of children, savages or the great mass of uneducated common people; and to this extent, they had a limited value as parables. But they could not be considered as evidence of divine or even demonic intervention. He had never come across a ghost story, he concluded, that could be considered as evidence of a scientific phenomenon deserving the serious consideration of men of education.

He called the book *The Anatomy of Ghosts* and had it printed at the small printing works he owned in Maid Lane on the Surrey side of the river. He advertised it in the newspapers and sold it from the shop in Leadenhall Street. It caused a small stir. An anonymous reviewer in the *Gentleman's Magazine* accused him of being the next best thing to an atheist. Two dissenting ministers denounced the work as blasphemous. The vicar of St. Ethelburga's in Bishopsgate preached a violently hostile sermon, excerpts from which were published in the *Daily Universal Register*, and therefore discussed in thousands of private parlors and public places up and down the country. As a result, sales were respectable, which was just as well because, after Georgie died, little else made a profit.

The shop sold old and new books, pamphlets, materials for writing, and a range of patent medicines. Unfortunately, two months before Georgie's death, Holdsworth had taken out two substantial loans, one to extend the premises and the other to buy the library of a private collector whose heirs had no use for reading. Holdsworth was rarely at the shop after Georgie's death. A careless assistant stored the newly acquired collection in the cellar, where a damp winter ruined two-thirds of them. Meanwhile, the manager of the printing works fell ill and left; Holdsworth let his deputy take over the enterprise, but the man proved a rogue and a drunk, who took what he could from the business. One night the deputy's carelessness proved even more damaging than his criminality: he left an unguarded candle burning when he went home and the entire works, along with its contents, were gutted by the morning. In the fire, Holdsworth also lost the stock he had transferred from Leadenhall Street, including almost all the surviving copies of *The Anatomy of Ghosts*.

Maria seemed unconcerned by these disasters. Apart from her trips to chapel, she stayed at home in the house on Bankside near Goat Stairs. She spent most of her waking life either on her knees or closeted with the woman who could talk to ghosts, and who brought the consoling messages from Georgie.

In March, Holdsworth managed to penetrate her absorption at last, though not for a reason he would have wished. Their lease was due to run out on Midsummer Day, and he was compelled to tell her that they would not be able to renew it, even for another quarter. He was not bankrupt, he said, but he was perilously close to it. They would have to move away from the house near Goat Stairs.

"I cannot remove from here," Maria told him.

"I regret the necessity, but we have no choice."

"But, sir, I cannot leave Georgie."

"My love, he is not in this house any longer."

She shook her head violently. "But he is. His earthly presence lingers where he was born, where he lived. His soul looks down from heaven on us. If we are not here, he cannot find us."

"Pray do not upset yourself. We shall carry him with us, in our hearts."

"No, Mr. Holdsworth." She folded her hands on her lap. She was a small, calm woman, very neat and self-contained. "I must stay with my son."

Holdsworth took her hands in his, where they lay cold and unresponsive. She would not look at him. He did not care that the printing works were gone, and what was left of the Leadenhall business would go under the auctioneer's hammer in a week's time, and that there might not even be enough to pay their debts. But he did care that his wife had become a beloved stranger to him.

"Maria, we still have some weeks to grow used to this. We shall talk it over, we shall decide when and how we shall come back here, if that is what you wish. Why, we may walk past the house any time we choose, if not come inside it. By and by, we shall become quite accustomed to the idea."

"Georgie sends his bestest love to Papa," said Maria, lisping like a child. "He says Mama and Papa mustn't leave his dearest home."

A sound like rushing water filled Holdsworth's ears. He hit his wife, and his blow sent her cowering into a corner of the parlor. He broke a chair and put his fist through the window that overlooked the river.

He had never hit Maria before and he never hit her again. Afterwards he stood in the parlor, with the blood running down his hand where her teeth had broken the skin over the knuckles. He wept for the first time since he was a child. Maria stared up at him from the floor, her eyes full of pain and wonder. She touched the side of her head and stared at the blood on her hand. There was blood on her lips too. Blood spotted the bare boards. Who would have thought that one blow could do so much damage?

He picked his wife up and kissed her and cuddled her and told her that of course all three of them would soon be together again in heaven. But it was too late.

That night they went to bed early. To his relief, Holdsworth slept deeply. Sleep was the one refuge that remained to him, and when he stumbled on it, he embraced it greedily. In the morning he awoke to the sound of hammering on the door of the house. Maria was no longer by his side in the bed where Georgie had been both conceived and born. She had gone to the water by Goat Stairs.

It is strange how soon a life can collapse if the foundations are removed. In the moment of that abrupt awakening, it seemed to Holdsworth that he had lost everything of substance about himself. He still moved through a solid world in three dimensions, a world existing in time and populated with flesh-and-blood people; but he was no longer constructed from the same materials as they were. It was as if his body had passed through a chemical process that had altered its composition. He had become as formless as the fog over the river.

Unlike Georgie's, Maria's body was unmarked, apart from a split lip and a wound, little more than a graze, on the left temple. The wound was the color of a damson and about the size of a penny piece. She was fully dressed.

At the inquest it was established by Holdsworth and two of his neighbors that Maria often took the air early in the morning, and that she was in the habit of walking to and fro along Bankside, often lingering in the neighborhood of Goat Stairs where her son had died in the unfortunate accident the previous November. Much was made of the fact it had been very misty. Two watermen who had been about at the time said that you could barely see a few yards in front of you, let alone the dome of St. Paul's across the water. Then there was the condition of the stairs themselves, which were worn and much marked with green slime, and therefore slippery. The coroner, a humane man, had no hesitation in bringing in a verdict of death by misadventure in the absence of evidence to the contrary.

A few days later, Holdsworth watched his wife being lowered into the earth of the burial ground. They laid her in the same grave as her son. Holdsworth averted his eyes in case he should glimpse Georgie's little coffin.

At the funeral, Ned Farmer stood at Holdsworth's side, and Mrs. Farmer was among the little crowd of mourners that clustered behind them. When they were young, Holdsworth and Farmer had been apprentices together. Farmer had been a big, bumbling, good-natured boy, and now he was a big, bumbling, good-natured man. The one astute decision in his life had been to marry the daughter of a wealthy printer in Bristol, though that decision had not been made by him but by the lady in question. Now her father was dead, and she his sole heiress, she thought it time for them to move to London and strike out there, for the capital was where fortunes were to be made in the printing and bookselling trade. She persuaded Ned to make an offer for what was left of the business that Holdsworth had built up over the years. It was not a generous offer but it was at least a certain one, whereas proceeding with the plan of auctioning everything carried a strong element of risk. Moreover, Ned said they would take over the lease on the house on Bankside too.

"Betsy has taken a fancy to it, for the sake of the river and the convenience of it," he explained. "And she refuses to live over the shop. But I beg your pardon, John, the subject must be painful."

"It's not the river pains me," Holdsworth said. "Or the house."

"No, of course not. But tell me—do you know where you shall live?"

"I have not considered it yet."

"Then, if it would not distress you, you must live with us until you find your feet."

"You are very good. But perhaps Mrs. Farmer . . . ?"

"Pooh, Betsy will do as I bid her," Farmer said. Optimism was another quality that had survived intact from Ned's boyhood. "Consider it settled."

Remaining in the house by the river, staying with the Farmers, was not a desirable arrangement. But it was a convenient one and avoided the need to make yet another decision.

Holdsworth knew that it would not answer for very long. In the old days, Maria used to say that he slept like the dead. But on his first night in the house at Bankside as the Farmers' guest, he did not sleep like the dead, he dreamed of them instead.

He dreamed that, when they were burying Maria, he had seen Georgie's tiny coffin at the bottom of the open grave. The lid was ajar and the wood was splintered, as if someone had tried to get in or out. The clergyman would not stop talking. A black tide rose out of the coffin. It came in waves, ebbing and flowing with the sound of the clergyman's prayer, sucking back on itself only to surge ahead even farther.

Holdsworth woke but the tide continued to rise, crawling up his legs like treacle. Higher and higher it climbed, soaking his nightshirt. A hammer pounded his chest. He could not breathe and the pain was so savage he could not even scream.

Soon the black tide would reach his mouth. Then his nostrils. Then he would drown.

3

ON THE MORNING OF TUESDAY, 23 May 1786, John Holdsworth woke before it was light. He listened to the creaking of the timbers, the sighing of the winds in the casement, and the snuffling snores of the servant on the other side of the partition. He watched the first cracks of light appear between the shutters and gradually grow stronger. Shortly after dawn, he dressed, went downstairs in his stockinged feet, and slipped out of the house before even the maid was up. He had heard the Farmers quarrelling about his presence in the house the previous evening. He knew that Mrs. Farmer had the stronger will, and it was only a matter of time before her side of the argument prevailed.

It was a fine morning: the great dome of St. Paul's shone white across the water, its outline sharp against the blue sky, and a drift of clouds like a convoy of sails lined the eastern horizon. The river itself was already crowded with wherries and barges. The tide was low, and the scavengers were out on both banks. The gulls wheeled and shrieked and snapped among them. The day was clearer than usual and the smoke that struggled up from innumerable chimneys might have been drawn with ink.

He walked beside the Thames to London Bridge. Only poor people seemed to be about at this hour. Poverty, he told himself as he made his way across the river, was a state that favored useful instruction in the follies and weaknesses of human nature. He had never really noticed the poor in the days of his prosperity, except as irritants like lice or, at best, as bystanders in the great drama of existence in which their betters performed the speaking parts. He murmured these words aloud and a man who was passing gave him a wide berth. The only knowledge worth having was that a hungry belly made you a little mad.

At Leadenhall Street, one of the apprentices was already taking down the shutters. Holdsworth kept his barrow and what was left of his stock in a small brick outhouse in the yard at the back. In the old days a binder had worked there, but Ned Farmer subcontracted that part of the work because Mrs. Farmer believed, probably correctly, that it would be more profitable to do so.

Holdsworth uncovered the barrow and wheeled it slowly down the alley from the yard. He set off down Leadenhall Street. On some days he wandered as far west as Piccadilly. He never stayed long in one place. The multitude of streets was one great emporium, and every itinerant vendor was jealous of the territory he occupied. The books on his barrow were on the whole of little value, the dross left over from the sale. Still, they made it possible to earn something rather than nothing; they kept him from absolute penury and complete dependence on the kindness of Ned Farmer.

That day he ate a meager dinner of bread, cheese and ale in a mean little tavern on Compton Street. Afterwards he made his way by degrees back to the City. On the corner of Leadenhall Street, a man selling singing birds was packing up for the day. Holdsworth set down the barrow. The pitch was convenient for the shop and he used it whenever he could.

The afternoon was fine, which was good for trade. It was not long before Holdsworth had three or four men turning over the stock. The majority of the books were sermons and other devotional works, but there was poetry also, some bound numbers of the *Rambler* and assorted editions of the classical authors, their value considerably diminished by damp stains or smoke damage. One of the browsers was a hunched little man in a snuff-colored coat. His complexion was dark and leathery, almost a match for the binding of the book he was examining, a folio of Horace's *Odes*. Holdsworth watched him, though without appearing to do so. The man looked respectable—an apothecary perhaps; something in the professional way—but then so had the fellow the previous week, a man he had taken for a clergyman up from the country, who had slipped a duodecimo Longinus into his pocket while Holdsworth's attention had been distracted by another customer.

The little man scratched his neck with his right hand, the fingers slipping like hungry little creatures under the unseasonably thick scarf he wore. His eyes met Holdsworth's. His hand withdrew. He gave a little bobbing bow and edged a little closer.

"Have I the honor of addressing Mr. Holdsworth?" he said in a hoarse voice, little more than a whisper.

"Yes, sir. You have." It happened not infrequently that a customer from the old days would recognize Holdsworth in his changed situation and would seek to pass the time of day, out of curiosity, perhaps, or pity. He did not discourage them, for sometimes they would buy a book and he could no longer afford to be proud.

"I hoped as much," the man said.

There was a lull in the exchange while a youth with sad eyes purchased Law's *Serious Call*. The little man stood to one side, while the transaction was in progress, turning the pages of the Horace. When the customer had departed, he looked up from the book.

"I called in at Mr. Farmer's." He cleared his throat, wincing as if the exercise was painful to him. "If that is not an indelicate way to refer to it."

"You speak no more than the truth, sir. The establishment belongs to him."

"Indeed. Ah—at any event, he said I might find you here."

"And how may I serve you, sir? Are you looking for a particular book?"

"No, Mr. Holdsworth. I am not looking for a book. I am looking for you."

"Well, sir, you have found me. And what do you want with me?"

"I beg your pardon. I have not introduced myself. My name is Cross, sir, Lawrence Cross."

They bowed to each other across the barrow of books. The other browsers had now drifted away.

"I wish to put a proposition to you."

"By all means."

"It is not a subject that can be discussed in the street. When will you be at leisure?"

Holdsworth glanced at the sun. "Perhaps another half an hour. Then I need only enough time to wheel my barrow to Mr. Farmer's."

Mr. Cross rubbed his neck again. "That would answer very well. Would you be so kind as to favor me with your company at St. Paul's Coffee House? In forty minutes' time, shall we say?"

Holdsworth agreed, and the little man walked swiftly away.

Twenty minutes later, Holdsworth wheeled the barrow down the street and laid it up for the night in the yard behind the shop. He had hoped to leave unnoticed but Ned Farmer bustled out of the shop and laid his hand on his arm.

"John, that's damned uncivil, sneaking away without a word." He clapped Holdsworth on the shoulder. "Where were you this morning? You must have slipped out of the house at cockcrow."

"I rose early. I could not sleep."

"Yes, but now."

Holdsworth explained that he had an appointment. He could not give his other reason, that he found Ned's cheerful conversation almost as trying as his unfailing kindness. Away from the house, away from Mrs. Farmer, he showed it without restraint, which Holdsworth found harder to bear than he would have imagined possible.

"There was a man asking if I knew your direction," Ned rushed on, for he was not insensitive. "Wizened little fellow like a brown monkey with a bad cold. I said he might find you on the corner." A frown passed over his broad red face. "I hope I did not act amiss."

"Not at all."

"So he found you? And?"

"I am meeting him later. That's my appointment."

"I told you! A man of your reputation must attract offers from every quarter. It is only a matter of time, John. Sit tight, and all will come right again." Ned flushed a deeper red. "Damn my tongue, always running away with me. I ask your pardon. I meant merely in terms of money, of course."

Holdsworth smiled at him. "I don't know what he wants yet."

"Perhaps he wishes to buy books," Ned suggested. "And he needs you to advise him."

"He did not look like a man who has much to spare on luxuries."

"Pooh," Ned bellowed. "Books are not luxuries. They are meat and drink for the mind."

Though Holdsworth was before his time, Mr. Cross was already at the coffee house, seated at one of the small tables by the door.

"I have ordered sherry," he murmured. "I trust that will be agreeable?"

Holdsworth sat down. Mr. Cross showed no inclination to rush into the business that had brought him here.

"You are a tall man," he observed. "And broad with it, are you not? I marked you in the crowd when you were some distance away. I thought you would be older but you are still quite a young man."

"But not inexperienced, sir."

"I do not doubt it."

While they waited for the sherry, Cross talked doggedly about the warmth of the weather, the crowdedness of the streets, and the intolerable stench from the river. The waiter came soon enough, and Holdsworth was pleased to see that the man had brought biscuits as well. The first mouthful of wine seemed simultaneously to glide down in a warm flow to his stomach and to move up in an equally warm vapor to his brain.

Mr. Cross set down his glass and drew out a snuffbox made of horn. He tapped the lid but did not open it.

"It cannot be easy for you."

"I beg your pardon, sir?"

"No, the shoe is upon the other foot. Pray forgive me if I seem impertinent but I was watching you this afternoon. You bear your misfortunes with great patience."

Holdsworth inclined his head, thinking that the man presumed much on so slight an acquaintance.

Mr. Cross took a pinch of snuff, closed his eyes and sniffed. A few seconds later, he sneezed with such an explosion of sound that the conversations around them faltered. He took out a stained handkerchief, wiped his streaming eyes and blew his nose. "Pray believe me, sir, I did not mean to offend. Tell me, have you sufficient leisure at present to accept a commission?"

"That would depend upon its nature."

"You have a considerable reputation as a bibliopole. They say you are a man who knows the value of a book."

Holdsworth remained silent.

"You catalogued the Mitchell library, for example," Mr. Cross went on, "and handled its sale. I understand Sir William was most gratified by the outcome. And then of course Archdeacon Carter's collection."

Holdsworth nodded. Cross had done his research. His arrangement with Sir William Mitchell had not been public knowledge.

The older man loosened the scarf around his neck. "So it would be no more than simple truth to assert that cataloguing and valuing such libraries is a task well within your competence?"

"Of course."

"And are you also able to advise on the care and maintenance of valuable books?"

"Naturally. Both printing and bookbinding are part of my trade. Am I to understand that the commission you mentioned involves cataloguing a library?"

"That might be part of it."

"And is it your own library, sir?"

"It belongs at present to my employer."

"And what precisely would you wish me to do for him?"

"My principal is a lady, sir." Mr. Cross refilled Holdsworth's glass. "Tell me, does the name of Oldershaw mean something to you?"

"The late Bishop of Rosington?"

"Precisely. Were you acquainted with him?"

"No, sir. I did not have the honor of being of service to his lordship. I knew him only by reputation. So his library has not been broken up?"

"Not as yet. It is now in the possession of his widow. His lordship reposed perfect confidence in Lady Anne's judgment. I believe the collection to be considerable, in both extent and value."

"That was certainly the common report."

Mr. Cross rubbed the stubble on his chin. "Well, sir. You tell me you are at liberty to accept a commission of this nature. So far as I may judge, you appear well qualified for the task. But of course the decision must rest with Lady Anne herself."

Holdsworth inclined his head. "Of course."

Cross made a great to-do of helping himself to another pinch of snuff, which was followed by the same explosive ritual as before. He looked up quickly, as though aware that Holdsworth was studying him. "It remains only to fix a time for you to wait on her ladyship."

"One moment, sir. Why has your choice fallen on me? There are many others equally competent to carry out such a commission. Some would say more so."

"I am afraid I cannot say," Mr. Cross said with calculated ambiguity. "Her ladyship informs me that it will be convenient for you to wait on her tomorrow forenoon."

"Very well. I assume her ladyship must be in town?"

"Yes. I will give you her direction."

Holdsworth drank his sherry and nibbled another biscuit, trying not to wolf it down. Meanwhile, Cross took out a worn pocketbook, tore out a leaf, scribbled a few words in pencil and passed the paper across the table.

"Thirty-five Golden Square," Holdsworth read aloud. "Eleven o'clock."

"The house is on the north side." Cross pushed back his chair and stood up, signalling to the waiter. He turned aside to pay the score. He seemed suddenly in a hurry to be gone. He turned back to Holdsworth and bowed. "I am obliged, sir," he whispered. "Indeed I am. I give you good day."

Holdsworth returned the bow and watched the little man slipping like a shadow through the crowded room and into the street. He ate the remaining two biscuits and drank the last of the sherry. Until now, he had felt elated at the prospect of employment. But, as he pushed away his empty glass, it struck him that Mr. Cross's gratitude seemed out of all proportion to the nature of the arrangement they had just concluded. More than that, for an instant his countenance had betrayed an emotion that looked curiously like relief.

In Golden Square, Lady Anne Oldershaw sat on a low mahogany armchair beside the marble fireplace in the back drawing room. Despite the warmth of the day a fire burned in the steel grate. She wore mourning and as usual her face was completely white, a monochrome intrusion in a colorful world. On her lap was an open book, and her maid was mending linen at the table by the window. Lady Anne had come here as a bride, for the house and its contents had been part of her marriage settlement. In this room, little had changed since then. The heavy velvet curtains had faded to a dusty amber, and there were pale patches on the painted walls where a generation of servants had rubbed at candle smuts.

Elinor Carbury curtsied from the doorway. With great condescension Lady Anne held out a hand to her and even indicated that Elinor might kiss her cheek.

"It is good of you to come all this way," she said, "and by the public coach, too. I shall insist on sending you back in my own chaise. But you will not hurry away, I hope?"

"I must return on Thursday," Elinor said. "The Doctor says he cannot spare me for longer on this occasion. He is not entirely himself at present. The warmer weather unsettles him."

With a mechanical courtesy of the very well bred, Lady Anne methodically satisfied her curiosity about Elinor's journey, the state of the weather and the health of Dr. Carbury. There was a right way to do everything, and a wrong way too. Lady Anne had known Elinor since she was a baby, and since the death of her father Elinor had lived in the Oldershaws' household for months at a time. Lady Anne probably loved Elinor as much as she loved anyone else alive, with the exception of her son; and she missed her almost as a daughter when she did not see her for any length of time. But Elinor was not of the same rank as herself, and she would never forget that fact.

At last the servants left them alone, and shortly after that the civilities were completed.

Lady Anne folded her hands on her lap and stared at the fire. "Have you news of Frank?"

"Dr. Carbury sent to inquire yesterday afternoon, ma'am, and I am happy to say the news is good. His body is mending, and his spirits are much calmer than before. Dr. Jermyn enclosed a letter for you, which I have here."

She handed it to Lady Anne, who put it aside and asked whether Elinor would take any refreshment after her journey. But her eyes kept straying to the letter, so Elinor hinted that she herself had a great desire to know how Mr. Frank did and wondered aloud whether Dr. Jermyn's letter might expand on his necessarily brief verbal message to Dr. Carbury. At this, Lady Anne found her spectacles, took up the letter and broke the seal. She scanned the contents rapidly and then looked up.

"Dr. Jermyn writes that Frank does very well. But that we must not hope for an early cure." She compressed her lips. "Well, my dear, we shall see about that."

"Dr. Jermyn is very able, they say."

"No doubt. But, you know, should not Mr. Richardson bear some responsibility for what has happened? After all, he is Frank's tutor. I hope I did not act unwisely in placing Frank in his care. At the time, I had some doubt about the choice, but Frank liked him and was very pressing in his favor. Tell me, my dear, has he said anything that might explain Frank's behavior? I cannot help wondering whether, if he had exercised more control over his pupil, this might not have happened."

"It is not always easy for a tutor to supervise his charges, madam, especially when"—Elinor searched to find a term that would be suitable for Lady Anne's ears—"especially when he has a pupil with such a decisive nature as Mr. Frank's."

"True, even as a boy, he found it natural to take the lead," Lady Anne said. "He is a Vauden through and through: but Frank is still young—he needs the guidance of older and wiser heads."

There was a knock on the door and the footman appeared. He announced that Mr. Cross was below and begged the favor of a word.

"Ask him to step up," Lady Anne said. "No, my dear, you may stay," she added to Elinor, who was rising to her feet. "I should like you to hear what Mr. Cross has to say. He has been assisting me in my little project."

Mr. Cross slipped into the room and bowed very low to Lady Anne, and rather less low to Elinor. He was the Oldershaws' steward, and had in fact known Lady Anne for longer than anyone in the house, for he had grown up on the Earl of Vauden's estate near Lydmouth and received his early training in the steward's office there.

"Well?" Lady Anne demanded. "You may speak quite freely before Mrs. Carbury."

"I have seen Mr. Holdsworth, my lady. He will wait upon your ladyship tomorrow morning."

"And what did you tell him?"

"I mentioned only the possibility of his cataloguing and valuing his lordship's collection, and perhaps advising on its maintenance. Although he never had the honor of having dealings with his lordship, he was of course perfectly familiar with the reputation of the collection."

"But you said nothing else?"

"No, madam. I followed your directions to the letter." He cleared his throat. "He did, however, ask why I had come to him rather than to someone else with his qualifications. I was obliged to tell him that I was not able to say. I hope I did not do wrong."

"It is quite all right, Mr. Cross," Lady Anne said graciously. "How did the man seem to you?"

"He is in much-reduced circumstances, I fear, and his misfortunes have weighed heavily on him. But there is no doubt that he has the ability to deal with the library—as you instructed, I made extensive inquiries on that point before approaching him. As to the man himself, he is younger than I expected. He has a fine person—vigorous, and well set up."

"A point in his favor," Lady Anne said. "You may continue."

"He said little, but what he did say was very much to the point, madam. I would say he has a prudent nature and is a man of some determination. All in all, my first impression was favorable."

Lady Anne thanked him and the steward withdrew. When they were alone again, she turned to Elinor.

"You see, my dear. I have taken your hint."

"Dear madam, I pray the plan will not go amiss. I would not for the world—"

"Then let us hope it does not go amiss," Lady Anne interrupted, her voice suddenly sharp. "Tomorrow we shall discover whether the author of *The Anatomy of Ghosts* believes he can practice what he preaches."

4

THERE WAS MONEY HERE but not extravagance. A trades-man grows acute in judging such matters. The house in Golden Square had been new and fashionable at the turn of the century but it was neither of those things now. But it had an air of sober comfort, Holdsworth thought, rarely found in the houses of those who are newly rich or who live high on long credit.

The footman conducted Holdsworth across the hall, through an anteroom and into a long and shabby apartment at the back of the house. The books were everywhere—in cases ranged along the walls, stacked on tables and the floor, overflowing from the door-way of a closet at the end of the room.

"Mr. Holdsworth, my lady," announced the footman.

Lady Anne Oldershaw was sitting by the nearer of the two win-dows with a volume open on the table beside her. She signalled Holdsworth to approach. She was small and thin, with features so sharp and delicate they might have been cut in wax by a razor. She could have been almost any age between forty and seventy. Her face was coated very thickly with ceruse, so perhaps the skin be-neath had been scarred by the smallpox; for that was an evil that neither wealth nor breeding could guard against.

"Mr. Holdsworth," she said in a dry, remote voice. "Good morn-ing to you."

"Madam." He bowed low. "I am honored to be of service to your ladyship."

"You have not been of service yet. It remains to be seen whether you will be."

"Yes, my lady."

He waited for her to say what she wanted. She remained silent, studying him with a complete lack of self-consciousness. After a moment he looked away from her white face. Despite the room's contents, he thought, it was clearly only a makeshift library. The books had been arranged by someone who neither knew nor cared that they were undoubtedly valuable. His eyes fixed on a precarious pile standing on an open escritoire between the windows; they should not have been left like that. There was a similar pile on the table beyond it beside an armchair—

There was another person in the room. The armchair placed before the second window had its back to the room. Holdsworth saw a woman's cap over the top of the chair and, on one of the arms, an open book with a long hand resting motionless on the page.

Lady Anne clicked her tongue against the roof of her mouth. She looked past Holdsworth at the footman. "I shall ring if I need you, James."

The footman bowed and silently withdrew.

"Mr. Cross has told you that I wish to discuss the disposal of my late husband's library," Lady Anne said. "You see some of it in this room. There are more books, but they are still in the country. You are familiar with the collection, I apprehend?"

"Only by reputation, madam."

"I have decided to dispose of the bulk of the library. But first I wish to know what it contains, and indeed what value it has."

"Would you wish to sell what you dispose of as a single lot, or in—?"

"I do not intend to *sell* any of it. In any case I do not wish to consult you solely or even chiefly about the books."

"I'm afraid I do not catch your meaning, madam."

"That is because I have not expressed it to you yet." She waited while half a minute crawled by, emphasizing her power to control the pace and direction of the interview. "I wish to consult you about ghosts."

"I beg your pardon, my lady. I did not quite catch what you said."

"I think you heard me perfectly well. I wish to consult you about ghosts. About a particular ghost."

After that, silence fell on the room. It was broken only by a rustle as the woman in the armchair turned over a page of her book. Lady Anne sucked in her cheeks, and for a moment he had a fancy that instead of flesh and blood there was nothing but a skull in a lace cap looking up at him.

"I am a bookseller by trade, ma'am. I am not a ghost hunter or anything of that nature. Your ladyship must look elsewhere."

"I do not agree. I have read your—your squib. You seem eminently qualified to advise upon the subject."

Holdsworth spread his hands wide. "I wrote in anger. As a way of assuaging grief."

"I do not doubt it, sir. But that is not to the point. I understand that your late wife was preyed upon by one who claimed falsely to be in communication with the world of ghosts. You set out to expose the cheat, but you did more than that. You revealed that the claims of those who believe in ghosts are baseless. With the possible exception of direct divine intervention, such stories may all be reduced to instances of popular superstition in the minds of the uneducated, or to tricks and pranks played upon the credulous, often in the hope of material advantage. That was your argument, which you pursued with great force."

"Nevertheless, I cannot put myself up as an authority."

"You do not need to do so." She sounded bored now. "I wish to put a proposition to you."

"About his lordship's library?"

"I told you: I wish to consult you about an apparition. An alleged apparition. But as it happens the matter is inextricably entangled with his lordship's books and what becomes of them. So I offer you two commissions: and if you accept the one, you must accept the other."

"Madam, I do not understand what you wish me to do."

"There is no mystery about it. You have shown that those who prey on the credulous with their tales of ghosts are frauds. You began with a particular case, it is true, but you argued from that to the general. The tools that such people use for their foul trade are spirits, apparitions, hauntings and superstitions; but they trade in dreams, Mr. Holdsworth, they trade in other people's dreams. You have brought the resources of reason to bear upon their evil practices and you have shown them for what they are: traps to gull fools, snares to entangle the fearful. They are nothing but leeches, and they prey upon the sorrows of the innocent. You made all that as clear as day."

"Much good it did me. Or anyone else."

He caught a movement at the edge of his range of vision. The woman by the other window had craned her head round to the back of her chair and was looking at him. He had a brief impression of a long face with heavy, dark brows above the eyes and a fringe of hair below the cap.

"You have done it once," Lady Anne said. "You will do it again. You will not find me ungenerous, for I have a particular reason for desiring you to do this. And there is also considerable work to be done with the bishop's library. I offer you the chance to better yourself while doing me a very material service. Moreover, in doing so, you may be able to help save a soul from despair, if not from perdition. Surely both self-interest and your duty as a Christian must point in the same direction?"

He said nothing. The ceruse gave her face the chalky whiteness that counterfeited death. Maria had been just such a color at the end, though without the benefit of white lead. He wondered how Lady Anne knew so much about his case. He wondered even more what on earth she really wanted him to do.

She tapped her fingers on the surface of the table. "Well, sir?"

"Madam, I—I am undecided."

"It is a simple enough decision, Mr. Holdsworth."

"But there is much I do not understand."

"Then I shall try to enlighten you." Lady Anne fell silent. She turned her head and stared out of the window, which gave on to a narrow yard bounded by high brick walls. Soot-spotted shrubs lined a gravel path that bisected the area. "Let us discuss the matter of the library first. Are you familiar with Jerusalem College?"

"Jerusalem?" For a moment he thought he must have misheard. "Ah—perhaps you refer to the college in Cambridge, madam?"

"Exactly so." She looked at him again. "My family has a connection with it. Indeed, one of my forebears was its Founder and the bishop was once a fellow there. So I have been turning over in my mind whether I might donate his books to the college. But before I decide, I wish to inquire into the present state of the college's library. I do not choose that my husband's collection should go to an unworthy recipient."

"Would your ladyship wish me to go to Cambridge on your behalf?"

She ignored the question. "And then there is the matter of the collection here, which needs to be catalogued and valued before I make my decision. I may decide to hold back some of the books. Indeed, some of the collection may not be appropriate for a college library."

Holdsworth thought it very likely. He had seen the libraries of too many men, both living and dead, to be surprised by what they contained. A man's library was like his mind: some of its contents might not be suitable for young gentlemen at the University, or indeed for his grieving widow or his fatherless children.

"And there is another reason," Lady Anne went on, "why I wish you to go to Cambridge. It has to do with my son, Frank. He was admitted a fellow-commoner at Jerusalem last year. He has not been well. I wish you to investigate the circumstances that have led to his ill health and to bring him home."

"Madam, I am neither a physician nor a nursemaid." He wondered when they would come to the ghost. "I am afraid I must decline at least that part of the commission, because I can be of no earthly use to your son."

"Earthly use?" she repeated, and she pulled back her lips revealing beneath the whiteness of her face three yellowing teeth set in glossy pink gums. "Earthly use?" she said once more. "Some would say that is not what is needed. Mr. Holdsworth, my son is not strong. His body is indeed robust, but his mind—that is where his infirmity lies. He is now in the care of a physician in Barnwell, a village near Cambridge. I must be plain with you but first I must require you to treat what I have to say as a confidence that must not be repeated to anyone outside the walls of this room."

Holdsworth's eyes strayed involuntarily towards the younger lady by the other window. "If you choose to honor me with a confidence, you may depend upon its remaining safe with me."

Lady Anne was silent. Holdsworth listened to the sound of his own breathing, suddenly unnaturally loud. There was a creak from the younger lady's chair.

"The long and short of it is that my son believes he has seen a ghost," Lady Anne said abruptly. She glared at him, as though expecting him to challenge this statement. "He is an impressionable young man, and this wild misapprehension, which was almost certainly exacerbated by youthful high spirits and the taking of too much wine, is the immediate cause of his state of health. You will apprehend now why your qualifications are of particular interest to me. I believe my son is not beyond reach of reason. You will look into his alleged sighting of this apparition on my behalf. You will demonstrate to him that it was a delusion. I believe it may be the first stage towards his cure. Indeed, it may be all he requires."

Lady Anne stopped speaking and looked straight ahead. It was an unnerving experience, as if she had suddenly turned herself into a statue.

"A delusion, madam? Was it caused by a mere accidental combination of circumstances? Or was there"—and here he hesitated, remembering poor Maria's case—"was there another party involved, and therefore something deliberate or contrived about it?"

"That I cannot tell. There is much that is obscure. So long as you find out the truth of the matter and can prove it to the world, it don't much signify."

"Young men at the University have been known to play waggish pranks upon one another."

"An action with such evil consequences could not be classified as a mere prank. If this happened by design, I am persuaded that there is malevolence behind it."

"Had the ghost a name, my lady?" Holdsworth asked.

"My son is convinced that he encountered the deceased wife of an acquaintance, a Mrs. Whichcote. The circumstances of her death may perhaps be germane to the matter. If necessary, you will inquire into them."

"There can be no guarantee of success. Not with a commission of this nature."

"But you will be successful. And when you are, I will lend you the money you require to discharge any debts you have, and on terms you will not find ungenerous. Moreover I shall instruct Mr. Cross to pay you an honorarium for the business you transact on my behalf, and the expenses you incur in doing so, whether the business has to do with my son or with the cataloguing and disposal of my late husband's library."

"I am overwhelmed by your ladyship's kindness," Holdsworth said. "But I have not yet decided whether—"

She held up a small hand. "Stay a minute, sir. I do not wish you to decide before you know the full circumstances, before you know exactly what you may meet with in Cambridge. I could not allow that to lie on my conscience. Be so good as to ring the bell."

He did as she asked. A moment later the footman entered the room.

"Ask Mr. Cross to step in here."

The servant withdrew as silently as he had come. Holdsworth heard movement at the other end of the room. The lady by the window had at last left her chair, and was advancing towards him. She was almost as tall as he was. She was plainly dressed and appeared perfectly self-possessed. Her thin face and heavy features would have prevented her from being considered beautiful. But she was undeniably striking.

Lady Anne smiled at her. "Well, Elinor?"

"I should like to see how Mr. Cross does for myself. And besides, perhaps I should make myself known to Mr. Holdsworth. After all, it is possible that we may meet again."

Lady Anne nodded. "Elinor, may I present Mr. Holdsworth? And Mr. Holdsworth, this is Mrs. Carbury, my goddaughter."

He bowed low. She gave an almost imperceptible curtsy in return, examining him as though appraising his value in pounds, shillings and pence. Her eyes were blue, with the whites very bright and pure, and fringed with long dark lashes. Holdsworth thought that her eyes and her skin, which was unblemished, would probably be accounted her best features. Something about her struck him as familiar. But he could not have met her before.

"If you go to Cambridge," Lady Anne said to him, "you will see something of Mrs. Carbury. Her husband is the Master of Jerusalem."

There was a tap on the door, and Mr. Cross entered the room. He wore the same brown coat and scarf as before, and his right hand was stained with ink as if he had been engaged in writing when Lady Anne's summons had come to him.

"I have unfolded my proposition to Mr. Holdsworth," Lady Anne told him. "At least in outline. However, I cannot in all conscience allow him to move any further in this matter without showing him why he would be advised to go cautiously if he wishes to avoid any— any discomfort."

Mr. Cross glanced at Holdsworth and then back to her. "As I said, Mr. Holdsworth is strong," he observed in a whisper. "He has that on his side."

"Indeed. Pray remove your scarf."

Mrs. Carbury came a step closer.

Mr. Cross undid the loose knot that held the scarf, let the ends fall away, and freed his neck from its folds.

Holdsworth stared fixedly at what was revealed. Mrs. Carbury sighed.

"Mr. Cross will not object if you inspect more closely," Lady Anne said to him. "Of course these things look worse as they begin to heal."

Holdsworth came closer to the little man and looked down at his neck. Mr. Cross obligingly tilted his head this way and that. The skin above the Adam's apple was marked with a smudged and swollen circlet of purple and blue. He swallowed, and a grimace passed across his face as though even that movement caused him discomfort.

"You must be on your guard if you see my son, sir," Lady Anne said. "He tried to strangle Mr. Cross."

5

WHEN HOLDSWORTH LEFT Golden Square that morning, he did not know whether he would accept Lady Anne's commission. He could not rid himself of the memory of Elinor Carbury's face. He walked slowly down towards the river. It was only when he reached the Strand that he realized Mrs. Carbury reminded him in some way that he did not entirely understand of Maria. Maria had been fair-complexioned and small of stature, whereas Mrs. Carbury was dark and tall. But the two women had a similar build, and a similar habit of looking very directly at one.

The Strand was full of shoppers and noise. He walked slowly towards the City. After all that had happened, he was very tired. He was forced to stop on Ludgate Hill, where three sedan chairs and their bearers had entangled themselves; the chairs were swaying dangerously and the bearers were swearing, and the chairs' occupants were rapping on the glass and, in one case, screaming. Through the racket, Holdsworth heard somebody behind him say his name. When he turned he found Mrs. Farmer was at his shoulder with a basket on either arm. Her face was pink, the skin damp with the heat.

"Madam—good day to you." Holdsworth tried to bow but the crowd made that difficult.

"I looked for you this morning, sir," she said, "but you had slipped out of the house before I was awake."

"I am in the habit of rising early. May I relieve you of those baskets?"

She thrust them at him. "I wish to speak to you, Mr. Holdsworth. We cannot do it here. Let us cross the road—I am going home."

She threaded her way between a stationary wagon and a coach and passed unscathed on to the other side of the road. Nature had made her a short, broad woman with a nose like a beak and the smallest of chins. With a little help from Ned, she was now broader than ever, for she carried within her their first child and she was within a month or so of her term. Holdsworth followed, marvelling at the way the woman strode through the foot passengers in an unswerving straight line as though they were the Red Sea and she had been miraculously assured that they would part before her, as indeed they did. With Holdsworth in her wake, she set off down Newbridge Street. She was taking him out of his way—so far as he had any plan, he was making for Leadenhall Street.

As they were passing the Bridewell Hospital, Mrs. Farmer stopped so sharply that Holdsworth almost collided with her. "Have you seen Mr. Farmer today, sir?"

"Yes—I have."

"And did he find the opportunity to mention that we shall soon need your room?"

"No, ma'am."

"We both regret the necessity," she said in a perfunctory way. "But when the baby is born, we shall need to house the nurse somewhere. Besides, I am sure you yourself must wish to remove somewhere more convenient."

Holdsworth did not ask in what way convenient, or for whom. Instead he listened to the mournful rattle and clanks of the treadmills and stared through the hospital's gates at a group of vagrants picking hemp under the shelter of the arcade. He did not wish to become one of those. He did not want the poorhouse, either.

"It will not take you long to find somewhere," Mrs. Farmer assured him, or even herself. "I am sure Mr. Farmer will give you every assistance; that is, everything within his limited powers, though of course his resources are much stretched at present. But perhaps there may be somewhere in Leadenhall Street."

He bowed. A corner in a cellar, perhaps, or the bench in the workshop where he left the barrow. Mrs. Farmer might even have calculated that he would be useful there, a nightwatchman who required no wages.

They crossed Blackfriars Bridge and turned along Bankside. Neither of them spoke. The house came into view, with Goat Stairs beyond. He fixed his eyes on the worn paving slabs beneath his feet to avoid looking at the stairs themselves and the water slapping and rustling at the foot of them. Gulls flew up around him, their wings beating with a swift, irregular rhythm. On the ground he saw the head and tail of a dead fish, lying among its own entrails. Above him, the wheeling birds cried savagely, waiting to return to what was left of the fish. They twisted in the air like scraps of charred paper above a bonfire.

Gulls would eat anything. He had seen men and women pulled from the water with their eyes pecked out and the fleshy parts of their faces eaten away. It was lucky that Maria had been found so soon, her body wedged against a cable a few yards downstream, or she might have suffered the same fate. It came to him very suddenly, and with the force of a revelation, that he did not want to be here any longer. He did not want to be beside the river. He did not want to be in Leadenhall Street either. He would not be a ghost in his past life.

"What's that?" Mrs. Farmer said, for she had sharp ears when she wanted to hear, and he had muttered the last words aloud.

"Nothing, madam."

A moment later they entered the cool, dark hallway of the house on Bankside. Holdsworth left the baskets on the kitchen table.

"I do not wish to be inhospitable, sir," Mrs. Farmer said, resting her hands on her great belly.

"You are kindness itself," Holdsworth said and stared at her until she looked away.

The mound was near the west wall. The earth was no longer freshly turned, no longer as shockingly naked as a suppurating wound. Nature had scabbed it over with a tangle of weeds and grass. The wooden marker was askew and Holdsworth had abandoned the struggle to make it stand upright. Sprays of herb Robert had sprouted around it, a green ruff, and Maria had liked green, growing things. She had tried to grow plants in tubs in the dark, damp yard behind the house but the experiment had not been a success.

When the mason in Queen Street had finished his work, and when Holdsworth had paid him, there would at least be a proper headstone. The stone itself was waiting in the yard. Unless Holdsworth could pay the balance of the money, it would soon have another inscription. But at present he could not even find the price of a good dinner and new shirt.

In the early days, he had worried that he would come to the grave and find it robbed. He had no faith in the gatekeeper's honesty, and in any case the boundary walls of the burial ground were ruinous in several places. Despite attempts to prevent them, the resurrection men had plied their grisly trade in the past. A few weeks ago, Holdsworth had found an old woman weeping inconsolably beside the empty grave of her late husband.

As Holdsworth passed out of the gate at the corner of Red Cross Street, he saw a familiar figure leaning against a mounting block and paring his nails with a pocket knife.

"John," Ned Farmer said. "I thought I might find you here."

"You might have saved yourself the trouble and found me at home."

Farmer pushed up his wig and hat and scratched his scalp. "I wanted to speak to you away from the house."

"Then let us walk back together, and you may speak all you wish."

Farmer took his arm and they set off in the direction of the river. "First, I am to command your presence at supper."

Holdsworth looked sideways at him. "I should not like to intrude."

"Mrs. Farmer will not brook a refusal. It is all arranged. I saw Sal coming in with our supper not twenty minutes since, and she is dressing it at this very moment. The nicest-looking veal cutlets you could hope to see, wrapped in a cabbage leaf and accompanied by a most tasty-looking rasher of ham. You must not disappoint us."

He looked so anxious that Holdsworth said he should be glad to accept the invitation. He did not usually eat with his hosts—Mrs. Farmer had contrived to make it clear that though he lodged in her house, he was not part of her household.

"I am much obliged," Ned said as though he were the invited guest. "And John—I know Betsy seems a little harsh sometimes, but the truth is, she is a good woman and has all our best interests at heart."

"Indeed she has."

"She has a head on her shoulders, too—and—and she is wonderfully devout. I sometimes think she is almost too strict with herself on that score, and the devil of it is that sometimes the strictness rubs off in the way she deals with others. Yet there's no help for it, John, and as I say she means it for the best."

Holdsworth touched his arm. "There is no need to run on like this. I am perfectly convinced that Mrs. Farmer is an admirable woman. And words cannot express my gratitude to you both for offering me shelter for so long."

Ned strode onwards. He was a good man, and Holdsworth gave Mrs. Farmer all credit for recognizing that. But she had also recognized that Ned was malleable, someone she could make something of. She had brought more than money to their union: she had brought resolution and a sense of purpose.

"I wish I could do more," Ned burst out. "You know it. Yet between you, what can I do? You are as stiff-necked as a hidalgo, whereas Mrs. Farmer—well, she examines the books every night, you know. She watches every penny. By God, she is a better man of business than I shall ever be."

Holdsworth told him that he did not doubt it, at which Ned laughed at him and Holdsworth laughed back.

"There," Ned said. "That's better. Seems an age since I saw you laugh. Are you in a more cheerful humor than you have been? Were you offered a commission by the little monkey man?"

"I was. I think he is a man of business or something of that nature. A steward, perhaps. At any event, he is acting for Lady Anne Oldershaw."

"Widow of the late bishop? Ah—I begin to see which way this is tending."

"Not entirely, I think. Her ladyship asked me to catalogue and value the bishop's collection. But then it became apparent that the library was only part of the reason she had summoned me. She wishes me to go to Cambridge as her emissary. She has it in mind to donate some or all of the books to Jerusalem College there."

"Admirable. You are the very man for the task. And all this will occupy you for weeks, months even."

They reached Maid Lane, where the crowd was thicker and the noise louder. Neither of them spoke until they had crossed the street and passed into a rent leading up to Bankside. The alley was so narrow that they had to walk in single file.

"There is another reason why she wishes me to go to Cambridge," Holdsworth said over his shoulder. "Her ladyship wants me to lay a ghost."

"What? Are you raving?"

Holdsworth stopped and turned back to him. "It is perfectly true. She has read my little book and is convinced that I am the very man to send ghost hunting."

"You are funning me."

"I assure you, I am not. Watch your step." Holdsworth held up his arm just in time to stop Farmer walking into a neat coil of human excrement in the middle of the path. "She has a son at the University and he is convinced that he has seen a ghost."

They emerged from the fetid little alley into the comparatively pure air of Bankside. Holdsworth glanced upriver towards Goat

Stairs. The gulls were still quarrelling, this time over something that lay in the water.

"Shall you go?" Farmer asked.

"I am undecided. The mother does not give a fig for the books, of course. She cares only for the boy."

Farmer grunted. "There's money there. And of course by birth she's a Vauden, is she not? That means she will have the ear of those who have something more valuable than mere money at their disposal."

"When the fit is on him, the boy is violent," Holdsworth said. "He tried to strangle your monkey man. I have seen the bruises."

"Ah. That is not so good."

"The likelihood is that I should be of no use to the lad at all. In which case I can expect nothing but trouble from the mother."

Farmer laid a hand on Holdsworth's arm. "Who's that, I wonder?"

He pointed to a tall, plainly dressed man thirty yards ahead. He was knocking at the Farmers' door. As Sal opened it, Farmer and Holdsworth reached the house. Hearing their footsteps, the stranger turned. It was the footman from Golden Square. He held out a letter to Holdsworth.

"Her ladyship desired me to wait for an answer, sir."

Holdsworth broke the seal and unfolded the letter.

Sir,

Her Ladyship hopes it will be convenient for you to travel to Cambridge on Friday. All arrangements will be made on your behalf. Pray call at Golden Square tomorrow at eleven o'clock to make a preliminary survey of his Lordship's collection, and to receive any further instructions she may have. She has instructed me to enclose a banknote for five pounds to defray your expenses. Pray sign the enclosed paper to acknowledge receipt of the money and hand to bearer. I am, sir, yr humble & obdt. servant,
L. Cross

Mrs. Farmer came into the hall to see what the fuss was about. She eyed the banknote with curiosity. Her face looked softer, almost girlish. Money was a powerful thing, Holdsworth thought, the true philosopher's stone, with the power of transmuting dreams.

Farther along Bankside, the gulls rose in an angry, squabbling group, their cries growing louder and more savage. Were there gulls in Cambridge? Surely not so many, surely not such predatory birds as these?

He handed the letter to Ned and went into the house. He turned into the little parlor. It was here that Maria and her friends had done their praying and wailing, their talking to ghosts. He found pen and ink on the table by the window and scrawled his name on the receipt. He sanded the paper, folded it and returned to the footman waiting at the door. He felt giddy, as though he had swallowed a bumper of rum.

The footman bowed and left. Mrs. Farmer and Sal retreated towards the kitchen, where supper was moving towards the final phase of its preparation. It was a fine evening, and Holdsworth and Farmer lingered outside by the river. Holdsworth watched the gulls, which were quieter now but still darting and gliding about the water near Goat Stairs. He felt calmer than he had done for months.

"Well," Farmer said. "She had already decided you were to go, and that is that. The wheel of fortune turns, eh?"

Holdsworth patted the pocket in which the banknote lay. "It is a bribe."

"It was delicately done. Not that a present of money needs any delicacy whatsoever."

"I shall call in at the mason's yard in the morning," Holdsworth said.

"To settle the matter of the headstone? Surely that expense might wait a little?"

"Twenty-seven shillings and sixpence. That's what the man wants. I shall have enough left over."

"I still think it might wait a little."

"No, I must do this for Maria if nothing else. I owe her a little square of stone." He hesitated, still staring downstream to Goat Stairs. "Then perhaps she will leave me alone."

Ned frowned. "You're full of fancies this evening. What do you mean now?"

Holdsworth waved his arm, taking in the river before them and the City beyond. "Sometimes I am—well, no—not haunted, not that, of course, never that. But my mind plays tricks at times, just for the merest instant, for the twinkling of an eye. I think I see the curve of a shoulder across the road, I hear her voice in a crowd, or—or—well, even a child weeping." He watched two apprentices sculling upriver against the tide and thought of black treacle rising to engulf him from the grave that Maria shared with Georgie. He said softly, "Perhaps the headstone will settle the business."

"This is grief speaking," Ned said. "It is nothing else. It is a natural consequence of an overactive imagination, exacerbated beyond endurance by the melancholy—"

"Stop prosing. Advise me instead. Should I buy a shirt tomorrow morning? A new hat? I shall be calling on the quality, after all. I must be shaved—I must have my hair dressed. I shall dazzle Mrs. Farmer and Sal with my splendor."

Farmer shook his head. "You must go cautiously in this matter."

"You have become very serious all of a sudden."

"Money makes it serious. Her ladyship has given you all this before you have lifted a finger for her. She will expect a return. The rich always do."

Holdsworth smiled at him. "That is why they are rich."

6

ON THURSDAY, Elinor Carbury breakfasted by herself. Lady Anne rose late, and rarely came downstairs before the middle of the morning. The chaise had been ordered for eleven-thirty. Elinor would travel post to Cambridge in far more comfort than by the public coach, and the journey would be two or three hours shorter.

After breakfast, she had a brief interview with Lady Anne, who was not in the best of humors because Elinor would not stay another day.

On her way downstairs she went into her chamber where her maid was packing. Susan was a plump, dark girl with brown eyes and thick ankles. She beamed at her mistress.

"Anything I can do for you, ma'am? Anything at all?"

"Try not to crush the silk this time."

The beaming continued. As a rule, Susan was inclined to be sulky but, a few months earlier, Elinor had given her an unwanted cloak and the maid would revert to being all smiles and sycophancy when she was hoping for another gift. To escape this proleptic gratitude, Elinor fled to the long room with the bishop's books. She sat down in the chair by the window and took up the volume she had been looking at the previous day. It was Lady Anne's own copy of Mr. Holdsworth's *The Anatomy of Ghosts*. Lady Anne had bought it at Elinor's suggestion when Frank's misfortune fell upon him. Now, as Elinor reread the first chapter, she paid particular attention to the unhappy case that Mr. Holdsworth described there in some detail, since it had aroused his curiosity about ghostly phenomena. He wrote that the wicked fraud had been practiced upon "a lady of my acquaintance," who had recently lost her only child in a tragic accident.

Shortly before eleven o'clock, she heard what she had been waiting for—a knock on the front door, followed by the sound of the porter's husky voice as he let a visitor into the hall. The footman, James, ushered Mr. Holdsworth into the room. Elinor slipped the little book on the nearest shelf and rose to her feet.

"Madam," he said, bowing. "I beg your pardon. I shall return another—"

"Pray do not go, sir. I hoped to speak with you before I leave. Tell me, does your presence here mean you are quite determined to go down to Cambridge?"

"Yes, madam."

"You may not find your task an easy one."

"I apprehend there may be difficulties."

She stared at him, sensing a hint of impertinence in his words. "In that case, I wish to warn you of another circumstance, which may help you to discharge your new duties."

Holdsworth bowed again but did not speak. The man was stiff and proud, she decided suddenly. And plain almost to the point of being ugly. But she wished he were not so tall. It gave him an unfair advantage. Still, there was no help for it: she must use what materials lay to hand.

"I wish to assist you with some information before you go."

"Then I am obliged to you, madam."

She frowned at him, once again uncertain whether he intended impertinence. "It concerns the lady whose ghost Mr. Oldershaw is alleged to have seen."

"Mrs. Whichcote?"

"Yes. She died suddenly in February."

Elinor stared out of the window. The glass seemed blurred, as if by rain. The sill was stained with whorls and smudges of soot.

"How did the lady die?" Holdsworth asked.

She turned her head towards him. "Mrs. Whichcote was found drowned in the Long Pond at Jerusalem College."

"Drowned?" For an instant his face crumpled as if an invisible fist had squeezed the features together. "*Drowned?* Had she fallen in?"

"It was put about that she must have missed her footing in the darkness."

"But you would have me believe otherwise?"

"No, sir. But there are those who say—well, it doesn't signify—there are always those willing to make bad worse."

"So they say it was a case of self-murder?"

She nodded.

"They take the one to confirm the other, I suppose?" he said.

"What?"

"They believe that if Mrs. Whichcote's ghost has been seen, it strengthens the notion of suicide. And vice versa—since she committed suicide, her ghost would be likely to walk abroad. It is one of those circular flights of speculation that defy counterargument."

"Mrs. Whichcote's name means little or nothing to most people," Elinor said in a low voice. "I do not wish it to attract further notoriety."

He seized upon a detail. "You say it was dark—at what hour did the accident happen?"

"At night. We do not know the precise hour. She was found by the night-soil man early in the morning."

"But what was she doing in a college at that time? Surely it is not usual for ladies to wander in college gardens, alone and unprotected, in the dead of night?"

Elinor felt her color rising. "It appears that Mrs. Whichcote suffered on occasion from noctambulism. She often visited me at the Master's Lodge by day, and she had her own key to the Master's Garden. It was convenient for both of us that she should be able to come and go as she pleased without passing through the college itself."

"So you believe she was sleepwalking? That in her sleeping mind she intended to pay you a visit?"

"It seems the most likely explanation. It was the one that satisfied the coroner."

After a pause, Holdsworth said, "Her ladyship's mind is much fixed upon her son."

"Now she is widowed, he is very dear to her. He is her only child yet living."

"Then why does she not go to his aid herself?"

"Her health does not permit her to travel," Elinor said. "She had a fall—she has to be carried everywhere like a baby now. She is exhausted this morning because of the effort she made yesterday."

"I am surprised she does not rely wholly on you to act for her in this matter. She clearly values your opinion. You are in Cambridge already. You know her son."

"You forget, sir. I am a mere woman. Lady Anne holds firm views on the respective duties of the sexes."

"But in that case her ladyship could put the matter in the hands of Dr. Carbury, could she not? Or there must be several other gentlemen almost equally well qualified for such a delicate commission, including Mr. Frank's tutor."

"She has decided that they would not answer—she prefers to send you."

"Because she can hire me?"

Elinor stared at him for a moment without speaking. She said, "And because you know something about the subject of ghosts. Now may I put a question to you?"

He bowed.

"I do not wish to pry into your private circumstances. And you may not wish to answer. It shall be just as you choose. But pray believe I do not ask from idle curiosity—I have a purpose. Mr. Cross tells me that you have recently suffered the loss of your wife, and that it is widely believed that she was the anonymous lady whose case you describe so feelingly in your book—the lady whose innocent credulity had been imposed upon with such terrible results."

He nodded but said nothing.

"I wish with all my heart that it had not been so. And so the ghost—?"

"Was said to be that of our son." He stared at her. "However, this is not to the point. I am here to help Mr. Frank Oldershaw." He glanced around the room. "And to look at books."

"But it is to the point, sir. Ghosts, whether real or alleged, usually have an identity, and that is, in itself, of significance."

"I do not catch your drift."

"I hope it will not wound you if I speak plainly. Just as your ghost was important to you, so this one is to me. I do not wish Mrs. Whichcote's reputation to be dragged even further in the mire."

"The sentiment does you honor, madam. I assure you I will pursue my researches as discreetly as possible."

"The death of an obscure woman in an obscure accident does not in itself arouse the world's curiosity. Unless—" She broke off, and a sigh escaped her. "You understand me, I think. We have been fortunate that this rumor of suicide has not reached the public press in Cambridge, let alone London. Dr. Carbury has exercised all his influence, and so has the Vice-Chancellor. This foolish ghost story has not had much currency, either. But if it gets abroad . . ."

"Suicide and a ghost? A lady abroad in a Cambridge college at the dead of night? And of course Mr. Frank Oldershaw." As he spoke, he held out his right hand, counting off the elements of the matter with his fingers, one by one. "Yes, you're right. The combination would send tongues wagging all over the country. Within a week, they would be selling penny ballads in every alehouse."

"Mrs. Whichcote has suffered enough. Pray oblige me in this. I ask your goodwill, sir, nothing more—your assistance in preserving a lady's reputation."

"Madam," Holdsworth said, his voice suddenly harsh. "Her ladyship has retained my services. A man may not work for two masters."

She waved her hand to dismiss the notion. She would have liked to use the same hand to slap his face. "I do not ask you to betray the trust of an employer. I do not wish you to work for me."

"May I ask why this lady's reputation is so near to your heart?"

"Because Mrs. Whichcote was my friend." She hardened her voice because otherwise it would have trembled. "I do not lightly ignore the ties of friendship. Why should we permit death to sever them?"

A little after one o'clock, the footman entered the library with a tray holding a light nuncheon of bread, cheese and small beer. He also brought the compliments of Mr. Cross, who hoped that Mr. Holdsworth would do him the honor of dining with him later that afternoon. At four o'clock, the servant reappeared and conducted Holdsworth to a small, dark room furnished as an office.

Mr. Cross was standing at his desk, casting up columns of figures. His neck was still swathed in a scarf but he looked happier than before. He removed his spectacles and greeted Holdsworth briskly, saying they would not delay dinner. While they ate, Mr. Cross worked his way methodically through the arrangements for Holdsworth's journey and for his stay in Cambridge.

"It is a pity you could not have gone down to Cambridge with Mrs. Carbury today," he observed. "Or that she could not have waited for you. But she was in a hurry to return, I understand."

An inside seat had been booked for Holdsworth on the stagecoach that ran from the Green Dragon in Bishopsgate Street. Once at Cambridge, he was to make his way to Jerusalem College, where he would stay with the Carburys at the Master's Lodge.

"You will be there as Lady Anne's emissary, remember," Cross said in his low, husky voice. "You are there to examine the college library, but no one will be surprised if you call on poor Mr. Frank in Barnwell to see how he does on behalf of his mother. I have a letter here for you to give to Mr. Richardson—he is the senior fellow, and he is not only the college librarian but also Mr. Frank's tutor. Her ladyship has asked him to give you every assistance in his power."

"Does he know the full extent of my commission?"

"Apart from the Carburys, no one knows that you have been entrusted with the task of examining the alleged sighting of Mrs. Whichcote's ghost."

"This ghost," Holdsworth said. "What exactly occurred?"

"I am afraid I do not know the details. You must apply to Dr. Carbury for those. And perhaps even Mrs. Carbury."

Mr. Cross hurried on, emphasizing that Lady Anne expected regular reports from him. Unless circumstances warranted it, Holdsworth was to spend no more than a fortnight in Cambridge. When he returned, he was to bring back Mr. Frank with him.

"Her ladyship has a mother's desire to have her son with her under her own roof," Cross murmured. "And by that time, of course, she hopes his health will be much improved."

"And if it isn't?"

Mr. Cross gave a little shake of the head. "I'm sure it will be. Lady Anne has every confidence . . ."

He changed the subject swiftly, and became almost cheerful when dealing with the matter of money. He advanced Holdsworth fifteen pounds for his expenses, and gave him a letter of credit addressed to an attorney in St. John's Lane, whom Holdsworth might approach if he needed more funds. At this point, Mr. Cross looked very serious and said that her ladyship would expect to see detailed accounts for all his expenditure, down to the last farthing.

As the meal drew to its close, Mr. Cross mellowed and became almost confidential. "I must confess I am glad not to be going back to Cambridge myself. Mr. Frank's behavior came as a terrible shock. I am not as young as I was."

"There was no reason for it?"

"None that I could see. All I said was that I was come to take him back to her ladyship, and she would soon make all well again. And then he gave a great cry and lashed out at me. I have seen the young gentleman fly into a passion before—most young gentlemen do—but nothing like this. I took it very hard, sir, very hard indeed. When he was in short-coats I used to dandle that boy on my knee."

"You must not refine too much upon it, sir. He is clearly not himself."

Mr. Cross shook his head. "I know not what he is now. It is Cambridge that has done this to him. Ever since he went there, he has been a different person. Tell me, do you know the place?"

"I was never there in my life."

"Then have a care, sir," Mr. Cross whispered. "It is meant to educate our young men but to my mind it blights them. And you must be constantly on your guard at Jerusalem. Lady Anne has a good deal of influence there but she is not universally beloved." He broke off suddenly, as if aware he was straying into dangerous territory. "To put it in another way, the college has its own interests to protect, which is quite natural." He pulled out his watch. "But I run on. I am sure you have much to do before tomorrow morning."

"What is the college's interest in this? How does it differ from hers?"

"Oh—that." Mr. Cross stuffed the watch back in one waistcoat pocket and took out his snuffbox from the other. "Well, you see, this business—it is not good for them at all."

"Because her ladyship may turn against them?"

"Not exactly. Though that is a consideration. But these scandals attached to Mrs. Whichcote and Mr. Frank have the power materially to affect them in more ways than one. A college does not attract young men of rank and fortune overnight. It has taken Jerusalem years to develop its reputation as a desirable establishment for them. I understand there are fashions in these things as in all else. What has been built up over years may be blown away in a matter of days. No, sir, when you are at Jerusalem, you must never forget that for many of the gentlemen there this is more than a little matter of a ghost, a suicide and an unfortunate boy: it is also a matter of money."

7

ON FRIDAY, 26 MAY, after dining as usual by herself, Elinor Carbury sat in her parlor at a table by the window, which overlooked the Master's Garden. The garden was still laid out in the old-fashioned style with parterres, shrubs and trees, all deployed with the mechanical regularity of a regiment of soldiers upon a parade square. It was bounded largely by the sweeping curve of the Long Pond, beyond which were more college gardens.

In front of her on the table was Dr. Johnson's *Rasselas*, a novel she had read several times before. She heard a muffled knocking on the hall door downstairs. She turned a page and appeared absorbed in her reading when Susan, squirming with excitement, announced Mr. Holdsworth.

He bowed from the doorway. Elinor responded with a civil inclination of the head. She closed the book and stood up. "Dr. Carbury had hoped to be here to greet you, sir, but he was unfortunately called away. I trust your journey was uneventful?"

"Yes, madam," Holdsworth said.

"Would you care to take some refreshment, perhaps?"

"No, thank you."

She disliked the way he stared at her almost as much as his lack of conversation. He was uncouth, she decided, a veritable bear of a man. He must have intimidated that poor wife of his. The maid lingered in the room, eyeing the visitor with ill-concealed interest. Elinor told her to leave them.

"I understand that Mr. Cross has informed you of all you need to know," she said when they were alone. "So—"

"I wish that were true."

"Sir? You are pleased to be droll?"

"No, ma'am, I spoke no more than the truth. For example, Mr. Cross told me little about Mr. Oldershaw's encounter with the ghost. When I inquired further, he referred me to you and Dr. Carbury."

She offered him a chair, partly to give herself time to regain control of the interview. She returned to her seat at the table and looked sternly at him. "There is little to say. Mr. Oldershaw was in low spirits already, why I do not know. On the evening before he saw—whatever he saw—he had drunk a good deal of wine and his gyp says he also took a dose of laudanum as he retired to bed."

"His gyp?"

"A gyp is a species of servant we have at the University—they condescend to work only for those undergraduates who can afford to pay their exorbitant charges."

"A reliable witness?"

"I do not know the man. His name is Mulgrave. Dr. Carbury says he is nobody's fool, and he is sober in his manner of life. When Mulgrave left Mr. Oldershaw at the end of the evening, he believed he was asleep. The rest is speculation, until the porter on duty heard a great shouting and splashing near the Long Pond. If you wish, you may see the spot from here."

He joined her by the window. The unfashionably large cuff of his shabby black coat brushed her shoulder.

"You see the water, sir?" she said. "And the great plane tree on the further bank? That was where they found him. He was bellowing like a baby."

"What time was it?"

"A little after two o'clock. The porter raised the alarm and pulled Mr. Oldershaw out of the water. He fell into a swoon, and indeed his life was despaired of for several hours, for he was chilled to the bone. When he awoke after dawn, it was found that his reason had fled, and that he could babble of nothing but ghosts." She paused. "Or, to be more precise, of Mrs. Whichcote's ghost. In a day or two it became clear that his reason had still not been restored, though in other respects he was recovered. Dr. Carbury communicated with Lady Anne, and she ordered his removal to Dr. Jermyn's."

"Tell me, madam, why—"

A knock at the door interrupted them. Susan announced Mr. Richardson. Elinor hoped her face did not betray her irritation. A small, slightly built clergyman came towards her, took the hand she held out to him and bowed low.

"Your servant, ma'am," he said in a soft voice. "A thousand apologies—I did not realize you had a visitor."

"I am afraid the Doctor stepped out after dinner, sir," she told him. "I believe he intended to call in at Trinity."

"No matter. I shall probably see him later this evening."

Elinor turned to Holdsworth. "I beg your pardon, sir. May I present Mr. Richardson? And this, sir, is Mr. Holdsworth, who is come down today from London."

The two men bowed to each other. Richardson was about fifty, a good-looking man with a gentlemanly manner. He had neat, delicate features and bright eyes like chips of glass.

"Mr. Richardson is our senior fellow," Elinor continued when they were all sitting down. "Dr. Carbury informs me that this University holds few scholars who can match the breadth of his learning and the penetration of his intellect."

"The Master is so very kind," Richardson replied with a smile. "But perhaps my reputation sounds more glorious to the ears of a stranger than in fact it is." He turned the smile on Holdsworth. "I fear that scholars are such a minority in this University now that the labors of those who remain shine with a luster they do not necessarily deserve. And you must be Lady Anne's emissary, sir. Dr. Carbury told me you would arrive today or tomorrow."

Holdsworth bowed again. He took out his pocketbook and removed a letter from the inner flap of the cover. "Her ladyship asked me to give you this, sir."

Richardson thanked him with rather more warmth than was necessary. He slipped the letter into his pocket without opening it and turned back to Elinor. "And of course you are just returned from seeing Lady Anne, I collect. I trust her ladyship is in better health?"

"She is no worse."

"I am rejoiced to hear that, at least. And, Mr. Holdsworth, you must do me the honor of dining with me while you're here. Where do you lodge?"

"Why—here, of course," Elinor said, hoping to make it quite clear to both men where Holdsworth's loyalties should lie.

"Then Mr. Holdsworth is indeed fortunate." Richardson turned again to Holdsworth. "The college is a perfect desert of masculinity. But the Master's Lodge"—he bowed to Elinor—"thanks to this charming lady, is become an oasis of femininity. Still, since you are come to look over the library, I hope I may be of service to you. You, too, are a scholar?"

"Not I, sir," Holdsworth said. "I have been a printer and a bookseller."

"Then I shall be particularly interested to hear your views on our collection," Richardson replied smoothly. "I have only recently taken over the direction of the library. It has been sadly neglected for at least a generation. All in all, our books are not as I should wish them to be." He smiled again at Holdsworth. "You may depend upon it, sir, I shall examine you very thoroughly on the subject."

Elinor asked if they would take tea. Mr. Richardson declined, saying that he had promised to look over some lecture notes for a colleague before supper, and took his leave, apologizing again for disturbing them. At the door he turned, raised himself slightly on the balls of his feet, and bowed again.

"Well, sir," she said to Holdsworth when they were alone. "And what did you think of Mr. Richardson?"

"I cannot imagine it much signifies one way or the other."

"He came here only to look you over."

"I thought he looked in to see Dr. Carbury."

"That was a mere *façon de parler*," Elinor said. "Mr. Richardson knew that he would see Dr. Carbury later this evening, and I am sure he already knew that the Doctor was not in college. Mr. Richardson knows everything about Jerusalem. Or almost everything. He will have known of your arrival. Hence his curiosity to see you."

"Then I hope he was satisfied with what he saw."

Elinor said softly, "You must be on your guard with him, sir."

"He is Mr. Oldershaw's tutor, I understand?"

"Oh yes—and he made a particular pet of the boy as he was Lady Anne's son. But I regret to say that he and her ladyship do not always agree."

"I do not understand all this," Holdsworth said abruptly.

"Understand what?"

"This place. This talk of masters and tutors and fellows."

"That is because Jerusalem is a world within a world. So is any college in this University, or perhaps at any University. A college is a world with its own laws and customs."

"It might be a world of savages for aught I know."

Elinor repressed a most unladylike desire to laugh, converting the bubble of mirth into a cough. "I was situated as you are when I first came here. Worse, indeed, for I am a woman, since a college is a place exclusively composed of men. I might have made landfall on some undiscovered island on the far side of the world, but for the fortunate circumstance that the inhabitants speak English."

He looked surprised. And then he smiled. "Suppose, madam, that I too have made landfall on this island. Suppose I am a shipwrecked sailor, another Crusoe. But I have been fortunate enough to come across you on the strand the waves have cast me upon; and you are kind enough to enlighten me as to the place where we find ourselves."

Holdsworth's smile took her by surprise after his surly, almost boorish behavior earlier. "First, sir, you must consider that Jerusalem is a species of miniature country. It is governed by a handful of gentlemen, who are obliged to follow, at least in theory, a regimen laid down for them by the college's Founder, and enshrined for perpetuity in the statutes. Jerusalem was founded by one of Lady Anne's ancestors in the reign of Queen Elizabeth. We attach much importance to our Founder's kin at Jerusalem: for not only do they have some influence upon how we may interpret our statutes, they also have the power to appoint two of our fellows, and they have been the source of many benefactions. So you see that—"

A loud, low voice was speaking indistinctly on the stairs. Footsteps were approaching, dragging and heavy. A moment later, Susan flung open the door and a large, elderly man built like a barrel advanced into the room.

"Dr. Carbury!" Elinor cried. "How—how delightful. I did not dare expect you so early."

"Your servant, madam." The voice was like the man: full, slow, deep and a trifle unsteady. "I tore myself away as soon as I could. I did not wish to delay the pleasure of welcoming our visitor."

It was nine o'clock before they sat down to supper. The room was lit by candles on tables and in wall sconces, creating uneven and shifting pools of light among the gathering shadows. The portraits of dead masters on the walls were granted a dim and spurious life by the flickering flames that illuminated them. The balcony above the screens at the far end of the room was almost invisible.

The high table was on a dais at the eastern end, flanked by two great bay windows. There were some ten or twelve men scattered round the great slab of oak, with Dr. Carbury, as of right, in the middle. Beneath the dais, several long tables stood in the body of the hall. Only one of these was occupied. It was at the farther end, nearest the buttery and the kitchens. Here sat a dozen or so young men. They were eating rapidly as though their very lives depended on the speed with which they consumed their food.

"I had expected to see more undergraduates, sir," Holdsworth said to Dr. Carbury, who was fighting his way through a large slice of mutton pie.

"Eh? Nowadays the majority take supper in their own rooms or in those of their friends. The ones you see below are of the poorer sort—sizars in the main, that is to say, undergraduates who are supported by the foundation."

"It is a fine thing for them to have such a chance of advancement."

"Very true. But I wish they were not such a hangdog, out-at-elbows crew."

Mr. Richardson, who was sitting opposite, leaned towards them. "Why, as to that, Dr. Carbury, one might turn the argument upon its head. If you look around this table, at least half or more of the men you see were once sizars, here or at another college. Most of our other undergraduates do not trouble themselves overmuch with work. Many do not take a degree. So the college needs its sizars as much as they need us. Most of our scholars will come from their ranks."

"Well, sir, it is natural that you of all people should—"

At this point there was a burst of drunken laughter in the court beyond the big window on Holdsworth's left. Dr. Carbury broke off and looked sharply in the direction of the sound.

"Ah," said Richardson blandly. "I believe I recognize the merry tones of Mr. Archdale. At least our sizars are not noisy. You must allow that."

Carbury picked a shred of meat from his teeth. "That young man grows rowdy."

"I am afraid so, Master. *Dulce est desipere in loco.*"

A tall young man sitting near the end of the table said with a gasp of half-suppressed amusement, "I believe he has been dining with Mr. Whichcote, sir. I fancy that might explain it on this occasion."

"Indeed, Mr. Dow." Carbury glowered down the table at him. "You do not seek to make excuses for Mr. Archdale, I trust? You would not make light of his behavior?"

"No, no, Master. A virtuous mind allied to a cultivated understanding must ever—"

"Depend upon it, I shall have a word with Mr. Archdale tomorrow," Richardson put in smoothly. "A word in time saves nine, as they say. After all, Horace's recipe advises only a dash of folly in one's wisdom, and Mr. Archdale appears to have mistaken the proportions in his moral cookery."

The little witticism raised a general laugh around the table, though Holdsworth noticed that Carbury did not join in. When the meal was over, the company moved to the combination room, which lay immediately behind the dais. Two tables had been set up, each with its own kettle to hand; one was for the tea drinkers, and the other for those who preferred punch. Some of the party continued with their wine.

Mr. Richardson was among the tea drinkers. He turned to Holdsworth with a smile and offered him the chair on his left. Dr. Carbury took the seat at the head of the table with the decanter at his elbow. He leaned towards Holdsworth, and was on the verge of speaking when he was interrupted by a shout of laughter from the other table, where most of the younger fellows had gathered.

"What is it?" Carbury asked. His thick lips were stained purple with wine. "Why are they making that damned racket?"

"Mr. Miskin has proposed another wager, Master," Richardson answered. "No doubt we shall soon learn its nature."

Not five minutes later a college servant appeared at Richardson's shoulder and murmured that Mr. Miskin begged permission to enter a wager in the wager book. Richardson graciously gave his consent.

"The younger men derive much enjoyment from their wager book," he told Holdsworth. "And some of the older ones, I am afraid. We shall soon find out what it is—before the wager is officially enacted, it must be approved by me; and to do that, I must see the book and initial the entry. By virtue of being the senior fellow, you see, I am president of this combination room."

"We must not bore our guest with the minutiae of our parlor," Carbury interrupted. "His time is too valuable. Mr. Holdsworth, sir, will you take a glass with me?"

Holdsworth could not decently refuse. Richardson watched them, and for an instant the pink, wet tip of his tongue flickered between his lips.

"You must let me know how I may be of service to you," Carbury said once he had drained his glass. "I shall place myself quite at your disposal."

"Yes," Richardson said, drawing out the monosyllable. "After all, Mr. Holdsworth is here on behalf of Lady Anne, and I know you like to oblige her ladyship. As of course we all do."

The words seemed innocuous, but Carbury flushed a deeper color.

Richardson turned to Holdsworth. "I wonder, sir, when would you find it convenient for me to show you our library? I am at liberty tomorrow morning."

"I'm afraid I shall be engaged in the morning." Holdsworth saw in Richardson's face a fleeting change of expression, a sharpening of interest, instantly smoothed away. "But after dinner, perhaps, if you could spare me an hour or so?"

"With all my heart. At six o'clock? Would that be agreeable? I shall speak to my library clerk, too—you must call on him for assistance while you are here."

"At what hour do you dine?"

"Three o'clock," Richardson said. "We are sadly rustic, I am afraid. Indeed, until a few years ago we continued to dine at one o'clock, just as our fathers and grandfathers had done. In Cambridge, three o'clock is considered almost shamefully *à la mode*. Shall you join us tomorrow, Mr. Holdsworth? I do hope so."

"Unfortunately, I cannot say for certain at this moment. My time is not my own."

The combination-room servant was now hovering with a tray bearing pen and ink, and a quarto-sized book bound in leather. Richardson told the man to lay it on the table in front of him.

"Now, let us see what they propose to do this time." He opened the book and turned the pages. "Ah—Mr. Miskin wagers Mr. Crowley two bottles of wine that—ah—" He broke off, frowning slightly; but after a moment he picked up the pen and initialled the entry.

Richardson glanced across the table at Carbury. He turned the page to the previous set of wagers, angling the book so the light was better for Holdsworth to read by. "Some of the bets are trivial matters of interest only to ourselves, but others touch on University affairs or even matters of national moment. You see? Here is one about Mr. Pitt's changes to the administration; and here is another about the plane tree in Herodotus. And here—oh dear—Mr. Miskin wagers Mr. Whichcote that he can arrange the fellowship in order of weight. Mr. Miskin is one of our livelier young men. I regret to say that in that case we were obliged to bring in the buttery scales to establish the victor."

"Mr. Whichcote?" Holdsworth said, playing the innocent. "The gentleman who was mentioned earlier, who was dining with Mr. Archdale? Is he a fellow of the college too?"

"Oh no. But he is something of a personage at Jerusalem. He often makes an appearance in the wager book."

Richardson's head was very close to Holdsworth's own. Immediately behind Richardson on the table was a candlestick, and the light from those flames threw his face into shadow and illuminated Holdsworth's.

Holdsworth said carefully, "Have I heard the name elsewhere? It seems familiar."

"It's possible. Or you may have come across other members of the family. Their principal seat is in Northumberland. Our Mr. Whichcote belongs to a cadet branch. He was admitted at this college as a pensioner some ten or twelve years ago but he did not take his degree. Like so many of our young men, he was not what you would call a hard-reading man. However, he still resides in Cambridge and has many friends here."

He would have said more but Dr. Carbury had a fit of coughing and spluttering. The servant was at his side in a moment, offering a glass of water. Carbury took a sip and waved the man away. His complexion had become mottled, and he was sweating. He pushed his chair back and stood up.

"Pray excuse me," he said to Holdsworth. "I have some reading to do before bed. My servant will wait up for you in the Lodge. We shall meet again at breakfast, no doubt."

Saying a general good night to the company, Carbury hurried from the room. The conversations around them began again, at a higher volume than before.

Holdsworth glanced down at the book on the table and turned the page. Here was the wager that had just been recorded: *The Revd. Mr. Miskin wagers Mr. Crowley two bottles of wine that the ghost will not appear again before the end of term.*

"So the college has a ghost?" he said.

"No, sir, we merely have a foolish story." Richardson closed the book and handed it to the servant. "The undergraduates make up tales to frighten each other."

8

THE GARDENS OF LAMBOURNE HOUSE ran down to the north bank of the River Cam. The previous owner, Mr. Whichcote's great-uncle, had built the elegant pavilion there; its tall windows had a fine prospect over the water, with Jesus Green and Midsummer Common beyond. On the ground floor was a loggia where one could sit and take the air on fine afternoons. The pavilion seemed far removed from the bustle of Cambridge, though in fact Mr. Essex's Great Bridge into the town was only a few hundred yards away in one direction, and the jail in the castle gatehouse a few hundred yards in another.

The principal apartment was on the first floor, a large, south-facing room in the form of a double cube. Mr. Whichcote's great-uncle had used it as a gallery to display his collection of antique statuary; he also applied himself there to the main occupation of his declining years, a biographical and critical study of Archbishop Ussher. The room was entirely separate from the house, which was why Philip Whichcote usually entertained his bachelor parties there. Some of his visitors preferred to be discreet about their comings and goings, and for these retiring souls the river frontage had much to recommend it, particularly in the warmer weather.

On Friday, 26 May, Whichcote played cards after dinner with a group of young friends, some from Jerusalem, some from other colleges. Despite its noble proportions, the room did not look its best in the merciless early evening sunlight. It was better in the evening, when candlelight cast a forgiving glow on ragged curtains, on frayed Turkey carpets spotted with burns, and on walls stained with smoke and with the damps of winter.

By now most of the guests had gone. Only Harry Archdale was left. He sat with his host at a table beside one of the windows. He was a plump youth with large, wet lips and a small chin. When and if he reached the age of twenty-five, he would acquire complete control of a fortune estimated at nearly £3,000 a year. He was playing piquet with Whichcote and was inordinately excited because he had won the last game. This had distracted him from the fact that he had lost not only the previous five but also the *partie* as a whole.

Augustus, the little footboy, slipped into the room and sidled around the walls until he reached his master's chair. He murmured in Mr. Whichcote's ear that Mr. Mulgrave was waiting his pleasure up at the house.

"Well, I had you on the run that time, eh?" Archdale said, beaming and perspiring and seeming plumper than ever, as though someone were inflating him with gas. "You can't deny that—you'd better look to your winnings! Another *partie*?"

Whichcote smiled at his guest. "I regret we must postpone it. I have a small matter of business to attend to."

The animation slipped from Archdale's face. "Philip," he said in a rush, "I rode out to Barnwell yesterday afternoon and tried to see Frank. But they wouldn't let me in. There's nothing wrong, is there? I thought you said he is on the mend?"

"Indeed he is. Your feelings do you credit, Harry, but you must not disturb yourself in the slightest. I have it on very good authority that he is making excellent progress. Why, I believe he may soon remove to London to be with his mother. They would not let him travel if he were not in good health, would they?"

"I suppose not. But why is he like this? I cannot understand it."

"It's simple enough. His imagination is disordered. You saw what he was like that last day when you dined with him at the Hoop.

Full of fears and fidgets. I had supper with him in college that evening, you know, and he was in such a melancholy state one could hardly distinguish it from mania. Poor fellow, I have seen this happen before—he had been living too hard; some men can take it, others can't. Frank is not as strong as you, I'm afraid."

"I've always been robust."

"Quite so. But not everyone is so fortunate in his constitution. Frank's nervous prostration is nothing out of the way. All that is needed is a little time away from the world. Nine times out of ten, tranquillity is the best medicine. If I've seen it answer once I've seen it answer a dozen times. You may depend upon it that after the Long Vacation Frank will be back among us and quite his old self."

"Still, I wish they'd let me see him."

"I am sure they soon will." Whichcote smiled at him. "Now—much as I wish you would stay, did you not tell me you had invited a party of friends to supper?"

"Supper?" Archdale pulled out his watch, a handsomely enamelled French piece. "Good God, is it as late as that? Devil take it, I had meant to work at my exercise for Mr. Richardson before supper."

"Ricky will wait, I am sure."

"You do not understand. This is to be my entry for the Vauden Medal. And my guardian wishes to see it before I submit it. He dines in Jerusalem on Sunday, and he has a most particular interest in the medal, because his brother won it."

"Surely that's no reason why you should trouble yourself in the matter?"

"It is if I wish him to increase my allowance. I must at least enter for it. No, I must go. I must not waste an instant."

Whichcote summoned Augustus. Archdale pushed back his chair and stood up. Almost immediately he lost his balance and was forced to cling to the table, knocking over his glass and spilling what was left of his wine. The footboy steadied him. Archdale pushed the servant's arm away.

"Clumsy oaf," he said. "Look what you made me do."

Whichcote had crossed the room to a writing table. "You may as well sign these now," he said. "Then we're square for next time."

Archdale staggered to the writing table and scrawled his signature at the foot of a note of hand for sixty-four guineas. Afterwards, Whichcote conducted his visitor to the punt moored at the little jetty on the river bank. Augustus followed, carrying Archdale's cap and gown with a certain reverence. Archdale was a fellow-commoner, so the cap was velvet with a gold tassel, and the gown was richly trimmed with gold lace. Whichcote and the footboy maneuvered him from the safety of dry land.

Cursing and puffing, Archdale settled himself on the cushions. He lay back, legs splayed apart, twitching like an upturned turtle. Signing away sixty-four guineas had raised his spirits again. He waggled his finger at Whichcote on the bank. "I've got you on the run, eh?" he crowed. "Soon we shall have another *partie*, eh, and this time you shall find me quite merciless."

At a sign from his master, Augustus worked the pole out of the mud and expertly punted the unwieldy craft into the center of the stream. Whichcote raised his hand in farewell and walked slowly up the garden to the side door of the house.

Mulgrave was sitting on a bench in the hall. As soon as Whichcote opened the door, the gyp sprang to his feet and bowed, a little awkwardly because of his lopsided shoulders. The two men had known each other ever since Whichcote had come up to Jerusalem at the age of seventeen.

"I thought you'd want to hear right away, sir," Mulgrave said. "Her ladyship's man came by the coach this afternoon."

"What's his name?"

"Holdsworth. They say he's a bookseller from London."

"A bookseller?" Whichcote repeated, amused. "I expected a physician or a lawyer. Where does he lodge?"

"With the Master, sir."

"How did he strike you?"

"Holdsworth?" Mulgrave looked at Whichcote, his face guile-less. "A big man. Bigger than poor Mr. Cross, and younger too. Just as well." He paused a moment. "He don't look as if he smiles much."

On the same Friday evening, Mr. Philip Whichcote called on Mrs. Phear. The lady lived on the east side of Trumpington Street, op-posite Peterhouse, in a small double-fronted house, with four prim windows overlooking the street and a fanlight and a lantern above the front door. The doorstep was white-stoned every morning by a gangling maid named Dorcas, a poorhouse apprentice who feared Mrs. Phear far more than she feared Almighty God because He at least was reputed to be merciful.

Whichcote arrived in a sedan chair. He paid off the bearers and rapped with the head of his cane on the front door. When Dorcas saw who was waiting on the doorstep, she curtsied and stood back.

"Madam is in the parlor, sir."

He found Mrs. Phear engaged with her needle and thread in a chair by the window. There was still a little light outside but two candles were burning on her worktable. She had been working for several weeks on a small tapestry showing the destruction of Sodom, or possibly Gomorrah; it didn't much signify which. The tapestry was designed as a sampler to aid instruction at a small school attached to the Magdalene Hospital, a reformatory for fallen women in London. When Mr. Whichcote was announced, Mrs. Phear set aside her embroidery and began to rise.

"Pray do not disturb yourself, ma'am," he said, coming forward. "No need to stand on ceremony."

She ignored him, however, rose to her feet and curtsied. Smil-ing, for he understood the game perfectly, he bowed to her.

"Mr. Whichcote, I am rejoiced to see you. I hope I find you well?"

They passed a minute or two in what Mrs. Phear called, when instructing some of those who paid for her services in other capaci-ties, "the civilities of genteel intercourse." Mrs. Phear was a tiny, dumpy woman with a widow's cap pulled low over her plain face. Whichcote had known her since he was five years old, when she came to be governess to his sister, and she had later married a neighboring clergyman, who had died shortly afterwards.

The maid was summoned, and the materials for making tea were brought to the room and set beside Mrs. Phear's chair.

"Dorcas," Mrs. Phear said. "Go to the kitchen and clean the knives. Do it directly. They are sadly in need of it."

When they were alone, Mrs. Phear unlocked the caddy and busied herself in measuring the tea into the pot. She stirred the leaves into the water and stared into the vortex of black, swirling specks. She sat back and looked at Whichcote. "Well?"

Whichcote drummed his fingers slowly on the arm of his chair. "There you are, my dear madam, sitting like patience on a monument. I have come to inquire whether matters are in order for Wednesday."

"Pray lower your voice. And yes—all is in order. A nice, plump little bird. On the young side."

He said nothing but raised his eyebrows.

"Ready for the plucking, I assure you," she went on. "And it won't be for the first time, though she knows how to make it seem so. Who is it this time?"

"Young Archdale. Also ready for the plucking, in his own way. You are sure she will be here in time?"

"You need not be anxious about that."

"But I am anxious," he said. "Consider what happened last time. Of course I am anxious."

"Last time we were unlucky, my dear," she said, handing him his cup.

His hand shook, and tea slopped into the saucer. "Unlucky? Is that what you call it?"

"How could we have known what would happen? What's done is done. At least we brought Tabitha Skinner back here, and the coroner made no difficulties about either fatality."

"It was the worst night of my life. First her." He stared at the embroidery. "Then Sylvia."

"This time there will be no difficulties. Not with the girl."

"What should I do without you, dear madam?" he said sourly.

"There is no point in wasting your smooth words on me, my dear."

He burst out laughing, and she smiled at him. Then, serious again, he said, "You do not think it is too soon to have another dinner, another meeting? The long and short of it is, I need ready money, and that is the only resource left to me, besides cards."

"It is a private party, Philip, not a rout. Besides, what has your club to do with propriety? Your boys will admire you all the more. You will be confirmed as a bold spirit, a man who cares naught for petty convention."

"I have another difficulty to lay at your feet, ma'am."

"The little matter of the ghost?"

He nodded. "And—worse than that, much worse—Frank Oldershaw. I feel like a man walking underneath a black cloud and expecting at any moment the heavens to open."

She sipped her own tea. "Has he regained his reason? Does he have lucid intervals?"

"Not to my knowledge. I should hear it if he does. But there has been one development—her ladyship has sent a man to pry on her behalf. He arrived at Jerusalem today."

"Ah—her ladyship. That is the root of the difficulty, I fancy."

"No, madam," Whichcote snapped. "The root of the matter is Sylvia. How could she do this to me? How could she, ma'am?"

"I told you at the time you should have done better than the daughter of a country attorney with hardly a shilling to her name."

Whichcote stood up and moved restlessly about the room. "It is as if she haunts me, as if she finds ways to goad me, even now. Do you know, I thought I saw her today? Sitting in the pastry-cook's in Petty Cury. It was someone else, of course, but—"

"This is childish talk, Philip. Why do you not sit down?"

He glared at her, but a moment later he resumed his seat.

"There, that is better." Mrs. Phear smiled at him. "Yes, if it pleases you, I shall agree that it is Sylvia's fault."

"I did not mean that exactly, I—"

"Sylvia is dead, my dear. That is the point. Now you must begin afresh. You are still a young man. And once you have dealt with the little matter of Mr. Frank, you must forget that Sylvia ever existed."

9

THE AIR IN THE COMBINATION ROOM was thick with the fumes of punch and tobacco. Holdsworth's head was aching, and his eye sockets felt as though they were lined with fine sand. He begged to be excused. At once, Richardson rose from his seat and offered to walk with him.

"Thank you, but I do not think I shall lose my way."

"I am sure you won't, but should you like a turn or two in the garden before you retire? I find that a little fresh air and healthful exercise clear the head and promote sleep."

Holdsworth accepted the invitation. Richardson led him outside into a court surrounded by buildings faced in palely gleaming ashlar. On the right were the lofty bay windows of the combination room and the hall. Richardson nodded at the nearer window. It was uncurtained, and the men they had just left were seated at the two tables in a haze of fellowship.

"They are clubbable fellows, by and large," he remarked. "One cannot begrudge them their dull potations. But some of them will have sore heads in the morning."

He took Holdsworth's arm, and they strolled along the arcade in front of the chapel. There were lighted windows in the building on the other side of the court, directly facing the hall and the combination room. From one of them on the first floor came a burst of laughter and a muffled thumping as though many fists were pounding against a table.

Richardson sighed. "Mr. Archdale continues to enjoy the pleasures of society."

A voice began to sing, at first uncertainly but then finding the tune and gaining in volume. Other voices joined in. The sound was not melodious but it was undoubtedly vigorous. The thumping continued, beating time to the song. Holdsworth and Richardson lingered in the shadows under the arcade. The verses were short and many of the singers appeared not to know the words. All of them, however, joined in the refrain with great gusto.

> *Jerry Carbury is merry*
> *Tell his servant bring his hat*
> *For 'ere the evening is done*
> *He'll surely shoot the cat.*

"Some of our young men do not treat the Master with the respect he deserves," Richardson murmured. "That vulgar ditty has attained a lamentable popularity among them. It is unkind indeed—Dr. Carbury has a weak stomach, and was once compelled to vomit in public."

A door opened further along the range, and a gowned man was briefly illuminated by the lantern hanging above the archway. Glancing towards the sound of the singing, he then set off at a fast pace towards the screens at the western end of the hall.

"Mr. Soresby?" Richardson called. "A moment of your time, please."

The man changed direction and made his way towards them. He was tall and thin, and he did not so much walk as scurry. He doffed his cap and bowed awkwardly to Mr. Richardson. He looked towards Holdsworth, who was in the shadows of the arcade. Richardson did not introduce him.

"Mr. Soresby," he said gently. "Would you oblige me by stepping up to Mr. Archdale's? Pray present my compliments and inform him that he would do me a great service if he would close his windows and moderate the volume of his singing."

"I—I believe there is a porter in the lodge, sir. Perhaps it would be fitter if—"

"I should be so very grateful, Mr. Soresby."

"Yes, sir. Of course, sir."

The man slipped away to the doorway leading to Archdale's staircase. Richardson laid a hand on Holdsworth's arm, detaining him. Once again, the light above the doorway fell on Soresby's stooping figure and shabby gown. The singing continued for a few minutes more and then tailed away. To Holdsworth's surprise, Richardson did not move. Next came a silence, followed swiftly by a great burst of laughter. In another moment, the two sash windows belonging to the room were closed and the shutters were drawn across. This was followed almost immediately by a thumping sound, as if someone had fallen down a flight of stairs, which terminated in a gasp of pain. Richardson made a sign to Holdsworth, and the two men walked away.

The arcade, which ran the entire length of the eastern range, backed on to the chapel in its center but on either side of this were two bays that opened on to the gardens beyond. Stretching south from the arcade was another range, which the tutor said was known as New Building.

Mr. Richardson led Holdsworth on to a path running eastwards into the gathering darkness. Holdsworth's eyes became accustomed to the gloom. The flagged path glimmered before them. The stars were beginning to emerge. On their left was the chapel, and then a stretch of water crossed by a humped wooden footbridge.

"Mr. Soresby did not have an enviable task by the sound of it," Holdsworth said.

"He is a sizar," Richardson replied. "It is not an enviable position."

"They are the very poorest of the undergraduates?"

"Indeed they are. The statutes laid down that they should be supported partly from the foundation but that they should also earn their keep through working as menials. That has largely changed, I am glad to say. But when I entered this college as a youth of sixteen, they still waited upon the fellows and fellow-commoners as they ate, and then they dined from the scraps left over. Some of them would even act as private servants to the fellows. Even now, many are poor devils who scrimp and save to take a degree, who are not too proud to run errands to make ends meet. Yet we may be sure that among them are those who will go on to earn distinction both in the University and in the wider world. In point of fact, I was once a sizar myself."

The night was very still. The revelry in Chapel Court had died away and they might have been in the depth of the country. Most of the windows of New Building were in darkness. They passed under the shadow of a great tree.

"Soresby serves as my library clerk—you will meet him again tomorrow." Richardson gestured at the shadows above and around them. "By the way, we are beneath the Founder's oriental plane. We are very proud of it here. Sir Walter Vauden planted it with his own hands. Some say it is the greatest tree in Cambridge, and certainly there is none quite like it."

"There was a wager concerning a plane tree."

Richardson chuckled. "Members of this college take notice of plane trees wherever they find them. That one is in Herodotus. The Emperor Xerxes conceived an admiration for it and ordered it to be adorned with gold."

"Is this water called the Long Pond?" Holdsworth asked.

"Yes."

Holdsworth waited but Richardson made no mention of the body that had been found in it earlier in the year.

The pond curved to the left and the path came to a gate set in a wrought-iron screen. Richardson unlocked it and they passed through.

"This is the Fellows' Garden," he said. "The ancients would have called it a *hortus conclusus*."

"An enclosed garden?"

"Just so. Enclosed and inviolate." Richardson's voice was so quiet now that the other man had to strain to hear it. "The college itself becomes a fortress at night when its gates are locked. But here, in the Fellows' Garden, we are doubly enclosed, and so doubly inviolate. Look to your left, my dear sir, through that opening among the branches on the other side of the water. There you see Dr. Carbury's private garden. It runs all the way from here up to the Master's Lodge."

Holdsworth stared through the gap at the farther bank. Directly ahead was a lighted window on the first floor of the Lodge. The window was open, and the sound of raised male voices came faintly through the still night air. Beside him, Richardson was as rigid as a dog scenting game.

As they watched, a figure appeared at the window. Holdsworth saw only a fuzzy silhouette, outlined by candlelight in the room behind, but the shape was almost certainly Carbury's. The lower sash scraped downwards and hit the sill with the sound like the rapping of a gavel.

Carbury tugged the curtains across the window. The light vanished.

"Ah," said Richardson, letting out his breath in a lingering sigh. "And now all is darkness."

Out of the darkness.

"Georgie? Georgie?"

The voice pulled Holdsworth towards consciousness. *Maria.* This was his first thought, instantly suppressed.

It was still dark. *Am I dreaming?* He was too warm, his body shrouded in the bedclothes. His mouth was dry, which was not surprising after so much wine at supper. And he was uncomfortably aware of another source of discomfort, as shameful as it was urgent. He was as stiff as a ramrod.

"Georgie? Come to Mama."

Let me consider this analytically, he thought. I am not an animal.

His wife returned to his sleeping self more often now than just after her death. Sometimes it was only the echo of her voice or a smell lingering in the air—or even a painfully sharp awareness of her absence, as though she had very recently been there. Or not there, depending on how you looked at it. Because that, surely, lay at the heart of the thing: it was not really she who was or had been there. It was a personalized emptiness—a sort of enclosed nothing, a longing for something that no longer existed, or not in this world.

But still—one could give a name even to an irrational sensation. Why should he not call this one Maria? It was a species of philosophical shorthand.

He tried to turn his body in the bed but the blankets still held him fast. All the abortive movement achieved was the application of sweetly uncomfortable pressure to his *membrum virile*.

My love, forgive me. My prick misbehaves.

Somewhere between waking and sleeping, he sensed Maria's presence. He fancied he saw her outline, just for a moment, a shadow among shadows between the bed and window, but somehow darker than the shadows that surrounded it.

He was breathing too fast, and he couldn't suck in enough air. He tried to slow the rhythm but something stronger than his will increased the tempo instead. Soon his nightshirt was drenched with sweat. He shivered, and once he had started he could not make himself stop.

Slowly the dream, if that was what it was, filled with gray light, a sort of illuminated mist that cloaked as much as it revealed. He was no longer in his bed but standing in the Fellows' Garden and looking down at the Long Pond, just as he had with Richardson a few hours earlier. The transition did not strike him as in any way strange. He looked down and there was Maria, floating face upwards on the water, her body submerged an inch or two below the surface. Despite this apparent handicap, she was speaking, or rather he heard her voice quite distinctly.

"Georgie," she cried. "Georgie, I am here now. Come here, my little one."

Maria, who had drowned in the Thames, was now drowning in the Long Pond. In the logic of the dream, the water was the same, and perhaps all times and places flowed through the same essential nexus of circumstance, and you saw one or the other—in this case the Long Pond at Jerusalem in May or the Thames at Bankside in March—according to your perspective on the matter. In the dream, this speculation seemed entirely rational and he wondered why he had not thought of it before.

"Come out!" he shouted. "You'll drown. Take my hand. Quick."

But Maria did not hear. She was still calling for Georgie, and telling him that Mama loved her own boy, and that he was Mama's little sugar plum.

He shrieked wordlessly at her.

"Georgie, Georgie." Her voice was fainter now. "Mama's own little boy."

Her body was no longer there. Indeed, now there was nothing left except the thick, black water of the Long Pond, and it was rising higher and higher.

"Georgie?" The voice was no more than a whisper on the edge of silence. "Georgie?"

Holdsworth groaned. His ears hurt, and he had the curious sensation that his skin had been stripped away from the bleeding flesh beneath. His hands tingled. Underlying everything was still the disgusting, desperate desire to copulate.

Stiff as a ramrod.

"Maria?" he muttered. Something puzzled him, but he could not pin it down, a monstrous and unspeakable anomaly of some sort. "Maria? Maria?"

It was only then, as he said her name for the third time, that he realized what the anomaly had been. It was quite inexplicable that he had not noticed at the time. The face he had seen distorted in the water had not been Maria's face. The voice had been Maria's. But the face had belonged to Elinor Carbury.

Pain lanced into his chest. An iron band tightened around his ribs. It tightened, squeezing the breath from his lungs. He opened his mouth to scream but the rising tide of black water now covered his mouth. As his lips parted, the darkness flowed inside him. His body convulsed.

He wrenched himself from the blankets. He was falling. A jolt ran through him.

Full consciousness flooded over him, and he knew that he was in the bedchamber at the Master's Lodge, lying on the bare boards between the bedstead and its surrounding curtains. His left elbow, which had borne the brunt of his fall, was exquisitely painful. He flailed with his arms and succeeded in finding the gap between the curtains. A cooling draught brushed his cheek. And there was a little light, too—a faint vertical line where the shutters failed to meet across the window.

Dear God—Elinor Carbury? He pushed the thought of her away. He despised himself and his treacherous, sin-ridden body.

A nearby clock with an unfamiliar set of chimes struck the three-quarters. Holdsworth stood up, steadying himself on the bedpost. He tore off his nightcap and rubbed the sleep from his eyes. He shuffled across to the window and opened the shutters. His body ached. To the east there was a pallor in the sky, an easing of the darkness. Thank God, it would soon be day. His erection slowly shrivelled.

The air was chilly. The window seat had a strip of cushion running along the top. He perched on it, drawing up his legs, wrapping the hem of the nightshirt under his feet and hugging his knees like an overgrown child.

Outside the window, light crept back into the gardens of Jerusalem. He grew steadily colder. He made an irrational decision, again like a child who invents a purpose because even an invented purpose is better than none: that he would permit himself to return to bed as soon as he saw or heard another human being, an incontrovertible sign of life and sanity returning to the world.

He had not long to wait. Through the glass of the window came the rattle of iron-rimmed wheels on stone. He craned his head and caught sight of a hunched figure trundling a little barrow along the flagged path at the back of the Master's Lodge. It was a man in a long dark coat and a slouch hat. He was making his way to a cluster of outbuildings on the left, near the northern boundary of the college.

The night-soil man. There was no one else it could be. The man who had found Sylvia Whichcote in the Long Pond.

The night-soil man. There was no one else to see. Not Maria. Not Elinor Carbury.

10

A FTER BREAKFAST, Ben, the Master's manservant, directed Holdsworth to a stationer's, where he purchased a plan of the town and its environs. Guided by this he set out on the road to Barnwell, which lay to the east of the town in the Newmarket direction. It was not quite a village and not quite a suburb of Cambridge, but something indeterminate between the two. Carbury warned him that parts of the neighborhood were not agreeable. There were disreputable taverns and houses of ill fame, which attracted low characters from both the town and the University.

None of this was visible on Saturday morning. The road was busy, mostly with traffic going the other way towards the town's market and shops. The house Holdsworth was seeking was on the eastern edge of Barnwell, where the houses were fewer and the air of the place was notably more rural.

The exercise and the morning sunshine made it possible to put the terrors of the night into perspective. A rational man need not chastise himself for his dreams, Holdsworth reminded himself, for they were quite outside his control and by their very nature replete with absurd fancies and sensations. There were difficulties enough in his waking life without wilfully manufacturing more.

Dr. Jermyn's establishment stood in its own small pleasure ground. The demesne was surrounded by a wall almost as high as

Jerusalem's. The gates were locked. There was a bell pull mounted on the right-hand gatepost, together with a notice advising visitors to ring and wait. Holdsworth pulled the handle. Thirty seconds later, the front door opened and a manservant came unhurriedly down the drive and inquired civilly enough how he might be of assistance.

"My name is Holdsworth. I believe Dr. Jermyn is expecting me."

The servant bowed and took out a key for the gates.

"You are well guarded against the world," Holdsworth said.

"It's not only to keep people out, sir." The servant locked the gate again when Holdsworth was inside, and began to lead the way up the drive. "It's to keep them in."

As they walked up the drive, Holdsworth glimpsed three or four men in the grounds. One of them appeared to be pruning a bush; another was hoeing a flower bed. There was nothing curious in that except for the fact they were attired not as gardeners but as gentlemen. Even at a distance, Holdsworth could see the black coats, black silk breeches and white waistcoats; and at least two of them had their hair powdered and arranged, as though at any moment they were due to pay a morning call upon a lady.

At the door of the house, the servant rang the bell as though he too were a visitor. Another servant admitted them and showed Holdsworth into a small drawing room, saying that Dr. Jermyn would be with him directly.

Holdsworth prowled about the apartment. He came to the window and stared out over an expanse of sunlit lawn at the side of the house, with an extensive shrubbery beyond. At this moment the door opened, and Dr. Jermyn appeared.

"Mr. Holdsworth, your servant, sir," he said briskly. "Mr. Cross wrote me that you would probably honor us with a call this morning."

The two men exchanged bows. Jermyn was a young man, little more than thirty, with a pleasant, open face. He dressed soberly and neatly, and wore his own hair.

"I see you were examining our windows, sir," he said. "Were you expecting bars across them?"

"I did not know what to expect. Were those your—your patients I saw in the garden?"

"Indeed. Honest toil in the open air has much to recommend it. I am glad to say that a number of our gentlemen condescend to assist us."

Holdsworth felt in his pocket. "I have a letter of introduction from her ladyship."

The doctor offered Holdsworth a chair. Murmuring an apology, he broke the seal of the letter and read it slowly. At length he looked up. "These matters are always delicate. And I apprehend that Mr. Oldershaw's case is so in more ways than one. Her ladyship writes that you have her complete trust, and instructs me to give you every assistance in my power."

"And how is Mr. Oldershaw?"

"In terms of his eventual progress towards a cure, I have great hopes of him. His constitution is robust, and his temperament naturally sanguine. His family and friends wish him all that is good. There is no lack of resources. In short, I have seen many patients in far worse circumstances. Indeed, I have had some of them under this roof."

"I do not doubt it," Holdsworth said.

"Nor, in some respects, is his case uncommon. There are many young men who come up to the University ill-prepared to meet the temptations and trials that they find here. Some have never been away from home before. Without firm guidance or, in many cases, the support of carefully inculcated moral principles, they unite the follies of youth with the opportunities of independence and, by degrees, slide towards catastrophe."

"You speak generally, sir," Holdsworth said. "But what of Mr. Oldershaw?"

For the first time Dr. Jermyn hesitated. "Pray, sir, what exactly have they told you? I would not have you meet him unprepared."

"I have seen Mr. Cross's neck."

"Ah. That was indeed unfortunate."

"Her ladyship informs me that her son's temperament from his earliest years has been mild and good-humored."

A noise broke out somewhere above their heads, a distant howling, followed by rapid footsteps and the slamming of a door.

"One must allow for a mother's partiality," Jermyn said. "I should perhaps preface my remarks by saying that there are aspects of Mr. Oldershaw's case which may not be easily comprehensible to those who are not physicians. Indeed, sir, I suspect that perhaps even the majority of my professional brethren would be quite at sea. Only a physician who has made a particular study of maniacal disorders is really in a position to appreciate the finer points."

"Then pray allow me to manage as best I may with the coarser ones, sir. Why was he brought to you and not to some other medical man in the locality?"

Jermyn stared down at his hands, which were small, white and very clean. Then, perhaps recollecting who was paying the bills, he looked up with a smile.

"Why, as to that, there are not so many of us who specialize in such cases within easy reach of Cambridge. I flatter myself that my name is not unknown in the University. The local physicians, though many of them are admirable men, have not had time or opportunity to study such conditions, let alone the modern science of moral management." Jermyn nodded, as if in approval of himself. "We have come a long way since the days of our grandfathers."

"And who recommended you to Lady Anne?"

"Why, the lad's tutor—Mr. Richardson. It seems that Mr. Oldershaw had not been himself for several weeks—since February. I wish they had called me in earlier. They waited until his condition had worsened considerably. That was in March."

"And what precisely was his condition?"

Jermyn joined his hands together and made a steeple of the fingers. "To put it simply, in lay terms, his melancholy had deepened to the point where he found life insupportable. The proximate cause appears to have been a nervous collapse within one portion of the brain, inducing a form of delirium. Now, we physicians distinguish in these cases between melancholia and mania. Some believe that the two conditions are generically separate, but I hold with Professor Cullen that in fact the difference between them is not one of kind but only of degree. If you consult his *Nosology of Mania* you will find the doctrine explained in great detail."

Holdsworth thought of Maria: of the effect on her of Georgie's loss, and then of the news that she must leave the house where he had lived and where they had brought his battered little corpse: in Jermyn's terms, when melancholia had slipped into mania. "You do not think there was a particular, external cause? A shock of some sort to his system?"

"I do not say that precisely. It is rather that I look to the physiology of the brain to provide my answers, rather than to any events, real or imaginary, that may or may not have taken place outside it."

"And so what of the ghost?"

"Ah—our ghost." Jermyn smiled again. "I wondered when we might arrive at this fabled creature. My dear sir, it is a symptom of Mr. Oldershaw's mania, not a cause."

"I am informed that Mr. Oldershaw was walking in the garden at Jerusalem late one night, and that he believed he saw the ghost of a lady who had recently died, a lady with whom he was acquainted as she was the wife of a friend. And it was this that drove him to attempt to take his own life."

"That is to put the cart before the horse. Consider his unprovoked attack on Mr. Cross. Here we have his mother's steward, an old man he has known since childhood. Mr. Cross barely had time to enter the room where Mr. Oldershaw was sitting when the young man leaped up and attacked him. Had not an attendant and myself been at hand to restrain him, the consequences for Mr. Cross might have been fatal. There is no conceivable *external* reason why Mr. Oldershaw should have attacked him, any more than there is any reason why he should have attempted to destroy himself in the college pond. No, in both cases he was in the grip of the delirium of mania. The technical phrase for it is *mania furibunda*; that is to say, mania attended by violence."

"Let us not be technical for a moment, sir," Holdsworth said. "Had anything happened to make him believe Mr. Cross was his enemy?"

"Not as far as I know." The doctor leaned forward. "Sir, I cannot yet fully explain these particular manifestations of mania, but I believe I know the general phenomenon that makes them possible. You are perhaps familiar with Locke's *Essay upon Human Understanding*?"

"I have glanced over it, yes."

Jermyn permitted himself another smile. *"Inter alia*, it deals with how we discern, and other operations of the mind. And Mr. Locke makes acute remarks on the subject of why madmen fail to discern matters correctly. *In fine*, he argues that madmen are perfectly capable of rational thought. In this, by and by, they differ from idiots, who are constitutionally incapable of reasoning." The physician's voice had imperceptibly acquired the inflections of the pulpit. "But for madmen, the difficulty arises from the propositions they reason from, rather than—"

"Forgive me, sir, but I do not understand how a philosophical error could result in Mr. Oldershaw's mania," Holdsworth said. "And I am also puzzled to understand what his physiology has to do with it."

"You have strayed into the province of the physician, sir, and I'm afraid some confusion is inevitable. It is usually safe to take Mr. Locke as a guide on such matters. Believe me, when you have seen as many of these unfortunate young men as I have, Mr. Locke's theories may not seem so improbable."

"But you are still unable to attribute a cause to his mania? That is the long and the short of it."

"I'm interested in the *fact* of Mr. Oldershaw's delusions, not their content. In general, the ravings of a madman signify no more than the wanderings of a will-o'-the-wisp, and tracking the course of their vagaries is equally beside the point. What does signify, however, is the fact that he is raving. Like everything in the universe, from the orbit of the sun to the migration of swallows, melancholia and mania follow immutable laws. Such laws are like the master keys that permit us to unlock the mysteries of nature, including those of the human mind. They are all we need."

"And all Mr. Oldershaw needs is to recover his senses," Holdsworth said. "What course of treatment do you follow, sir?"

"I practice a system of moral management. I believe it the only effective way. The physician must achieve a benign domination over his patient, both in the psychological and the physical spheres. Once this is done, he can set to work on the defects of understanding that lie at the heart of the patient's malady. Much depends on the physician's ability to master his patient. It is not unlike training a child."

"Moral management," Holdsworth repeated. "You make your patients obedient to you? Like a dog?"

"In essence, yes. It is a system of re-education. We insist on their following appropriate lines of thought, speech and conduct. I confess that with Mr. Oldershaw, I was over-sanguine. I advised Mr. Cross to say to Mr. Oldershaw that he would soon take him home to her ladyship and that, since he was so much improved, it might be agreeable to have a little dinner party here—for Mr. Oldershaw to act as host, and to invite not only Mr. Cross and myself but also some of his acquaintances in Cambridge."

"Who?" Holdsworth said.

"Oh, only three other men. His tutor, Mr. Richardson, of course. And Mr. Whichcote, a most reputable gentleman of some substance, who goes much in society here; recently widowed but he still dines out at small private parties. He made something of a pet of Mr. Oldershaw. And the other man is called Archdale, a fellow-commoner at Jerusalem—he and Oldershaw were always together. I hoped a small dinner for Mr. Oldershaw's intimates would be the first step to restoring him to society. In the event, all was in vain. He became increasingly agitated and, most unfortunately, my attention was distracted for a moment, and as you know he lost all control and tried to assault Mr. Cross. *Mania furibunda* operates in just such a way—as impossible to predict as summer lightning."

"I should like to see him, if I may."

"I cannot advise it, sir. It may provoke—"

"I must insist. Her ladyship has charged me to see him with my own eyes."

With another of his smiles, Dr. Jermyn rose to his feet. He held open the door. There was something shiny and impervious about him, Holdsworth thought, as if he had been coated with a veneer of resin. Neither harsh words nor arguments seemed to reach the interior of the man: they remained on the outside, and drained harmlessly away.

"Very well," Jermyn said. "Even a physician must bow before the tender curiosity of a mother."

II

PHILIP WHICHCOTE STOOD in the doorway and gnawed his forefinger. He did not like looking at the bed but he could not stop himself staring at it. It was an ugly, old-fashioned thing, too big for the room; Sylvia's mother, who had been inordinately proud of it, had given it to them as a wedding present. The bare mattress rested on the wooden skeleton of the frame. The four carved posts at the corners supported a canopy that had always reminded him of the top of a hearse.

Here Sylvia had lain, night after night. Here he had lain with her. Her warm body had pressed down on that mattress, and he had pressed his body against hers. Night after night.

The still, silent room oppressed him for more reasons than he cared to count, but the bed was the worst part of it. He would like to have been able to order them to break it up, take it downstairs to the kitchen garden and burn it, along with the mattress. Instead he would have to sell it for what he could get.

Whichcote went next door to Sylvia's sitting room. He walked rapidly to the nearest window and pulled up the blind. Midday sunshine streamed into the room. Motes of dust danced in the air. He tugged the dust sheets from the furniture. The bureau bookcase was a handsome piece, which had come from his great-uncle. It should be worth something. He pulled the volumes at random from the shelves. Her books should fetch a few guineas at least as well. He'd call in someone from Merrill's or Lunn's and see what they would offer.

He opened the bureau and poked his fingers into its recesses and compartments, hoping he had overlooked something of value the last time he looked. There were rusty nibs, paper, dried-up ink, sealing wax and string. Sylvia had left surprisingly little trace of herself. It was as though she had barely existed. She had spent half her life writing to other women, to her mother in the country, to Elinor Carbury at Jerusalem. But she had not kept the letters she received. She had not kept a diary, either. There was nothing left of her.

Dead. Dead. Dead.

He closed the bureau flap. Behind him, there was a squeak as Augustus cleared his throat. The footboy aimed to produce the discreet cough of a well-trained servant advising his master of his presence. But nature decreed otherwise.

"What is it now?"

"If you please, your honor, Mr. Mulgrave is below."

"Send him to me in the study."

Whichcote locked the door leading to Sylvia's apartments and went downstairs. Almost at once, Augustus announced Mulgrave. The gyp came slowly into the room, his body leaning to the left as it always did because his left leg was shorter than the right.

"Well?" Whichcote demanded.

Mulgrave shrugged. "Not much change, sir. Mr. Oldershaw is quiet enough, they say. They keep him dosed up so he's sleeping most of the time. He's eating like a horse. But there's no life in him, any more than that there sofa."

"Do his attendants believe their master will cure him?"

"They say the doctor's mended a lot of people." Mulgrave smiled. "Made a deal of money out of it at any rate. But he don't seem to have got very far with Mr. Oldershaw. He shouts at him, like at the others—says do this, do that, do the other thing, kiss my arse—but mostly Mr. Oldershaw just sits there. Or he starts yelling and crying fit to burst himself."

"Mind your tongue. Is that all?"

"Still having these violent fits, sir, if that's what you're asking. Not very often, but he's a big lad, Mr. Frank, and you don't want to get in his way when the fit is upon him."

"When do you next visit?"

"Tuesday, sir, unless I hear contrariwise beforehand. Usual thing—shave him and dress his hair, brush his clothes, see to his linen. One thing, though—I hear Mr. Holdsworth's been to Barnwell too."

"Her ladyship's man?"

"Yes." Mulgrave frowned. "Dark horse, that one."

"I should like to hear more about him. Come and see me after you have visited Barnwell again—or before if you have information, especially about Holdsworth."

"As your honor pleases."

Whichcote turned away and stared out of the grimy window. "You may go."

Mulgrave coughed. "Begging your pardon, sir, but there's the little matter of my bill."

"Not now."

"It's mounting up, sir."

"I gave you something the other day," Whichcote snapped.

"A couple of guineas on account in late March, sir." Mulgrave took out a pocketbook and opened it. "March twenty-ninth, sir, to be precise. That was when the account was thirteen pounds, eight shillings and fourpence. Bit more than that now, I'm afraid, not far off twenty pounds."

"Damn it, you shall have it. But not now, man."

Mulgrave held his ground. "Begging your pardon, sir, but these last few months, I can't help noticing you're not as flush as you were. You've sent the footmen away, haven't you? There's only that boy to wait on you, and the women."

"My domestic arrangements are nothing to do with you, and I don't choose to discuss them. Leave me."

"And then there's also your note of hand, sir. When there was the trouble with the livery stable."

Whichcote held back his temper. "Your bill isn't due yet. Anyway, the money is as safe as the Bank of England. This is merely a question of a temporary shortage of ready money in the house."

"Oh yes, sir, I don't doubt it. Why, I dare say you could make a completely fresh start if you mortgaged this place, or even sold it, for it must—"

"Damn your eyes, Mulgrave."

"Listen, sir, I don't want to be disobliging, and you and me, sir, we've known each other for a long time. But a man must live. I've got my dependents, same as you." Mulgrave raised his eyebrows very high. "I could apply to her ladyship, I suppose."

"What ladyship?" Whichcote said in a voice hardly louder than a whisper, knowing the answer before he asked the question.

"Why, Lady Anne, of course, sir. Seeing as I've done so much for Mr. Oldershaw since he was admitted at Jerusalem, and now especially at Dr. Jermyn's. I ain't sent in my bill yet. Anyhow, her ladyship might find it a comfort just to talk to me about how he does." He patted his waistcoat. "I feel for her, sir. I'm a parent myself."

"There's no need to trouble her," Whichcote said. "As for the bill, if you wish, I shall look into the matter directly and see if we cannot manage something further on account."

"In full, if you please, sir. With the note of hand, it comes to a little under eighty pounds." Mulgrave opened his pocketbook once again. "I have the exact figure here, sir."

"Something on account, I said," Whichcote repeated.

It was as though the ground itself were giving way beneath him. One winter's day, when he was an undergraduate, he had been shooting in the Fens and the earth beneath him had done just that: what had seemed solid became liquid mud, drawing him down and down and down. If a party of Fenmen had not been within earshot, he would have drowned. They had pulled out his shivering body in its sodden, stained clothes. They had stood around him and laughed.

"Yes, sir," Mulgrave said. "In full. You could raise something on the house, I'm sure. Do it easy."

"Get out," Whichcote said. "Just go. Now."

Mulgrave moved unhurriedly to the door. Before opening it, he stopped and glanced around the room. "I'm sure old Jeevons would oblige in a trice, sir. You know him? Corner of Slaughterhouse Lane. Very reasonable, all things considered.

"There's always a way, your honor, always a way."

They walked side by side up the broad, shallow stairs. A clock ticked in the cool darkness at the back of the hall. The air smelled of beeswax, lemon juice and vinegar. The house radiated normality so powerfully and so perfectly that it made normality itself seem sinister.

On the landing, Jermyn paused. "You may not get much sense out of the poor fellow," he murmured. "As his physician, I cannot sufficiently stress the importance of his treatment continuing. His treatment here, that is—it is imperative not to uproot him."

A private asylum was a commercial enterprise. Holdsworth doubted that Jermyn's motives in setting up the establishment were solely or even primarily scientific, let alone philanthropic. He wondered what Lady Anne was paying the man for her son's board, lodging and treatment, and for all the sundries that no doubt accumulated when a young gentleman of Mr. Oldershaw's standing was residing here. Five guineas a week? Six? If Jermyn had half a dozen patients like this, he must be making a handsome competence. If he had a dozen, say, his income would outstrip that of most landed gentlemen.

On the first floor, the doors leading off the landing were closed. Jermyn entered the nearest on the right without knocking. Holdsworth followed him into a large bedchamber. There were two windows, which overlooked the pleasure grounds at the back of the house. The air smelled sweet.

A broad, muscular man rose to his feet from a chair by the door. Jermyn raised his eyebrows, a silent question. The man nodded. They both looked at a youth sitting at a card table in the corner farthest from the door. He was concentrating on something in front of him. He did not look up.

Jermyn advanced towards his patient. "Well, Frank? And how do you do today?"

The young man did not answer. Holdsworth could not yet see his face. He was dressed plainly but well in black. Like many young men he wore his own hair.

Jermyn beckoned Holdsworth to come forward and turned back to his patient. "Ah, good, Frank, very good indeed. I like to see you engaged in a useful activity."

As he moved across the room, Holdsworth noticed a sturdy wooden armchair standing against the wall near the fireplace. There were broad leather straps attached to the arms, the legs and the back. The straps had the supple, flexible appearance that leather acquires with use.

On a woman, Frank Oldershaw's face would have been called beautiful. He was looking downwards, frowning slightly, like an angel brooding over the imperfections of humanity. On the table before him were several dozen small wooden cubes. Each face of each cube had a little picture on it. Six of them were lined up on the table, with the visible faces matching those of their neighbors so a broader picture was beginning to emerge. The cubes looked unexpectedly familiar, and suddenly Holdsworth recognized them for what they were. They formed an instructive puzzle for use in nurseries. The pieces could be assembled to make six different pictures. The markings on the little engravings ensured that each piece must match its neighbor. One was a genealogical table showing the kings and queens of England back to King Arthur. Another illustrated episodes from the Old Testament, with particular emphasis placed on the prophets, arrayed in their proper order. Frank Oldershaw was working on a table of useful knowledge, rationally displayed. Holdsworth had stocked the puzzle in the Leadenhall shop for a few months but it had not sold well.

"Frank, you must interrupt your labors for a moment. There is a visitor to see you."

Very slowly, Frank placed the cube in his hand on the table and looked up, first at Jermyn, then at Holdsworth.

"Pray rise, sir," Jermyn said. "It is what we do in polite society when we are introduced to somebody."

Slowly, Frank rose to his feet. He was a large youth, nearly as tall as Holdsworth himself though less broad; his movements still had an adolescent gawkiness, as if he had not quite learned to live with the unaccustomed length and weight of his limbs. Despite the beauty of his face, there was nothing effeminate about his appearance. He stood in front of them, shoulders rounded, head lowered. Holdsworth bowed. Frank responded with a twitch of his head.

"Good," Jermyn said. "This is very agreeable. We are getting on famously, are we not?"

He paused but no one spoke.

"Her ladyship has sent Mr. Holdsworth down to see you," Jermyn went on. "Who knows, if you continue as you do for a few more weeks, he may even be able to take you back to London."

Frank Oldershaw came to life like a sprung trap in a covert. He whirled round, arms outstretched, and swept the wooden pieces of the puzzle from the table. Jermyn stepped back, his face expressionless. Equally abruptly, Frank reversed the direction of his movement. He sent the little table flying into the corner.

The episode was over almost as soon as it had begun. The attendant rushed across the room and grasped Frank in such a powerful hold that he could not move his arms. The young man heaved and strained and stamped. But he could not break the grip.

Jermyn rang a bell in the wall beside the fireplace. The door opened and two more men appeared. Between them they forced Frank into the armchair and strapped him in. All this time no one said a thing. It was as if such episodes were so familiar that there was nothing left to say about them.

Holdsworth picked up the table and set it upright. As he did so, he trod on one of the cubes. He bent down and picked that up too. He put it down on the table. Animal husbandry was uppermost. He turned it over and got the sacrifice of Isaac instead. He looked up suddenly. Frank was staring intently at him.

"That was very wrong," Jermyn said sternly, bringing his face down to the level of Frank's. "You must not allow these fits of temper to master you."

Frank's mouth gaped wide. He stuck out his tongue and waggled it from side to side. "Quack," he said. "Quack."

"You must apologize," Jermyn went on. "To me, and of course to Mr. Holdsworth, who, as your mother's emissary, deserves your particular attention. And to poor Norcross, who was obliged to restrain you again."

Frank bowed his head, shutting them all out.

Jermyn seized his patient by the hair and yanked his head back. Frank stared up into the doctor's face. "Look at me, Frank," Jermyn said firmly. "Look at me and tell me who is master here."

Frank screwed his eyes shut, retreating into a private darkness.

Jermyn nodded to Norcross, who came forward, stood behind the chair, and prised open Frank's eyelids with his thumbs. He pulled back the head so Frank was looking directly into Jermyn's face, hardly six inches above his own.

"Look at me," Jermyn said. "And tell me who is the master here."

Frank's eyeballs twitched and rolled as though he were having a fit. He spat at Jermyn. The doctor stood back and carefully hit his patient twice, left palm to right cheek, right palm to left cheek. He took out a handkerchief and wiped spittle from his face and the sleeve of his coat.

"You are here for your own good," Jermyn said in a deep, resonant voice, speaking slowly and rhythmically. "It is for your own good that you must obey me in all things. Who is the master here?"

Frank's tongue appeared briefly between his lips as though he were moistening them. He made a gargling sound deep in his throat.

"Who is the master here?" Jermyn repeated, and as he spoke he glanced up at the attendant, who responded by jerking Frank's head farther backward and digging in his thumbs more deeply to the eye sockets.

"You are," Frank burst out, his voice little more than a hoarse whisper.

"Say it like this," Jermyn commanded. " 'You are the master here, sir.' "

"You—you are—the master here."

"Sir!" roared Jermyn.

"Sir," Frank muttered.

Jermyn stepped back from his patient and Norcross released his hold. The doctor turned smiling to Holdsworth.

"There you see it, sir," he said cheerfully. "The modern system of moral management in action. Sooner or later it answers in every case. But you must show them who is master. Everything follows from that."

Frank's head fell to his chest. He closed his eyes. The lashes gleamed with moisture.

"I wish to talk to Mr. Oldershaw," Holdsworth said.

"By all means." Jermyn waved towards his silent patient. "However, I do not think his replies will necessarily be much to the point."

"I should prefer to talk to him alone, sir. I have private matters to discuss."

Jermyn smiled courteously. "I do not doubt it, sir. But I cannot permit it."

Norcross picked up a leather gag from the mantelpiece and looked at Jermyn for instructions.

The doctor shook his head. "Later. It is better our visitor should understand what we have to deal with."

Frank drew a long, sobbing breath. He threw back his head and howled like a wolf.

When the noise had abated, Jermyn turned to Holdsworth. "Now, sir," he said briskly. "Now do you understand?"

12

HARRY ARCHDALE TRIED TO GET UP—but as soon as he swung his legs over the side of the bed, he felt intolerably dizzy; and the movement triggered violent internal activity that required him to plunge head first out of bed with his arms out-stretched for the chamber pot. After he had vomited, he was obliged to lie down again to recover.

He drifted into an uncomfortable doze, during which fragmen-tary memories of the events of the previous day floated like lethar-gic fish through his semiconscious mind. He rather thought he had lost the deuce of a lot of money to Philip Whichcote—not be-cause of any lack of skill but because of the way the damned cards had fallen. If Whichcote dunned him for money, which he might well do, Archdale would have to apply to his guardian for another advance on next quarter's allowance, which would lead in turn to another ugly scene, as a consequence of which he might not be able to visit Paris in the Long Vacation after all.

The unwelcome recollection of his guardian's existence led to another, equally unpleasant thought. It must be Saturday today. Sir Charles, who was also his uncle, would be in Cambridge by this evening: he was putting up at the Blue Boar, and tomorrow he was to attend divine service in Great St. Mary's and then dine at Jerusalem. It was of prime importance not to upset the old man. But this would not be easy. His guardian intended to discuss his ward's progress with Mr. Richardson. There was the little matter of his debts—and of course his uncle would see only those from the college and from licensed tradesmen, which came directly to Richardson; but there were others—gambling debts, for example, and all the little sundries of life. To make matters worse, Sir Charles had a bee in his bonnet about Archdale's going in for the Vauden Medal.

Somehow tomorrow had to be managed in a discreet and mutually agreeable way that would leave Archdale in tip-top condition for the excitements of the club meeting on Wednesday evening. He did not want to miss that for the world, for he was due to become an Apostle. The Holy Ghost Club was reputed to be the most select dining club in Cambridge with its members drawn from the first rank of society. There was nothing more desirable than to be one of the Twelve Apostles. But his uncle was quite incapable of appreciating the importance of this. If the curmudgeonly old brute was in an ill humor, he might well withdraw his nephew from the University. He had threatened to do so in his last letter if Archdale failed to live within his allowance and apply himself to his studies. Something must be done, therefore, some little gesture, some *coup de théâtre* that would turn Sir Charles into a paragon of benevolence.

Archdale hauled himself into a sitting position and groaned aloud. There was a tap on the door, and his bedmaker cautiously poked her red face into the room.

"Did you call, sir?" she inquired, her eyes swinging to and fro, taking in the disordered bedclothes, the heap of discarded clothes on the floor, the overflowing chamber pot and Mr. Archdale huddled on his bed.

"No," he bleated. "That is to say, yes. Where's Mulgrave? I need Mulgrave."

"He's not in college this morning, sir."

"That's so provoking. I want—I need—" He ran out of words and chewed his lower lip in silence, waiting for the pain in his head to subside a little.

The bedmaker made up her own mind. "You want tea, sir," she told him. "And I'll send to the buttery for one of their special mixtures. I'll be back directly."

"Yes—no—oh, all right. No, stay. There's something else. I must see Mr. Soresby without delay. Step upstairs and see if he's in the way. They—oh God."

Archdale broke off and reached for the chamber pot. The bedmaker slipped away.

After a while, the inner turbulence subsided, though the headache remained as did the foul taste in his mouth. The bedmaker returned with his tea and a tankard containing the nauseating and extremely expensive restorative the buttery provided for undergraduates in Archdale's situation. She also brought the news that Mr. Soresby would be down in a moment.

The restorative was worth its price. It would be hours before Archdale was fully himself again but soon he was sufficiently recovered to drink his tea in the armchair by the window. Idly, he watched the foreshortened black-clad figures in Chapel Court below. The sight of Mr. Richardson moving diagonally across the lawn towards the Fellows' combination room reminded Archdale that yet again he had missed morning chapel without taking the precaution beforehand of providing himself with a *dormiat*; there would be another fine to pay, and possibly an unpleasant interview with old Ricky.

Archdale's attention was caught by a stranger, who came by himself into the court from the passage leading to the combination room and the Master's Lodge. He turned right and walked beside the hall. Archdale assumed he was heading towards the entrance to the street. He was a tall, broad man, shabbily dressed in black, though not a clergyman.

At that moment there was a tap on the door. Soresby shambled into the room. Beside him could be heard the voice of the bedmaker, warning him to watch where he trod.

Soresby made his bow. "Mr. Archdale, I trust I find you—"

"Yes, yes." Archdale flapped his hand impatiently. "I say, who's that fellow down there?"

Soresby joined him by the window. The stranger was now talking to Mepal, the head porter.

"I've never seen him before in my—" Soresby broke off. "No, I think I saw him yesterday evening. He was with Mr. Richardson."

"Friend of Ricky's, eh?"

"That I cannot say. It looks as if he's asked Mepal where the library is. He won't have any luck there. The door's locked."

"Can't think why he'd want to go there. Dreary old place."

"Pray, Mr. Archdale," Soresby said, his voice sharpening. "Do you remember seeing me last night?"

"Not sure I do." He took a mouthful of tea, wincing because it was hot. "Did I?"

"Yes. When Mr. Richardson sent me up with a message."

Archdale rubbed his head. "Now you come to mention it, that does sound familiar." He frowned and then with an effort actually did recall something of what had happened. "Yes, one or two of the men were rather elevated in their spirits, I'm afraid. We were singing, were we? Anyway—so that cove down there, he was with Ricky?"

"I think it was him. It was dark, of course, and he stayed in the shadows. I believe his name is Holdsworth."

They watched the man trying the door of the library. Afterwards, he retraced his steps.

"You wanted to see me, Mr. Archdale?" Soresby pulled at his fingers and one of the joints cracked, a small, unsettling explosion he appeared not to notice. "I must confess that after last night—"

"Yes, yes, I'm truly sorry about that. I told you, some of the men were a trifle foxed and got carried away. A thousand apologies. Hope you weren't incommoded. No bones broken, eh?"

"No. Only bruises on my arms, and this graze on my—"

"Good, good—I'm heartily relieved to hear it. Now look here, Soresby, never mind that now—you've simply got to lend me a hand. Two things I need you for. First, I want you to collect something from Pranton's this afternoon—you know? The tailor's in Green Street?—and keep it for me until tomorrow evening. My guardian's coming, you see, and he's dead against a fellow buying a decent suit of clothes occasionally. And Ricky wouldn't approve either, because we're not meant to go to Pranton's, he's not on the college list, which is why it has to be collected. I'd ask Mulgrave to go, but the damned rogue isn't in the way this morning. Isn't that servants all over, eh? Always there when they're not wanted, and vice versa . . . Where was I? Yes, and the other thing, that's even more important. You see, he's got this idea that I should enter for the Vauden Medal, and there'll be the devil to pay if I don't."

"I beg your pardon—who?"

"I told you—my uncle, Sir Charles. He is quite settled in his mind that I shall shed luster on the family name. He's dining in college tomorrow, and he writes that he expects the pleasure of reading my entry for the Vauden afterwards. I meant to talk to you about it weeks ago, but somehow it slipped my mind. It's all damnably awkward, I tell you. I haven't even started the damned thing. And at present I particularly want the old gentleman to be in a philanthropic frame of mind."

Soresby frowned but did not speak. He unfolded a long arm and pushed a strand of hair away from his forehead.

"You could do it in your sleep, my dear fellow," Archdale rushed on, sensing opposition. "Each to his own, eh? Can you see your way clear to helping me? If we sit down together we can turn out something in a trice. Only it must be done soon. I must have at least something to show my guardian tomorrow or I can't answer for the consequences."

"The pity of it is, I'm pressed for time," Soresby said slowly.

"But I'm depending on you! A man like you, always with his nose in a book—why, upon my honor, I wager you could have turned out a creditable set of verses when you was in short-coats."

"But, Mr. Archdale, pray consider, there's very little time if you must have something to show for tomorrow. And a good deal of preliminary work must go into an entry for the Vauden Medal. And in your case, no doubt your guardian may wish you to discuss what you have done with him, which means you must show at least some familiarity with the material."

"You must help me," Archdale burst out. "Come, to a man of your parts it will be next to nothing. Consider—one needs a theme, of course—that could be anything, so long as it proves the existence of God according to the regulations. Isn't that what it's meant to be about? God or something? Then all we need do is turn it into a set of Latin verses. And I wouldn't worry too much about the old fellow— my uncle is no great scholar himself, which makes it so damnably unfair that he should expect me to be one. I promise you won't re-gret it." A thought struck him. "Oh—you are not entering for the medal yourself, are you? Is that why you are dragging your feet?"

Soresby shook his head. "I won it last year, Mr. Archdale. The regulations do not permit a man to win it twice."

"Ah—and what was the prize?"

"A guinea, Mr. Archdale, and the medal of course."

"Pooh—was that all? I call that downright shabby. I tell you what, I'll give you three guineas if you help me to write a passable entry."

"Three guineas?" Once again, a finger joint popped. "Dear me, Mr. Archdale, that is a great deal of money."

"It need not win the damned medal, either. The only thing is, I must have it now. Or at least a draft of the damned thing."

"Perhaps I might possibly be able to assist you in this."

"I knew it! Clever man like Soresby, I told myself, sure to find a way."

"I do not say it would answer, mind. But I have an idea."

Archdale bounced up and down in his seat. "What is it?"

"Last year I tried more than one theme for the medal before I settled on the one I used." Soresby cracked another joint. "I believe I may be able to lay my hand on my notes."

"Now that's a fine idea. Pray do not make that noise with your fingers again, my dear fellow, it makes me start."

Soresby colored. "I'm sure I beg your pardon."

"It's nothing, nothing at all. Pray continue."

"I had only laid the groundwork for the project, Mr. Archdale. I had sketched the theme—I had drafted perhaps a third or a half of the verses but I thought them a trifle pinguid."

"Eh?"

"Pinguid, Mr. Archdale—which is to say, unctuous, even turgid, as Tully called Asiatic rhetoric."

"If you say so. Anyway, that would be more than enough for my uncle to be going on with. He might like it, in fact—he verges on the pinguid himself." Archdale could feel his hangover drifting away from him. "Go and fetch it right away. After dinner, and after you've been to Pranton's, you shall cram it into me as far as you've got, and then you can work on the remainder at your leisure. You will not be the loser for it, I promise. Here, ring the bell, will you? I believe I could take a little toast."

❧ 13 ❧

MR. RICHARDSON WAS SEATED at a table in his parlor. Standing beside him was a portly young man. They both turned towards Holdsworth as he came in.

The tutor stood up. "Mr. Holdsworth—this is an unexpected pleasure."

"But I see you're engaged, sir," Holdsworth said. "No matter—I shall have the pleasure of seeing you later at the library."

"No, pray stay—Mr. Archdale and I have finished our business. Mr. Holdsworth, may I present Mr. Archdale, one of our fellow-commoners? And Mr. Archdale, this is Mr. Holdsworth."

Archdale blinked rapidly and sketched a bow to Holdsworth. The young man had a pink, round face dominated by large, loose lips that looked as if their owner's tongue might slip between them at any moment. "Your servant, sir," he muttered. "Charmed, I'm sure."

"Mr. Holdsworth has already heard you, if not seen you," Richardson went on. "We were strolling through Chapel Court last night and you were in full cry."

Archdale became even pinker. "I—I beg your pardon, sir. Some—some of the men—were a little merry."

"I am sure it will not happen again, Mr. Archdale." Richardson smiled at him. "Well, I am glad that you will have something to show Sir Charles tomorrow, and I shall inform him of the good news when I call on him this evening. After I have seen him, I should like to discuss the course of reading you should pursue next, and your plans for the Long Vacation. Perhaps you would make it convenient to call upon me on Wednesday. At about seven o'clock?"

Archdale stopped, his hand already on the door. "I regret it infinitely, sir, but I'm already engaged."

Richardson raised his eyebrows. "Indeed?"

"The HG Club, sir. I have been elected to it."

"Ah yes." A flicker of emotion passed over Richardson's delicate features. "You will not wish to miss that."

"Mr. Whichcote was most pressing."

"In that case, let us make it Thursday. Seven o'clock. You shall come and drink tea with me." Richardson looked consideringly at him. "You must go carefully at the HG Club. It has something of a reputation, I understand."

"Yes, sir. Much obliged, I'm sure."

Archdale bowed, first to Richardson and then to Holdsworth. The door closed behind him.

The tutor sighed. "We have too many young men like that, Mr. Holdsworth. No harm in him, but sadly dissipated. The tragedy is, he's not entirely a fool and he has some shreds of scholarship about him. He could do well enough if he were to apply himself. Still, I must not weary you with my little concerns. You've been to see Mr. Oldershaw this morning, have you not? How did you find him?"

"Sound in body, but not in mind," Holdsworth said.

"No improvement then?"

"It would appear not. Dr. Jermyn is sanguine but only if Mr. Oldershaw stays with him. The doctor has great faith in his system."

"Moral management," Richardson said. "They say it transforms the treatment of the insane."

"I cannot say I like what I have seen of it so far. It is more like bullying than anything else."

"In all events, it is kinder than chaining the poor devils to their beds as they used to do, and leaving them to rot in their own filth. Were you able to talk with Mr. Oldershaw?"

Holdsworth shook his head. "When Dr. Jermyn introduced me, he became violent and had to be restrained. Which reminds me: Mr. Archdale mentioned Mr. Whichcote just now. I heard his name at Dr. Jermyn's too."

"As I think I said yesterday, Mr. Whichcote is much at Jerusalem."

"And so, I believe, was his late wife."

Richardson raised his eyebrows. "Ah. I see we have no secrets from you. Not that the poor lady's death is in any way a secret, of course. There are some who say that Mr. Whichcote goes into society more than he should so soon after his bereavement. But we should be charitable, I believe. We should not begrudge the poor man his consolations."

"Why should Mr. Oldershaw believe he had seen the ghost of Mrs. Whichcote?"

"There you have me, my dear sir. Why indeed? He knew the lady, of course. But the poor fellow's wits are disordered. He does not need a reason for his fancies, surely?"

"Were there signs that his wits were disordered before that?" Holdsworth asked. "Her ladyship wishes to know all there is to know so you will not mind if I press you a little further."

"I cannot tell you much more than you already know. Mr. Oldershaw was at Lambourne House the very evening before Mrs. Whichcote died. The circumstance had affected him—he was a little melancholy, I should say. But that's nothing out of the way—young men always find something to sigh about, do they not?"

"How did he seem on the day before he saw the apparition? And what was he doing in the garden in the middle of the night?"

"I believe he dined at the Hoop with Mr. Archdale, and supped privately in college with Mr. Whichcote."

"Perhaps that brought the memory of Mrs. Whichcote to mind in a particularly vivid way."

"Perhaps. In any case, I fancy he must have woken in the middle of the night and wished to visit the necessary house—the undergraduates' privies are on the other side of the garden."

"I wonder if I might see Mr. Oldershaw's rooms?"

"Nothing would be easier. They are as he left them. Her ladyship did not wish to alarm Mr. Oldershaw's friends unnecessarily. A sudden recovery seemed perfectly possible at the time of his confinement, and even now we live in hope of such a happy eventuality." Richardson's eyelids fluttered. "Lady Anne has given out that her son is indisposed, his nerves are fatigued from his labors at the University."

"When would be convenient?"

"We might pay a visit now if you wished." Richardson stepped up to the window overlooking the court and looked up at the clock on the pediment. "We have a good half an hour before the dinner bell."

He shrugged himself into his gown, locked his door and led the way outside. They walked up to the door in the south-eastern corner of the court. Among the half a dozen names painted on the board inside the entrance to the staircase were those of Oldershaw and Archdale, who had the sets of rooms on the first floor. When Richardson turned the key in Oldershaw's heavy outer door, nothing happened. He frowned and increased the pressure. Still the key would not move. He reversed the direction of the turn and the lock immediately engaged with a loud click.

Frowning, he glanced at Holdsworth. "Strange."

"The door was unlocked?"

Richardson twisted the key again, pulled open the outer door and turned the handle of the inner door beyond. It led into a spacious room, larger and loftier than Richardson's. Directly in front of them stood a small man in dark clothes. He was carrying a pile of shirts.

"Mulgrave!" Richardson said. "What the devil are you doing here?"

"Fetching clean linen for Mr. Oldershaw, sir. And Dr. Jermyn asked me to bring in a few of his books."

"Why did you not come to me for the key?"

"Beg pardon, sir. Didn't want to bother you, and Dr. Jermyn gave me Mr. Oldershaw's key."

"It's most irregular, Mulgrave, as you very well know. We cannot go about handing college keys to all and sundry."

"Yes, sir. Beg pardon, sir. As it was Mr. Oldershaw, I thought you'd made an exception."

"I had not," Richardson said. "You must surrender the key to me."

"Very good, sir. I'm due to see him again on Tuesday, sir. I expect I'll have to trouble you later in the week."

"You need not concern yourself with that."

Mulgrave limped into the room and laid the shirts reverently into a valise that stood open on the carpet.

"How often do you see Mr. Oldershaw?" Richardson asked.

"Two or three times a week, sir. Dr. Jermyn tells me what to bring and when to call. I shave the poor gentleman and dress his hair, and run any little errands that the doctor thinks he needs." Mulgrave strapped up the valise and rose to his feet. "It was Dr. Carbury who told me to go. But I give my bills to Dr. Jermyn and he puts them on her ladyship's account."

"They should come through me, as you know very well. I'm Mr. Oldershaw's tutor."

"Yes, sir, but the Master said it's different because the young gentleman's not in residence at present."

"I see. Very well. Pray have the goodness to remember that Mr. Oldershaw is my pupil, and in future I shall take it kindly if you make it your business to tell me how he does."

"Yes, sir."

"Now leave the key on the table and be off with you."

Mulgrave bowed again, lifted the valise and limped to the door.

Richardson waited until the door shut behind Mulgrave. His face had grown pale. "It is insupportable. The Master has gone behind my back and no doubt Mulgrave was well paid to keep quiet about it. He's a gyp in more ways than one."

"I don't understand," Holdsworth said.

"Eh—oh, the word 'gyp' is said to be derived from the Greek word for 'vulture.' If so, it is entirely apposite. Such parasites make a fortune from their fees and vails." Richardson paused, breathing deeply. "You see, a gyp is not like the ordinary run of college servants. He works for himself, and offers his services to whomsoever he chooses. Were I able, I should exile the entire tribe of gyps from Cambridge."

"You speak with some heat, sir."

"I speak as I find, Mr. Holdsworth. Forgive me, however, I have allowed my feelings to become overheated. When one spends one's life in a college, seeing the same men day in, day out, these little things can mean a great deal to us. Little passions grow vast, and take monstrous shapes." He forced a laugh. "When I was a sizar here, thirty years ago, the gyps looked upon us as their rivals, and treated us accordingly. I remember Mulgrave then—he was but a boy, of course—he used to hop about and take great pleasure in humiliating us."

Holdsworth moved to the nearest window, one of the pair looking out over lawns towards the Long Pond, with the wall of the chapel immediately to the left and the great dome of the oriental plane tree beyond. Had Frank Oldershaw stood here on the night he saw the ghost? Had he seen something that drew him outside?

Richardson, his self-possession now entirely restored, smiled. "You must do me the honor of allowing me to be your Cicerone. When our Founder laid down our statutes, he included a stipulation that there should always be a suite of apartments for any of his descendants who might wish to study here. I think I may say without fear of contradiction that only the Master has better accommodation. This is the principal apartment, the parlor or keeping room, as we often style it here. That door there leads to a bedroom and the one beside it to a study. And the little door beyond the fireplace leads to what we call the gyp room, which is the province of Mulgrave and the bedmaker."

"It is splendidly furnished."

"Lady Anne saw to all that. Naturally she wished her son to live in a manner suitable to one of his rank and expectations."

Holdsworth moved from room to room. The little study overlooked a small, sunlit garden on the southern side of the range.

The room itself was square and high-ceilinged, almost a perfect cube. Here was some evidence that Frank Oldershaw had occasionally pursued his studies—a few volumes of Tacitus, Virgil and Livy, and several works on mathematics, such as Waring's *Meditationes Analyticae* and Vince's *Conic Sections*.

"Did Mr. Oldershaw apply himself to his books?" Holdsworth asked.

"Rarely. His mind is not framed for scholarly pursuits. What he really cared about was racing his phaeton against Archdale's, or the number of snipe he could bring down in a morning's sport."

Holdsworth opened the door opposite the window and found that it gave into a closet containing a commode and a large wardrobe. The door on the other side of it communicated with the bedroom. He looked through the clothes—wigs and coats, breeches and stockings, and shoes and boots and hats and gloves and topcoats.

"There's enough to clothe an entire village," he said over his shoulder to Richardson. "A village inhabited solely by the quality."

"Her ladyship never stints him anything that may increase his consequence. He will have a great position in the world when he comes of age, and will move in the first rank of society. Which is why his present situation is particularly galling to her."

"Because of pride?"

"That's certainly part of it. I do not mean, however, that she does not feel a mother's love for her son. But few of us can boast of simple sentiments, unalloyed by considerations of self-interest. Even the great ones in this world." Richardson pulled out the sleeve of a bright green coat. "This is the livery that Mr. Archdale will wear with such pride on Wednesday. The HG Club. The buttons have the club motto on them—*Sans souci*. A sad irony for Mr. Oldershaw, wouldn't you say?"

Holdsworth looked down at the cuff. "It's lost a button."

Originally there had been a line of three gilt buttons on the cuff. Now there were only two.

"It's on the dressing table." Richardson glanced out of the bedroom window. "The chapel clerk is on his way to ring the dinner bell. But one thing before we go, sir." He laid a hand on Holdsworth's sleeve. "Pray, have a care."

"What do you mean?"

"It pains me to say this, but Dr. Carbury serves only himself. If he sees a means of gaining advantage with Lady Anne at your expense, he will not scruple to use it. You must be on your guard."

The bell began to toll.

"Now we must hurry," Richardson said in a bright, cheerful voice. "If I do not take my seat at high table before they read grace, I shall have to pay a fine of two bottles of wine."

14

AFTER DINNER, Elinor Carbury ordered her maid to bring the tea things to the parlor. She had hardly settled herself before she heard voices in the hall below and steps on the stairs. The door burst open and Dr. Carbury advanced into the room. Behind him was Mr. Holdsworth.

"Ah—Mrs. Carbury!" her husband exclaimed, clinging to the back of a chair for support. "And that is the tea urn! What is it that Cowper says? 'The bubbling and loud-hissing urn throws up a steamy column, and the cups that—that . . .'"

"'Cheer but not inebriate,' sir, I believe," Elinor said, acknowledging Holdsworth's bow.

"Yes, yes," Carbury said, throwing himself in a chair with such force that its legs moved an inch or two backward.

"Pray be seated, Mr. Holdsworth," Elinor said. "I am about to make the tea, and I am sure Susan is already bringing more cups." She smiled at him and saw an answering smile on his face; it quite transformed his countenance. "This is an unexpected pleasure. I had thought you engaged with Mr. Richardson this afternoon."

Carbury suppressed a belch. "Later. The bishop is dining at St. John's, and Mr. Richardson wished to wait on his lordship. For the usual reasons, no doubt."

Elinor was still looking at Holdsworth. "Dr. Carbury means that the bishop may be able to put Mr. Richardson in the way of preferment."

"I do not hold out much hope in that quarter," Carbury said. "We shall have to put up with him a while longer."

Elinor stirred the teapot with unusual vigor, and the clatter of the spoon was enough to stop her husband in his stride, as she had hoped. He broke off, and swiftly changed the subject, asking Holdsworth how Frank Oldershaw was. While Holdsworth was talking, Elinor passed the cups to the men.

"Ah—poor fellow," Carbury said. "So the long and the short of it is that Jermyn is making no progress?"

"He believes it will come in time."

Carbury took a sip of his tea, wrinkled his nose and set down the cup, spilling some of its contents into the saucer. "But something must be done now! This brings the college into disrepute, it displeases her ladyship." His voice rose in volume. "And what about this ghost, Mr. Holdsworth? If you could show it's nothing but the boy's wild imaginings, that would be something. A ghost means gossip, and there's been too much of that already. Why, I fear we shall have fewer admissions next year, and merely because of this wretched story. No one wishes to send his son to an establishment with a ghost." He broke wind in a long rumble. "It is scarcely genteel. If you can scotch that foolish rumor, we shall be eternally grateful to you."

"It would be helpful to know more of the circumstances in which Mrs. Whichcote's body was found."

"Why, pray? There is no question about her identity."

"In case I can employ some fact about her discovery to undermine at least part of Mr. Oldershaw's conviction that he encountered her ghost. For example, how did she get in?"

"She had a key," Carbury said. "She often visited us at the Lodge. My wife had given her a key to our private gate from Jerusalem Lane so she might come and go without having to suffer the disagreeable experience of passing before so many masculine eyes."

"The gate was locked," Elinor said. "The key wasn't found."

Her husband scowled at her. "Because it's probably in the mud at the bottom of the pond."

"What was the lady wearing when she was taken from the water?" Holdsworth asked.

"A gown," Elinor said. "Her feet were bare. She wore stockings but they were torn and muddy. We—"

"We tried to avoid that circumstance becoming generally known," Carbury interrupted. "But the servants prattled. No doubt the shoes came off in the water and were washed into the culvert that drains the pond. Or perhaps she lost them as she ran through the streets—and on a night like that!"

Holdsworth rubbed his eyes, which were bloodshot and weary. "But why would Mrs. Whichcote come to Jerusalem at that time?"

"To see Mrs. Carbury, of course. Noctambulants are not, strictly speaking, irrational in their actions. I have discussed the matter with Professor Trillo, who has made something of a study of the subject as it occurs in classical antiquity. The actions of sleepwalkers are often guided by considerations which would have seemed reasonable to their waking selves."

"Still—forgive me, sir, if I labor the point—was Mrs. Whichcote feeling low? Despair is the foe of reason, is it not? One may commit terrible actions under the influence of despair."

Carbury broke wind again, and winced. "Mrs. Whichcote was not in despair, sir. You will oblige me by not mentioning even that possibility to anyone. It might create a misleading impression. One would not want the lady's reputation to be stained posthumously by a baseless suspicion of self-murder." He edged forward in his chair and rose unsteadily to his feet. He tried to bow to Elinor but the movement was converted into an awkward nod. "I—I find I must withdraw for a moment. Pray excuse me."

Elinor listened to his stumbling footsteps on the stairs and the bang of a door below. She turned to Holdsworth and found that he was looking directly at her. She looked away.

"I hope the Master is not indisposed," Holdsworth said.

"No—I'm sure not. He—he sometimes is obliged to withdraw after he has dined. But to return to Mr. Frank. I shall write to Lady Anne today. Should I say that he is in good health as far as the body is concerned? And, as to the infirmities of his mind, he is at least no worse. May I say more?"

"It is a part of Dr. Jermyn's regime that he oversees very strictly any intercourse his patients have with the outside world. I wish I could talk privately to Mr. Frank, if he would let me. He seemed perfectly placid at first. Then the doctor said I had come from her ladyship, and that I might be able to convey him back to her in a few weeks if his progress continued satisfactorily. After that Mr. Frank flew into a passion, and there was no point in my staying. I should like to see if it would answer to talk to him in private, without the doctor, or the attendants. It is necessary, too. He believes he has seen the ghost of Mrs. Whichcote. How can I attempt to disprove it unless I know the precise nature of the delusion? Only he can tell me that."

"Surely Dr. Jermyn could enlighten you?"

"Unfortunately not. Indeed, he evinced a perfect lack of interest in the subject of the ghost. His method, you see, does not concern itself with such matters. He takes the view that his patients are mad, and therefore their delusions are by definition unworthy of rational consideration—they are meaningless nonsense. Instead he places his emphasis on the treatment, which seems to revolve around teaching them to reason from correct propositions. He grew quite philosophical while he was explaining it to me."

"Locke," Elinor said, and enjoyed the flash of surprise on Holdsworth's face.

"Indeed, madam," he said. "Dr. Jermyn made considerable mention of him."

She did not reply.

"Tell me," he went on, "what was Mrs. Whichcote like?"

Elinor rose and fetched a folder from a drawer in her bureau. She laid it on the table by the window and undid the ribbon. She turned to Holdsworth, who had risen to his feet when she had. "Come here and you shall have your answer, sir."

She opened a folder and took out a sheet of paper. Holdsworth was standing beside her now, and she was very conscious of his eyes and the smell of wine on his breath. He looked down at the paper, at a head-and-shoulders sketch of Sylvia Whichcote, informal in its nature, and done rapidly in pen and ink. The clock ticked on the mantelpiece. Elinor's breathing accelerated. His forehead was wrinkled. Like a good housewife, she wanted to stretch out her hand and make it smooth again.

"Yes," he said at last, moving away. "Yes, I see. She was very beautiful."

"It was not just how she looked, sir," Elinor said, suddenly desperate to make him understand. "Though indeed she was lovely of face. But what counted for more than that, far more, was the charm of her manner, her conversation—something indefinable about her. Something unpredictable. It drew people. God knows—it drew Philip Whichcote, and if she could do that, she could draw anyone. He was head over heels in love with her at one time. I suspect he loved her still in his way, though I fear the marriage was not a happy one."

She shut the folder and tied the ribbon with fingers grown suddenly clumsy.

"I would count it a favor if you would tell me more about her," he said.

"She and I were children together. My father kept a school in Bath, and she attended it as a boarder. We became intimate friends, and remained so. When I married Dr. Carbury, she visited me in Cambridge and encountered Mr. Whichcote. At the time it seemed providential—a way of continuing our friendship."

"Who was it who did the portrait of her?"

"I did."

"You are skilled with the pencil, ma'am. Is the portrait a recent one?"

"The likeness was taken seven or eight months ago."

Elinor looked up. Holdsworth was staring at her again.

They heard Dr. Carbury returning. Elinor stood up and returned the folder to the drawer. Her husband came slowly into the room, walking cautiously as if on the deck of a boat that might be expected to sway at any moment.

"Still here, Mr. Holdsworth? I'm glad—I wanted a word in your ear. A word of warning. I had hoped it would not be necessary, but I find there's no help for it. Mrs. Carbury tells me that yesterday you had scarcely arrived before Mr. Richardson called to make your acquaintance. And he has made a dead set at you ever since, eh?"

"As you know, I saw something of him yesterday evening, sir," Holdsworth said. "And I called on him earlier because I wished to look over Mr. Oldershaw's rooms. He was so kind as to conduct me there."

"Just so," Carbury said, nodding. "Kind, eh? Kind to himself, I'll warrant. I regret to say this of a senior member of our society, but I would be failing in my duty if I did not put you on your guard against him. He has been all smiles and smooth talk to you, eh?"

"He has made himself very agreeable."

"Ha! I knew it."

Elinor rose to leave, but her husband waved her back to her chair.

"Pray do not disturb yourself, my dear. This will not take a moment and besides, you know all this and more already." He stuck his thumbs in his waistcoat pockets and stood legs apart with his back towards the empty fireplace. "When my predecessor as Master died, Mr. Holdsworth, we had, as is customary in these cases, an election for his successor. The fellows are the electors. By statute, anyone may be put forward as a candidate as long as he has an MA and is of course a communicant of the Church of England. Very often the candidates are chosen from among the fellows themselves, as is natural. And this was the case in the last election. The candidates were myself and Mr. Richardson."

Elinor coughed. "I'm sure we must not tire Mr. Holdsworth with our little affairs, sir. He has—"

"Pray be silent, Mrs. Carbury, and leave these matters to those who understand them."

Elinor felt herself flushing and turned her head away.

"As I was saying, I had allowed my friends to put me forward, but in truth I cared very little about the result." Dr. Carbury stared at the ceiling. "Mr. Richardson, on the other hand, felt very strongly about the matter. So much so that the methods he employed to advance his case were not—well, I shall not say they were actually corrupt, though I fear others have suggested as much. But I will say that they were certainly not those of a gentleman. Still, as I said to Mrs. Carbury only the other day, one cannot make a velvet cap out of a sow's ear. Mr. Richardson's origins are humble, you know, and despite his undoubted abilities there is a meanness about him that one does not find in a man of breeding. You must not allow his agreeable manner to blind you to his real nature, Mr. Holdsworth. We were undergraduates here together, and his true nature was apparent even then. Some of the more unkind students knew him as 'Dirty Dick.' They affected to believe that an unfortunate odor clung to him, for his father had been a tanner's journeyman, and you know how difficult it is to get rid of the smell of stinking hides."

Carbury paused. He looked at Holdsworth, as if expecting a comment from him.

Holdsworth said, "Yes, sir, indeed I do. As it happens, my father was a tanner too."

15

SORESBY WAS PARING his nails with a penknife under the western arcade of Chapel Court. The tunnel of the college's principal entrance was behind him and the gates beside the porter's lodge were open. The outer archway framed a view of St. Andrew's Street, the bustle from which struck the one discordant note that disturbed the dignified tranquillity of Jerusalem.

When the sizar saw Holdsworth approaching he flushed unbecomingly and slipped the knife in his pocket. He doffed his cap. "This way, sir."

"Mr. Richardson tells me you are the library clerk, Mr. Soresby," Holdsworth said, lingering outside. "What do your duties consist of?"

"I open up the place in the morning, sir, and close it at night. I restore the books to the shelves in the proper order. And I maintain the loans book."

"They keep you busy."

"Oh, there is more, sir. I keep the accounts, too, under Mr. Richardson's direction, and I am often called on to help those who wish to find a particular volume on the shelves."

"All this and you have to pursue your own studies too?"

"Yes indeed, sir. If you would be so good as to precede me up the stairs. Mr. Richardson is waiting."

Holdsworth walked ahead, wondering what Soresby earned for his labors. At the top of the stairs was a door that stood open, revealing a long room beyond. It was lit by rows of windows on both sides. Late-afternoon sunlight, heavy and golden, slanted through the windows on the right. The walls were lined with shelves and cupboards. In the center of the room was a heavy oak table, its top stained with ink and scarred with cuts and scratches.

Mr. Richardson advanced towards them with a book in his hand. "Mr. Holdsworth, you are delightfully prompt—"

"Please, sir," Soresby interrupted. "Will there be anything else?"

"No, I suppose not just now. Unless Mr. Holdsworth wishes to talk to you."

Holdsworth shook his head.

"But stay—I desire to talk to you about the loans book," Richardson went on, glancing down at a ledger lying open on the table. "I am not perfectly convinced that your method of recording them is the best possible."

"Please, sir, I have an errand."

"Very well—but we shall discuss this later."

"Yes, sir." Soresby bowed low and almost ran out of the room. "Thank you, sir."

"Forgive me, sir," Richardson said to Holdsworth. "I must pay constant attention to the minutiae of this library if it is to run smoothly. I try to ensure my procedures are followed in every particular. Now, how may I be of service to you?"

"Pray continue with your work, sir," Holdsworth said, wondering if the scene with Soresby had been laid on for his benefit, to create an impression of competence and industry. "I would not disturb you for the world. I wish merely to make a preliminary inspection."

"Let me know if you need anything unlocked. The keys are here. Our more valuable books are in the wall cupboard on the left of the fireplace."

Richardson sat down. Holdsworth made a slow tour of the room. There were smaller tables set for studies at right angles to the windows so they would catch the light. The bookcases had clearly been built for this place, and by somebody who knew what he was about.

The shelves were protected by glazed doors. There were cupboards and drawers beneath. Everything that opened had a lock to keep it secure. At first sight, however, the contents of the bookcases were less impressive. The bindings were in poor repair. Many of the books dealt with theological matters no longer considered essential or even desirable to the education of future clergymen of the established Church. The classical authors were poorly represented, as were mathematics and all branches of mechanics.

When he had made a full circuit of the place, Holdsworth turned back to Richardson. "Tell me, does the library have a fund for the purchase of new books and the maintenance of its old ones?"

"Not—not as such, sir. From time to time, the fellows grant a sum of money to the library for a particular purpose. And occasionally we are favored with presentation copies from authors, or even a bequest."

"In other words, any additions to the library are on an ad hoc basis?"

"Yes. It is not a perfect situation, I am afraid, and I wish we had a regular provision of funds. But we are better off than many other colleges. And of course we benefited from the generosity of the late earl, her ladyship's father, which allowed us to fit out this splendid room."

"The room is splendid. The same cannot be said of the books it contains."

"We live in an imperfect world," Richardson said drily. "No one is more aware than I of the library's deficiencies. Or of the world's."

When Holdsworth had finished his inspection, he went downstairs and walked slowly through the court. He heard footsteps and turned his head. Soresby was walking behind him with a large parcel clasped in his hands. The sizar was breathing heavily and there was sweat on his pale forehead.

"Mr. Soresby," Holdsworth said, stopping. He nodded at the parcel. "Have you been making a purchase?"

"Oh no, sir—this is not for me. It is Mr. Archdale's. He asked me to collect it from his tailor's. Though heaven knows—" Soresby broke off, flushing.

"Heaven knows what, Mr. Soresby?"

"I—I was merely about to observe that Mr. Archdale will not require the coat until Wednesday so there does not seem to be a great rush. Still, he has been very particular about it, very pressing. He needs it for the HG Club dinner. The coat is in the club livery, and perhaps it is a matter of great moment to him."

Soresby's tongue flickered between his lips. He had been speaking in a level and unemotional voice but the tip of the tongue gave a suggestion of malice to the words.

"The HG Club—what is it exactly?" Holdsworth spoke partly from idle curiosity and partly to sustain the conversation with Soresby, for he guessed the man might feel slighted by an abrupt dismissal; a man in a sizar's position would have a thin skin for insults.

"Why, sir, it has been going for years, in one form or another. HG stands for the Holy Ghost."

This put an unexpected slant on young Mr. Archdale. Holdsworth said, "So the society's purpose is a religious one?"

"Not exactly." Soresby grinned, transforming his long face into something impish and likeable. "At Jerusalem, the Holy Ghost has quite a different meaning. It's a dining club. Its amusements have nothing to do with religion, as far as I know. When you are a full member of the club, you're entitled to wear the coat." He glanced down at the parcel in his arms. "It's a most elegant livery. The tailor showed it me."

"Elegant and no doubt expensive."

"Yes, sir. And the entertainments are said to be extraordinarily lavish."

"Do they meet often?"

"Not since February. Usually, you see, they meet at Mr. Whichcote's, as he is the president, but he has been recently widowed. But on Wednesday—"

"Hoy—I say!"

Soresby and Holdsworth looked in the direction of the shout. Archdale himself was standing in the doorway to Frank Oldershaw's staircase. He waved impatiently at Soresby.

"Have you got it?" He took in Holdsworth's presence. "Beg pardon, sir, don't mean to interrupt." And then he was gone, retreating abruptly inside the building.

"I'd better go," Soresby said. "Mr. Archdale does not like to be kept waiting." He bowed.

"One moment," Holdsworth said. "I've heard that Mr. Frank Oldershaw is a member of this club."

"Oh yes, sir." Soresby, who had already set off, stopped and looked back. "I believe he was inducted on the occasion of its last meeting. A most affable gentleman, sir, most affable." He pulled his fingers. A knuckle cracked. "That was the very last club dinner. But then Mrs. Whichcote died. They found her body floating in the Long Pond over there on the very morning after."

The day had been warm and increasingly close. Elinor came downstairs and took the side door leading to the Master's Garden. She walked up and down the gravel paths, this way and that, aimlessly crisscrossing her route as though she were lost in a maze. The ruler-straight gravel paths passed between beds that were mainly triangular in shape. All of them were bordered with low hedges of box and yew in the Dutch style. She hated their stiff, masculine conformity. She would like to have it turned into a place of grass and trees, of wild and romantic irregularities and hidden corners.

Time and again, her eyes returned to the trees in the Fellows' Garden and beside the Long Pond, and in particular to the cool green cave beneath the oriental plane. Whichever path she took, sooner or later they all seemed to lead her to the pond, to the spot directly opposite the plane tree. Here the water was wider than elsewhere. Mepal had once told her that the largest of the carp, and even a mighty pike, lay hidden in the murky green depths. The water lilies clustered like a ruff around the patch of water where Sylvia Whichcote's body had been found.

Elinor caught movement from the corner of her eye and with a stab of annoyance realized she was not alone. On the farther bank, something black was moving in and out of the dappled shade cast by the overhanging branches of the plane. She swung round and followed the path along the length of the Long Pond, glancing every now and again across the water at the Fellows' Garden on the other side.

She took a diagonal path to the opposite corner of the garden, where the water on her side was bordered by a high thick hedge, also of box. The path led to a wrought-iron gate set in the hedge, and on the other side of it was the little Frostwick Bridge leading to the main garden. She stood for a moment beside the gate, staring through the grille at the green and sunlit space beyond.

Holdsworth was walking towards Chapel Court. His slanting shadow sliced across the grass on the other side of the bridge. She began to move aside but she had left it too late. He caught sight of her and bowed, and she was obliged to curtsy in return. He changed course and came on to the footbridge.

"Was your visit to the library of service to you, sir?" she asked.

"I have made a start, ma'am, nothing more." He crossed the bridge and reached the gate. "I have just been talking to the head porter."

"Mepal? Is there anything you require?"

"I wished to ask him about the discovery of Mrs. Whichcote's body."

Elinor tried the handle on the gate. It would not open. "I regret it exceedingly, sir, but the gate is locked. It seems unfriendly to speak to you like this."

He smiled at her and she noticed that he had a full set of teeth. He was a well-made man, she thought, with nothing flabby about him. She wondered what his dead wife had been like and how she had felt about him.

"Pray do not trouble yourself," he said. "It doesn't matter."

"Was Mepal helpful?"

"He showed me where they found the body." Holdsworth hesitated. "I hope the subject does not pain you."

She shook her head. "No more than it usually does. Mepal helped pull her out of the water."

"Yes, he and the night-soil man who raised the alarm. Mepal told me where I might find him."

"I doubt you will learn much from him. Dr. Carbury says he can barely string two words together."

"I must pursue every line of inquiry."

She said nothing. There was dark hair on the back of his hand. He had not shaved that morning, and the stubble outlined his cheekbones and his jaw.

"After all, what else can I do?" he went on, sounding irritated, as if she had objected.

"Yes, but what is the use of it, sir?" To her horror, Elinor felt her eyes filling with tears. "What can any of us do that's any use? We cannot turn back time. We cannot bring Mrs. Whichcote back to us. She's dead. And that's an end to it."

"Not an end," he said. "Not yet, I'm afraid. But would you help me with a little matter of geography? Mepal says that Mrs. Whichcote was found in the water there, just beyond the great plane."

"So I apprehend."

"Then where did her body go into the water?"

She stared at him. "How should I know, sir?"

"The general assumption is that Mrs. Whichcote must have fallen in from the Master's Garden, because she had the key to the private gate from Jerusalem Lane. But—in theory at least—she could equally well have entered the pond from the Fellows' Garden or from the college's main garden."

"She must have fallen from the Master's Garden. She could not have found her way into either of the others."

"But we don't know how she died, do we?" he said in a slow, quiet voice. "We do not know the full circumstances, or whether she was alone. We do not even know if it was accident, suicide or murder."

The tears spilled from her eyes and rolled down her cheeks. She felt terribly faint. She gripped the vertical bars of the gate to steady herself. His grave face shimmered, distorted by the water and fragmented by the iron. Then, for a brief but shocking instant, she felt the warmth of his hand on hers.

"Madam," he said urgently. "Are you unwell? Shall I fetch your maid? Some water?"

Elinor shook her head. She turned so that he could no longer see her face and, without a word of farewell, walked rapidly towards the garden door of the Lodge. She despised herself for displaying such weakness. She hated Holdsworth for witnessing it. And she despised herself and hated him even more for the strange, tingling warmth that spread through her body from the touch of his hand.

She did not look back but she knew that he would be standing there still, beside the gate, looking through the grille at her retreating figure.

16

THE GATES WERE STILL OPEN. As Whichcote came into college, he glimpsed Mepal in the porter's lodge angling his newspaper to catch the lamplight. In Chapel Court, he walked over to the staircase in the south-eastern corner, climbed to the first floor and rapped on Archdale's door with the head of his stick.

"Go away!" Archdale shouted.

Whichcote turned the handle and threw the door open. The rooms were smaller than Frank Oldershaw's on the other side of the landing and had fewer windows. But they were similar in layout. Archdale was not in his sitting room but in the little study beyond. He was visible through the open door, sitting at a table beside the window, with a pile of books before him and a pen in his hand.

"Damn it, I told you—" He broke off when he saw who it was. "Philip! What are you doing here?"

Whichcote stood in the doorway of the study and looked down at him. "A fine welcome. And what the devil do you think you're up to?"

Archdale was wearing nothing but shirt and breeches, and round his head he had wrapped a damp towel in an untidy turban. His breeches were unbuttoned at the knee and the waist for better ventilation.

"Had you forgotten my uncle is in Cambridge?" he said. "He's already here—Ricky's doing the polite at the Blue Boar with him now. Didn't ask me, mind you—I'm sure the old fellow's plotting something. He has a bee in his brains about the Vauden Medal."

"He thinks you might win it?" Whichcote said, so surprised that he did not bother to keep the incredulity from his voice.

"And why not?" Archdale said.

"I've never seen you at your books before."

"I've done a lot of reading in my time," Archdale said truculently. "Just because a man likes other things, it don't follow he never opens a book. Anyway, I haven't got to win the damned thing, thank God, and I've got a sizar to help. I've merely got to make my uncle think I'm having a stab at it. The trouble is, if I don't, he's threatening to withdraw me from the University. He's cutting up savage about some of the bills, though he don't know the half of it yet."

"When do you show it him?"

"Tomorrow. He dines in college after church. And afterwards he and Ricky will put me through my paces."

Whichcote leaned against the jamb of the door. "But you'll not fail us on Wednesday, I trust? We're depending on you, Harry. But if you've got cold feet, let me know now. I've a list of postulants as long as my arm."

"No, no." Archdale waved at the books and papers in front of him. "Upon my honor, once I've disposed of this, I shall think of nothing else. They sent me the suit of clothes this afternoon. I've tried it on already and it looks most handsome. *Sans souci*, eh?" He smacked his lips. "That's me. All the preparations are made? The—sacrifice awaits?"

"Oh, indeed. You need not trouble yourself on that score."

Archdale wiped the sleeve of his shirt across his forehead. "Damn me if it ain't growing hotter."

"I shall leave you to your labors." Whichcote began to move away but stopped, as if a thought had suddenly struck him. "By the way, a word in your ear about Mulgrave. I've discharged the fellow."

Archdale's mouth fell open. "I thought—I mean, you've employed him for years."

"I don't choose to any more. I caught him thieving—I've suspected it for some time. I advise you to consider very seriously whether you wish to continue using him."

"Good God." Archdale sat back in his chair. "That's a bit of a facer. He's a most obliging fellow—seems to know where to get anything one wants."

"But he's not to be trusted," Whichcote said. "And there's an end to it."

Archdale was following his own line of thought. "Ah—I wonder if Ricky's heard something too?"

"What?"

"Since Frank's been away, Mulgrave's been in and out of his rooms, fetching what he needs. Frank must have let him have a key. But Ricky went in there with Lady Anne's man just before dinner today, and they found Mulgrave there. There was hell to pay. He took Mulgrave's key away."

Whichcote frowned. "Lady Anne's man?"

"I met him in Ricky's rooms this afternoon. Name of Holdsworth."

"I know."

"He probably works under that old steward of theirs—what's his name? You know—the one who looks as if he's almost dead."

"Cross," Whichcote said. "Holdsworth's been to see Frank. Did you know that?"

Archdale glanced at him. "And?" Alarm flared in his eyes. "Have they heard something, do you think?"

Whichcote laughed, though he was privately concerned about that himself; Archdale didn't know the half of what had happened during that night in February. "How could an old lady in London know anything? But enough of this—I'll leave you to your labors. Until Wednesday, then. And mind you are in the pink of condition. You cannot be half-hearted when you make such a sacrifice to the gods."

The entrance to the Angel's yard was off the Corn Market. Holdsworth went into the coffee room, where a waiter directed him to a porter, who, with the encouragement of a sixpence, was willing to conduct him to an outhouse beyond the kitchens. The shed stank like the midden in the stable yard. A man lay snoring on a heap of sacks in the corner.

"There you are, sir," the porter said. "Tom Turdman at your service."

He seized the shoulder of the sleeping man and gave him a shake that would have unsettled a sack of coal. The night-soil man groaned, opened his eyes, rolled on to his side and vomited on to the floor.

"Easy come, easy go," said the porter. "Dined on beer and a drop or two of spirits by the smell of him." He gripped Tom's ear between finger and thumb and hauled him into a sitting position. "Gentleman to see you. Look sharp."

"Thank you," Holdsworth said to the porter. "That will be all." He waited until the man had gone and turned back to Tom Turdman, who was wiping his mouth on his sleeve. "Mr. Mepal at Jerusalem sent me."

"I done nothing wrong, sir. I told Mr. Mepal, I have to do my job, and I can't help the noise the wheels—"

Holdsworth took a shilling from his waistcoat pocket and held it up. The words stopped as if the tail of the sentence had been chopped off with an axe. Tom's mouth hung open. In one smooth movement, his hand swooped on the coin, scooped it up and slipped it into the pocket of his breeches. He swayed on his feet and almost overbalanced. He was a small, bent man, probably ten or twenty years younger than he looked. He still wore his long brown coat. His Fen accent was thick and murky, like mud, and at first Holdsworth could make out barely one word in three.

Holdsworth took him into the yard, where the relatively fresh air revived him a little.

"Done nothing wrong, sir," Tom repeated, "just my job."

"I want to ask you about the body you found."

Tom looked cunning. "Which one?"

"Don't gammon me, not if you value Mr. Mepal's kindness. Tell me about the lady at Jerusalem. In the pond."

"Thought it was a sheet or a gown in the water, sir."

"Why? Was it dark?"

"Near enough. Just before dawn. I fell in the water. God's death, the cold. And—and I touched her hand—" He broke off again, his face working. "Thought it was t'other one."

"What other one?" Holdsworth asked, bewildered.

"His honor's lady, sir."

"The Master's wife, Mrs. Carbury?"

Tom nodded. "But it weren't her abroad, not this time. Were the pretty one."

"You knew her face, then?"

The night-soil man's face cracked into a toothless smile. "Wouldn't forget her, sir, once you seen her. Used to come visiting the other one. I knew who she was soon as we laid her out on the bank. Looked stark staring mad, she did, like she seen a ghost. Lot of ghosts at Jerusalem, they say, and they walk at night, like that other one, other ghost—"

"Nonsense. Ghosts have no existence outside the minds of fools and children. But I shall not argue the point with you." Holdsworth fought down his rising anger, aware of its absurdity and disconcerted by its very existence. Something in his mind surfaced briefly and then vanished. He struggled to retrieve it but failed. "Go back to the point where you fell in the water, when you discovered the thing was a body. Was it face up?"

"Don't know, sir."

"What did you do?"

Tom closed his eyes. "It was cold, sir, mortal cold. I yelled, and I screamed, and I thought I was drowning. But then I was standing on the bottom and the mud and weeds were clinging to me like they wanted to drag me down."

"Stop this nonsense. Even if there were mud and weeds, they did not want to drag you down. They have no feelings in the matter either way."

"Yes, sir. Ask your pardon, sir. I was a-hauling myself on to the shore, when Mr. Mepal came running up and he dragged me out." An expression of pride settled on the man's face. "And I fainted quite away with the horror of it, sir."

"You damned fool," Holdsworth said.

"Yes, sir, but I came round in a flash. And Mr. Richardson came, and we got the poor lady out of the water and laid her on the bank. That's when I see who it was. Mr. Richardson told Mr. Mepal to get some men and bring back a door so we could lay her on it." The man hesitated, looking warily at Holdsworth. "Queer thing was her face. She did look terrible afraid. God's truth."

"What did you think had happened?"

"I thought the lady had been staying with Mrs. Carbury, like she did sometimes. And she come out for a breath of air, and maybe tripped. Fell and hit her head, sir, that's it, then she tumbled in the water."

"Hit her head? What's this?"

"Because of the wound, your honor."

Holdsworth stared at him, and Tom Turdman looked guilelessly back at him. Neither of them spoke for a moment.

"The wound?" Holdsworth said casually. "And what wound was that?"

"On her head, sir." Tom touched his own head in front of the left ear.

Despite the warmth of the evening, Holdsworth shivered. "A fresh one?"

"Yes, sir. We was waiting for the door to lay her on, see, and Mr. Richardson was looking to see if there was any life left in her. And I was sitting on the bank near him. He saw it too."

"But you said it was before dawn," Holdsworth said. "How can you have noticed all this?"

"It was growing light all the time," Tom said with a note of reproach in his voice. "Saw that wound plain as I see you."

"A bruise or a wound? Was the skin broken?"

"Both maybe, your honor. The skin was cut, for certain."

"Was it bleeding?"

"No, sir. The blood must have washed away."

Holdsworth stared at him. He saw with hideous clarity the little parlor in Bankside, where Maria used to pray, and where they had carried her dripping body. No one had commented on the broken window overlooking the river or the broken chair or the spots of blood on the floor. Someone had closed Maria's eyes, and he had been glad of that. Even dead eyes accuse. The side of her head was grazed. The wound had been on the left temple, half masked by strands of wet hair.

The color of a damson. The size of a penny piece.

He prayed that the river had given her that wound. Because if it hadn't happened then, as she was falling into the water or just afterwards, then it must have happened earlier: when he hit her, when he sent her flying across the room.

"Anyhow it don't mean nothing," Tom said. "Mr. Richardson said it don't signify, it was dark, and the poor lady fell in the water and drowned herself."

"How big was it?" Holdsworth demanded.

"You what, sir?"

"The wound on her head, damn you." Holdsworth seized the lapel of Tom's coat. "For God's sake, tell me how big?"

Tom held up a trembling hand. He made a circle with thumb and forefinger.

The size of a penny.

17

When holdsworth had finished with Tom Turd-man, he gave the little brown man another of her lady-ship's shillings and strolled up to the marketplace. He did not know what to do. He did not want to drink, for his head was already aching. He did not want to sit in the combination room at Jerusalem. Most of all he did not want to think about a wound the size of a penny on a woman's temple.

It was as if the weather in the hot, restless streets had transferred itself to the interior of his head. The marketplace was full of drunken people quarrelling, gambling, embracing, singing, vomiting and sleeping. At the corner of the Corn Market and the Garden Market, a vicious little fight was in progress between three townsmen and four undergraduates.

He tried to conjure up Maria's face but he could not remember what she looked like. She was reduced to an aching absence, like an amputated limb. But, in contrast, it was all too easy to visualize Elinor Carbury. Even thinking about the Master's wife seemed a form of disloyalty to poor, drowned Maria.

Holdsworth plunged into a dark and narrow street running to the south. Out of necessity he walked slowly. There were fewer people here and fewer lights, but the buildings pressed in on either side and the air seemed no cooler. The alley was cobbled, with a gully running down the middle. The stench was very bad. Heaps of refuse oozed across the footpath. There was a constant pattering and scuffling of rats, and every now and then he glimpsed their scurrying long-tailed shadows.

The trouble was, he told himself, he had been sent to Cambridge to talk reason to Frank Oldershaw, and in the event he had failed to say anything at all to him. He had also been engaged to find a ghost and instead he had found a dead woman with a wound on her head.

A wound like Maria's?

But the Jerusalem authorities, certainly Richardson and Mepal, had decided not to make public the injury to Mrs. Whichcote. The most likely explanation was the merely venal one, that the college had decided for the sake of its own reputation that it would be better to minimize any gossip about Sylvia Whichcote's death. It did not necessarily follow that her death had been anything other than suicide. The wound might have been caused by her plunging into the pond, and perhaps hitting her head on a stone. Or, in her journey towards the college through these ill-lit and ill-paved streets, she might have slipped and fallen; indeed, it would have been strange if she had not. Nor could the night-soil man be considered a reliable witness. It did not take long for a man to learn that the more sensational a story, the more attention the teller of it earned.

A wound the size of a penny piece: the phrase repeated itself in his mind like a curse.

More by luck than good judgment, Holdsworth discovered that he had navigated his way through the narrow lanes and emerged into an open space shaped like an axe-head. He recognized it from his walk earlier in the day as the Beast Market. Along its southern side ran Bird Bolt Lane. If he turned left, he would be back at Jerusalem within a few minutes.

Dear God, even here the strange, unseasonable heat was terrible. It tampered with the very fiber of his being. It stripped away the defenses of his reason. Now, in a sudden and hideous reversal, he could not stop his mind imagining the cool white skin of Elinor Carbury.

The size of a penny piece, he muttered aloud, a penny piece. It was if that damned wound, whether Sylvia's or Maria's, was a key. The key unlocked a door inside him that was better left fastened for all eternity. If he let the door open, God alone knew what might come out.

He wanted a woman now, for the first time in months, almost any woman, but he wanted Elinor most of all. She was no beauty, or not as the world estimated such things, but she had something stronger than beauty, a quality as much of mind as of body. God forgive him, but he did want her, and he could not deny it.

He saw Elinor's hand on the gate of the Master's Garden. He remembered how it had trembled slightly under his touch, and also the way she had caught her breath as if he had pricked her with a pin, just before she turned and walked away.

But what if she had stayed? If she had allowed her hand to remain beneath his? And what if they met again in the garden, and by night. Tonight. He thought of Elinor's smooth fingers running up his arm and then—

Real footsteps destroyed the sweet illusion; the dream became instantly insubstantial and tawdry, revealed for what it was, a mere lubricious fancy.

The size of a penny piece. *Oh, Maria, forgive me.*

Someone was coming down the lane from the direction of Jerusalem. Holdsworth drew back into the shadow of a clump of trees and shrubs on the corner of the market. At this time of night, you never knew who might be abroad. And here, on the fringes of the town, the conditions were well suited to robbery. On the other side of the lane was the Leys, the stretch of unenclosed fields and marshy waste that bordered the town on the south.

Forgive me.

A lamp burned feebly above the doorway of a building on the opposite corner of the market, illuminating a few yards of the paved footpath. As Holdsworth watched, a small, stout man walked slowly into the patch of light and paused. He stood with his hands in his pockets, looking towards the darkness on the other side of the road.

Not looking? Showing himself?

There were other, lighter footsteps. A woman crossed the road towards the man. She must have been sheltering in or near the Leys. She stood beside him, their heads close together. They had a short conversation, conducted in whispers. The man took the woman's chin and tilted her face so he could see it in the light. Holdsworth felt a twinge of envy: it was quite clear what they were discussing. Coins chinked. Then the woman moved away from the lamplight. The man waited. He looked up and down the lane, turning his head, which allowed Holdsworth a glimpse of his profile.

It was young Mr. Archdale. Holdsworth's envy turned to disgust. So that was how you found yourself a whore. You showed yourself under the light in the Beast Market and waited for one to come to you, a moth to your candle. If he stayed here, if he waited under the light, Holdsworth could find himself a whore of his own. Had he come to this, he wondered, that he lusted after such pleasures? A grieving widower at least retained a little dignity. But surely a man who paid to fornicate in the dark had none?

Harry Archdale walked quickly over the road. In hot pursuit of the last favors, he plunged into the Leys, moving deeper and deeper into the darkness that had already swallowed up his whore.

Forgive me.

Few people found it easy to sleep that night. There was a storm coming.

When Mr. Richardson left Sir Charles Archdale at the Blue Boar after supper, he could not bear to return immediately to college but walked aimlessly through the streets. The unnatural heat made him itchy, and he scratched himself as he walked, especially under his wig. The air was particularly bad—he sniffed and caught a trace of the foul and familiar stench of tanning hides.

It had not been an agreeable evening—Sir Charles was overbearing by nature, and enjoyed the sound of his own voice. He also disliked what he had heard about a fatality at Jerusalem, and the tutor had been obliged to handle him carefully. But now it was over, Richardson still could not relax. He had much to occupy his mind and he could not see his way clear.

As Richardson passed St. Michael's Church, he thought he heard someone murmur his name. Or rather, not his name but one like it. *Richenda.* He told himself he had taken too much wine, though now he felt suddenly and unpleasantly sober. He hurried on.

Tobias Soresby was walking through the streets like Mr. Richardson, though unlike the tutor he was perfectly sober. His loping progress was erratically punctuated with tiny cracking sounds, as he tugged at his finger joints. The sizar was trying with growing desperation to weigh up the pros and cons of a decision so complex and so momentous that it frightened him. He had heard today that Mr. Miskin might soon resign the Rosington Fellowship. That was most unexpected. It might change everything.

In his wanderings Soresby passed the little house in Trumpington Street where Mrs. Phear was working by candlelight at her tapestry showing the destruction of Sodom, or possibly Gomorrah. When her eyes grew tired, she summoned Dorcas, checked the bolts and locks on doors and windows, and prepared herself for bed. But after she had blown out the candle, Mrs. Phear could not sleep. She too had a great deal on her mind. Above all she was worried about Philip Whichcote. She did not want to worry about him but had long ago resigned herself to the fact that she had no choice in the matter. If she had had a child of her own it might have been different. She blamed Sylvia above all for Philip's troubles.

Mrs. Phear had thought everything would be better with the woman dead, but in the event everything was worse.

On the floor above her mistress's bedchamber, Dorcas undressed herself and lay down on her bed. She was completely naked. The sweat poured off her. Her room was immediately under the roof, and all the heat of the day seemed to have gathered there.

Dorcas said the Lord's Prayer in the usual way and then again, backwards, just to be on the safe side. In her left hand she held a corm of garlic, which a gypsy in the market had told her was an infallible specific against ghosts.

In February they had laid Tabitha Skinner on the bed next to Dorcas's and drawn the blanket over her head. Dorcas had spent a wakeful night with a dead girl. Everyone knew that the soul lingered near its earthly habitation until the body was consigned to a Christian burial. And in cases like Tabitha's, where the circumstances surrounding her death were sinful, the soul might linger much longer in the place where its body had been.

And now when she did sleep, Dorcas sometimes dreamed that the girl pushed aside the blanket, sat up in bed and talked to her. Sometimes Tabitha talked when Dorcas was awake. But Dorcas could never make out what she was saying. Once she had a nightmare in which Tabitha got out of her bed and climbed into Dorcas's. On that occasion, Dorcas woke up screaming, and Mrs. Phear came upstairs and whipped her.

Dorcas prayed, but it did not help. The memory of Tabitha, alive and dead, lingered like a bad smell, and so did the dreadful heat. She lay there with her right hand resting between her legs and wondered exactly what they had done to Tabitha.

"Tab?" she whispered into the darkness. "Tab? Go away now, please, there's a good girl."

Mulgrave, who lived not far away from Lambourne House in a cottage backing on to the castle ditch, dozed in his chair after a late supper. He had spent much of the evening reckoning up his worth—the house he lived in, several hundred pounds in the bank, and nearly as much again in gilts.

He made money from catering to the whims of wealthy puppies, just as Tom Turdman made money from shit. It was tiresome work but lucrative. On the borders of waking and sleeping, he turned over in his mind a scheme to reduce his labor while increasing his profit. After all, bankers and lawyers had their clerks, tradesmen their apprentices and beneficed clergy their curates. Why should a gyp be any different?

In Dr. Jermyn's house in Barnwell, Frank Oldershaw lay on his back in his chamber. He was snoring. After the outbreak in the morning, Jermyn had ordered the attendant to dose him thoroughly with laudanum. Every hour the porter unlocked the door and shone a lantern on his face to make sure he was still there and still breathing.

Harry Archdale was in the Leys. He had taken hardly a drop of wine since dinner. He had finished working through his notes for the Vauden Medal, together with Soresby's detailed commentary on it. Rather to his own surprise, he was confident that he had sufficiently mastered it to acquit himself respectably under examination by his Uncle Charles, whose erudition was more commonly admired than displayed. He doubted that the results would fool Mr. Richardson, but that did not concern him. Ricky would not want to upset Sir Charles any more than Archdale did.

He had discovered that the combination of study and unaccustomed sobriety had invigorated him quite remarkably. The girl said she was called Chloe, a likely story, but she knew her business well enough. He pushed her up against a tree and dealt with her manfully—he fancied that she would not soon forget the vigorous thrusts of his mighty *membrum virile*. Archdale wore his armor for the encounter, for in his way he was a prudent youth, though there was no denying the protection affected the pleasure of an amorous engagement. But he would not need his armor at the Holy Ghost Club because the girl there would be a virgin.

Only a virgin was suitable for the occasion. It was, after all, the Holy Ghost Club, and the Holy Ghost insisted on a virgin. That was the point of the whole thing.

In the Master's Lodge at Jerusalem, Ben was dismissed for the night. He left college and went to his room in Vauden Alley, hard by the northern wall of Jerusalem.

Elinor Carbury's maid, Susan, the only servant who slept in college, went to her attic bedroom and bolted the door. She opened her box. She took out the special clothes she wore on her days out and laid them one by one on the bed. She kneeled before them, holding up the candle so she could see them better.

At last she made her choice. She chose the velvet cloak that Mrs. Carbury had given her. It was her favorite, the most magnificent thing she owned, and looked so neat and fresh it might have been delivered but yesterday from Mr. Trotter's shop in St. Mary's Lane. Despite the warmth of the evening, she draped it around her shoulders. The rich, soft folds fell to the floor, enveloping her. She breathed deeply, sucking in their smell, absorbing the cloak's essence and making it a part of her.

She closed her eyes, stroked the fabric and thought of Ben.

Elinor Carbury also went to her bedchamber and also did not sleep. She sat in the darkness in her chair and listened to the sounds around her. She heard footsteps on the landing, and she knew which ones were Holdsworth's. She tried to persuade herself that it was unprofitable to look back at one's mistakes, in marriage as in all else. One must make the best of things. After all, if one had a roof over one's head and food on one's plate, there was no need to despair. The condition she feared above all was poverty.

She wondered what Sylvia Whichcote would have thought of Holdsworth, and he of her. Would she have enchanted him, as she had so many men? Holdsworth was clearly a man of parts and had some elements of cultivation about him. However, there was a ruthlessness about him, a sense that it didn't much matter whether he walked round an obstacle in life or simply kicked it out of his way. Perhaps the death of his wife and son had made him sour and fanatical. All in all, Elinor was not entirely comfortable with him as her guest, or even with him at Jerusalem. She wondered whether there was something she might say to Lady Anne that would shorten his stay at the Master's Lodge. On the other hand, she didn't want him to go.

Time passed. The clocks on colleges and churches rang the quarters. The air grew hotter and stuffier. It was not until well after midnight that the first heavy drops of rain fell on warm lead on old roofs, on dusty, stinking streets, on parched gardens and on those few people still abroad.

Beyond the river, in Lambourne House on Chesterton Lane, Philip Whichcote was still wide awake. He was sitting at his desk in the study. The pile of papers on top seemed to have grown larger and more confused than earlier in the day, as though the bills had been breeding among themselves with feckless enthusiasm during his absence.

The rain pattered against the window. Whichcote shouted for his footboy, who was dozing on a chair in the hall. The child stumbled into the room, rubbing the sleep from his eyes. Augustus was such a grand name for such an insignificant boy.

"Bring more candles. Stay a moment—how old are you?"

"Thirteen, your honor." Augustus dropped his eyes. "Well, in September, anyway."

"Come here. Stand before me."

Augustus advanced slowly towards him, coming to a halt when he was four feet away from his master. Whichcote turned his chair around so they were facing one another. He looked up at the scrawny child before him. The boy was trembling slightly. He expected a blow.

"How long have you been part of my household?"

"Nearly nine months, sir."

"You wish to remain in my employ?"

"Oh yes, your honor. If you please. There's eight of us at home, you see, and Ma can't feed us all." There was a note of panic in the boy's voice. "I like my position, truly, sir. I hope I give satisfaction."

"That remains to be seen. Fetch the candles now."

When the boy returned, Whichcote ordered him to light him upstairs. On the landing, he unlocked the door to Sylvia's apartments. Once he was inside, he told the boy to put down the candles and go away. When he was alone he wandered from room to room with a candle in his hand. He would put Sylvia's furniture up for auction on Monday. It would send a signal that he was short of money to his creditors but it couldn't be helped. At least he would have something in hand and he wouldn't have to look at that damned bedstead any longer.

Sylvia had kept secrets from him. He knew that now. So she might have hidden valuables from him. It was worth making absolutely sure that he had overlooked nothing—a ring, perhaps, a few guineas; anything would help.

He opened the bureau and set the candlestick on the flap. He stretched out his hand towards the back of the recess. In the poor light he misjudged the distance. His fingertips jarred against the mounting that held the little drawers and pigeonholes. He felt it give a little at his touch. He took out one of the drawers and tugged at the mounting. It moved smoothly away from the back of the bureau.

Whichcote lifted it out and set it on the floor. He shone the candlelight into the wide, shallow space behind it and ran his fingers along. To his disappointment, there was nothing but powdery dust. He came to the corner and felt the outline of a small, shallow recess in the side of the desk. There was something inside it.

He almost upset the candle in his urgency. He took out a scrap of yellowing paper, folded into a little parcel. Dear God, he thought, a banknote, please let it be a banknote. But as he turned it over in his shaking hands, something sharp stabbed his finger and he cried out, as much in surprise as in pain. A rusty pin was attached to the paper.

Holding it close to the candle flame, he unfolded the sheet completely. The pin held in place a lock of dark, wiry hair. Sylvia had labelled it *My Dearest Philip*.

To his consternation, Whichcote felt his eyes filling with tears. It was a strange and uncomfortable thought that this was what Sylvia had hidden in her most secret place, carefully wrapped away for a future that had not come to pass. He remembered now that when he had wooed her, he had begged a lock of her own hair, that he had gone down on bended knee to do so, and that she had blushed and after long argument agreed to his request. And she had asked for one of his in return.

He folded the paper carefully and slipped it into his waistcoat pocket. He said softly, "Sylvia?"

The flame of the candle flickered. There was a faint sound from the bedroom. A sigh? A moan of pain, instantly suppressed.

Nonsense. Nothing but wind and rain in the chimney and the rustle of water in the downpipe outside the window.

He sucked his finger where the pin had pricked it. The wound was deeper than he had thought. His blood was salty. What had he done with the lock of hair she had given him? He had no idea.

Still with the finger in his mouth, he carried the candle to the bedroom door. He stood in the doorway and stared at the shadowy outlines of the great bedstead.

A cage of wood, he thought, a prison for shadows and secrets.

"Sylvia?" he whispered. "Sylvia? Is that you?"

18

WHEN SUSAN WOKE HER, Elinor Carbury told the girl to open the window as wide as it would go. The sky was cloaked with high gray clouds. The air was cool and smelled pleasingly of damp earth. The rain had been heavy for much of the night but by dawn it had quite fallen away. She asked after her husband and learned that Dr. Carbury had not risen yet.

Elinor decided she would take her breakfast downstairs. It would only be civil, she told herself, for otherwise Mr. Holdsworth would breakfast alone. She was not habitually a vain woman but she changed her cap and ribbons twice before leaving her room.

The Carburys' dining parlor was a small square chamber overlooking the open court on the west side of the Master's Lodge. Holdsworth was already at the table with a bowl of tea in his hand. As she entered, he rose and bowed. They asked after each other's health, and speculated with polite insincerity that the noise of the storm had prevented Dr. Carbury from sleeping well. Elinor inquired, very delicately because she did not wish to seem unduly forward, about Mr. Holdsworth's plans for the day.

"I believe I shall go to Barnwell again, ma'am."

"Are you expected?"

"No."

Grim-faced, he drank the rest of his bowl of tea. Elinor continued to crumble the roll she had been failing to eat; her own tea was untouched.

He looked up suddenly and caught her staring at him. He drew in a breath and seemed to come to a decision. "If I am to understand the nature of Mr. Oldershaw's delusion, I must speak to him directly, without any intermediary or interpreter or eavesdropper. If I am to move at all in this matter, I must begin with him, whether he is mad or not. But Dr. Jermyn is opposed to this. No doubt he has his reasons."

"You will probably not find Dr. Jermyn at Barnwell."

"How do you know?"

"He and Mrs. Jermyn come to church in Cambridge every Sunday. They attend Holy Trinity. She is most devout, and she will make a particular point of it this Sunday, for Mr. Revitt is preaching, and all the Evangelicals will be there in force. Afterwards they generally dine at Mrs. Jermyn's parents' in Green Street."

He smiled, taking the hint at once. "I'm obliged to you, ma'am."

Elinor began to smile back, and then made herself look serious. Mr. Holdsworth's manner could not be said in any way to be flirtatious, and yet it was almost as though he were flirting—or rather attempting to flirt—with her. She reminded herself sternly that he was but recently a widower, that he was a guest in her house and moreover that he was a tradesman in humble circumstances. And then she thought also of her absurd behavior yesterday afternoon when she had looked at him through the gate of the Master's Garden, and when he had inexplicably and no doubt accidentally touched her hand.

"If you see Mr. Frank this morning, and if—if he gives you the opportunity, pray give him my compliments."

"You may depend on me to do so, ma'am. And may I wait on you later today when I know the result of my visit to Barnwell? In case there is news?"

She nodded and began to crumble another roll. "Of course."

He thanked her again for her kindness and left the room with a want of ceremony that verged on rudeness. Elinor became aware that her plate was almost entirely obscured by a mound of crumbs.

The streets were quiet, and they smelled sweet because the rain had settled the dust. Most of the people Holdsworth encountered were on their way to church. He pulled his hat low over his eyes and kept his head averted from the passing carriages that rumbled past him, splashing through the puddles from last night's storm. He did not want to encounter Dr. and Mrs. Jermyn on their way to Holy Trinity. As he came into the village, he saw and almost immediately recognized a small figure limping in front of him. He accelerated and drew level with him.

"Mr. Mulgrave—good day to you."

The gyp bowed. "And to you, sir." He showed no surprise at the meeting.

"Are you going to see Mr. Oldershaw?" Holdsworth asked.

"No, sir. I see him next on Tuesday, I believe. But it's cooler this morning after the rain, and I thought I would walk over with my account for Dr. Jermyn."

"I thought he was at church."

"Indeed he is, sir." Mulgrave's dark eyes were full of malicious intelligence. "Saw him and his lady on the road not ten minutes ago."

"What happens at the doctor's house on Sunday? Do the people go to church?"

"A parson comes in to read prayers in the morning, sir, and in the evening Dr. Jermyn often takes some of the gentlemen to church. The more sober ones, sir, if you take my meaning."

Holdsworth nodded. They walked on in silence, with Holdsworth shortening his stride to fit with Mulgrave's.

"You work for quite a number of gentlemen, I apprehend?"

"Oh yes, sir. A man must make ends meet the best he can. And it is not always easy, however hard a man works, because not all gentlemen are prompt payers. And some of them run up bills they can't hope to pay."

Holdsworth glanced at him. "When I kept a shop, I could not help but notice that gentlemen have a very different view of money from the rest of us. Indeed, some of them appear not to have any view at all, nor indeed any money. Yet that did not stop them spending what they had not got."

"Young gents ain't so bad. You can always have a word with their tutors, and they generally knows what's what. The trouble is the older gents. That Mr. Whichcote, for example." Mulgrave turned his head and spat on the roadway. "Trying to get money out of him is like trying to get a pint of blood out of a veal cutlet."

There was another silence. They covered another hundred yards of their road.

"I like a man who pays his way," Holdsworth observed, jingling the loose coins in the pocket of his coat. "You may know that I am here on Lady Anne's business."

Mulgrave looked sharply at him.

"She has a mother's tender feelings for her son's plight," Holdsworth said.

"As is very natural, sir."

"It is indeed. She wishes me to talk to him as soon as possible, to see how I may best help him. However, I find that Dr. Jermyn is fixed upon a certain method of treatment that does not allow of a patient to have a private conversation with his own mother's representative. It is most vexatious."

Mulgrave shook his head solemnly. "Dr. Jermyn can be very set in his ways, sir."

"I shall of course write to her ladyship and obtain the necessary permission," Holdsworth went on. "But that will take time. I have very real grounds for believing that I can be of material assistance to Mr. Frank in his plight, and I would not wish to extend his distress by another minute if I could help it. Nor would her ladyship, I am sure."

The two men walked along, side by side, with Holdsworth jingling the coins in his pocket.

"Her ladyship is not one to forget a service," he said. "Nor for that matter am I."

They were now only a few hundred yards from Dr. Jermyn's gates.

"They know me here pretty well," Mulgrave said. "I come and go for Mr. Frank, and I've been here before many a time, for other young gentlemen."

"So they will make no difficulty about admitting you at the gate this morning?"

"Lord bless you, sir—why should they? Did you meet Mr. Norcross?"

"I believe that was the name of the attendant in Mr. Frank's room."

"Just so, sir. George Norcross is my brother-in-law. He's in charge when Dr. Jermyn is away from home. I've always found him most obliging and reasonable."

"I should take it as a great favor if he would allow me to speak privately to Mr. Frank, or at least to attempt to do so. So would her ladyship." Holdsworth abandoned the coppers in his coat pocket, inserted two fingers into the pocket of his waistcoat and drew out a half-guinea. "I wonder whether this might help? And another when I have seen Mr. Frank."

Mulgrave stopped, and so did Holdsworth. Mulgrave looked at the coin between Holdsworth's fingers.

"Mr. Norcross would not wish to imperil his position, sir."

"That goes without saying."

"However, the man that opens the gate, seeing us together, and knowing your face, might think it all quite in order. If we arrived together, he might assume we'd come together."

"He might indeed."

"Nothing is certain in this world, sir," Mulgrave said piously. "I cannot answer for Mr. Norcross, for example. And even if you were to see Mr. Frank, the poor gentleman may be too disordered to talk sense to anyone."

"That is entirely understood. But there is half a guinea for both you and Mr. Norcross whatever the outcome. If I am able to talk privately with Mr. Oldershaw, whether or not his wits are disordered, there will be another half-guinea."

Mulgrave nodded. "You can't say fairer than that. And on the nail?"

"Her ladyship would insist on it."

"So that makes half a guinea apiece now," Mulgrave said with the air of one making an interesting arithmetical discovery. "And another half-guinea apiece if all goes well."

Mr. Norcross was taking his ease in a small parlor next to the butler's pantry. He sat in an elbow-chair by the open window with a pipe in his hand and a jug of ale on the sill. He had removed his wig and his coat, and unbuttoned his waistcoat. When he saw Mulgrave in the doorway, he sat up and made as if to stand.

"Pray do not disturb yourself, George," Mulgrave said quickly. "I brought Mr. Holdsworth with me because he begs the favor of a private word." Here Mulgrave winked in a knowing fashion. "If you're quite at leisure, that is. As you know, he comes on her ladyship's business."

Holdsworth lingered in the passage, examining a large basket containing vegetables newly brought in from the garden. Mulgrave murmured confidentially in his brother-in-law's ear. Mr. Norcross nodded and slowly rose to his feet. The top of his skull was a dome of gray bristle. He had no visible neck, and something about his appearance reminded Holdsworth irresistibly of an unwashed potato. He put on his coat in a leisurely way, clapped his tie-wig on his head and came over to Holdsworth. It was almost as if without his coat and wig he had not been able to see his visitor beforehand.

"Mr. Holdsworth, sir," he said. "I hope I see you well."

"Well enough, thank you."

"Always glad to oblige her ladyship," Norcross went on. "And a gentleman like yourself. However, there's ways and means." He tapped his nose at this point and nodded. "I don't think I see you standing there, sir."

"I beg your pardon?"

Norcross appeared not to have heard Holdsworth either. "When Mr. Mulgrave came this morning, there you were at the gate at the same time. And the porter knows Mr. Mulgrave, of course, he knows he's coming up to see me, and that's all right, and so he thinks you're with Mr. Mulgrave, as you happen to be exchanging the time of day with each other. And along you come, up to the house, I shouldn't wonder, and you see the gentleman working outside and you slip away before I have a chance to clap my eyes on you. You want a private conference with Mr. Oldershaw, and no doubt you turn the matter over in your mind and think maybe he's working in the garden with the others. And as chance would have it, you direct your steps behind the stables, which is where the kitchen gardens are. If you did that, I shouldn't be surprised if you was to catch sight of Mr. Oldershaw among the lettuces and such-like. But you could put it another way, and say I shouldn't be surprised in any case because I wouldn't know anything about it. Do you follow me so far, sir?"

"Perfectly," Holdsworth said. "Will an attendant be watching over Mr. Oldershaw?"

"Yes, sir. Of course. We look after our gentlemen very carefully here. I should think an attendant will be in the kitchen garden the whole time. I expect he will be sitting on the bench by the door, or keeping an eye on one or two of the other gentlemen working there. He'll see your black coat, and maybe he'll think you're one of the doctor's colleagues. After all, you was here with him only yesterday, so that would be a natural mistake to make."

"How is Mr. Oldershaw today?"

"Quieter than yesterday, that's for sure."

"Is he capable of rational conversation?"

Norcross shrugged. He pulled out a watch. "I am doing my rounds upstairs now," he informed them. "That's why I didn't catch sight of you."

Without a word of farewell, he walked away, his heavy body rolling from side to side as though his thighs were made of granite.

Mulgrave joined Holdsworth in the passage. "This way, sir." He directed Holdsworth to a side door to a gravel roadway. "Follow the path past the stables, sir. The kitchen garden's beyond."

A groom looked curiously at Holdsworth as he passed the entrance to the stable yard but made no move to stop him. On the edge of the lawn, five or six elegantly clad gentlemen were trimming the grass along a belt of trees. Another man was standing on the bowling green, reading from a volume of Thucydides in a loud and carrying voice as if addressing a large but invisible public meeting. Two attendants chatted in the shade nearby.

Holdsworth opened the gate into the walled kitchen garden. A third attendant sprawled on a bench near the door with a newspaper spread open across his knees and a pipe on the seat beside him. He looked up and then away, as if satisfied that Holdsworth was not one of the inmates absconding from his allotted work.

Three men were at work among the vegetables. Two of them, both middle-aged, were hoeing weeds. At the far end of the garden was Frank Oldershaw, a solitary figure on his hands and knees.

Holdsworth walked down the brick path that bisected the enclosure. Frank's coat and waistcoat were draped over a wheelbarrow nearby. He was kneeling in the freshly turned earth in black silk breeches and a fine white shirt. In his hand was a little fork with which he was harvesting radishes. He must have heard Holdsworth's footsteps on the path but he did not look up.

"Good morning, sir," Holdsworth said. "Would you allow me a few words?"

There was no reply.

"We met briefly yesterday," Holdsworth went on. "I give you my word, I shall not act in any way you do not wish."

Frank paused in the frantic digging. Still he did not look up.

"If you do not wish me to be here, if I do anything that is not agreeable to you, you have only to call to that attendant and say I am troubling you, that I have no license to be here. The doctor has no knowledge of my visit. He has forbidden me to talk privately to you."

For the first time, Frank turned his head and looked up at Holdsworth. Despite the quality of his clothes, he hardly looked the gentleman now. The face was smeared with mud, the hands grimy, the fingernails broken. He was still on his hands and knees, and he swayed slightly to and fro, as though the weight he supported was too much for him to bear.

"I must finish this row," he mumbled, "and the next. Else they will not give me my dinner."

"There is time enough for that," Holdsworth said. "Let us talk a little."

Frank stuck his little fork in the earth, rolled his body over and squatted on the brick path. "I am so tired. I could sleep forever."

"It is because they drug you."

Frank nodded. "To murder grief."

"What? Do you grieve? Why?"

Frank shook his head but did not answer.

"They tell me you saw a ghost," Holdsworth said, speaking casually, as though seeing a ghost was of mild interest but nothing more. "I suppose it was Mrs. Whichcote's?"

Frank let his head fall forward to his breast.

"So it was? How did you know it was she?"

"Who else could it be?" Frank muttered. "Where else would Sylvia walk?"

"Why? Because she died there?"

With his forefinger, Frank drew a circle, a zero, in the earth.

"Tell me, pray—why did you go outside that night? Were you going to the necessary house?"

Frank shook his head. His face filled with flickering animation, the muscles twitching and dancing under the skin. "Couldn't sleep," he said. "Wanted air. Nothing mattered."

"You went outside," Holdsworth said. "You wanted air, and nothing mattered. I see."

Frank shook his head with a vigor that was almost manic. "You don't. You're stupid. I could do anything. Don't you understand? I was free. I was God. I was the Holy Ghost." He put his head in his hands. "And now I'm mad. My wits are disordered, do you hear? I do not understand anything. Nor do you. You're a perfect blockhead."

Holdsworth stood up. A shift had taken place in the conversation. Frank had spoken to him as an angry young gentleman talks to an inferior.

"I am the Holy Ghost," Frank went on in a quieter voice. "And so I saw a ghost. *Quod—quod erat demonstrandum.*"

"Are you happy here?" Holdsworth asked after a pause.

"I hate the place and all who live here."

"If you wish, perhaps you may leave."

"I cannot go home," Frank said. "I will not go home."

"Is that why you attacked Mr. Cross? To stop them sending you home?"

Frank lowered his head and drew another circle in the earth, another zero. "Poor Cross. The fit was upon me—I could not help it. I can help nothing now. It would be better if I were dead. I wish I were."

Holdsworth had felt the same way himself when they brought first Georgie home and then Maria. Unhappy people spoke a common language. He would have given his life for Georgie. Hadn't Maria known that? He would have given his life to save hers too, but instead he gave her a wound the size of a penny piece and a desire for death.

Forgive me.

"Tell me," he said to Frank. "What if I could persuade her ladyship to order Dr. Jermyn to release you into my custody?"

"How can I trust you? You would take me back to my mother. You would take me somewhere worse, for all I know, worse than this."

"I cannot force you to trust me. So let me appeal to your reason."

"I have no reason."

"You have enough reason for this, sir, I think. At all events, let us suppose you have. If I ask her ladyship to release you into my custody, and if we find somewhere quite retired where we shall live—will that not be better than this? As for this matter of trust—consider it from my perspective. I can only carry out this suggestion with your mother's agreement. If anything happens to you, if anything at all undesirable occurs because of this move, then her ladyship will lay it solely at my door. Simply for reasons of self-interest, I cannot afford to do you anything but good. Even if there is nothing I can do to cure you, at least you will be away from here. You will be away from Dr. Jermyn and his moral management."

Frank drew another zero in the earth. "I do not want to see my mother or Cross or Whichcote or Harry Archdale or my tutor or any of them. Anyone at all."

"That would be entirely understood. If you permit me to raise the matter with her ladyship, I shall say that you and I must live in seclusion. That would be a necessary precondition."

Frank looked up sharply. "What if I shouldn't want to be cured? Have you thought of that? What then?"

Before Holdsworth could reply, there was a sudden commotion behind them. Holdsworth and Frank turned. Two men had come into the kitchen garden—Norcross and Jermyn himself. Norcross had a mastiff on a short leash. The other attendant leaped to his feet, his newspaper fluttering to the ground. The only people who appeared quite unaffected were the two middle-aged patients, who continued with their work as if nothing had happened.

"Shall I write to her ladyship?" Holdsworth said in an undertone. "Yes or no?"

"You, sir," Jermyn called. "Come here this instant or I shall order my man to unleash the dog."

"Yes," Frank whispered. "Quickly."

19

AFTER DIVINE SERVICE, a sea of caps and gowns flooded through the doors of Great St. Mary's and gradually dissipated itself among the streets, alleys and colleges. Holdsworth paused outside the railings of the Senate House to watch the spectacle. Most of the worshippers were in academic dress, and their gowns and hoods were of many colors and textures. Some slouched, some strolled; some walked in chattering groups, others in silence, one or two with their noses in books. Here was the University in its Sunday finery, and the sight was both magnificent and slovenly.

Holdsworth was in no hurry to reach Jerusalem. On his way back from Barnwell, he had called at Lambourne House in Chesterton Lane, but the little footboy who answered the door told him that Mr. Whichcote was not at home to visitors. Holdsworth declined to state his business. As he had turned to leave, he had glimpsed a gentleman with a lean, handsome face looking down at him from an upstairs window. Whichcote probably took him for an importunate tradesman with an upaid bill, and the footboy had fobbed him off with a polite fiction.

Afterwards Holdsworth had walked about the town at random. Cambridge was like a place in the grip of an occupying army. The streets were mean and crowded, the houses small and ugly, huddled in among themselves as though for protection. The citizens scurried about with surly faces as though they had little right to be there—the true masters of the place were the gowned figures who lived behind the gates and walls of the colleges. Occasionally he had glimpsed above the rooftops a tower, a soaring pinnacle or, through a great stone gateway, a quiet grassy court surrounded by gracious buildings, some modern, others Gothic and picturesque. In Cambridge, he thought, appearances were deceptive: it was a place that jealously guarded its secrets and its beauties. And perhaps its ghosts, as well.

When the crowd outside Great St. Mary's had diminished, Holdsworth crossed the road and walked into St. Mary's Passage, which ran along the south side of the church. He saw the dapper figure of Mr. Richardson thirty yards ahead, walking beside a tall, stately man swinging a gold-headed cane. Another, smaller figure sauntered behind them, swaying with exaggerated motions from side to side in a manner that caricatured the movements of the man with the cane. It was young Mr. Archdale indulging in his sense of humor.

Holdsworth followed them back to Jerusalem. Mepal made his obedience with particular reverence as the little party passed the porter's lodge. The three men paused in Chapel Court, standing in the watery sunshine. The tall man looked about him with a proprietorial air. Holdsworth, judging that his presence might not be welcome, was about to slip by when Richardson murmured something to his companions and turned aside to greet him.

"Mr. Holdsworth—this is well met, sir: I had hoped to see you before dinner. You will be in the library after dinner, I apprehend? I shall be with Sir Charles. But Soresby will be your guide—he is very able—he knows almost as much about it as I do, I believe. I saw him after chapel this morning and reminded him of the engagement. Pray ask him anything you want. He will place himself entirely at your service for as long as you wish."

Richardson said goodbye to Holdsworth, and scampered after the Archdales, who were strolling across the sacred square of grass in the center of the court. Holdsworth walked through the passage by the combination room to the door of the Master's Lodge. When

Ben admitted him, he said that his master was now up and dressed; he was with Mrs. Carbury in her sitting room.

Holdsworth went upstairs to join them. Carbury was in his armchair. He was dressed in a smarter black coat than usual, newly shaved and with his hair freshly powdered, but he looked old and ill. Elinor was seated by the window. Holdsworth was uncomfortably aware of her presence.

"I hope you are fully restored, sir," Holdsworth said once the greetings were out of the way. His eyes slid towards Elinor of their own volition.

"Yes, yes. I am very vexed, however—that fool Ben let me sleep late and I had intended to go to church. Tell me, sir, was you there?"

"No. Although I happened to be passing Great St. Mary's as they were coming out."

"Sir Charles Archdale was to attend the service," Carbury said. "I wish I had been there."

"I believe I saw him coming out with Mr. Richardson and young Mr. Archdale."

Carbury scowled. "I shall have the pleasure of meeting Sir Charles at dinner."

"Sir," Elinor said. "Is this wise? You are not entirely yourself yet."

"I am perfectly well," Carbury said without looking at her.

"Indeed you are, sir." Elinor rose from her seat and came to stand by her husband's chair. "Still, we must not weary Mr. Holdsworth with these little details. He hoped to see Mr. Frank this morning, you remember, and perhaps he has good news for us, and for her ladyship."

Carbury looked sharply at Holdsworth. "Yes, how did you do? Would they admit you without an appointment?"

"As it happened, the doctor was not in the way when I arrived." Holdsworth exchanged another glance with Elinor. Neither of them mentioned their conversation at breakfast, and the shared knowledge was a kind of treachery. "And I was able to have some private conversation with Mr. Frank."

"Could you get sense out of him? Was he in his right mind?"

"They had dosed him up so much that it was hard to say where he was, sir. He is fearful—and I am not sure of what. His wits are wandering but I would not call him mad. The one thing I am sure of is that he is not suited to the regimen of that place. It is doing him no good. I asked him whether he would consent to be released into my custody, on the understanding that we would live apart from the world for a while without seeing anyone from his former life, including his mother. I think he would be agreeable to that. Such a course could not harm him and might indeed be of benefit. We cannot do worse with it than he is doing now."

"We must have Jermyn's opinion on this," Carbury said. "We must proceed in the proper way."

"I doubt he would be in favor, sir. He came upon me unexpectedly while I was talking with Mr. Frank, and he was not at all pleased. He had me escorted from the premises."

Elinor said in a low voice, "If Mr. Frank went from Dr. Jermyn's, and that fact became known to the world, would it not seem that his health had improved? Would it not suggest that his wits were no longer disordered?"

Carbury grunted. "That is certainly a consideration, madam. It does not help the college's reputation that Mr. Frank Oldershaw is known to be in Dr. Jermyn's madhouse. So if he is not there, if he seems cured, it can only be to the good."

"I believe it to be a matter of urgency, sir," Holdsworth said. "If he is not mad already, that place will soon make him so."

"This is all very well, but you cannot move at all in such an important matter without Lady Anne's leave."

"If we sent an express tomorrow, we should hear from her by Tuesday," Elinor said.

"Would you support the plan too, sir?" Holdsworth asked. "A letter from you would carry far more weight than one from me."

"Perhaps." Carbury gently rubbed his stomach. "Yes, it will help no one if Mr. Frank is made worse. Very well, I shall write to Lady Anne directly. It is worth trying. But I shall emphasize that the notion is yours, Mr. Holdsworth. After all, her ladyship has deputed you to act for her in this. Where would you take Mr. Frank if you could get him out of Barnwell?"

"I wondered whether perhaps we might hire a cottage a few miles distant from Cambridge. I would prefer that to taking lodgings. The people of the house might talk."

"You would need someone to look after you, sir," Elinor put in. "What about Mulgrave? He would be a familiar face and he already knows how Mr. Frank is, and would be quite prepared for what he would find."

"Let me think on it," Carbury said. "The college has a number of estates near Cambridge, and there may be something there. I will look into it in the morning." A bell began to toll in the distance, and he heaved himself out of his chair. "Well, well, it is time for dinner."

"Are you perfectly convinced of the wisdom of dining in hall?" Elinor said. "I could send Ben to the kitchens and have them bring you something up."

Carbury, now swaying on his own two feet, waved his hand. "I shall go down."

"But sir—"

"I am not at all fagged now, and I hope I do not need you to teach me anything about my duty, madam."

Holdsworth saw Elinor coloring. She turned away without saying anything.

Holdsworth and Carbury went downstairs slowly together, with Carbury clinging to the banister rail.

"Why must women fuss a man so?" Carbury said, not troubling to lower his voice. "It is unamiable, is it not? Still, I suppose one must not blame the fair sex for their weaker understanding."

In the passage they met Mr. Richardson, coming in from Chapel Court. He greeted the Master and Holdsworth with a bow and a smile.

"Where is Sir Charles?" Carbury demanded.

"He and his nephew are coming directly, Master. Why, Sir Charles is such an agreeable man, is he not? So genteel, and yet so unaffected." Richardson paused with his hand on the door of the combination room. "By the way, Master, have you heard the news? Miskin has had the promise of a living in Gloucestershire—a snug little parsonage and seven hundred a year."

"I know," Carbury said. "He told me yesterday."

"We shall miss his merry laugh in the parlor, eh? The present incumbent intends to vacate after Christmas, so we shall need to elect a new Rosington fellow in the new year."

"I'm obliged to you, Mr. Richardson," Carbury said, sweeping into the combination room. "But you need not trouble yourself in the matter. According to the terms of its endowment, the Rosington Fellowship is in the Master's gift. You may safely leave it to me."

Dinner on Sunday was a lengthy affair, and one that had an air of celebration. They began with a fresh salmon boiled and garnished with fried smelts, anchovy sauce and shrimps, with a calf's head, chicken pie and a chine of roasted mutton. The second course involved a haunch of venison with gravy sauce and currant jelly. There were also collared eels, a green goose, lobsters and tarts. Holdsworth wondered whether they always dined in such style at Jerusalem high table on a Sunday, or whether this was in some sense a special occasion, perhaps because of the presence of Sir Charles Archdale.

Harry Archdale sat beside his uncle. His debauches on the previous evening had not harmed his appetite. Holdsworth stared at the sizars' table in the body of the hall. The fare was simpler there. Soresby was hunched over the board, his elbows protruding and the sleeves of his stained black gown trailing on either side of his plate as he shovelled food into his mouth.

The conversation at high table was largely sustained by Carbury and Richardson, operating in competition, each attempting to monopolize the attention of Sir Charles. After dinner, Holdsworth found himself next to Harry Archdale in the movement towards the combination room. Holdsworth said nothing but stood back to allow the young man to precede him through the doorway. They were the last persons left on the dais, apart from the servants behind them who were busy clearing the table.

Archdale hesitated. "Pray, sir, how is poor Frank? You must not mind my asking. Mr. Richardson told me that Lady Anne sent you here to see how Frank does, as well as to look over the library."

"His health gradually improves," Holdsworth said quietly. "But he is still not entirely himself."

"I wish you would oblige me by telling him when you see him that Jerusalem is devilish dull without him. If—if it is convenient, that is."

Afterwards, Holdsworth drank a cup of tea in the combination room and made his excuses. He walked down to the western arcade and climbed the staircase to the library. Soresby must have heard or seen him coming, because he was standing in the doorway and bowing low as Holdsworth appeared. On the big table behind him were several open volumes and a sheaf of loose, handwritten papers.

"I hope I have not interrupted your studies, Mr. Soresby," Holdsworth said.

"Not at all, sir. I am quite at your disposal."

Holdsworth looked about him. "Is this the collection in its entirety?"

"Apart from those on loan."

"Do you know how many books the library contains?"

"No, sir. I do not believe anyone does." Soresby's fingers plaited themselves together. "I would hazard a guess that there must be somewhere between fifteen hundred and two thousand volumes."

"Is there a catalogue?"

"Mr. Richardson's predecessor attempted the task. Unfortunately it was left incomplete at his death."

"And has the library other materials, apart from what we can see here?"

"What you see on the shelves, sir, are all the bound volumes we have." Soresby gestured at the cupboards below the bookshelves. "But in the past many fellows have left the college the fruits of their scholarship, and we store their papers here. It would be a formidable task to catalogue them. Also, we have a number of manuscripts of considerable antiquity, the earliest of which I understand goes back to the reign of King John. But these are kept in the Treasury along with the college plate, the deeds, the leases and so forth."

"I am obliged to you," Holdsworth said. "I shall need to make a survey. It may take several days. But there is no need for me to trouble you, or not in the normal way of things, for I work better at my own pace. If I have any questions, you may be sure I shall apply to you directly."

"Will you begin now, sir?"

"No. And I shall not take up any more of your time this afternoon." Holdsworth indicated the books on the table. "I see you are already at work."

Soresby tugged at the index finger on his left hand with sudden violence. "I must read every moment I can, sir."

"Because you wish to take a good degree?"

"I cannot afford not to, sir. I have not sixpence in the world. If I am to make anything of myself, it is not enough merely to take my degree, I must be highly placed on the list, the Ordo Senioritatis, I hope as a Wrangler." He broke off. "Forgive me, sir, I prattle too much of my own affairs."

"Indeed you do not. I asked you a question and you most courteously answered it. In fact, you would do me a great service if you would allow me to satisfy my curiosity a little further. You must understand I am not familiar with the ways of the University. If you take a good degree, what happens then?"

"I hope to attain a fellowship and take orders."

"What is the advantage to a young man in your position?"

"Why, sir, as to that a fellowship gives one an income and a place to live. Besides that, it offers the chance of improving one's lot with a little private tuition, perhaps, or a lectureship. And the college has a number of livings at its disposal and, in the course of time, one of these may fall vacant, and so preferment within the Church is not an impossibility."

"I hear the Rosington Fellowship may become vacant soon."

Soresby's expression changed: his face narrowed and sharpened. His features might have belonged to a starving man. "If I were to get the promise of it, my situation would improve beyond all recognition. But it's in the gift of the Master." He paused and then added in a sudden, savage rush, "It's all of a piece, here at Jerusalem, sir: one can hope for nothing, large or small, without the support of Dr. Carbury."

20

ON TUESDAY MORNING, Elinor sent Susan to rinse collars and cuffs in the washhouse, which was in the little service yard. It was always damp and gloomy because it was overshadowed by the high blank wall of Yarmouth Hall on one side and the back of the Master's Lodge on another. Later that morning, Elinor passed through the yard herself on the way to the necessary house. The door to the washhouse was ajar, and she heard Susan laugh softly.

Elinor paused. She was about to go in to see Susan when a man said something. Her maid wasn't alone. Suddenly Susan cried out, and the sound was like a dog's yelp when someone treads on its paw. The cry was hastily smothered. Elinor took a step towards the door and then stopped again as she became aware of a rhythmic movement inside the washhouse. It rapidly gathered momentum.

She could now see a little way inside. Two people were lying on the brick floor. She could see only part of their legs and their shoes—Susan's shoes and stockings, a man's square-toed shoes, part of his breeches and a flash of white muscular thighs pumping up and down.

"Ah, yes," said Susan. "Ah! Yes!"

Susan was lying there with Ben. What they were doing was foul. It was immoral. By rights Elinor should sweep in there and instantly dismiss them both. Instead she felt herself flushing, and her breathing accelerating.

Ben grunted urgently.

"Hush!" Susan whispered.

Elinor went back in the house, slamming the door behind her. The words formed in her mind: *My servants are copulating in the washhouse, snuffling and grunting like pigs in their sty.* She was trembling. How dared they? And to do it in broad daylight, where anyone might stumble across them. Such brazen behavior beggared belief.

She found Dr. Carbury was sitting in an armchair drawn up to the window of the little dining parlor at the Master's Lodge. His mouth was open, his feet were up on a footstool and a book was open on his lap. He was so very still that for an instant Elinor thought he was dead. He sat up and looked around wildly before his eyes fell on her. He looked old and unwell.

"My dear sir," she said. "What is it?"

"Nothing—nothing in the world. I was merely dozing a little, that's all. What do you want?"

She had intended to complain to him about the lewd behavior of their servants. But she could not trouble him when he was in this state. Then she was distracted by footsteps in the hall behind her.

"Is that Mr. Holdsworth?" Dr. Carbury asked. "Pray ask him to step in here."

Holdsworth was already coming towards them. What if it had been Holdsworth with Susan in the washhouse? *Snuffling and grunting like pigs in their sty.* The very notion was absurd and fantastical but she felt a sensation strangely like jealousy.

Jealousy?

But if it had been herself with Holdsworth? *Snuffling and grunting like pigs in our sty.* She turned aside, shocked by the wanton immorality of her own imaginings. She made as if to straighten a salver on the sideboard.

"I have not been idle, Mr. Holdsworth," Carbury was saying. "I think I have found somewhere where you may stay with Mr. Oldershaw, at

you to stay within earshot when we are at the mill. I must repeat what the Master said: for the time being you are working solely for me as her ladyship's representative. For no one else. I wish to make that quite clear."

The chaise edged forward through the press of traffic.

"Mr. Archdale asked where I was off to, sir," Mulgrave said. "He wanted to know why I would not wait on him tomorrow as usual."

"What did you say?"

Mulgrave shrugged. "I said you'd hired me to look after Mr. Older-shaw. I didn't say where and he didn't ask. Lord, his head was so full of this evening, he couldn't spare a thought for anything else."

"The Holy Ghost Club?"

"That's it, sir. He becomes a full member and wears the livery for the first time. He was parading up and down in front of the glass for half the afternoon, pleased as punch. He'll be the worse for wear tomorrow morning, though, I'll warrant. And Mr. Which-cote will be a little richer, I daresay, not that any of it will come my way."

"A little richer?"

"Lord love you, sir, Mr. Whichcote don't do all this from the kindness of his heart. The young gentlemen have to pay their sub-scriptions and they ain't cheap. And there's always play at these meetings, too, and the stakes are high. I've heard hundreds turn on one card, one throw of the dice. Still, it's not my place to say anything about how gentlemen choose to amuse themselves. As long as they pays their way."

The motion of the chaise suddenly accelerated. Holdsworth stared out of the window. They would soon be at Jermyn's house.

"There was something else I wished to ask you," he said. "About the supper you served Mr. Oldershaw on the night of his—his seizure."

"As nice a little supper as I've ever served, though I say it myself. Everything neat and handsome."

"And how were the gentlemen? In spirits?"

If Mulgrave saw anything strange about the question he made no sign. "No, sir—Mr. Whichcote was quiet and serious, and Mr.

Oldershaw was low-spirited. Had been for days. I believe he'd dined with Mr. Archdale that day and afterwards they sat a long time over their wine, so his wits was already a little cloudy. And by the end of the evening, he must have been a lot more than half seas over, judging by the empty bottles and the state of the punch bowl."

They came to a halt outside the gates of Dr. Jermyn's establishment. The carriage lurched as Ben scrambled down from the box and rang the bell.

"When we leave with Mr. Oldershaw," Holdsworth said softly, "you will ride outside with Ben."

Mulgrave shot a sly glance from the opposite corner of the chaise. "Are you sure, sir? If he has one of his reckless fits—"

"Quite sure."

"You want the young gentleman to have his privacy, sir, I shouldn't wonder. Very natural, I'm sure, and of course you could have him restrained. Just as a precaution. I am sure Norcross would lend you a straitjacket for a consideration."

"I'm obliged to you, but I don't think I shall want a straitjacket."

The gates opened and the chaise rolled slowly up the drive. At the house, Ben remained on the box. Mulgrave opened the door, jumped down from the carriage and let down the steps for Holdsworth. Now the gyp was in the public view, he had transformed himself with the swift efficiency of his kind into a perfect upper servant, a mere machine ingeniously designed to gratify the desires of his employer.

When the door opened, Holdsworth found himself face to face with Frank Oldershaw. Norcross was on one side of him and another attendant on the other. The young man was dressed immaculately in black. He looked at Holdsworth and then past him at the chaise waiting on the gravel sweep in front of the door.

"There's a couple of portmanteaus here, sir," Norcross said. "No doubt her ladyship will send for the rest of his things."

"Thank you, I'm obliged to you. Where is your master?"

"Dr. Jermyn's compliments, sir, and he regrets he is not at liberty to receive you."

"Very well. We need detain you no longer. Mr. Oldershaw, would you be so good as to enter the chaise?"

At these words, Mulgrave brought his heels together like a soldier coming to attention and opened the carriage door. Ignoring Holdsworth, ignoring Norcross and the attendant, Frank walked down the steps, across the gravel and climbed into the carriage. Holdsworth followed. Mulgrave shut the door behind them and folded up the steps. Frank was sitting in the farthest corner, facing forward. Holdsworth sat down diagonally opposite. Mulgrave mounted the box. There was a jolt and the carriage moved away.

"I have her ladyship's authority to take you to a cottage north of Cambridge, sir," Holdsworth said as they were travelling slowly down the drive. "It is a secluded place and we shall see no one. Mulgrave will attend us. There will be no one else."

Frank said nothing. He was staring at the empty seat directly opposite him.

"We are obliged to drive back through Barnwell and then Cambridge to reach our destination," Holdsworth went on. "To avoid inconvenience, I propose we put up the glasses and lower the blinds until we are past the town."

He put up his own glass and drew down his own blind and then he leaned across and did the same on Frank's side of the chaise. The young man made no move to stop him.

They drove slowly through Cambridge, often travelling no more than a footpace. The interior of the chaise was gloomy and close. Holdsworth's limbs ached. It seemed to him that he had spent most of the last three days cooped up in a carriage. It was easy enough to monitor their progress by the speed they were going, by the surface under their wheels and by the noises that reached them from the outside world. First came cobbles and paved roads. The timbre of the wheels changed as they rolled across the great bridge near Magdalene College. They picked up speed briefly and then slowed for the hill beside the castle. Beyond the castle, they turned right, leaving the main road to Huntingdon, and travelled in a northerly direction on a road whose condition grew steadily worse.

"We may raise the blinds if you wish, sir," Holdsworth said.

Frank made no reply.

Holdsworth raised the blind on his own side and light flooded into the carriage. He lowered the glass, too. They were running down a long, straight lane with huge flat fields on either side.

Suddenly there was a flurry of movement on the other side of the carriage. Frank raised his blind and lowered the glass. He poked his head half out of the window. The wind of their passage ruffled his hair and sent the powder flying away in little curls and puffs. Holdsworth watched him but did not move.

In a moment, Frank withdrew his head and sat back. He said as casually as if it were the most natural thing in the world, "I—I am obliged to you, sir. It is Mr. Holdsworth, is it not?"

"Yes, sir. You remember that her ladyship has sent me. She hopes that you will soon be restored and able to return to her."

Frank screwed up his features and turned his head away. "As to that, what's the point of her wishes?" he muttered. "I am the un-happiest wretch alive. I wish I were dead."

21

WHICHCOTE RAISED THE MONEY for the dinner on the strength of his wife's furniture. He had a long-standing arrangement with the landlord of the Hoop, who lent Whichcote his French chef and several of his waiters for the occasion. Some of the food was prepared in the inn's kitchens. After breakfast, three footmen arrived, a father and two sons. They had worked for Whichcote before and, like the landlord of the Hoop, insisted on payment in advance. They needed nearly an hour to curl and powder their hair and dress themselves in the livery that Mr. Whichcote provided. The coats were sadly shabby now and they did not fit their new wearers very well.

In the afternoon, Whichcote retired to his study and bolted the door. In a corner of the room out of sight from the window and from anyone standing in the doorway, a tall cupboard had been built into an alcove. There were two keyholes in the panelled door but no handle. He unlocked the two locks and opened the door.

The cupboard held the archives of the Holy Ghost Club, together with a number of items associated with it. On one shelf was a selection of glasses, punchbowls, plates and curiously designed cutlery. On the top shelf was a line of leather-bound volumes recording the membership, activities, accounts and decisions of the Holy Ghost Club over the three decades of its existence. Here too were the wager books and cellar books.

Whichcote took down the current cellar book. The club kept its own stock of wines, a subject of great and abiding interest to its members, and the source of considerable expense for them. He had already selected the wines for the evening and withdrawn them from that part of the Lambourne House cellar reserved for their storage. But, on reflection overnight, he had decided that there would be no harm at all in bringing up another dozen of claret and the same of port. He had overseen the withdrawal directly after breakfast. Now he carried the book to his desk, made a note of what had been removed, and replaced the volume on the shelf.

He ran his index finger along the row of spines. He had read, or at least skimmed the pages of, all of them. The club had been founded by Morton Frostwick in the 1750s. Full membership was restricted to the president, known as Jesus, and twelve Apostles. Its entertainments rapidly became legendary in Cambridge because their nature was both mysterious and lavish.

Both these qualities were due to Frostwick. He had spent many years as a servant of the East India Company in Bengal, where his activities had been immensely profitable. When he returned to England, he visited Cambridge and found the fellows' combination room at Jerusalem so congenial a place that he had himself admitted to the college as a fellow-commoner. He enjoyed the society of younger men, and his munificence earned him the title of Nabob Frostwick. He presented the college with the little foot-bridge across the Long Pond, a replica in miniature of Mr. Essex's famous wooden bridge at Queens' College.

At his own cost, Frostwick had bought wines for the club's cellar, and also glasses, cutlery and plate, all curiously adorned, which were still used at club dinners today. Among them was a ceremonial glass from which all who desired admission were still obliged to drink: it ingeniously resembled an erect penis, complete with testicles; it had the capacity to hold about half a pint of wine, and each postulant was required to swallow its contents in one go. Frostwick left Cambridge unexpectedly after an episode rumored to involve one of the sizars at Jerusalem, and went abroad, where it was said he kept a harem of catamites and died of cholera.

Members of the Holy Ghost Club had always had a keen interest in the deflowering of virgins, as the archives amply testified. Frostwick had pointed out that nothing could be more appropriate to the name and aims of the club than to signal the elevation of a disciple to apostolic rank with an outpouring of virginal blood. Was not he himself, in his capacity as Jesus, the son of the Virgin? Was not the very wine they drank at their meetings emblematic of blood? And were they not, by definition, Holy Ghosts, and therefore obliged to lie with virgins whenever possible, in respectful imitation of a similar episode in the Gospels? In Frostwick's time, this part of the admission ritual had been enacted in front of Jesus and the assembled Apostles. After his departure, however, his successors had decided that it would be more genteel to allow the deflowering to take place in private after the rest of the ritual, as a sort of reward that set the seal on all that had gone before.

Philip Whichcote restored the book to its place in the cupboard. As he was locking the door, Augustus entered the study, his eyes sliding from side to side as though he expected to find monsters lurking in the corners.

"If you please, sir, it's Mr. Richardson from the college."

"Show him in, you booby."

The tutor advanced into the room and bowed gracefully. His wig was perfectly powdered, his coat was perfectly cut; there was a smile on his freshly shaved face. Only the eyes were unsettling, restless and flecked with amber.

"Your servant, sir," Richardson said. "I hoped you would not be engaged. You must have so many calls on your attention."

"I hope I shall always have leisure enough to greet my old tutor."

"You are too kind. I hear that your club meets this evening and I am sure such occasions require a vast deal of work beforehand."

Whichcote smiled. "Not at all, my dear sir—these things arrange themselves. The servants know what to do."

"Indeed." Richardson adroitly switched the course of the conversation to the weather, which led by degrees to the recent ill health of the Master, which Mr. Richardson prayed would not recur. "For I am sure that he is sensible of the difficulties his indisposition causes in the college. Nothing of any importance can be done without him." Richardson hesitated. "For example, had he been in better health, he might have been in a position to help poor Mr. Oldershaw."

"The unhappy fellow. Is there any change in his condition?"

"Not that I am aware of. Of course, he is a member of the HG Club too. In fact, now I come to think of it, I believe his melancholy dated from the last of your dinners." Richardson leaned forward, his brow creased with anxiety. "But the subject must be inexpressibly painful to you. Pray forgive me."

"I'm sure no offense was intended," Whichcote said. "And certainly none was taken." He knew that Richardson was the last person in the world to speak without calculation. "As for poor Frank, I believe I perceived signs of his melancholy long before that night. He opened his heart to me on more than one occasion."

Richardson inclined his head, acknowledging Whichcote's superior knowledge.

"I believe you yourself were not a member of the HG Club?" Whichcote said.

Richardson changed countenance. "No. I did not move in those circles when I was an undergraduate."

"But you must have known our Founder, I fancy. Was he not a Jerusalem man? Morton Frostwick—a fellow-commoner, if I remember rightly, and past the first flush of youth."

Richardson turned his head away. "Yes, I believe I knew him very slightly."

Whichcote smiled. "Sometimes I while away an idle hour by glancing at the club archives. Mr. Frostwick figures largely there, as you may imagine."

"I hardly remember him."

"Really?" Whichcote allowed his disbelief to seep into his voice. "There are so many diverting stories about him."

The senior tutor gestured gracefully with his right hand, displaying fine white fingers. "It is always agreeable to recall the scenes of one's youth, but alas I have a more pressing concern on my mind. You are aware, perhaps, that Mr. Archdale is one of my pupils?"

Whichcote nodded. "He is fortunate indeed."

"And I understand that he is to be advanced to full membership of the HG Club today."

"I am sure that he will be a popular addition to our little society."

"No doubt. However, I had some discussion with his guardian on Saturday, and again on Sunday when Sir Charles dined in college. He is most anxious about his nephew. May I speak in confidence, my dear sir?"

"By all means," Whichcote said.

"Sir Charles fears that the lad may be following a mode of life that can not only harm his future prospects but also undermine his health. As you are intimate with him, I thought it my duty to have a word with you on the subject. He respects you greatly. A word from you in season may work wonders."

"I feel you have too high an opinion of my abilities, sir."

"I do not think so." Richardson rose to his feet. "I must trouble you no further, sir. I know I may rely on your good offices, and I shall be infinitely obliged."

Whichcote accompanied his visitor into the hall, where Augustus opened the door and bowed very low as Mr. Richardson left. Whichcote stood on the step, his hand raised in farewell, as his visitor walked briskly down the short drive towards the main road. He had received a warning. Richardson had no wish for another club scandal touching a member of Jerusalem College.

It was a great pity that before the tutor reached the gates, Mrs. Phear turned into the drive, with Archdale's little whore for the evening walking behind her. Richardson uncovered and bowed to Mrs. Phear as he passed. He looked curiously at the girl from the Magdalene Hospital, who passed him with downcast eyes.

The meeting was unfortunate, Whichcote thought. He hoped it was not an evil omen.

The Apostles arrived in ones and twos, some on foot, flaunting the full glory of the club livery in the afternoon sunshine, others preferring to conceal their splendor in sedan chairs or hackneys. The hired footmen ushered them down to the pavilion at the bottom of the garden, where Whichcote waited to receive them in the great room overlooking the river.

Mrs. Phear and the girl from the Magdalene Hospital were in the small white bedchamber below. The girl was called Molly Price. She was not as pretty as Tabitha Skinner, but she knew what she was about. Mrs. Phear had looked over the arrangements, visited the kitchen, and made her presence felt among the servants. This was all to the good, for there was no getting away from the fact that the servants were a slovenly, greedy crew who needed careful watching. They would serve the company, wait at dinner, clear away and serve supper. But once supper was on the table, they would go, leaving the club to serve itself, with a little help from Augustus if necessary. Then the real business of the evening would begin.

Harry Archdale was one of those who arrived in a sedan chair. His face had lost its usual high color, and the pallor of his complexion contrasted curiously with the careful arrangement of his hair, which he had had thickly powdered in a shade of white with a distinctly pink tinge. Whichcote smelled brandy on his breath.

Before dinner, the members of the club strolled in the garden. It was, all in all, not a bad turnout. When dinner was announced, Whichcote led the way upstairs, where they arranged themselves around the table in the order of precedence. He placed Harry on his right hand.

He had spared no expense with the food. The first course consisted of cod, a chine of mutton, some soup, and a chicken pie as well as many puddings and roots. For the second course they had fillet of veal with mushrooms, pigeons and asparagus, roasted sweetbreads, a hot lobster, apricot tart and, in the center of the table, a great pyramid of syllabubs and jellies. Dinner was more than a meal: it was an investment.

Afterwards, some members, including Archdale, showed a tendency to linger over their wine, but Whichcote weaned them away to the card tables set up at the far end of the room. This was, after all, the lucrative part of the proceedings. He did not encourage club members to engage in such games as piquet, which took too much time and involved only two people. Simpler, shorter games were much better, both cards and dice. With these, the players won and lost with such rapidity that they became infected with a mania for play; and each loss was obliterated by the hope of winning next time.

Whichcote moved from group to group. He carried loaded dice in a concealed pocket of his waistcoat and had also taken the precaution of opening a pack of cards, filing the corners of some of them and carefully resealing the pack in its original wrapper. Not that he liked to rely on such shabby shifts. Usually there was no need: if he kept himself sober and took the trouble to calculate the arithmetical odds, he would win the cost of the dinner within twenty minutes.

The hours passed agreeably. The invisible servants, who screened off the table from the rest of the room, came and went, making preparations for supper. The drinking continued steadily, and the laughter and the voices grew louder as the last of the daylight ebbed from the room. The air filled with smoke, shifting in the draughts, and the muddy glow of candles swayed with it.

Whichcote's winnings, partly in ready money but mainly in notes of hand, steadily increased. As he moved from table to table, he kept an eye on Harry Archdale. The young man was drinking as heavily as anyone in the room. His face had lost its pallor and was damp with sweat. His elaborately arranged hair was a ragged mop and the shoulders of his green coat were sprinkled with dislodged powder. He was playing so wildly that he had already lost at least a hundred guineas, and not all of it to his host.

It was after another loss that Archdale suddenly pushed back his chair and stumbled behind a screen in the corner where a line of commodes had been arranged along the wall for the convenience of the guests. Five minutes later, when he had not returned, Whichcote went in search of him. The young man was slumped on a window seat. His face was pressed against the glass.

"Harry—what ails you?"

Archdale turned his head sharply and straightened up on the seat. "It is nothing—it's so damned hot in here—I wanted air."

"Then let us take a turn in the garden."

Whichcote led the way downstairs. The sky was now dark. A lamp burned in the doorway, and two or three more beyond, marking the path up to the side door of the house. They strolled along the gravel path between the pavilion and the river. On the far side of the water, Jesus Green lay in darkness, apart from the soft gleam of lights from the college itself and, farther to the right, the lights of the town.

"You seemed a little melancholy just now," Whichcote observed.

"It was nothing," Archdale said hastily. "The closeness of the air made me feel a little fagged—I am perfectly restored now."

"I am rejoiced to hear it," Whichcote said. "After all, you have a man's work to do tonight. You must go to it with a will, eh?"

"Oh I shall, I shall indeed."

They were now walking along the rear of the pavilion on the side facing the house. Archdale swayed. Suddenly he stopped, leaning against the wall. He stared fixedly at the row of ground-floor windows.

"Is—is she already here?"

"The sacrifice? Oh yes," Whichcote said. "The virgin awaits your pleasure."

"Does she know what is to happen?"

Whichcote laughed softly. "How can she? She's a maid. Her knowledge of such matters must be entirely notional."

"But she knows I will lie with her?"

"It is all arranged. You are to have the way of a man with a maid. You need not trouble yourself in the slightest about her. If she puts up any resistance, you must not scruple to overcome it. Indeed, many of us find it adds relish to the conquest. The fruits of victory are all the sweeter if hard won."

"Yes, yes—Philip, would you excuse me one moment?"

Without further warning, Archdale stumbled away from the path and made his way blindly to a large shrub standing in a pot. Whichcote waited, listening to the sounds of retching. Archdale returned, wiping his mouth on a scented handkerchief.

"Very wise," Whichcote murmured.

"What? I beg your pardon?"

"Your decision to vomit. As the French say, it is a case of *reculer pour mieux sauter.*"

"Yes," Archdale said weakly. "Yes, that's it. Vomiting for that purpose was much practiced by the ancients, I believe. Seneca refers to it somewhere in the *Moral Epistles*, I fancy, and Cicero tells us—I believe it is in the *Pro Rege Deiotaro*—that Caesar himself was not a stranger to the habit. It also—" He broke off. "I ask your pardon, sir. I allow my tongue to run away with me."

Whichcote said nothing. Archdale set out to play the part of a rake but somewhere inside him was a scholar. He touched Archdale's arm, and they moved away. They passed the shuttered window of the whitewashed bedchamber where Molly Price was waiting with Mrs. Phear.

"I wish Frank was here," Archdale said.

"So do I. We all do."

"I asked him how it was that night—when he became an Apostle. He would not tell me."

"That was very proper of him. He swore a most terrible oath never to reveal what passed on that occasion to anyone who was not an Apostle. And so will you when your time comes. But since you are so nearly one of us, I may tell you in confidence that Frank dealt manfully with his virgin, just as you will, I am sure."

They reentered the pavilion and went upstairs. Whichcote had presided over too many initiations to be surprised by what had occurred. For two pins, Archdale would have slipped away from the club. But he was too rich a prize to lose. That was the point of the ceremony—and of the ceremony with the virgin in particular. Archdale had mentioned Caesar: well, Caesar had crossed the Rubicon when he invaded Italy and, in doing so, had taken a step that could not be reversed. Archdale would believe he had done the same when his manly ardor overcame the feigned resistance of Molly Price.

They reached the head of the stairs. Whichcote stopped. They heard the hubbub of voices in the room beyond. Some of the Apostles were singing.

Jerry Carbury is merry
Tell his servant bring his hat
For 'ere the evening is done
He'll surely shoot the cat.

Archdale blinked rapidly. He looked on the verge of tears.

"And now we shall have supper," Whichcote said quietly. "The servants will leave us to wait on ourselves. We shall have the toasts—we shall have the initiation—and you will be canonized. St. Bartholomew is the title reserved for you. And then, when you are finally one of us, you shall be conducted to your trembling virgin."

❦ 22 ❦

SUPPER PASSED IN A DREAM; then came the interminable
toasts; then, at long last, the initiation ceremony. Archdale
kneeled before Whichcote, very grand on a throne-like chair
flanked with black candles; and Whichcote, as Jesus, read out a list
of apostolic tenets couched in bad Latin, to each of which Archdale
was required to assent.

Archdale took the phallic glass, filled to the brim with wine, and
drained it without lowering it from his lips, to the accompaniment
of apostolic whoops and cheers. He committed himself to the Holy
Ghost for all eternity. Amen. He swore to abominate the Pope of
Rome and all his works and to leave no bottle unemptied, no toast
undrunk and no virgin undefiled. Amen, amen, amen, amen.
There were more tenets and more wine and his head spun around
and around. He noticed that the thread at the front of Whichcote's
left shoe had frayed and the sole was beginning to come adrift from
the upper. He mumbled the required responses and drank the required toasts. He would have given everything he possessed to lay
his aching head on a cool pillow and fall asleep for ever. Amen.

When the ceremony was over, a procession formed up around
him. Jesus was on his right and St. Peter on his left. St. Andrew led
the way with one black candle, St. Simon followed with the other
and St. John wielded a handbell. Jesus and the Apostles marched
Archdale downstairs, chanting as they went an obscene variation

of the Angelus that dwelled at some length on the phallic splendors of the Holy Ghost. The procession halted in the corridor. The discordant voices swirled around Archdale, mingling with the clanging of the bell.

Apart from the candles, the only light came from a lamp burning near the far end of the hallway. Archdale thought he glimpsed the footboy Augustus cowering in a doorway and for an instant felt a stab of relief that he was not alone in his fear.

St. John rapped smartly on one of the nearer doors, ringing the bell and calling on the occupants to open in the name of the Holy Ghost. The Apostles formed an arc facing the door with Archdale at its centre. As the door opened, it revealed the shadowy outline of a small woman, childlike in size, enveloped in a nun's habit and with her face obscured by a domino.

"In the name of the Holy Ghost, an Apostle demands the virgin sacrifice," the Apostles chanted in ragged unison.

The masked nun stepped back and pushed the door wide. The Apostles cheered. Jesus and St. Peter led Archdale forward. He stared wildly around the little white cell. Only two candles were alight, one on the table near the fireplace and the other near the bed. There was his virgin, lying on the white coverlet, her limbs lashed to the bedposts. She wore a plain white shift with a loose neck. She stared up at him with wide and terrified eyes.

"You may take her trussed like that," Whichcote murmured in his ear. "Or if you want her loose, you may untie her. But be warned, the little minx may struggle."

St. Peter patted Archdale's shoulder. "Go to it, my lad," he urged. "Show the maid her master."

Archdale heard the door closing behind them. Someone outside began to sing the drinking song about Jerry Carbury again. The apostolic footsteps receded into the distance. Even the nun was gone. He was alone with the girl.

He stared at her, and she stared back. She was not ill-favored, he thought, taken all in all, and she was certainly young. She seemed clean, too, and in that she compared favorably to Chloe the other night. As he watched, she licked her lips and he noticed that they were full and prettily formed. He pulled off the green coat and draped it over the chair by the table. Still with his eyes on the girl, he slowly unbuttoned his waistcoat. His fingers were clumsy and it seemed to take an age. His head hurt and his mouth was dry. There was wine on the table but what he really wanted was water. Why was there no water to be had?

He pushed the embroidered waistcoat over his shoulders and let it fall to the floor behind him. There were now two beds in front of him, and two virgins, and if he had not known better, he would have sworn that they were both smiling at him. He tugged violently at his necktie and the movement overbalanced him. He staggered to the right and tried to steady himself on one of the posts at the foot of the bed. His hand unaccountably missed the post. He fell forward and his face collided with it. He yelped with pain. The next thing he knew he was sprawling half on and half off the end of the bed.

The necktie felt as if it were strangling him. He tore it off and flung it on the floor. He looked at the girl, furious that she should be witnessing this moment of weakness. But her face was unchanged. Her eyes stared up at him.

Archdale used the bedpost to pull himself into an upright position. He kicked off his shoes and glanced over his shoulder again at the girl. He had to deflower her by force. That was the whole purpose of his being here. It was unthinkable that he should fail to carry out the task. Everyone would know—Whichcote, the other Apostles, the little nun, even this girl here. She would blab about it, of course she would. There was no help for it, he would have to do it.

He unbuttoned his breeches and stood up. The breeches fell about his knees. He pushed them lower and stepped out of them. At the last moment, he tripped and plunged forward on to the bed, landing partly between the girl's legs and partly on her body. The impact made her gasp. Frowning, he pushed up her shift, exposing her fork. He pushed his hand under his billowing shirt and grasped his penis.

To his utter, unbearable horror, his m   stra
flaccid in his hand. He massaged it, first   bod
ously. Nothing happened. Sweat broke out o1   witl
his eyes and tried to concentrate, to force t.   N
ercise of will. Still nothing happened.   A

The girl cleared her throat.   The

It was as though a waxwork had made a   was
dale opened his eyes and stared at her. Here   the
his shame. He could not see her clearly but   ter
she was looking at him with grave, unblink   his
an expression of sorrow in her face.   the

"I can give you a hand, sir," she said in a l   an
whisper.   wo

"Eh? What's that? What?"   wo

"Sometimes a gentleman likes a little enc   sic
attention, sir."

"Yes, yes, that's true." He pushed himself   is
the bedpost and leaned his cheek against it.
know?"

She laughed softly. "Oh, bless you, sir, wh   lo
gether at night, they talk of all sorts of thing
about what gentlemen like, and how we may   w:
time comes. If you untie me, I'll show you."   in

Archdale dragged himself up and shuffle
doing the four knots. The bonds were so loo: fi
that the girl could easily have extricated herse   w
When she was free, she sat up and pulled
her shoulders. She drew Archdale down besic   s
kissed him several times and encouraged   a
against her little breasts, all of which he wou.
able enough in normal circumstances. Unfor   I
escape that sense of underlying panic, a sus
failure.   a

Murmuring endearments, some of which
able for one who was a maid, she pushed him d

dled his legs. She tugged up his shirt, exposing his soft pink
  She set to work on his penis, first with her hands and then
her mouth.

thing happened.

ter two or three minutes of her attentions, Archdale groaned.
girl raised her head and then sat back on her haunches. This
ailure, Archdale knew, unalterable and absolute. Soon Jesus,
postles and the lesser disciples would be roaring with laugh-
him. He was but half a man, a poor womanish creature, and
adequacies would be exposed before the world. He imagined
ews flying around Cambridge, whispered in coffee houses
lubs, and finding its way at last to London, where men and
n would laugh at him in the street, and Sir Charles Archdale
l cut off his allowance and disinherit him. He wanted to be
he wanted to cry, he wanted to die.

u poor love," the girl cooed. "It is the wine, nothing more. It
nkind of them to press you to take so much."

chdale blinked. "Yes—yes, the wine."

r fingers strayed to his penis again. "And you have such a
little lad down here. Oh, how I desire it inside me."

e possibility occurred to Archdale that perhaps this virgin
ot quite the maid she was meant to be. She appeared surpris-
at home with a man's anatomy.

'hat wouldn't I give for the honor of losing my maidenhead to a
entleman like you, sir?" she murmured. "Why, in an hour or two
you're recovered, I wager you'd make me swoon with pleasure."

chdale felt tears prick his eyelids. Life was so unjust. The occa-
vas one for rejoicing. The time was right. The girl was agree-
Yet his body would not allow him to play his part.

ut what does it matter, sir, if you do it to me now or tomorrow?
l one."

s, but you do not understand. The others will—" He broke off
tared miserably at the little white canopy above his head.

e girl was still stroking his thigh. "The others aren't here. None
m. Only you and me, sir. So they'll know only what we tell 'em."

Archdale lowered his eyes and looked at the girl's face. There still appeared to be two of her. "You mean—?"

"We say you had your way with me, sir. As I'm sure you will when you're yourself again."

"You—you are a virgin, aren't you?"

She stared guilelessly at him. "Oh yes, sir."

"There—there would be signs."

"Not always, sir. Besides, I have a plan."

She dismounted him as though he were a horse and she had been riding astride him. She went to the fireplace, picked up a covered basket that stood beside it and set it on the table. She uncovered it and took out a little phial containing a dark liquid and sealed with a cork. She held it up between finger and thumb. By chance, it was on a direct line between Archdale's eyes and the flame of the candle on the table.

Two flames, two phials, of course, and in the center of each phial was a dull red spark.

"A few drops of that on the sheet, sir, and there's my maidenhead."

"But how did you come—?"

"Hush, sir. Don't speak so loud. A maid must look ahead."

She returned to the bed and uncorked the phial. He was lying with his legs apart and his shirt rucked up. She scattered a few drops of red fluid between his thighs.

"There, sir," she said, sitting down beside him and taking his hand. "Now there needs only one more thing and we are done."

He frowned up at her. "One more thing? What?"

She opened her mouth wide, exposing blackened teeth, and screamed.

23

ON THE FIRST NIGHT at Whitebeach Mill, Holdsworth slept badly, his limbs crammed into a little box-bed built into the wall. He had given Frank Oldershaw the larger of the two upstairs rooms, the one with a decent bedstead. Frank was only a few feet away, on the other side of the lathe-and-plaster partition. The bed creaked as he moved about.

When the dawn came and the little room filled with light, Holdsworth was unexpectedly reminded of the house on Bankside near Goat Stairs. His window at the cottage overlooked the garden, beyond which was the millpond and the muddy green river, hardly more than a stream compared with the Thames at London. Some trick of reflection cast a faint and flickering image of moving waters on the ceiling of the bedroom. It was a poor and insubstantial phenomenon compared to the shimmering light, Georgie's ghost water, that the Thames threw through the windows. But it was a connection between here and there, now and then.

Georgie and Maria had become less substantial like the light. For minutes at a stretch, they seemed removed from him, at once real and unreal like favorite characters in a play rather than the beloved dead.

Holdsworth rose early, dressed and crossed the little landing on stockinged feet. He looked in on Frank. The boy was lying on his back, one arm outstretched above his head, and appeared to be sleeping soundly. He looked very young, completely vulnerable. Holdsworth had not appreciated before how perfectly formed his features were. In the house at Barnwell, Frank had been considered a madman and he had looked like one too. Asleep in Whitebeach, he looked like an overgrown child.

Would Georgie have lain like this, with such careless and innocent abandon, if he had lived? Holdsworth had failed to save his son and so he would never know. But could he save this living boy in front of him? Would it be something to set against Georgie's death?

He went down the stairs, which were so steep they were almost a ladder. The interior of the cottage was gloomy because of the small windows and overhanging thatched eaves. There was a rattle of fire-irons in the kitchen. Holdsworth went into the garden. Early though it was, the gray dome of the sky was full of light. The unkempt grass was silvered with cobwebs and dew. He followed the flagged path down to the water. He stood on the bank for a while, watching a pair of moorhens who flew off at his appearance, oddly erect, with their legs dangling down. Both the water and the air were noticeably cleaner than in Cambridge. Apart from Mulgrave at work in the kitchen, there were no man-made noises. Holdsworth closed his eyes and heard drumming water, the call of a bird he could not identify, and a faint, shifting rustling of vegetation.

Thank God, he thought, thank God the boy is still here.

This had been his greatest fear—that Frank Oldershaw would take advantage of the sudden freedom and either flee or find some way of killing himself. Either of those things might happen in the future but at least that first night was past and the boy was still asleep.

Holdsworth walked round the house to the cobbled yard and washed his hands and face at the pump. The mill itself stood at right angles to the little cottage, its wheel raised out of the water. Beside it was a line of outbuildings thatched with reeds. Beyond the pump was the lane to the village. A ginger cat slipped under the gate and snaked around Holdsworth's legs with his tail erect. Holdsworth tried to nudge it away with his foot but the animal easily evaded him and purred as though it had been paid a compliment.

He was drying himself on his shirt-tails when he heard footsteps behind him. He turned and saw Frank.

"Mr. Oldershaw—you are up early."

The young man looked surprised to see him there. Frank's hair was tousled. He wore a shirt and breeches but his feet were bare.

"Would you like to wash?" Holdsworth asked. "I will send Mulgrave out with a bowl and a towel."

Frank Oldershaw raised his arms and threw them back as if he were preparing to dive. His face, which had been very serious in expression, suddenly broke into a smile.

"Quack," he said. "Quack. I am a duck."

He bolted out of the yard, taking the path that led round the gable end of the cottage and into the garden. Holdsworth pounded after him. As he passed the kitchen window, he saw Mulgrave's white face staring open-mouthed.

In the garden, Frank left the path and plunged into the tangle of long grass and weeds. As he ran, he flailed his arms and kicked out his legs with mad and joyous abandon. His feet kicked up silver sprays of dew. He was like a boy let out of school.

"Quack," he cried. "Quack, quack!"

In front of him lay the placid expanse of the millpond. Frank did not break stride. At the water's edge, he plunged into the air in a clumsy dive. His body hit the water with a crash that sent waves rolling over the pool. The waterfowl fluttered into the air in a panic of flapping wings.

"Mr. Oldershaw!" Holdsworth cried. "Mr. Oldershaw!"

Seconds later, the boy broke the surface about ten yards from the bank. He turned on his back, half submerged and splashing his arms and legs. "Quack, quack!"

"Pray come out," Holdsworth called. "There may be weeds or other hazards. I cannot save you—I cannot swim."

Frank stopped splashing and quacking. He stared across the water at Holdsworth.

Maria had not been able to swim either, nor for that matter had Georgie. And so the water had swallowed them whole and spat them up to the surface once it had siphoned the life from them.

Had Sylvia Whichcote been able to swim? Had she drowned just as Frank was about to drown?

Holdsworth opened his mouth but no words came out. Instead he sucked in breath. He could not get enough. Pin-like pains stabbed his chest. The great gray sky pressed down on him. Dear God, he was drowning in air.

Frank turned over on to his front and swam with leisurely strokes to the bank. All of a sudden the world had become sane again. Breathing heavily, Holdsworth stepped forward and held out his hand. Frank took it, and hauled himself out of the water.

"Dear God," Frank said, his teeth chattering, "it's so damned cold."

For the rest of their first day at the mill, Holdsworth and Frank Oldershaw circled around each other like animals who did not know each other but had been forced to share the same confined space. Until now, Holdsworth had followed where common sense or instinct had led him. He had had no doubt that removing Frank from the care of Dr. Jermyn would be in Frank's best interests and therefore in his own best interests too. Now he was not so sure. Indeed, he was not sure of anything.

Frank's behavior was unpredictable. He gambolled about like a large and energetic puppy, reminding Holdsworth inevitably of Georgie when a fit of excitement was on him. Frank sang discordantly, mingling drinking songs with nursery rhymes, and sometimes applying the words of one to the melody of another. He ate whatever was put before him, shovelling food into his mouth as though he had been half-starved at Barnwell. He resisted, or rather ignored, all attempts to guide him in any direction. Every now and then he fell asleep in the middle of what he was doing—again like Georgie—at table with his head cradled on his arms, on the grass in the garden or the cobbles in the yard, on the kitchen floor in the corner by the stone sink.

Mulgrave said and did nothing that did not relate to his own duties. He waited for Holdsworth's orders, and when he received them he obeyed them swiftly and fairly efficiently. He avoided being left alone with Frank, though Frank ignored him as he ignored Holdsworth. Mulgrave was a good servant and a worthless ally.

The only other living thing in the house was the ginger cat. Unlike the three humans, he appeared entirely unconcerned by the strangeness of the occasion. He approached each of the men with the same impersonal enthusiasm. He demanded to be petted and fed. To Holdsworth's embarrassment, he found himself stroking the animal when it leaped on to his lap, and he even fed it with a scrap of meat from his plate. When Holdsworth pushed it away, the cat leaped on to Frank's lap, and Frank absentmindedly stroked it just as Holdsworth had done.

On one occasion, when the cat had again been on Frank's lap, it grew weary of him and jumped down. It sauntered into the kitchen where it plagued Mulgrave. Mulgrave did not want its attentions and kicked it. The cat squawked with pain and surprise. It was this that unexpectedly affected Frank, who had been watching events through the open door.

He stood up suddenly, and his chair fell over behind him. The cat ran round the kitchen in momentary panic.

"Let him be," Frank said, his voice sounding thick and rusty from disuse. "Let him go freely wherever he wishes, do you hear me?"

Mulgrave bowed. He came forward and righted the chair. Frank frowned. He looked puzzled, as if wondering what had happened. He sat down on the chair without looking behind him to see if it was there. The cat jumped on to his lap again and purred loudly.

24

Y OU NEVER KNEW with Mr. Whichcote.

In the early hours of Thursday morning, Augustus slept fitfully for nearly two hours in a chair drawn up to the dying glow of the kitchen fire. Even in his dreams he heard the jangling of the bell over the kitchen door. He was not summoned, however, and he dozed until the scullery maid came down at five o'clock.

The girl, who was the next best thing to a halfwit, coaxed the fire into life and made an almighty clattering as she set pans of water to warm. One by one, in order of seniority, the other servants appeared—the wall-eyed maid, the old man who had tended the garden with gradually decreasing efficiency since the time of Mr. Whichcote's great-uncle, and finally the cook, a majestic but sour-faced woman who was at present working out her notice. None of the servants liked the day after a club dinner. The day itself was hard work, but it was a break in routine, undeniably exciting, full of strange faces, and with the tantalizing possibility of discarded trifles or unexpected tips. Afterwards, though, came the unpleasant task of clearing up.

A little after eight o'clock, Mr. Whichcote's bell rang. Augustus took his jug of warm water upstairs. When he returned thirty minutes later with tea and rolls on a tray, he found the jug had not been touched. Mr. Whichcote was still in his dressing gown, sitting up in bed and making notes in his pocketbook. He gestured towards

Augustus to leave the tray on the night table. As he did so, the footboy glanced down and saw that the master was adding up a column of figures, against which he had made a number of entries.

An hour later, there was a knocking at the front door. Augustus opened the door to Mrs. Phear. Her maid Dorcas was two paces behind her.

Mrs. Phear advanced into the hall, as implacable as a small black cloud in a clear blue sky. She addressed the air in front of her. "Where's your master?"

Augustus hastened to open the study door. Mr. Whichcote was already rising to his feet. Mrs. Phear said that she had brought her maid with her: the girl was so idle at home that a little work would be good for her.

Whichcote turned to Augustus and held out a key for him to take. "You and the girl will make the pavilion neat again. I wish to see it clean and swept and garnished, with everything restored to how it was."

Augustus bowed and turned, believing he had been dismissed.

"Stay. Come here." Whichcote towered over the footboy. "Only you and the maid are to work down there. I hold you responsible for that, as well as the rest. Now go."

Mr. Whichcote kept the pavilion locked. According to Cook, this was because the building was reserved for the master's obscene and blasphemous activities, especially those that occurred on the nights of club dinners, so the master's caution was entirely understandable. Cook said that she herself would not go in there alone for all the tea in China. Mr. Whichcote, she said, was a gentleman who made your blood run cold, which was one reason why she had handed in her notice; the other reasons being the death of her late mistress (God rest her soul), the impious activities of the master and his friends, and (worst of all) his inability to pay his servants on time. Cook also said that if Mr. Whichcote made your blood run cold, then Mrs. Phear made it freeze in your veins and turn your very heart to a block of ice; and Cook was right.

Augustus took Dorcas through to the service side of the house, where they collected the brushes, mops, cloths and buckets. He carried the key of the pavilion in his pocket and was conscious of its weight and the responsibility it signified. Dorcas, who was half a head taller than he was, stared straight ahead. She had a white and bony face with freckles like flecks of mud on her skin.

"We'll do the big room upstairs," he said as he unlocked the pavilion door. "Then the little room they used downstairs and the staircase."

"You please yourself," the maid said, still without looking at him. "I want to see the bedchamber first."

Augustus stared at her. "How do you know there's a bedchamber?"

"Because the girl told me. The one who had to lie in there last night all trussed up like a bird for the oven."

"You're making it up," Augustus said uncertainly. "I was here last night."

"But you weren't in that bedchamber, were you?"

"No more was you."

"That girl was, though. She had to pretend to be a virgin. But she's no more a virgin than my grandmother. She had this fat young gent come to her. He was too drunk to do it but he gave her three guineas."

"Where's she now?"

"Gone back to London."

Augustus opened the door, thinking that Dorcas must be telling the truth because she knew it had been the fat young gent, Mr. Archdale. She pushed past him into the lobby and looked about her.

"Where is it?"

Without waiting for an answer, she opened the nearest door, which led to the passage running the length of the pavilion's ground floor. With Augustus at her heels, she walked briskly along it, trying the doors until she found the bedchamber.

With a bucket in one hand and a mop in the other, Augustus stood in the doorway and watched Dorcas inspecting the room for all the world as though she were the mistress of the house looking for evidence of her maid's shortcomings. She tutted over the puddle of wax at the foot of one of the candlesticks on the table. She sighed loudly as she replaced the cork in a bottle of cordial. She raised her eyebrows at the heap of bedclothes on the floor and touched with her forefinger one of the silken white cords that were still attached to the bedposts. She studied the red stains in the middle of the sheet on the bed and wrinkled her nose.

"Up to all the tricks, that one."

"What?"

She stared at him not unkindly. She was three inches taller and nine months older yet her expression hinted that in her superiority to him she might just as well have been as tall as King's College Chapel and roughly as old too. "She lay with me last night and she wouldn't stop talking. That's how I knew all about the young gent being unmanned. Happens a lot, she says, and they have to pretend. It's worth their while, mind you."

Augustus felt hot and uncomfortable. He turned away, wanting to assert his control over the situation; after all, he was in some sense the host and besides he was a man and Dorcas was nothing but a girl. "Come upstairs," he said. "That's where the worst of it is."

He went out of the room without looking at her. He led her back down the passage and up to the long room on the first floor.

"Pho," Dorcas said as she passed through the doorway. "Worse than a midden on a hot day."

She walked round the room, with Augustus once again at her heels. The air stank of stale alcohol and tobacco and the smoke from the candles. Underlying that were other and less agreeable odors. Two of the chairs had been overturned. There were pools of wax and wine on the table and the floor. At least half a dozen glasses had been smashed, some intentionally, and the fragments of glass lay around the empty fireplace. There was a pool of vomit on a bowl of fruit at one end of the table. They found far worse behind the screen, the source of the worst smells, where one of the commodes had fallen on to its side and a chamber pot had smashed. The floorboards here were slippery with urine, more vomit and even a pile of excrement.

"Take days to set this to rights," Dorcas said, and for the first time she sounded awed and even a little scared.

Together they examined the debris on the table. Dorcas picked up a strawberry and ate it. Augustus found a half-eaten chicken leg. They foraged for a few minutes, cramming scraps of food into their mouths.

She wiped her mouth with the back of her hand. "Do you think they enjoy it?"

A door banged below them. There were footsteps on the stairs. Dorcas seized a brush and began to sweep vigorously. Augustus righted one of the fallen chairs. The door of the room opened and Mr. Whichcote appeared on the threshold.

"I don't pay you to be idle," he said to Augustus.

He might have replied that Mr. Whichcote did not pay him at all. Instead, he hung his head and blushed.

Dorcas curtsied low and said nothing, fixing her eyes on the ground.

"Begin by airing the place," Mr. Whichcote said. "What are you waiting for? Open the windows."

They sprang to obey him. Whichcote made a leisurely circuit of the room with a handkerchief raised to his nose.

"Remember," he said. "I do not choose to have what passes here to be talked about abroad. If there is foolish gossip in the town about it, I shall know that one or both of you have been talking out of turn. And if that happens, Mrs. Phear and I will know what to do." He looked from Augustus to Dorcas and then went on in the same low, unhurried voice: "It is a singular coincidence that neither of you has friends in the world, is it not? It follows that Mrs. Phear and I must stand in place of them. And you shall find that, just as we know how to punish wrongdoing, we know how to reward fidelity."

Without another word, he sauntered out of the room and down the stairs. Neither Dorcas nor Augustus moved until they heard the closing of the big door in the lobby.

"He'll kill us if we talk," Augustus blurted out.

He glanced sideways at Dorcas. He was alarmed to see that her eyes were full of tears.

"You remember the other girl, the one that died?" she muttered.

"The one who came in February? Tabitha? They said she choked."

"Who knows? Maybe they killed her. I tell you this, though—the mistress locked me in with Tabby's body that night. And now she never goes away."

"What do you mean?"

"Every night she's there," Dorcas hissed. "I see her shape in the bed next to mine. She talks and talks and I can't hear what she's saying."

Elinor Carbury sat in her sitting room and tried to reread Chapter 31 of *Rasselas*.

> *That the dead are seen no more, said Imlac, I will not undertake*
> *to maintain against the concurrent and unvaried testimony*
> *of all ages, and of all nations. There is no people, rude or learned,*
> *among whom apparitions of the dead are not related and*
> *believed. This opinion, which, perhaps, prevails as far as human*
> *nature is diffused, could become universal only by its truth:*
> *those, that never heard of one another, would not have agreed in a*
> *tale which nothing but experience can make credible. That it is*
> *doubted by single cavillers can very little weaken the general*
> *evidence, and some who deny it with their tongues confess it by*
> *their fears.*

But her mind refused to concentrate on the words before her. Her eyes drifted over the distressingly formal garden to the dark green mass of the plane tree. She thought of John Holdsworth and wondered how he was at the mill. She had felt his absence at breakfast. There was nothing reprehensible or out of the ordinary about this, she assured herself, for in the last few days she had seen more society than she often saw in as many weeks. John Holdsworth had simply been part of that society; and as his hostess she had been obliged to see a good deal of him. Still, there was no denying that she felt flat and dull.

The sitting-room windows were open, and so were other windows in the Master's Lodge. She became aware that Dr. Carbury had a visitor in his book room below. The rumble of their voices, her husband's and that of another gentleman, grew steadily louder. Their conversation was becoming heated.

She rang the bell. When at last Susan bustled into the room, Elinor asked who the visitor was.

"Why, ma'am, 'tis Dr. Jermyn from Barnwell."

Elinor sent the girl away. Had she imagined an alteration in Susan's manner? She had seemed strange for the last day or two— unnaturally cheerful but also watchful, almost wary.

In the circumstances, it was scarcely surprising that high words should pass between Dr. Carbury and Dr. Jermyn. Though Frank's removal from the asylum had had nothing to do with her husband, Jermyn would naturally believe that at least some of the responsibility was his.

What did surprise Elinor, though, was what happened next. The gentlemen soon lowered their voices, so they appeared to have made peace. Some ten minutes after that, she heard the garden door opening below her. When she craned her head, in a most unlady-like manner, she saw the foreshortened figures of Dr. Carbury and his guest walking along the gravel path and through the gate that led to the service yard where the washhouse was.

The gentlemen were gone for perhaps five minutes, and when they returned, their heads were close together and they were deep in conversation. Shortly afterwards she heard Jermyn leaving.

It was most curious, Elinor thought, and she could not for the life of her think what they had been doing in the yard. Surely it could be nothing to do with what had happened there on Tuesday morning?

Susan and Ben snuffling and grunting like pigs in their sty.

ᎦᏋᏋ

On Thursday, Harry Archdale recovered slowly from his promotion to apostolic rank. He faced fines for missing chapel, breakfast and his morning lecture; and he would almost certainly be obliged to endure an unpleasant interview with Dr. Richardson and possibly further punishments. He forced himself out of bed when he heard the bell ringing for dinner. But he could not bear to go down to the hall. He sat on the edge of his bed, his head in his hands, and moaned. He did not think it possible that he would ever want to eat another mouthful of food.

He dressed himself very gradually. The dinner was over by the time he had finished. His rooms were unbearably stuffy. He made his way downstairs, pausing at each step, moving his limbs as though they were made of glass and might be expected to shatter at the slightest shock.

In the court, the sun hurt his eyes with its brightness. Soresby passed him, wishing him good day, and the sound of his voice made Archdale moan.

Like a sick animal, he obeyed the promptings of instinct, not reason. He tottered through the arcade, past the chapel and into the gardens. He made his way down to the gate leading to the Fellows' Garden where as a fellow-commoner he was entitled to walk. The gate was unlocked. He walked very slowly along the path beside the Long Pond. It was cool and shady here, and after a while he began to feel a little better. But even the slightest exertion seemed intolerably tiring. He came to a rustic bench and sat down heavily, wincing as the impact travelled up to his head.

He did not know how long he sat. No one disturbed him. The bench was secluded, surrounded by a large box-hedge on three sides. He closed his eyes and dozed uncomfortably, enclosed in a universe of pain.

The sound of voices roused him. He opened his eyes. The voices came from the other side of the pond, from the Master's Garden. He yawned and rubbed his head. He glimpsed two black-clad figures crossing a gap between two hedges. First came the portly and unmistakable shape of Dr. Carbury himself, lumbering along like a large, tired animal. After him came Tobias Soresby, tall and hunched, his limbs moving with ungainly rapidity. Their conversation continued, the words indistinguishable.

Archdale frowned. Everyone knew that Soresby was Richardson's pet. That automatically meant that Carbury disliked Soresby, and anyway Carbury was no friend to poor undergraduates, as a class. So what was Soresby doing strolling in Carbury's garden? It made no sense.

Archdale dozed again. Again, a voice jerked him awake.

"Be damned to you," Carbury said loudly, then his voice became a mumble, swiftly diminishing into silence.

Archdale opened his eyes. No one was there. The Master's Garden might have been empty. Perhaps he had dreamed it. He closed his eyes.

This time he slept more soundly and for longer. When he awoke with a start, the sun was lower in the sky, and the air cooler. He felt a hand on his shoulder.

"Harry, I hope I find you well."

Archdale turned his head and looked up. Philip Whichcote was beside the bench, smiling down at him. He looked offensively sober and healthy.

"I am in very good spirits," Archdale said sourly. "Never better."

Whichcote sat down and stretched out his legs. "I looked for you in your rooms but you were not there. Mepal said I might find you here. You look a little pale, I am afraid. I hope you have not been spending too much time poring over your books."

"Go away, Philip," Archdale said feebly. "I am not in the mood for your funning."

"You will be as fit as a fiddle in an hour or two, you may depend upon it. Well, your prowess last night was much admired by your fellow Apostles. The general vote was that rarely had a maid screamed louder."

"Where—where is she?"

"The girl? How should I know? Gone back to London, I imagine. The reason I came was to see how you did, and to invite you to dine with me and a few of the others tomorrow. I thought we might run over to Newmarket."

"No," Archdale said, surprising even himself with his vehemence. "It—it would not be convenient."

They sat in silence for a moment. Archdale privately resolved that from this moment forward, if God spared him, he would become a hard-reading man. Never had sober scholarship seemed so attractive. Never had gambling, whoring and drinking seemed so foolish, unpleasant, expensive and unhealthy.

Whichcote laughed. "I should have waited until later, my dear Harry. You must not get in such a taking. You will feel more yourself directly, and then I shall ask you again."

"And I'll give you the same answer."

"You must tell Mulgrave to mix you one of his particular tonics. They would revive a corpse. Which reminds me, is he about somewhere? There is something I wish to say to him."

"Mulgrave? But you told me the other day he wasn't to be trusted, and you'd discharged him."

"So I have. But I still need a word with him."

"Well he's not here. And nor's he likely to be."

"What do you mean?" Whichcote said sharply. "He is always about the place like a bad smell."

"He is looking after Frank."

"He's gone to Barnwell?"

Archdale shook his head and winced. "Frank's not there any more."

"What?" Whichcote gripped Archdale's shoulder. "Are you saying that Frank is cured?"

"I don't know about that." Archdale moved away from Whichcote. "He's not at Barnwell, though. He's with that man that Lady Anne sent. Holdsworth. And Mulgrave's attending them."

"But where are they? Has Holdsworth taken Frank back to London?"

"I don't know." Archdale's hangover spilled over into irritation. "And I don't much care."

In the evening Whichcote laid a coin at one end of the mantelpiece. At the other end of Mrs. Phear's mantelpiece stood a lighted candle, the only one in the room. It was still light outside, and a small creature rustled among the leaves of a pear tree espaliered against the rear wall of the garden. Whichcote laid another coin on the mantelpiece, an inch apart from the first. It had been a long day, and he felt flat and weary.

"There will be more," he said. "This is merely an earnest of what is to come."

"Have you enough for your creditors?" Mrs. Phear asked.

"There is never enough for those vultures, ma'am. But thank you."

He laid another coin on the mantelpiece, this one on top of the first, and then placed a fourth on top of the second. Slowly the columns of gold grew taller. In total, the money amounted to a down payment of ten guineas. For Mrs. Phear, he knew, such a sum could bridge the difference between genteel poverty and a genteel competence.

"We have made up some lost ground," he said. "But there is more. Can we contrive another dinner before the end of term?"

"It is always the girl that takes the time. The next committee meeting at the Magdalene Hospital is not until the end of the month. It would not be easy to arrange before then."

"It is a pity. They are ready for another one. Or most of them are. And young Chiddingley burns to be an Apostle, and for that we need a girl."

"There's one way." Mrs. Phear stared out of the window. "What if we use the same one? Only Mr. Archdale saw her."

"But I thought we decided that the less they knew the better, and if we use one of them more than once—"

"That is true as a general principle. In this case, however, there is much to recommend a relaxation of the rule. This girl is a discreet little chit, I fancy. She handled Mr. Archdale very well last night."

"What was her name again?"

"Molly Price. She's no great beauty, I know, but she looks well enough for the part."

"A flower waiting to be plucked," Whichcote said drily.

"Think of the convenience of the thing—there is always trouble and risk in recruiting a new one. Also, it takes time. But if it's Price again, I can simply tell them at the Magdalene that I have hopes of another lady who's in want of a girl to train up into service."

"Still, it increases the danger, does it not? If the Price girl talks—"

"You may leave all that to me. I will answer for her discretion. Besides, there is nothing she can say that would be believed." Mrs. Phear's voice sharpened. "Pray, sir, pass me the money. I do not like to put temptation in the way of servants."

He scraped the guineas into the palm of his left hand and brought them to her. "Very well," he said. "I will talk to the Apostles in the next day or two and give you a date."

"The sooner the better."

"That's one difficulty disposed of, ma'am. But there's another that may not prove so easy. I saw Harry Archdale this afternoon. He told me that Frank is no longer in the care of Dr. Jermyn."

"What? Is he cured?"

"He must be."

"Either that or Lady Anne wished him removed—to the care of another physician, perhaps, or even to her house in London."

"All I have been able to establish is that Frank has left Barnwell. Her ladyship's agent in this seems to be the man Holdsworth, who has been staying at Jerusalem. He has gone too. Archdale said that Mulgrave is with them."

"The college servant?"

"A gyp—his only loyalty is to himself. But he's a shrewd fellow, unfortunately, and knows what he's about."

Mrs. Phear stroked her plump little hands, one with the other, looking down at them with an expression of concern in her face, as though the hands were naked little animals in need of consolation.

"We must wait and see," she said. "Even if Mr. Frank is cured, it does not follow that what he says will be believed. A man whose wits have been disordered does not make a reliable witness. It all depends on his word, after all. And he must be sensible that you could make counter-accusations. He does not come out well from all this, however one looks at it." She smiled at Whichcote. "I cannot but think that his mother has acted foolishly in allowing him to leave Dr. Jermyn's. With a young man whose wits are so far astray, anything might happen. He might kill himself and those around him before he's done."

Whichcote sighed. He crossed the room to the window and stood by Mrs. Phear's chair. They were so close and the room was so quiet that they could hear each other's breathing. They did not look at each other. They stared out of the window and watched the sky gradually darken above the pear tree.

25

AT WHITEBEACH MILL, time slipped away like the river itself. Day followed day, each as formless as the next. The weather continued warm, often sunny, the air heavy.

After the first night, Frank Oldershaw spent much of his time asleep. So did they all. It was as if they were convalescing after a long, wasting fever and the only remedy was time and rest. The most lively creature in the household was the ginger cat, though that was not saying much.

They had arrived at the mill on the evening of Wednesday, 31 May. After the first day, Frank became quieter. Though the water was still very cold, he swam a good deal, to and fro across the mill-pond, propelling himself with long, leisurely strokes. "Quack, quack," he cried at intervals, but in other respects he showed no signs of mental disturbance while swimming. At first Holdsworth tried to dissuade him from going into the water on the grounds that there might be an accident, but he might have saved his breath. Frank ignored him. Short of restraining his charge physically, there was nothing that Holdsworth could do.

Frank refused to talk about his madness or about the ghost. He became passionately angry when Holdsworth raised the subject of Lady Anne. Apart from that, he did what he was told, more or less. He did not treat Holdsworth and Mulgrave with consideration, but he did not make unreasonable demands, either. Bearing in mind the immense difference between their stations in life, his manner might almost have been called condescending.

Mulgrave had brought a valise of Frank's belongings from his rooms at Jerusalem. There was a chess set among them, also backgammon and draughts. On most evenings, Holdsworth would propose a game to Frank. When they played chess, Frank invariably won. There was nothing wrong with his powers of reasoning. He was good at draughts, too, but less successful at backgammon, where the element of luck made him rash.

Sometimes Holdsworth read aloud. He had brought Young's *Night Thoughts* with him, and he found a battered copy of *The Pilgrim's Progress* in his bedroom, where it had been used to prop a table leg on the uneven floor. Neither book was exactly cheerful in tone, but Frank appeared to find them soothing, often dozing off while Holdsworth was reading.

Mulgrave effaced himself whenever he could. He lived, worked and slept in the kitchen. He watched everything and said as little as possible.

On the evening of Monday, 5 June, he came to Holdsworth and murmured that their supply of food was running low. He could obtain bread, beer, milk, eggs and some vegetables from the farm, but he was obliged to go farther afield for anything else.

"Go to Cambridge tomorrow after breakfast," Holdsworth told him. "I want you to take a letter to Dr. Carbury and you can buy what we need while you're there."

"It's a long walk, sir. And there's the matter of weight on the way back. Mr. Frank said he wanted wine. And we need coals for the kitchen fire."

"You must call in at the farm in the morning and see what can be done," Holdsworth said. "If necessary, the carrier can bring the heavy items and leave them with Mr. Smedley. But in all events you must come straight back, and you must keep your mouth shut, do you understand? You must not say where you are, or with whom. You may speak openly only to Dr. and Mrs. Carbury."

"Yes, sir."

Holdsworth had a sense of foreboding. It was not so much that he distrusted Mulgrave, though he did not trust him either. It was more that, by leaving the mill, if only for a few hours, Mulgrave would destroy the illusion that the three of them were isolated from the outside world and its malign influences.

He slept badly that night. The mattress was lumpy. The box-bed enclosed him like a coffin. He was too hot and then, when he had flung back the covers, he was too cold. And all the while, he drifted in and out of dreams. There was a logic to the dreams that he could not grasp, though in their subjects they appeared completely unconnected. Once he woke with a start, believing that he was back in Bankside, and Georgie had woken in the night and was crying out that the drowned lighterman from Goat Stairs had come to drag him down to the bottom of the filthy river.

Now, wide awake, Holdsworth was by the steps, peering down into the water. But it wasn't Georgie's face he saw there: it was Maria's. He saw quite clearly the bruise on her temple. The color of a damson. The size of a penny piece.

But was it Maria? Or was it Sylvia Whichcote down there?

"Wake up! Wake up!"

Holdsworth was suddenly, painfully, awake. He was fighting for air as though it were he who was drowning. He sat up sharply in bed. The gray half-light preceding dawn filled the room.

Frank was holding Holdsworth's left arm and shaking it vigorously. "For God's sake, man, what ails you?" he demanded, for all the world like a young gentleman in perfect health berating an unfortunate servant. He stepped back and glared down at Holdsworth. "You woke us all with your damned noise."

Holdsworth blinked and rubbed his eyes. Mulgrave was standing at the head of the narrow stairs looking sideways into the room. He and Frank were wearing the shirts they slept in, and nothing else.

"What the devil is it?" Frank said. "Why were you shouting?"

"Forgive me—a dream—it was nothing."

The old dream. And there was nothing he could do to stop it, and there never would be.

On Monday evening, Elinor heard a familiar, heavy tread on the stairs. Dr. Carbury came into the sitting room, wished her good evening and sat down. He took out a handkerchief and wiped his forehead.

"You are early, sir," Elinor said. "Shall I ring the bell for the tea things?"

He shook his heavy head. Supper could only just have finished in the hall, Elinor calculated, and usually her husband would have lingered over his wine in the combination room for at least another hour. He patted his pockets one by one, searching for his snuffbox.

"You know, if Miskin goes, I am minded to reserve the Rosington Fellowship for Soresby," he said abruptly, as if they had been talking about this subject for some time.

He found the box, tapped the lid, opened it and took a pinch. She waited, her stomach clenching, knowing what would follow but not when. At last he gave an enormous sneeze, spraying fragments of snuff over his lap. When he had blown his nose, he fell silent, fanning himself ineffectually with his hand and moving restlessly in his chair.

"I thought Mr. Soresby had not taken his degree yet," she said.

"He will in January. And he is very able: he will almost certainly be highly placed on the list, and the terms of the endowment permit me to hold it open for him as long as I wish. I have been turning the matter over in my mind for some time."

"Your decision will please Mr. Richardson, I am sure. Is not Mr. Soresby one of his pupils?"

"I don't care a fig whether I please Richardson or not." Carbury was now speaking in a vehement, jerky voice. "It's a matter of serving the best interests of the college and of rewarding individual merit. That's all there is to it, ma'am."

Elinor held her peace. Her husband was coming it very high all of a sudden. She knew that something must have happened to bring about this extraordinary change of heart. Soresby was in

Richardson's camp, and in the ordinary course of things Carbury could expect nothing in return for his patronage. Unless, of course, Soresby had changed his allegiance.

Dr. Carbury took another pinch of snuff, spilling much of it on his waistcoat. He sneezed again and the two of them sat in a stunned silence, Carbury with his eyes closed. Elinor stared at her husband and thought how ugly he was. She told herself sternly that she should feel grateful to him for nearly everything that made life endurable, including the roof over her head.

"Mrs. Carbury, there is something else I must say to you."

She felt a jolt of guilt. It was as if he could read her mind, her thoughts about himself, even her thoughts about Mr. Holdsworth.

"I had intended to mention this for some time but it was never the right moment." His eyes were open now, watering from the snuff, and he was staring at her. "Perhaps it is never the right moment. You know that I have been concerned about my health."

"And so have I, sir."

"Indeed. And I'm much obliged to you. As you know I have long been troubled by a distemper in the guts." He dabbed his eyes with his handkerchief. "The English malady."

"Is not the remedy at least partly in your own hands, sir? If you were to change your diet, and perhaps not linger quite so long over your wine, I am persuaded your health would soon be the better for it. During the Long Vacation, you might even consider a course of sea bathing. I understand the waters of Scarborough are notably beneficial."

He raised his hand to block the flow of words. She fell silent. She felt inexplicably unsettled, almost on the edge of panic.

"You are very good, ma'am, but these remedies will not answer. I don't know whether you were aware that Dr. Jermyn called on me last week?"

"About Frank?"

"Yes. He grew heated, and I cannot blame him for that altogether. But he's no fool—he don't bear a grudge, or not for long. While he was here, I asked if I might consult him about my own case."

"You, sir? But surely you have no need for—for a man like him?"

"You mean for the services of one who makes his living from patients with maniacal disorders?" Carbury smiled awkwardly, almost shyly, at her. "No, I have not come to that. But Dr. Jermyn is of some eminence in other areas of his profession. I believe he is well qualified to treat any patient he chooses."

"Then why did you consult him, sir?"

"Because I desired a second opinion. Dr. Milton has already examined me and diagnosed my case with I believe tolerable accuracy. But old Milton is set in his ways, and I fear has not kept up with recent discoveries."

"But you said nothing of this to me."

"I did not wish to alarm you unnecessarily. But now Dr. Jermyn has confirmed the original diagnosis, the time has come."

She stood up and went to stand beside his chair. "Then what is it, sir?"

"I regret to say that I have a growth." He patted his abdomen with both hands. "Here."

"Surely a surgeon may cut it out?"

He shook his head. "It is impossible to remove it because of its position. I understand that the growth is in an advanced stage and that Dr. Jermyn thinks there may be similar malignancies in other places."

"Another opinion might say very differently, sir," Elinor said wildly. "You are still a comparatively young man. It—"

"No, no, my dear." Dr. Carbury rarely used even so mild an endearment as that: it seemed all of a piece with the dreadful news he brought. "I'm afraid there can be no doubt about it. Dr. Jermyn asked to examine my stools, and I took him out to the privy where I had reserved a sample. He tells me the signs cannot be interpreted in any other way."

Tears welled up in her eyes. She had seen the two men on their way to the outhouse from the window of this room. She tried to speak, and the words came out in a jumble. She was obliged to try again. "How long do they say you have?"

"Not long. Neither of them felt able to be precise. It may be a few weeks or it may be a few months." He looked up at her and smiled with unmistakable warmth. "You must not be so distressed, my dear. I am living under a death sentence and I do not know when the sentence will be carried out. But is that so very different from the generality of mankind? We all know we must die, but none of us knows the hour of his death." The smile broadened. "Unless he is to be hanged, of course, but I trust I may escape that fate."

"What can I do? How can I best help you?"

"There is nothing, thank you. Or not at present. But you must naturally be anxious about your own future. You are still a young woman. I will provide for you the best I can, but I am not a rich man. When I go, the house and income must go with me. But I shall do what I can."

With a series of grunts, he edged forward on the seat, gripped the arms of the chair and stood up. "I find I am a little fatigued. I wish you goodnight, madam."

He shuffled out of the room and closed the door behind him. Elinor listened to his footsteps on the landing as he made his way slowly and painfully to his own room. She knew now that the signs had been there for weeks, if not months. Dr. Carbury had not suddenly become a sick man. He had been dying in front of her eyes. She simply hadn't noticed.

She sat down again in her chair by the window and the tears rolled down her cheeks. She wept for her husband, and because she would be sad to lose him, even though she had never loved him. She wept because of what life would hold for her as a widow. She wept because she was desperately afraid she would be poor again.

And finally, she wept because she felt guilty: because part of her was glad that she would soon be a widow.

26

WHY WERE YOU SCREAMING?" Frank Oldershaw asked.
Holdsworth looked up from his book. "What?"

"Why were you screaming? When you woke us all at dawn."

"I told you, sir—a foolish dream. I cannot now remember it."

Frank leaned forward on his chair. "You must remember something. One always does remember something."

They were sitting in the garden on armchairs they had dragged out from the parlor. The heavy, overhanging thatch soaked up the air inside the house. The cottage had grown stiflingly hot.

The ginger cat strolled through the long grass and weeds towards Frank. It leaned against him and purred, its tail waving like a flag above its body.

"Quack," Frank said amiably. "Quack." He looked up and caught Holdsworth staring at him. "Quack," he said for the third time. "Now I wish you'd tell me what you were dreaming of."

"I cannot tell you what I do not know."

"Quack," Frank said. "It's so damned hot. I'm going on the water." He pointed towards a willow tree on the river just below the millpond. "There's a punt down there. We'll go out in that. And you can come too and make sure I come to no harm."

Without waiting for a reply, he stood up and walked down the garden towards the water. The cat glanced at Holdsworth and then stalked away. Holdsworth swore under his breath. Frank was no longer as docile as he had been when they first came here. Then, the regimen at Barnwell had reduced him to a cross between a child and a vegetable. Now he was more assertive, and appeared more capable of sustaining a rational conversation. Sometimes he would lapse and quack and talk nonsense; or he would allow a strange grief to master him; or converse with the cat as though it were his equal. But these episodes happened less frequently.

Now, Holdsworth thought, as he followed Frank through the long grass, there were glimpses of the true nature of the young man. He was physically vigorous. By nature and by upbringing, he was accustomed to lead and to believe that God had ordained him to do so. After all, Frank Oldershaw was a gentleman, and John Holdsworth was not. As far as Frank was concerned at least, it was in the natural order of things that a man like Frank Oldershaw should give the orders.

When Holdsworth reached the willow tree, he found Frank studying the punt. It was much heavier and more crudely built than the ones that Holdsworth had glimpsed on the river in Cambridge. It was no more than a heavy rectangular box constructed of rough planking. To Holdsworth's eyes, it looked as watertight as a colander.

"We shall be afloat in a moment," Frank said. "You take this side and I'll take this. We'll turn it on its side first and let the water run out. Then we'll slide it into the water."

"But there's no pole."

"That's what these branches are for." Frank nodded at two mud-streaked sticks leaning against the trunk of the tree. "Now lend me a hand, will you?"

Reluctantly, Holdsworth obeyed. They pulled the punt on to its side, emptied out most of the water and lowered it again. They maneuvered it slowly down the muddy bank. The punt scraped down the bank and slid into the river, where it rocked alarmingly. The cat watched from a safe distance.

"There's water coming in," Holdsworth said. "It's leaking. It is not safe to go on it."

"Nonsense. These old punts always leak. It's nothing to be frightened of. You may get your feet a little wet but these old tubs never sink. We'll take off our shoes and stockings and be none the worse for it."

For a moment, Holdsworth was tempted to assert his authority and insist that they stay on dry land. He held back, however, not least because he was not perfectly convinced he could make Frank Oldershaw obey him. There were other reasons. Headstrong though he was, Frank was behaving in a manner that was entirely rational, or at least entirely to be expected from one of his rank and age. In other words, he was growing better, and that surely should be encouraged. Also, Holdsworth himself was shamefully scared of going on the water. Was it possible to conquer somebody else's demons before you had conquered your own?

Frank tossed the branches aboard and scrambled after them. He held the punt to the bank by holding one of the roots of the willow. "In you come, man," he said. "Sit at that end."

Since the drownings, Holdsworth had avoided boats of all descriptions, even those that made such easy work of crossing the Thames. He climbed aboard and the punt rocked under his weight. His stomach lurched with it. Frank seized one of the branches and pushed off with a jerk. The boat inched out into the stream. In a moment the bank was out of reach.

"Why, you're as white as a ghost," Frank observed. He pointed at the shore with his makeshift pole. "Look, there's Puss watching us. Quack."

The ginger cat looked gravely at them.

"Sit quiet and you will soon be yourself again," Frank advised. "You seemed such a solid fellow I thought nothing in the world could disturb you."

Holdsworth gripped the side of the boat, squeezing the rough wood until he felt it biting into his skin. A pain tore into his chest. He forced himself to breathe. "It's not to be wondered at, sir. I cannot swim."

"That's soon remedied. Nothing to it. I'll teach you."

Frank threw down his pole and stood up. The punt swayed and rocked.

"Pray sit down, Mr. Oldershaw—have a care—the motion will overset us."

The punt tilted violently. Frank Oldershaw laughed. And as he was laughing, there was a blur of movement, a great splash and a shower of spray. A wave flooded over the side, soaking Holdsworth's breeches. Holdsworth shouted, a wordless sound, both a protest and a plea. And also a cry of fear.

Frank was now floating in the water, his white and spectral arms waving to and fro beneath the surface. "It's so refreshing. You see how simple it is. Our bodies are like pigs' bladders full of air, so we float." He swam to the side of the punt and gripped the edge with both hands. "If you jump over the side of the punt and hold on to the edge like this, you will find you are perfectly safe. In a moment or two you will grow used to the sensation of your body moving in the water. I assure you, it is delightful, if a little chilly at first. The body becomes so light. I think that angels must move through the air like this."

Maria, Holdsworth thought. Georgie. Drowned at Goat Stairs. He looked at Frank Oldershaw's smiling face and saw theirs behind his: and their faces were pale, wet and waxy with death.

"Take me back," he whispered. "Pray, sir, pray take me back."

Frank shook the side of the punt, making it rock. "On two conditions."

"What?"

"First, that you allow me to teach you to swim while we are at the mill. Not now, if you want, but later when you have grown more used to the idea, and nearer the bank, where you will be able to feel the bottom under your feet."

"Take me back."

"Promise me."

"No."

"And the second condition is this: that you tell me why you woke us this morning."

"I do not know." The punt rocked again. "Oh for God's sake, Mr. Oldershaw—"

"Of course you know. One always remembers one's bad dreams."

Oh yes, Holdsworth thought, the boy is right.

Frank laughed at him, though not unkindly. "Come, sir, I shall take your silence for assent. You shall tell me later. See—we are nearly back on *terra firma*."

Holdsworth turned his head. For the last few minutes, his misery and his fears had trapped him in a small bubble consisting of the punt, Frank and the stretch of water immediately surrounding it. It was only now he realized that all this time the current of the river had been moving them imperceptibly downstream. The river had entered a shallow bend, and the punt was now no more than a couple of yards from the bank.

Frank suddenly stood up. The water was little higher than his waist. He pushed the punt to the bank. Holdsworth groped blindly over the side for anything to hold on to. He seized a tussock of grass and it came away in his hands. The side of the punt scraped against the sloping bottom. He launched himself over the side, and landed heavily on solid land. On the grass around him were thistles and cowpats. A group of cows, sheltering under the branches of an oak tree in the corner of the field, turned their heads one by one to look at him. He lay there, trembling, wet and panting, and pressed his cheek against the hard, dry ground.

Frank scrambled out of the water and sat down. He was streaked with mud. He pushed back the wet hair from his face and turned towards Holdsworth. "I ask your pardon, sir," he said. "I should not have teased you like that. It was very disagreeable of me."

Holdsworth sat up and tried to control his rapid breathing with an effort of will. In the circumstances the apology was both unexpected and generous. It was also in its way a perfectly sane gesture. Not for the first time, Holdsworth wondered about the precise nature of Frank Oldershaw's madness.

"You were not to know," he said quietly.

"What was I not to know?"

Holdsworth shrugged. "That I—that I have such a deep-rooted aversion to water."

"There is more to it than that, I fancy."

Neither of them spoke for a moment. Holdsworth thought how very strange it was that he should be sitting with the grandson of an earl in a cow pasture beside a muddy river. His own life seemed no longer to make any sense whatsoever. It was as if the universe itself, with all its laws and regulatory mechanisms, had been struck with a fit of madness.

"You cannot swim," Frank said softly. "But that in itself is not a reason to fear water. So there must be a particular cause."

Holdsworth thought that the madness of the world had now re-arranged itself and become the new mode of being rational. It seemed quite as a matter of course that he should be talking of his night terrors and his sorrows to a youthful madman he had been hired to help. After all, who better than the sorrowful to help those who are sad? Who better than a lunatic to understand the ravings of a madman?

"I lived by the Thames for many years and it did not trouble me at all," he said. "I often went on the water. But then my little son drowned in the river, and a little later so did my wife. So that is why I fear the water. That is why I have bad dreams."

"I am not the only one who sees ghosts."

Holdsworth turned his head and looked directly at Frank. "I have accepted your second condition. And I shall accept your first as well. Will you teach me to swim?"

27

"YOU WILL DINE WITH US, I hope?" said Mr. Richardson. "Why, we have not seen you in college for an age."

Whichcote bowed and said that nothing would give him greater pleasure. The two men had encountered each other in Chapel Court. Whichcote had left Augustus to ferret out what he could about Frank's whereabouts, and he himself could do nothing on the matter until he knew more. But there was no telling what might be said in the combination room or at high table, what scraps of information might emerge. Carbury must know where Frank was, and almost certainly Richardson too; and perhaps others knew or guessed. Besides, Whichcote was hungry, and his own cook, as the day of her departure drew nearer, was inclined to grow more and more lax about her duties.

Dinner would not be for another twenty minutes. Richardson proposed a stroll to work up an appetite. The two men walked through the chapel arcade into the college gardens, and passed under the shade of the oriental plane. Whichcote smiled to show he was perfectly at ease at the spot near the Long Pond, so close to where his wife's body had been found, and where her ghost had allegedly appeared. But he thought it shockingly ill bred that Mr. Richardson should have suggested a walk here. By careful study, Richardson had acquired the manners of a gentleman but in Whichcote's opinion the imitation was only skin-deep.

They passed through the gate of the Fellows' Garden and walked by the pond.

"I was here with Harry Archdale the other day," Whichcote observed. "Have you seen him recently? I hope he is well."

"He was in rather delicate health after the last meeting of your club," Richardson said. "But I am happy to report he is entirely recovered. He has in fact been applying himself to his books, and with unusual assiduity. Sir Charles wishes him to enter for the Vauden Medal this year, and he is making a very creditable stab at it. Mr. Soresby—one of our most promising young men—has been reading with him."

"And poor Frank Oldershaw? Is there news from that quarter?"

"Alas, none that I know of."

"Harry tells me he is no longer with Dr. Jermyn."

"Yes, I heard that too."

"I wonder where they took him."

"It is very curious," Richardson said. "I have no idea."

When the dinner bell began to toll, Richardson and Whichcote made their way back to Chapel Court and entered the combination room, where ten or twelve of the fellows were already gathered. As the bell ceased, the door opened and the Master himself came in. Whichcote was struck by his haggard face. Carbury was a big, bulky man, but his weight seemed to have been redistributed, as if the internal framework sustaining it had lost its rigidity. He seemed in good spirits, however, and greeted the company with unusual amiability.

They went through into the hall, where the undergraduates were already gathered, waiting for the Master and fellows to take their places. When Carbury and the rest of them on the dais were standing by their chairs, a hush fell over the hall. Carbury looked towards the scholar at his lectern, a signal that he should say grace.

The silence had fallen very suddenly, and it was not quite complete. A young man at the bottom of the hall continued talking, addressing one of the buttery servants in a high, excited voice: "And a half-gallon jug of the audit ale, do you hear, and—"

Whichcote, who was almost opposite Carbury, happened to look at the Master's face. He had turned his head towards the disturbance, and he was smiling.

The scholar read grace, and the company sat down.

"Mr. Soresby is in cheerful spirits," Mr. Dow said.

"Audit ale, too," Mr. Crowley replied. "He must be in funds."

"Why, gentlemen, I think I can solve the conundrum," Carbury interrupted. "Mr. Soresby has received some welcome tidings."

The atmosphere changed. Whichcote sensed it, without at this point understanding why.

Glass in hand, the Master leaned across the table towards the two younger fellows. "You are aware, of course, that Mr. Miskin is resigning the Rosington Fellowship at Christmas? Well, I have decided to reserve it for Mr. Soresby, on the condition that his performance in the examinations justifies my expectations. I communicated my decision to him today, and I suspect this may have something to do with his ordering audit ale."

Carbury had spoken loudly enough for his words to be heard by everyone at the high table. A ripple of surprise ran round the company.

Richardson laid down his knife. "Surely that is unorthodox, Master? As you say, Mr. Soresby has not yet taken his degree."

"I am aware of that, sir, perfectly aware. If you take the trouble to consult the terms under which the fellowship was established, you will discover that not only is it in the Master's gift, but also that the Master has the power to reserve it *sine die*, should he so wish."

"I have no doubt you are right." Richardson wiped his mouth with his napkin. "And it is most gratifying to have one of my own pupils singled out for such a mark of approbation. Still, you will allow that it is unusual to appoint an undergraduate, even so promising a one as Mr. Soresby."

"Why, as to that, by the time Mr. Miskin leaves us Mr. Soresby will be on the very threshold of taking his degree. And I have no doubt whatsoever that he will be highly placed on the list." Carbury smiled, and it was not a pleasant sight. "I am sure you will agree with me, sir, that in these matters the merit of a candidate should be the only consideration. Many great scholars in this University have come from circumstances as humble as Mr. Soresby's. I do not doubt that with proper encouragement he will go far, and the college will greatly benefit from his presence."

Carbury emptied his glass as if toasting the propriety of his sentiments. Richardson murmured that what the Master had said was very true, very true. The conversation became general round the table. Richardson said little, however, and he picked at his food.

After dinner was over, Whichcote did not linger in the combination room. He found Augustus waiting for him in the arcade beside the chapel. They left college without speaking, the footboy several paces behind his master. Outside Christ's College, however, Whichcote beckoned to the boy to come up to him.

"Well?"

"I listened at the stables, sir. Ben's to collect the pony phaeton at ten o'clock in the forenoon tomorrow."

"Where are they going?"

"I don't know, your honor. They didn't say. But Mr. Mulgrave walked over today from somewhere. He's gone now but they say he called at the Master's Lodge."

Whichcote rubbed his cheek. Mulgrave was no great walker with that limp of his. The pony phaeton must be for Mrs. Carbury, probably with a man to drive her. So light an equipage wouldn't bear the Master's weight. No one would hire a pony phaeton for a long journey, either.

He stared down at the thin, grubby face of the footboy. "Well, you must go to the stable tomorrow, and wait till they leave, and then you must follow them."

"But they will go faster than—"

"Then you will have to run," Whichcote said. "After all, it is only a pony phaeton. It won't proceed much above a footpace. I want to know who's in it, where they go, and who they see. But you must not show yourself, boy, or I'll have you whipped until you're raw."

They must have walked for ten or twelve miles in that long mid-summer afternoon. They followed country roads that shimmered with dust and farm droves that were muddy even in this dry, warm weather. They marched along the high green banks of drainage cuts and dikes, as ruler-straight as their Dutch engineers had been able to make them. They splashed across fens where tall reeds waved above dark water stinking of rotting vegetation, disturbing countless waterfowl.

"If only I had a gun," Frank said not once but many times. "What sport we should have."

They met few people, and those they did were usually solitary—slouching men with muddy complexions who seemed as much a natural feature of this watery landscape as the reeds and the brackish water.

"Ha!" said Frank after one such encounter. "I wager they take us for father and son."

Holdsworth did not reply. Georgie, he thought, my darling son.

Despite the heat, they walked rapidly. They did not talk much. The flatness of the country and the clarity of the air conspired to make Holdsworth feel he was a mere speck, lost in the immensity of the heavens. Frank, on the other hand, appeared positively to relish it. At one point, standing on top of an embankment running along a drainage cut, he stood for a moment, raised his arms and slowly spun around. Then he glanced at Holdsworth, and smiled like a happy child. Without a word, he started walking again, at the same rapid pace as before.

It was after seven o'clock by the time they came in sight of White-beach again. As they passed Mr. Smedley's farm, the dogs began to bark, rattling their chains and rushing to the yard gate, where they stared with wild yellow eyes at the strangers.

Mulgrave, alerted by the barking, came to meet them in the yard of the mill. Frank greeted him carelessly and went into the cottage, calling over his shoulder that he wanted a bowl of hot water, beer, bread and cheese.

Holdsworth lingered. "Well? Were you able to get what was needed?"

"Yes, sir. Warm work, walking into town, I can tell you. But I got a lift back most of the way on a farm cart."

"Did you call at Jerusalem?"

"Yes, sir. Mrs. Carbury gave me a letter for you."

He took it from his pocket and handed it to Holdsworth.

"Did you see anyone else you know?"

"Only college servants, sir. Mr. Mepal at the lodge and the like."

"You did not tell them where we are, I hope?"

Mulgrave drew himself up, and went through the motions of looking affronted. "Of course not, sir."

Holdsworth dismissed the servant and sat down on the bench near the horse trough. His tiredness forgotten, he turned the letter over in his hands. There was a curious and almost sensual pleasure in the texture of the paper and the sight of his own name in that unfamiliar handwriting. He broke the seal and tore the letter open.

Jerusalem College, 6th June.
Dear Sir, Her Ladyship commands me to call on you to see how Mr.
Oldershaw does in his new quarters. I have arranged to drive over
tomorrow, and I hope you will both find it convenient to receive
me at about two o'clock. Believe me, yours faithfully, E. Carbury

Mrs. Carbury's handwriting was like her face, Holdsworth thought, too decided and too heavily marked to be called beautiful in any formal or customary sense of the word, but undeniably striking. He read the letter again, though there was no need to do so, as if to make sure there was not some last drop of meaning to be squeezed out of those few words.

The ginger cat walked lightly across the yard and made a figure of eight round Holdworth's ankles. He shivered at the touch of the animal's body, at the casual intimacy of it. He thought of Elinor Carbury's hand on the gate by the bridge.

Touch me, he thought. Touch me.

❧ 28 ❧

ELINOR HEARD THE SHUFFLE of Dr. Carbury's slippered
feet outside the door. A moment later her husband, still in
cap and dressing gown, came slowly into the sitting room, leaning
on a stick. She knew from one look at his face that he had not
passed a comfortable night. She went to him at once and guided
him to a chair. Since he had given her the news about his health,
her emotions had been in a jumble. She scarcely knew what she
should or could feel. She did not like being married to him but it
was preferable to not being married at all, and without him she
would have nothing to fall back on except the uncertain generosity
of Lady Anne. Strangest of all, she felt pity for him and even a certain respect. Here was a man who knew he was in the very antechamber of death. His plight seemed more a source of irritation to
him than terror.

As if purposely to destroy any sympathy he might have occa-
sioned, the Doctor broke wind lingeringly and with the unselfcon-
sciousness of a child alone in its own bed. "You go to the mill this
morning, I collect? I shall depend on you to examine Mr. Holdsworth very carefully. I do not know whether you will see Mr. Oldershaw himself—he may require restraint and be under lock and
key; you must allow Mr. Holdsworth to be your guide." He stared at
her with his small dark eyes, partly concealed by the folds of skin.
"I judge him to be reliable on the whole. Like ourselves, he has a

pressing reason to want Mr. Frank restored to health. What time does he expect you?"

"Two o'clock."

"Go earlier. One o'clock, perhaps, or even sooner. Take them by surprise, and you will see them as they really are. Her ladyship wants accurate intelligence above everything, and that is the way to obtain it."

"Very well. If you wish it, sir."

"And I should like us to give her ladyship what she desires," he said slowly. "I have a particular favor to ask her."

He paused, allowing Elinor time to conclude that the favor no doubt concerned herself, and what would become of her when she was a widow. Then she was distracted by the realization that her husband was trembling. She started up in her chair. His lips were quivering, and his great barrel of a chest shook slightly as though a small, heavy object were bouncing about inside. She opened her mouth to ask what was wrong, and in that instance became aware that there was no need: Dr. Carbury was laughing.

"I wish you had seen him, my dear Mrs. Carbury—Mr. Richardson, that is—it was most diverting. He did not know what to do or say."

"About what, sir?"

"About the Rosington Fellowship, of course. I told him when we were at the dinner, in front of everyone. The poor man almost fell off his chair." Carbury folded his hands over his great stomach. "He desires above all things to be Master of this college. If her ladyship will use her influence against him, it would be a great thing. And Soresby too may have his uses, for if he holds the fellowship, he will have a vote in the election." He winced as a spasm of pain struck him. Slowly it passed. Then he smiled at her so broadly that his eyes entirely disappeared in the surrounding folds of skin. "My dear Mrs. Carbury," he repeated. "You should have seen his face. You really should."

Elinor smiled and nodded, as a good wife should when her husband invites her to share his enjoyment. Her dying husband cared more about the fate of his enemy than about the future of his wife. In the antechamber of death, hate was more powerful than love.

The problem with the pony phaeton was that it had a single bench seat that Elinor was obliged to share with Ben. The servant was a large, perspiring man whose thighs had a way of spreading along the seat. It was hard to avoid all contact with him, and it was impossible not to think of his white thighs pumping up and down in the washhouse. The poor pony labored as it drew the phaeton up the gradient of the Huntingdon Road. The vehicle was a small four-wheeler, lightly constructed and with cane sides. Elinor would have been perfectly competent to drive it herself, and indeed it had been designed for ladies' use. But Dr. Carbury would not permit her to drive alone on the public roads.

Soon after leaving Cambridge, they left the high road and plunged into a network of lanes confined between high embankments and hedges. Streamers of white dust billowed behind them, marking their progress. The surface under the wheels became gradually rougher and the pony stumbled over ruts and potholes.

They rounded a bend, and about quarter of a mile away a handful of roofs came into view. Ben said that this was Whitebeach, and that the mill lay on the other side. Dogs barked in a ragged chorus as they drew closer. It was a hamlet, so small and insignificant it hardly deserved a name of its own. Two or three cottages huddled about a dilapidated alehouse. Beyond them was the farm, a more substantial house with a yard and barns, and the home of most of the dogs. Ben sat up a little straighter and gave the pony a flick with his whip. Distracted, it stumbled again, and the phaeton lurched towards the hedge on Elinor's side. The pony slowed. It was hobbling.

Ben swore under his breath. "Beg pardon, ma'am, the brute's lost a shoe."

"It will do us no harm to walk the last little way. We shall throw ourselves on Mr. Smedley's mercy."

He climbed down and helped his mistress descend from the seat. She walked as fast as she could, careless of the mud on her shoes and the dust on the hem of her skirt. Ben followed, leading the pony and the phaeton. The farm was at the other end of the village. Elinor heard the chink of hammering, metal on metal. Just before the farm was a small forge, and smoke was coming from its chimney. There might be no need to trouble Mr. Smedley.

She sent Ben into the smithy while she waited in the lane with the pony. In a moment he reappeared with the blacksmith himself, a squat, hunched fellow with narrow shoulders and huge forearms like a badger's.

"He can do it, ma'am," Ben said.

"How long will it take?" Elinor said, addressing the smith directly.

The man shuffled his feet and muttered something about maybe an hour, he couldn't rightly say.

"How far is Whitebeach Mill?"

He pointed with a blackened forefinger at the mouth of the track beyond the farm and on the other side of the road. He glanced back at her, running his eyes over her, assessing her condition as he might a horse's. "Five or ten minutes, maybe."

She came to a decision. "I shall go on," she told Ben. "When the pony is ready, come down to the mill."

"But, ma'am, shouldn't I go with you?"

"No," Elinor said. "I wish you to wait for the pony."

She set off at once, not allowing her resolution to wane, knowing that Ben would be looking after her, with that worried expression on his face. He had wit enough to know that his master would have preferred him to accompany his mistress.

In the track to the mill, the air smelled strongly of garlic because ransoms grew thickly in both verges. She walked more slowly now she was out of sight of Ben and the blacksmith. She was not carrying a watch, but she knew from the position of the sun that it could not be long after midday. It did not signify. If no one was in the way at the mill, which seemed unlikely, she would find somewhere to wait in the shade. To be by herself in public, even in this remote place, was a form of freedom. All her troubles were behind her in Cambridge—this business with Sylvia, her husband's illness and threat of a return to friendless poverty. Here she felt almost drunk with liberty, with the sense that she might do anything and there would be no one to stop her, no one even to witness it. She had not felt so happy for months. Not since Sylvia died.

Soon she would see Mr. Holdsworth. Frank, too, of course, but he was just a boy. How odd that she had only known the man for a fortnight; it seemed much longer.

The track passed through a little copse of limes and chestnuts, their leaves blindingly fresh with the green of early summer, and rounded a bend. Suddenly she was at her destination. In front of her was a gate, beyond which was the mill and its cottage. Smoke rose from a single chimney. In the shadow of the horse trough lay a ginger cat. It was watching her.

She opened the gate and crossed the cobbles. The enclosed yard was very warm. A path led her past the end of the cottage to an overgrown garden. The principal door of the house was on this side, and the windows into the downstairs rooms. She peered inside.

No one was about. There were signs of occupation, though—candlesticks, a pewter tankard and a book on the table; a coat flung carelessly over the back of a chair.

The door was ajar. She pushed it fully open and called a greeting, first softly and then more loudly. There was no response. After a moment's hesitation she went into the cottage, thinking that perhaps she would find Mulgrave in the kitchen, which she assumed must be the room at the side with the smoking chimney. But no one was there. She felt unpleasantly like a spy.

For the first time she also felt a hint of unease. Here she was, an unchaperoned woman in an empty house in the middle of the country. True, her servant knew where she was, but he was hundreds of yards away and out of earshot. Anything might happen to her and no one would be any the wiser.

She went back into what seemed to be the room they used as a parlor and for a moment even wondered whether she should arm herself with one of the candlesticks. She picked up the book that lay beside it instead—a copy of Young's *Night Thoughts*. She took it outside, intending to turn over the leaves while she waited.

The sunlight made her blink, for her eyes had already adjusted to the relative gloom of the cottage. The garden stretched down to the water; there was long, lank grass, tall weeds, foxgloves and, near the bottom, a ragged huddle of unpruned fruit trees and then a willow beyond. Something was moving among the branches of the trees, for there were flashes of white among the green. Perhaps Mulgrave had washed the shirts and hung them out to dry on the branches.

Then, as her eyes grew used to the light, there was a strange intermediate moment when she saw quite clearly what was only partly concealed by the branches on either side. The whiteness was not the whiteness of a shirt. It was skin, and the skin belonged to a tall, naked man.

Someone was speaking. The man half turned towards the sound, raising his arm and revealing more of his long, lean body. Drops of water flew away from him, scattering diamonds in the sunlight.

Elinor drew back into the shadows of the house. Her brain at last contrived to marshal the jumbled perceptions of the last few seconds and come to a conclusion.

John Holdsworth was in the garden. He was soaking wet and stark-naked.

29

Y OU SEE?" Frank said behind him. "You did not sink."
Holdsworth turned. He was still trembling, and the
drops of water flew from his body, glittering in the sunlight. "Only
because your arm supported me."

"Not all the time." Frank dragged himself from the water and
stood up, waving his arms to dry them. "You floated. More than that,
you kicked your legs—"

"I did not mean to. It was the act of a desperate man, and I was
quite unconscious of doing it."

"That don't signify. You kicked your legs and moved in, or rather
on, the water. We call it swimming, Mr. Holdsworth. That is the
technical word for it."

Laughing, Holdsworth unhooked his breeches from the branch
of the pear tree beside him and pulled them on. "We had better
prepare ourselves, Mr. Oldershaw. It must be after noon."

Frank's face lost its cheerfulness. "I wish Mrs. Carbury weren't
coming."

"There's no help for it." Holdsworth dropped his shirt over his
head, and it fluttered around him, the cotton muffling his voice.
"Her ladyship wishes to know how you do—that's natural enough
in all conscience."

"What will you say?"

"It is more a question—" Holdsworth broke off. As his head emerged from the shirt, he happened to be facing the open door of the cottage. He was almost sure that something was moving among the shadows inside. Hurriedly he turned round, now facing the water again. "Damnation, I think she may be here already," he said in a low, urgent voice. He hurriedly tucked in his shirt. "Where the devil's Mulgrave? Why hasn't he warned us?"

When they were decent, if not respectable, in shirts and breeches, the two men walked barefoot up to the cottage, with Frank lagging behind. As they approached the doorway, Mrs. Carbury rose from the chair by the table, with a book in her hand.

"A thousand apologies, ma'am," Holdsworth said. "Have you waited long?"

"I was before my time," Mrs. Carbury replied, her eyes on Frank, who was standing to one side and looking at the ground. "The wretched pony cast a shoe, so I left him with Ben at the smithy and came the rest of the way on foot."

"You must be fatigued, ma'am."

"Oh no—I wanted exercise."

There were hurried footsteps on the path from the mill. Mulgrave appeared, straightening his necktie and smelling strongly of tobacco. Leaving him with Mrs. Carbury, Holdsworth and Frank went up to their rooms. When they returned, suitably dressed for a lady's society, they found Mulgrave serving tea. Frank went to stand by the window, for all the world like a sulky schoolboy obliged to be civil to the grown-ups but burning to play outside. Elinor's color was a little higher than usual, Holdsworth noticed, which suited her to perfection. He could not understand how he had ever thought that her appearance was merely striking. Even a fool could see she was beautiful.

"Well, Mr. Holdsworth, how do you and Mr. Oldershaw like Whitebeach? Do you find it agreeable?"

"It serves its purpose admirably, thank you."

She gave a little cough, as if clearing an obstruction from her throat, and took a sip of tea. "Mr. Frank," she said. "I should like to take a turn in the garden. Would you be so good as to escort me?"

Frank gave an awkward bow and allowed himself to be led out-side. Holdsworth sat down at the table and watched them walking down the path towards the water, with Elinor's hand resting lightly on Frank's arm. Her face was turned up to his, and she was speak-ing; but Frank was staring at the ground.

Holdsworth admired the elegant shape of Mrs. Carbury's body as it swayed from side to side. A woman in motion was a lovely thing. During this visit he would have to speak privately with her. It would not be an easy conversation. Whatever they talked about, or failed to talk about, he would always be wondering whether she had seen him naked in the garden.

The question on Elinor's mind as she talked to Frank Oldershaw in the garden was one that she could hardly raise with him, or indeed with anyone else. Had Mr. Holdsworth realized that she had seen him as naked as Eve saw Adam before the Fall?

Even the desire to ask was mortifying. As it happened, she had never seen a fully naked man, apart from statues and in paintings, which did not count. It was true that members of the lower orders had offered her the occasional glimpse of those parts of their anat-omies that decency usually concealed. But when the disordered clothing of a drunkard or a beggar revealed something of this na-ture, it was both easy and desirable to avert one's eyes. The trouble was, she had seen Mr. Holdsworth naked in his entirety. She had seen all of him, white and hairy, in the sunshine beside the fruit trees, and part of her had not wanted to look away. Indeed, she had found the spectacle curiously fascinating.

Mr. Holdsworth had seemed perfectly happy with his naked-ness, too. Even Dr. Carbury, her own husband, had never revealed himself for what he truly was beneath his clothes. At the begin-ning of their marriage, on those very rare occasions when he had come to her in the night-time, it had been under cover of dark-ness; and, presumably to make absolutely sure that she saw noth-ing untoward, he had not removed his nightgown either. For her part, she had been glad of it: she had no desire to see her husband naked, any more than she wished him to see her in the same state.

All these considerations filled the back of her mind, heavy and stifling, like the atmosphere on the night of the great rainstorm. She tried to ignore their tiresome presence, reminding herself that she was here for a purpose.

This was the first time she had seen Frank Oldershaw since he had been removed to Dr. Jermyn's house. She was surprised by how normal he seemed. She had expected to see him unshaven, with hair unkempt, in his shirtsleeves, and perhaps with his limbs confined to a straitjacket. Instead, she walked up and down the little garden with what seemed to all outward appearances a perfectly respectable and healthy young man. Frank's hair, still damp from the river, had been neatly arranged. He was plainly dressed in a dark coat and his manner, though subdued and uncommunicative, had nothing out of the ordinary about it. When she asked him how he did, he turned his head away and muttered that he did very well.

"And do you prefer your present situation to Dr. Jermyn's?"

"Yes," he mumbled.

"And do you feel your health improves, sir?"

"Yes."

"Her ladyship will rejoice to hear it. She is most anxious about you, of course, and she will want to know everything I can tell her. But she would be so glad to have a word from you directly. Is there a message I may give her from you? Or even a letter?"

He shook his head violently. He was a very good-looking young man and if anything his recent experiences had improved his appearance, for in the last few weeks he had eaten and drunk far less than usual, and exercised more. But now he looked like a child in a fit of the sulks.

"Her ladyship lives only for you," Elinor said in a low voice. "She will be so happy to see you at her side once more. May I not at least say that you hope soon to be restored to her?"

Frank stopped walking and turned to face her. He swallowed, opened his mouth and moistened his lips. She waited patiently for him to speak.

"Quack, quack, quack," he said. "Quack."

Suddenly he was running down the garden. Still quacking, he waved his arms in a parody of flapping wings. He sprinted through the fruit trees and jumped into the water.

Holdsworth ran down the garden and stood on the bank. Elinor felt the air move against her cheek as he passed her. Mulgrave followed more slowly.

Have I driven the poor boy to take his own life?

Holdsworth called out something to Frank. She could not make out the words. But he sounded irritated as much as anxious.

The boy swam calmly in a wide circle, and then came to the bank, pulled himself out and allowed himself to be led up to the cottage. His sodden clothes clung to his body. He had lost one shoe in the water, and Mulgrave carried the other. Frank looked gawky and bedraggled, like an ill-made scarecrow caught in a rainstorm; he was no longer handsome. He did not look at Elinor as he passed her.

She walked up and down, feeling foolish, relieved and useless. At length, Holdsworth came out to her. She turned eagerly to him. "How is Frank?"

"You look more distressed than he does, madam." Holdsworth was close to her now, and she would have liked to lean against him, as one leans against a tree. "You must sit down and recover. Would you like more tea, or perhaps brandy?"

She shook her head. "I will do very well as I am, thank you, sir. Are you sure he is unharmed?"

"He is none the worse for making himself wet again. I am very vexed with him for frightening you, though. Mulgrave is upstairs with him, helping him change into dry clothes. I hope he will apologize to you in person before you leave. But in the meantime I do so on his behalf and my own."

"There is no need," she said. "He took me quite unawares. He seemed almost his old self at first, though subdued."

"What were you talking about when he lost control of himself?"

"I mentioned his mother, and how much her ladyship wished to see him. That was when he made that foolish noise and ran off. It's as if he's afraid of her."

"We cannot hope to have him cured in just a few days, madam. I wish we could. What will you tell Lady Anne?"

"I hardly know yet."

She felt suddenly very weary and allowed Holdsworth to escort her back to the cottage. She stumbled as she crossed the threshold, and immediately his hand was under her elbow, steadying her. For an instant she let him take more of her weight than she needed. She felt less steady than before. He guided her to a chair.

"I still believe that the only way to restore him to his senses is to find out what caused him to lose them in the first place," he said quietly when she was seated. "I think he trusts me a little now. Not much, perhaps, but it is a start. We need more time, ma'am. It is easy to forget how far he has already come."

"I shall tell Lady Anne as much."

He sat down beside her and leaned closer. She stared at him. There was a terrifying sense of inevitability about what was happening. Was this what Sylvia had meant? To have this absolute need for someone? A compulsion to draw closer, an irrational power of attraction which had no more to do with will-power than gravity itself.

"Madam? Shall I fetch you a glass of water?"

It was as if she had fallen from a cliff. The one thing she could not do was return to the clifftop and continue with her old life, with its familiar comforts and inconveniences. It was now merely a matter of wondering when she would hit the ground and what the impact would do to her.

Heavy footsteps were approaching on the path along the front of the cottage. Elinor drew aside from Holdsworth and took up *Night Thoughts*, which was at her elbow. He sat back in his chair and drummed his fingers on the table. Neither shifted their position more than by a few inches, but there was a suddenness about their movements, as well as an unsettling symmetry.

The doorway filled almost entirely with Ben's large figure. He blocked the light, and it was as if evening had come upon them with tropical rapidity.

He made his obedience. "Pony's done now, ma'am."

30

IT WAS AT SUPPER that Frank began to drink. He proposed toasts, he sang songs. He encouraged Holdsworth to match him, glass for glass. Holdsworth thought this must surely be a sign of returning health. It was, he reasoned to himself, natural for a young man to want to drink deeply. Frank, under Jermyn's care since March, had had little opportunity to do so for three months.

Mulgrave had set up a table for them under the fruit trees. They drank first one bottle, then another. Frank called for a third and ordered a fourth to be brought in readiness. They talked in bursts interspersed with comfortable silences that grew longer as the evening slipped away.

Frank was cheerful enough, increasingly loquacious and as rational as the wine would let him be. His manner see-sawed between that of a lordly host and that of an awkward, confiding boy, but there was more of the latter than the former. He described episodes from his childhood; he dwelled in particular on his long visits to his grandfather Lord Vauden's home in the West Country. When he spoke of the management of estates, he showed knowledge and enthusiasm. He asked Holdsworth about his apprenticeship, and Holdsworth found himself talking at length of the times he spent on the river with Ned Farmer and of their trips up the Thames.

With the third bottle, they grew quieter. It was still light, but only just. The air was soft and smelled sweet. Water rustled faintly.

Mulgrave had gone to his bed in the kitchen. A solitary candle burned in the window of the cottage. There were pinpricks of light in the gray sky.

"When did it happen?"

Holdsworth looked up. "What?" He could no longer make out Frank's face. It was as if a shadow had spoken. "When did what happen?"

"Your wife, sir," Frank said, his face a blur. "Your son."

Holdsworth did not reply. He heard the chink of glass on glass and the gurgle of wine.

"You see, I wondered what it must be like to drown when Sylvia died," said the voice in the darkness. "And I suppose you must wonder, too. I—I do not wish to pain you. I wish to understand."

"My wife died last March, my son the previous November," Holdsworth said.

"What were their names, pray?"

Holdsworth stared up at the sky. He caught the glimmer of another star. "Maria." He drained his own glass and stretched a hand out for the bottle. "Georgie."

"How did they die?"

Holdsworth told him. He told this rich, spoiled, mad boy things that even Ned had never heard. He told him about the little family on Bankside and the shop in Leadenhall, about the ghost light from the river, and about the day Georgie died at Goat Stairs. He told him about Maria's search for Georgie and the charlatan who had preyed on her, about *The Anatomy of Ghosts*, the barrow of second-hand books and the headstone he could not afford until her ladyship had given him her money. In the darkness, his voice might have belonged to someone else, and he himself was standing aside, listening but paying little attention because the story was already familiar.

Frank fumbled with the corkscrew and a fresh bottle. "So it's not to be wondered at, I suppose."

"What isn't?"

He eased the cork out of the bottle with a soft explosion. "That you don't like ghosts."

"And now it's your turn," Holdsworth said.

"My turn to what?"

"To tell me about your ghosts."

Frank said nothing. He drank.

"It's a night for ghost stories," Holdsworth went on. "It's good to let them out and give them air."

Frank laughed, and the sound erupted from him like a bubble from water. "You make ghosts sound as if they were our captives."

"Aren't they, in a way? And a humane regime should allow its prisoners to mingle occasionally in society. Did you see the lady only once?"

"Can ghosts appear in dreams? Some people say they can. In that case I saw Mrs. Whichcote many times both when she was alive and when she was dead. She was very beautiful, you know."

"I have seen her portrait."

"I saw her ghost only once, though, in the garden." Frank's voice was as slow and relaxed as a sleepy child's. "That is, only once when I was awake."

As a rational being, Holdsworth knew they were both drunk, that he was tired and Frank was overwrought. Nothing anybody said or thought or did was to be trusted. But, as Frank's sleepy voice went on, it seemed to Holdsworth that he was not hearing the story that Frank told, he was in some sense living it.

"Friday, the third of March," Frank said. "A fortnight after they found her body."

Holdsworth was there, lodged behind Frank's eyes, encased in Frank's skull, trapped in another time and place. He was haunting Frank, perhaps, or Frank was haunting him; he wasn't sure which. Did haunting flow in both directions? Was it a dialogue?

There and then, on the evening of 3 March, Frank was in a trance-like state in which his inert body seemed suspended in a heavy, clinging fluid. He bobbed just below the surface of consciousness, buoyed up by a sense of frantic excitement. His mental processes were in a ferment of activity. Frank knew, however—or Holdsworth knew, or both of them did, then and now—that after supping with Whichcote that evening he had taken several cups of coffee, along with wine, punch and laudanum, and all these things had something to do with his state of mind.

Frank was in his bedroom at Jerusalem, and it was cold.

At last the discomforts became too much for him. He rolled slowly out of bed, as slow and fumbling as an old blind man, and pushed his feet into slippers. He went into the sitting room, where the fire still gave out a little warmth and light.

The air was stuffy with the fumes of stale alcohol. He staggered towards the fireplace, drawn towards the orange glow, but faintness overwhelmed him and he was forced to stop and cling to the table. Nausea rose in his throat. His own unworthiness washed through him, rising like bile.

Sylvia would not leave him alone. It was worse, far worse, now she was dead.

Frank blundered across the room, seizing his gown and cap automatically from the hook on the wall as he passed, opened the inner door and unbolted the oak. His feet found the head of the stairs of their own accord. He stumbled downwards, drawn by gravity, and cannoned into the wall of the half-landing.

The cold enveloped him. But he was still carrying his cap and gown. With chattering teeth, he put them on. Holding the gown tightly around him, he negotiated the rest of the stairs, opened the door, slipped on the step and fell flat on his back upon the cobbles of the court.

He lay there for a moment, growing even colder. He was mildly surprised that he did not feel more pain. As the damp seeped into his bones, he considered life from this new horizontal perspective. Chapel Court was cold, monochrome and regular. To his left, a lantern hung over the archway leading to the main gate and the porter's lodge. Otherwise the only light came from the moon and the stars. Above the buildings was a black world with silver inhabitants, unimaginably far away. The weight of it all crushed everything into cold and unimportant dust.

He raised himself on hands and knees. He picked up his cap, settled it on his head and stood up.

Philip Whichcote had been right. What did it all matter? What did anything matter?

Frank Oldershaw had been nothing and he would be nothing again. His presence or absence, his actions or words or thoughts, were all alike meaningless. The stars would shine in their cold, black nothingness whatever he did or didn't do. If Bishop Oldershaw's God were somewhere out there, He didn't matter, for He didn't care a jot for what He had made and the world didn't care for Him.

Frank heard the rasp and crack of a latch from the direction of the porter's lodge. He slipped into the shadows of the chapel arcade along the eastern range of the court. He waited, but no other sound came from the lodge. There was a faint scraping, creaking noise from the other side of college or perhaps farther afield. That sound stopped, too. He was aware that in some part of his being he was growing colder, but the knowledge was unimportant. Cold was a necessary part of this strange amoral world where clarity of thought was possible, and where sin did not exist so there could never be any need for forgiveness.

He slipped from the arcade into the gardens. There were no lights here apart from those in the sky. On his right, thirty yards beyond New Building and partly screened by a line of bushes, was the Jericho, the undergraduates' boghouse. He walked in the other direction, into what seemed the deeper darkness beyond the east end of the chapel. The wet grass soaked into his slippers. Shadows shifted around him. He thought he saw something moving on the bridge. But as soon as he saw it, it was gone.

Something or someone?

Nonsense, there was nothing. He stood as straight as he could, holding out his gowned arms with their sleeves like black wings. He glided slowly over the grass.

"Now," he said aloud. "Now I know, I can do anything." He sucked in the cold air and drifted towards the Long Pond. "I can do anything," he said again, more loudly than before. "I am free. I am God. I am the Holy Ghost."

He crouched on the bank of the pond. The moon shone up from the black water. He palpated the surface with his fingers. His fingertips sent tiny ripples travelling away from him. The stars' reflections danced, and the moon swayed and fragmented, disintegrating into scores of lunar shards, a million moons above other planets.

"I am God," he repeated, watching the moving universes he had made. "I am the Holy Ghost."

He straightened up and a sound emerged from his mouth that was partly laughter and partly his teeth chattering. He came to a decision: he would walk down the Long Pond to the gate of the Fellows' Garden and then back. He would stare at all the universes in the pond. Then at last he would return to his rooms, climb into bed and sleep without dreaming. And when he woke up, Sylvia would be gone for ever and everything would be all right.

Frank could have taken the path, but he kept to the grass, feeling obscurely that the cold and the wet were in some manner connected to the value of what he was doing. His eyes had adjusted to the dark. On the other side of the water, he made out the tops of the trees in the gardens, black outlines against the sky like the tips of feathers. Black feathers, he thought, to match his own black wings. That must mean something too: for they had sacrificed a black cock one evening at the club, and it was meant to bring good fortune.

Where the pond curved, he passed into the greater darkness of the Founder's tree, whose cascading branches crouched down to the ground like a spider's legs. Hands outstretched, he walked slowly under its canopy.

His left hand touched something. He stopped, his mind racing to grapple with this unexpected piece of information. What was it? His mind defined it with negatives: not cold, not wet, not hard. His hands dropped a few inches and, for the briefest of moments, he touched a thick velvet material, beneath which was the outline of a woman's breasts, rising and falling like black water beneath his fingers. And there was something metallic under his fingertips, curving this way and that, not much larger than his thumb.

Frank screamed, a high-pitched sound like the scream of a woman or a child. There was a confusion of violent movement. He turned.

Black on silver. Not a man—a woman.

Frank screamed again. He began to run, blindly into the great spider blackness under the oriental plane, where it was too dark to see anything.

The ground gave way beneath him.

The Holy Ghost walks upon the water.

"What's that?" Holdsworth sat up with a start. "Over there."

They were the first words that either of them had spoken for several minutes, perhaps longer. Frank Oldershaw raised his head, which had been resting on the table, pillowed in his arms. The air was cooling and there was now very little light in the garden, apart from the candle in the window of the cottage, and the stars.

They listened in silence. They heard the faint rustlings from the water and the leaves. An owl hooted.

"A duck," Frank said. "Perhaps a fox."

Holdsworth rose to his feet and walked slowly down the garden to the millpond. He crouched on the bank, made a scoop of his hands and washed his face. He knew he must be drunk but he did not feel it now. The story that Frank had told lingered like a dream. He looked at the sky, as Frank had done on the night he had seen a ghost, and remembered Maria standing in the yard of the Bankside house a few weeks after Georgie's death. He found her there one night, standing in the December cold and staring upwards. She had moved her head from side to side like a sailor searching for land. It had been a murkier sky than this, but even over South-wark there had been stars.

"What are you doing?" he had said.

"Looking for Georgie," Maria had replied.

He had brought out a cloak, which he placed around her shoul-ders. Maria believed that Georgie was in heaven, and she believed too that Georgie had a location, somewhere in the stars, and that it was a place as real as the house on Bankside. If she looked hard enough she would see it. Like everyone else, she looked up into the immensity of the night sky and put whatever she wanted there.

He went back to the table. "Your head was full of fancies that night," he said to Frank. "The wine, the laudanum, the coffee, your dreams while you were asleep—each of these will fill a man's head with monsters. And how much more likely is it if you take them in combination? You must see how probable it is that your ghost was nothing more than a creature of the imagination rather than some strange aberration from the natural order of things."

Frank touched his sleeve. "You feel that? I felt the stuff of the cloak she wore. Soft to the touch—velvet."

"Others wear velvet. Perhaps it was a real person you touched."

"No, sir, no—there was a clasp on the cloak—in the form of the letter S. S for Sylvia, in the form of a snake. It was quite unmistak-able, it was there under my fingers. Besides, I saw someone on the bridge. I'm sure of it. I saw Sylvia."

Holdsworth sighed. "But if it really were Mrs. Whichcote's ghost, why should she choose to walk at Jerusalem?"

"She did not come to Jerusalem, sir. She came to *me*."

"Why?"

"Because without me she would still be alive."

A breeze had blown up, making the leaves rustle more loudly in the trees. All of a sudden, Holdsworth felt very tired. Frank was talking nonsense, but at least he sounded entirely rational. Was that progress?

"So is that all it is?" he said. "That is your ghost?"

Frank did not reply.

"If we can find a way to lay the lady to rest, then all will be well?"

"Things can never be well," Frank said. He got up from the table and walked slowly up the path towards the cottage. He muttered as he went, "You understand nothing. The ghost is only part of it. What does the ghost matter, for God's sake?"

31

ON THURSDAY MORNING, Whichcote had Augustus shave him—the lad was surprisingly deft—and dressed with particular care. Appearances were important when they were all one had. With the footboy, now in his ill-fitting livery, behind him, he strolled across Cambridge, acknowledging the greetings of friends and acquaintances but avoiding conversation. By the time he reached the house in Trumpington Street, the clocks around them were striking eleven.

Dorcas showed him into the parlor.

"He's in Whitebeach," he said without preamble after the door closed. "It's but four or five miles away from Cambridge."

Mrs. Phear said nothing. She sat down in her chair, an oddly graceful movement despite her small and dumpy figure. She motioned to him to sit and did not speak until he had done so.

"How do you know?"

"My footboy traced them. They're putting up at a watermill the college owns. He's with Holdsworth, and Mulgrave is in attendance. No sign of anyone else. Mrs. Carbury visited them yesterday."

"No doubt Lady Anne wishes to know how her son does. And how is he? Was your boy able to form an opinion?"

"He saw nothing of Mrs. Carbury apart from her arrival and her departure. Afterwards he watched the garden, where Holdsworth and Mr. Frank spent most of their time. But he was not close enough to hear what they were saying."

"So we know nothing except where they are, and who is with them." Mrs. Phear nodded. "Well, that is something."

"We know a little more than that, ma'am." He hesitated. "Not know, exactly. It is merely the impression of a foolish boy. Yet he seems to have sharp eyes, and he is perhaps not entirely foolish. He said that Holdsworth and Mr. Frank talked and talked into the evening and, as far as he could tell, the tenor of their conversation was entirely rational. There were no hysterical fits, no sudden movements, no shouting or weeping—in short, nothing to indicate that both parties were not as sane as you or I."

"You infer that Mr. Frank is cured?"

"It's possible. Or, at the very least, on the road to recovery. And if Mrs. Carbury reports as much to her ladyship—"

He broke off. They sat in silence for a moment. Whichcote caught the sound of movement somewhere in the house and a laugh, hastily smothered. Augustus and Dorcas were entertaining each other.

"All this over a ghost," Mrs. Phear said slowly. "Was there ever anything so ridiculous?"

"It is not the ghost that is our difficulty, ma'am. It is what happened at the club."

She frowned at him. "That is not entirely correct. We contrived something to deal with that, did we not? The difficulty came afterwards, and we know who was responsible for that."

"Sylvia," Whichcote said. "Will she never let me be? Did she not injure me enough when she was alive?"

As the days slipped by, Elinor allowed herself to hope that the worst was over. As soon as she reached Jerusalem after her visit to Whitebeach Mill, she had written to Lady Anne and sent the letter by express on Thursday morning. Lady Anne had written back the next day. She was overjoyed by the progress that Frank had made. She was graciously disposed to be appreciative of the efforts that the Carburys had made on his behalf. She enclosed a draft for fifty pounds on her Cambridge bankers to cover the new expenses that the Carburys had disbursed on her behalf.

Best of all, she had written as a postscript: "I am sensible of your labors on my behalf. You will find that I do not forget those who have served me, my dear."

"Very civil," Dr. Carbury commented as he read the letter. "And the money is convenient, too." He looked at Elinor and smiled. "And now you must make yourself easy about the annuity her ladyship has promised you in her will. I do not think there can be any doubt about it now."

Soresby called twice at the Master's Lodge, by invitation, setting the seal on his defection from the Richardson party. He drank tea with Elinor, who found him gauche and silent at first. He was not used to the society of ladies and treated her with a respect so profound it was almost embarrassing. She tried to set him at his ease, however, and by the end of the second visit he had become almost sociable, displaying a quick, nervous intelligence which seemed all of a piece with his fluttering movements and cracking finger joints.

"He will do," Carbury said afterwards. "His scholarship is not in doubt and he is no more of a scrub than Dirty Dick himself when he was a sizar."

"Mr. Soresby told me he has been reading with Mr. Archdale," Elinor said.

Carbury rubbed his hands together. "All the better. It will vex Mr. Richardson. And Mr. Archdale's uncle will be pleased, while Soresby cultivates an acquaintance he may find useful in later life. If he can contrive to lay Mr. Archdale under an obligation, so much the better."

"I had not set Mr. Archdale down as a reading man, sir."

"Nor I—but a taste for learning can take root in most unexpected soil."

For once they were almost cheerful in the Master's Lodge, or at least tried to give each other the impression that they were. But Jermyn's prognosis hung over them both like a shadow.

After breakfast on Monday, 12 June, Holdsworth walked into Cambridge with a satchel over his shoulder. He had decided to leave Frank to his own devices for a few hours. The boy was better, and one sign of this was that he chafed at Holdsworth's constant presence. The answer was to give Frank a taste of independence—and, in doing so, to show that Holdsworth believed he was better.

Nevertheless, it was a risk. He did not know what he would find when he returned to the mill.

He had now been in Cambridge and its environs for two and a half weeks. The town was becoming familiar. In Bridge Street, he called at one or two shops to execute commissions that Mulgrave had given him. It was nearly half-past two before he turned in at the main gate of Jerusalem. As he entered Chapel Court he saw Mr. Richardson walking under the arcade with Harry Archdale.

"The forty-seventh proposition is generally held to be the most difficult in the first book," the tutor was saying. "But you will conquer it with application. It would be worth your while to—" Seeing Holdsworth, he turned from Archdale. "My dear sir, how do you do? You have been sadly missed. Pray, will you take a turn in the garden with me? I have something most particular I wish to discuss with you. Mr. Archdale and I have almost finished, and I shall be with you in a trice."

After a flurry of bows, Richardson turned back to his pupil. "Yes, our own Mr. Dow has written most illuminatingly on the trickier propositions of Euclid. You will find his little book in the library, and I should advise you to look over it before attempting the problem. And while we are about it, you cannot do better than consult Maclaurin for your algebra." He glanced at the chapel clock. "But I will not detain you any longer, Mr. Archdale—I see it is nearly time for dinner."

The undergraduate looked towards Holdsworth as if he wished to say something. But Richardson gave him no opportunity. He took Holdsworth by the arm and guided him down to the chapel arcade and out into the gardens beyond. As they were walking down the path towards the gate of the Fellows' Garden, it began to rain. They sought shelter under the umbrella of the oriental plane. The rain was falling heavily now, but no drops of water penetrated the thick green canopy above their heads.

"Have you heard the news?" Richardson's face had lost its customary urbanity; anger twisted his features. He rushed on without giving Holdsworth a chance to reply. "I had not thought it possible, even of Dr. Carbury."

"Why? What's he done?"

"He has suborned one of my pupils. I can use no other word, sir. The Rosington Fellowship will soon become vacant, and he has offered it to Soresby of all people. But I have smoked him. It is clearly designed to buy Soresby's loyalty. And the pity of it is, such a mean stratagem as that appears to have succeeded. One can hardly blame the poor fellow for accepting, I suppose. What is mere gratitude worth, after all, when it is weighed in the balance against so substantial a temptation as the Rosington?"

The shower lasted no more than three or four minutes and, as it exhausted its course, so did Mr. Richardson exhaust his rage.

"You must pardon the force with which I express myself," he said, touching Holdsworth's sleeve. "It is foolish of me to let the matter rankle. But when we live cheek by jowl as we do here, it is not easy to keep a sense of proportion. But to have it reserved for a man who, however able, has not yet graduated as bachelor of arts is most irregular. I shudder to think what the other colleges are saying of us. But let us leave that aside—I wished to ask you about something of far more importance. It has been rumored that you have been with Mr. Frank Oldershaw. Is it true? How is the dear boy?"

"I am afraid I cannot break a confidence," Holdsworth said, smiling.

"Ah, so that's the way the wind blows, eh? Well, wherever he is, I hope his health improves. You must let me know if I may be of service either to you or to him. And if you should chance to see him, pray give my compliments."

The rain had stopped. The two men strolled slowly under the green shade of the tree in the direction of Chapel Court and New Building. Neither of them spoke. Over to the left there was a metallic rattling that continued for a few seconds and then stopped. It was the sound of iron-rimmed wheels rolling over flagstones. Tom Turdman was doing his rounds. The chapel bell began to toll.

"Ah—dinner time. Do you dine with us, sir? You would be very welcome."

"Thank you, no," Holdsworth said. "By the by, and under quite a different head altogether, I wanted to ask you about Mrs. Whichcote's wound."

"Her wound?" Richardson stopped, his eyebrows rising. "You have the advantage of me."

"When I talked to the night-soil man, he mentioned that there was a wound of some sort on her head. On the left temple."

Richardson laughed. "What Tom referred to as a wound was no more than a slight discoloration. An old bruise, no doubt—perhaps the poor lady knocked her head on a beam a day or two before her death. How typical of the uneducated mind to make a melodrama from the most mundane circumstance."

The Jericho was a brick outhouse that backed against the college boundary wall on the south side of the gardens. The door was at one end, raised about a yard above the ground, and with five stone steps leading up to it. There were no windows, only a line of long rectangular vents just below the eaves. Beyond the door and the steps was another lower door, as wide as the first but no more than four feet high. Both doors were open. Tom Turdman's barrow stood nearby.

Holdsworth went up the steps and stopped in the upper door-way. The chamber was empty. From below, however, came the sound of scraping, shuffling and spitting.

Along the right-hand wall ran a four-seater bench, each hole separated from its neighbor by a low partition that afforded the notion of privacy rather than its reality. Generations of under-graduates had scratched their initials and a selection of insults and obscenities into the wood.

The bell over the chapel continued to toll, calling members of the college to their dinner in hall.

As Holdsworth came out of the boghouse, Tom Turdman emerged from the lower door, hunching forward to duck under the low lintel. A heavy apron, soiled with excrement and urine, pro-tected his clothes. He carried a bucket overflowing with ordure and scraps of newspaper, which he emptied into the barrow. In his other hand was a stained handkerchief, trimmed with lace. Whis-tling tunelessly, he pushed the handkerchief into the mouth of a little sack hanging from the handle of the barrow. He straightened and blew his nose between finger and thumb. He saw Holdsworth standing over him.

"Are you later than usual?" Holdsworth said.

"I come when I can, sir." Tom knuckled his forehead in salute and turned back to the door of the cesspool chamber.

"Wait. I wish to speak to you."

"Me?" Tom repeated, sounding like a parrot and contriving to give the impression that he understood the word as much as a par-rot would have done.

"I want to ask you something."

"Best be getting on, sir. Always a rush on the Jericho after din-ner." He gave another of his toothless grins. "You wouldn't like to be down there when the young gentlemen is up above you, sir, upon my honor you wouldn't."

Holdsworth jingled a handful of change in his pocket. "About your discovery in the Long Pond."

"The ghost that murdered herself, sir?"

"Damn it, man, she did not murder herself and she was not a ghost and nor is she now. She was a woman of flesh and blood who had the misfortune to fall in the water and drown."

"If you say so, sir."

"I do say so. Now listen to me: when we talked in the Angel, you told me that when you found the body your first thought was that it was Mrs. Carbury because she was the only woman who slept in college."

"There's two of them."

"What?"

"Her maid sleeps in too." Tom Turdman chuckled. "Ain't natural, sir, is it? Two women, all these men."

"Listen: you said it wasn't her outside, not this time. So you mean to tell me that Mrs. Carbury sometimes walks out in the garden very early in the morning? At night, even?"

Tom shuffled nearer the low doorway, his bucket clanking. He did not look at Holdsworth.

"Well? Is that the case or is it not?"

The night-soil man glanced at Holdsworth and then away. "Sometimes, maybe."

"Does she know you see her?"

The man shrugged.

"Surely she must hear your wheels?"

"I ain't always moving around, sir. Sometimes I just stand somewhere and rest a bit."

"So you smoke a pipe or have a nip of something to warm you or fall into a doze? Very likely. And where do you do this?"

Tom Turdman waved vaguely, his hand describing an irregular arc that took in most of the college. "Ain't particular, sir. All I ask is a bit of shelter from the weather, a bit of quiet."

"Under that big tree by the pond, perhaps?"

Tom nodded.

"And where have you seen Mrs. Carbury?"

"In the Master's Garden, sir, walking up and down. Or sometimes she used to come out here. Through that gate on t'other side of bridge." He nodded towards the gate with the iron grille through which Holdsworth's fingers touched Elinor Carbury's. "Lady can't sleep, I reckon."

Holdsworth took a handful of coppers from his pocket. "Used to? Does she no longer walk abroad at night?"

"Don't know, do I, sir? All I know is what I see with my eyes. And hear with my ears. And I ain't heard her or seen her for weeks. Not that I've been looking out for her, though. Got my work to do, haven't I? So for all I know she might be walking here still. Or maybe the lady sleeps more soundly now."

Holdsworth held out his hand. Tom Turdman stared at the coins.

"I saw them both, one time," he said.

"What? Who?"

The night-soil man wiped his nose on his sleeve. "The Master's lady, sir. She was with the one that died, the ghost."

"When was this?" Holdsworth snapped.

Tom Turdman stared up at him with frightened eyes. "Months ago, sir. Before Christmas, before the pretty one died. They were walking in the garden under the moon."

32

IKE SHRUNKEN ACADEMICS, two hooded crows stalked across the sacred square of grass in the middle of Chapel Court. Cane in hand, Philip Whichcote entered the arcade by the porter's lodge. Everything about him was neat and genteel. The birds flapped ungainly wings and rose unsteadily into the air.

No one was about. Little happened at Jerusalem during the hour after dinner. Whichcote went to the staircase at the south-east corner and climbed to the first-floor landing. The outer door to Frank's rooms was still closed. Harry Archdale's oak was open, however, and he rapped on the inner door with the head of his cane. Archdale's voice called in answer.

"My dear Harry, how do you do? I have not seen you for an age."

Archdale, who had been standing beside a table sorting through a pile of books, put down the volume he was holding and came forward to greet Whichcote. "I've had a vast deal of reading from Ricky. I've hardly stirred from college for days."

"That will never do," Whichcote said. "Why, surely you must allow that too much reading is bad for a man; it curdles the intellectual faculties. And I have the very plan to take you out of yourself for a few hours. I have come to invite you to a little supper party. Only a few of our most intimate friends will be there. I thought perhaps we might amuse ourselves with cards afterwards."

"You are very kind, but I regret I am not at leisure."

Whichcote was too well bred to show surprise. "In that case we must arrange something else. It's a fine afternoon—shall we take a walk along the river?"

"I'm afraid I cannot." Archdale gestured towards the books on the table. "I have too much to do. When you came in I was about to go to the library."

"The library! Ah—I see: this is the doing of your guardian, is it not?"

"Sir Charles naturally wishes me to pay due attention to my studies," Archdale said awkwardly.

"Well, it's of no great consequence," Whichcote said easily. "I shall wait on you later when you are less engaged with your books. I wish to settle a day for our next club dinner, and I shall make a point of ensuring you're not engaged elsewhere before I do."

He talked of commonplaces for another moment or two to smooth away any abruptness their conversation might have had. As he was doing so, he sauntered to the nearest window and looked idly down at the court. A tall man was walking rapidly down the opposite side towards the passage by the combination room. It was the person whom Augustus had refused admittance at Lambourne House on the Sunday morning after the storm.

Whichcote turned back to Archdale. "Is that not Mr. Holds-worth?"

"Quite possibly. I believe I saw him myself before dinner. He came into college when I was talking with Ricky, and they went off together."

"I thought he'd left Cambridge for good with Frank. How is our friend, by the way? Is there fresh intelligence?"

"Ricky believes he must be much improved or Holdsworth would not be here."

"That is most gratifying. I hope we shall soon see Frank again in our midst." Whichcote looked out of the window again. Holdsworth was no longer in sight. "Does he mean to make a long visit here? Mr. Holdsworth, that is. I thought he had been commissioned to examine the college library."

"I don't know."

Archdale made no offer of refreshment, and showed no signs of wanting to prolong their conversation. Whichcote took his leave. He stepped into the porter's lodge, where Augustus was waiting for him. Mepal told him that Holdsworth had walked into college shortly before dinner time and that there had been nothing to indicate that he expected to spend the night here. Nor had Mepal heard anything about the whereabouts of Frank Oldershaw.

Afterwards, Whichcote stood irresolute outside the entrance to Jerusalem, weighing alternatives in his mind. He beckoned Augustus.

"I want a hack for the rest of the day. Go to the stables and tell them I shall be with them within the hour, and I shall wish to leave directly."

"Tell me the truth," Holdsworth said.

Elinor Carbury did not reply for a few seconds. Their footsteps crunched in time on the gravel path. This man constantly disconcerted her. With an effort, she gathered her thoughts together and turned her face towards him. "The truth, sir? And which part of the truth would you like me to provide?"

"I had in mind that part which deals with your noctambulism."

She stopped. "*My* noctambulism?"

"I mean the term in its literal sense. I do not mean to suggest that you walk in your sleep, madam. But the night-soil man told me that sometimes you walk about in the gardens at night-time."

She glanced about them. They were quite alone.

"It is true that sometimes I find I cannot sleep and so come outside for a little air. But I do not wish it generally known."

He bowed. "I understand. And I also understand that exercise can be an aid to sleep. Indeed, I often find it so myself, and take a turn or two outside before retiring. So you walk here, madam, in Dr. Carbury's garden?"

"Yes, of course. It is very secluded, as you know."

"And Tom says that sometimes you come through the gate and over the bridge into the college garden."

"Yes," Elinor said, and her eyes strayed towards the gate in question and the Founder's oriental plane. "Very rarely, however. Dr. Carbury does not like me to walk out by myself at night, even in our garden." She felt trapped, as so often in her life, and cast about for a means of escape. "Shall we go back to the house and see if he is returned? I cannot think what has kept him in the combination room."

"One moment, pray."

In his urgency, he had the temerity to touch her forearm. Her body grew warm under the thin material of her gown. She frowned at him. He appeared not to notice. He was not standing so close to her now, but had moved a little away as if to study her better.

"Tom saw you walking by night in the garden with Mrs. Whichcote."

She glared at him. "What has that to do with anything? She stayed with me at the Lodge sometimes. And she found it hard to sleep too."

"It shows that she was familiar with Jerusalem at night."

"What of it?"

"Is it possible that you were abroad on the night when Frank Oldershaw believed he saw Mrs. Whichcote's ghost?"

She did not answer. She turned away from him and began to walk slowly down the path in the direction of the Long Pond. His footsteps followed her. She wanted to scream with frustration. Why was he so provoking?

He drew level. "You understand what an alluring hypothesis it is, madam, I am sure."

She did not look at him. "Alluring?"

"Why, it is alluring because it answers every question at a stroke."

"Alluring," she repeated, with great care, as though the word were as fragile as a bird's egg and needed the most careful handling.

"Yes, alluring." Holdsworth was very close to her, and she wondered what echoes the adjective set off in his mind. "The hypothesis offers an entirely rational explanation for what occurred that night. On the one hand, we have young Mr. Oldershaw who, by his own admission, had drunk a great deal, and then rammed it home with copious quantities of coffee and laudanum. He woke suddenly from a deep sleep. He was in any case in low spirits. And there he was, wandering about in a dark garden, believing himself to be entirely on his own, when he encountered a woman where no woman should be. The death of Mrs. Whichcote in the very same place was lying heavily on his mind. It is not surprising that the experience should have temporarily overset his reason, given that he was already in a state of nervous exhaustion, and taking all the circumstances together. So, if true, the hypothesis would explain the alleged ghost. I am persuaded that it would convince Mr. Oldershaw and satisfy Lady Anne."

He stopped speaking and looked at Elinor. She ignored him, turning aside to study the surface of the pond.

"Madam," he said gently. "It is the truth, is it not? It is more than a hypothesis. It is what happened."

Still looking down at the water, she said in a voice scarcely louder than a whisper, "And does the night-soil man claim that he saw me then? Is this your witness?"

"No, ma'am. He was not aware of your presence that night. Indeed, he was not at Jerusalem at all until much later that morning. But this is not a court of law and it is not a matter of convincing the jury. It is merely a matter of finding a theory that covers the facts, such as we know them. And you must see the attraction of this one."

"Does it signify what I say, sir? You have already fixed on your theory, and if my answer does not suit, no doubt you will ignore it."

"I can never ignore anything you say, madam."

He stopped, but she did not speak, though she felt her color rising at his impudence.

"Lady Anne has laid a heavy responsibility on my shoulders," he went on. "I must discharge it as best I can. Were you in the garden that night?"

"It is only my word one way or the other. You will believe it or not, just as you like."

"I had rather hear it from your own lips, madam. Whether or not you were there."

"I was not," she said.

"It is my duty to try to restore Mr. Oldershaw to himself. Even if I cannot adduce absolute proof, this remains a perfectly valid alternative to the idea that he saw an apparition of a dead woman. Surely the very knowledge of this possibility may be of service to him?"

She turned and looked up at him. Her skin was hot and clammy, and it no longer seemed to fit her very well. "Pray say nothing of this notion to anyone. I know her ladyship. Her principles are firm, her judgement severe. She would be horrified by the very idea of a lady in the habit of rambling alone and unprotected at night, the only female in a college full of young gentlemen. She would not hesitate to condemn both the sin and the sinner. And there would be no appeal."

"Madam, I cannot believe—"

"Wait," Elinor interrupted. "That is but a part of it, and the smaller part. You are aware that Dr. Carbury is not in the best of health, I think?"

Holdsworth bowed.

"May I confide in you?"

"I should be honored, ma'am."

"If the worst happens, I cannot risk losing Lady Anne's friendship. There is no one else I shall be able to turn to. A friendless woman cannot afford to be poor in this world."

She looked up at him. She had never before noticed the lines that cut into his face, horizontally across the forehead and splaying out from the outer corners of the eyes. He had not shaved for a

"Mr. Holdsworth, the very man! Pray, sir, will you join us a moment? I am in urgent need of your advice."

There was no help for it. He allowed Richardson to draw him aside. Archdale waited a few yards away, shifting his weight from foot to foot.

The tutor lowered his voice. "I am afraid we have a thief in our midst, sir. Mr. Archdale went up to the library just now and found that the lock on one of the cupboard doors had been forced. It's the cupboard where we house our more valuable books and also those of a delicate nature. You remember it, no doubt? I pointed it out to you. To the left of the fireplace."

"Yes. Set in the wall. When did this happen?"

"Probably during or just after dinner. The library was unlocked, and few people were about. When he discovered the cupboard had been broken into, Mr. Archdale very properly sought me out. I've made a quick survey of the contents, and I believe only one volume is missing. A play by Marlowe."

"*The Massacre at Paris?*"

"Exactly so. A strange choice—there are more valuable books."

"Or astute?" Holdsworth suggested.

"How so?"

"It's an unusually unblemished copy of the earliest-known edition of the play and it appears to be in its original binding. But nobody knows how many copies were printed, how many still are in existence, or where they are. So if the thief took care to remove any marks of ownership from it, it would be relatively easy to dispose of."

"Ah. I catch your drift. So this is perhaps a thief who knows his work?"

Holdsworth bowed. "Perhaps."

"And what might such a book fetch?"

"That I cannot tell you. These things fetch what the market will bear. Marlowe is not much sought after these days but there are those who would be delighted to have a copy of it in their collection. If the thief is as clever as he seems to be, he would bide his time. He would look for a private gentleman perhaps, rather than a bookseller. The alternative is that he has stolen the book to order, as it were, and already has a purchaser waiting for it."

Richardson glanced at Archdale, just out of earshot. "Mr. Holdsworth, I have not told you the whole of it yet. There is another circumstance, and I scarcely know whether this makes it worse or better." He took something from his pocket and held it out on the palm of his hand. "When Mr. Archdale found that the cupboard had been broken into, he also found this inside. I can swear that it was not there this morning—I had occasion to open the cupboard then. So we can only conclude that it belongs to the thief."

In the palm of Richardson's hand lay a small penknife with a bone handle. The knife was open. The dull metal of the blade was pitted and scarred. Constant sharpening had worn it down to a shadow of its original self. The metal shone brightly only along the edge.

"You believe this was the instrument used to force the lock, sir?"

"So it would seem. And both Mr. Archdale and I have had occasion to see this particular knife before. It is quite distinctive in shape, you see, and there is a black smudge on the bone as if a redhot poker had lain there briefly, or something of the sort. I'm afraid there can be no doubt of it. It belongs to Mr. Soresby. I have seen him use it on countless occasions. He picks his teeth with it, pares his nails, even cuts his meat."

"Has Mr. Soresby been seen in the library today?"

Richardson shrugged. "Why, as to that, he comes and goes so often that no one notices him most of the time. After all, he's the library clerk."

Archdale had edged closer. "Look here, sir," he said to Richardson. "This is devilish unpleasant. I can't believe Soresby would be such a blockhead. And to leave his knife behind as well."

"We cannot be sure it was he," Richardson said, frowning. "Besides, who can trace the hidden springs of another human heart? When one hand commits a guilty act, the other hand may find a way to confess it. I am much obliged to you for bringing this to my attention, Mr. Archdale, and I would not wish to keep you from your studies any longer. But may I ask you not to say anything of this to anyone until I have had an opportunity to interview Mr. Soresby? There may be a perfectly innocent explanation."

It was an unpleasant business, and Holdsworth was anxious to be gone as well. Taking a step towards the porter's lodge, he said, "You have much on your mind, sir, and you will—"

"No, pray stay, Mr. Holdsworth," Richardson said. "May I trespass on your good nature and entreat a further favor? A matter as delicate as this needs such careful handling, such nice calculations. Your assistance would be invaluable. You see, on the evidence available to us, we have as it were *prima facie* good reason to suspect Mr. Soresby is responsible for this theft. But the evidence falls far short of absolute proof. As both librarian and Mr. Soresby's own tutor, my duty is to call on Mr. Soresby at once. It would be improper for me to see him without the presence of a witness, and you unite in your person the ideal qualifications for such a man. You are not a member of this college, but you have some knowledge of its workings and of the people involved. You are here on behalf of her ladyship, whose family has so many ties with Jerusalem. And you have a particular knowledge of our library and its contents."

Richardson took Holdsworth's arm and led him through the screens, the passageway that separated the lower end of the hall from the buttery and the kitchens, and into the open court beyond. Directly in front of them, beyond the railings, was Jerusalem Lane. On their right was the Master's Lodge. In the north-east corner, at right angles to the Master's Lodge and along the boundary of Jerusalem Lane, was Yarmouth Hall. Richardson led the way diagonally across the cobbled court to the building's entrance, a heavy oak door adorned with fragments of cracked Perpendicular tracery and set between two buttresses.

"It is a most inconvenient lodging for students," Richardson said, raising the latch. "It is very old and constantly in need of repair."

He led the way into a dark hallway with a stone floor. Passage-ways led off to either side and a staircase wound up to the floors above.

The tutor held a handkerchief to his nose. "I fear the air is not as healthy as it might be," he mumbled. "This way, sir."

He conducted Holdsworth up the stairs. Yarmouth Hall had been divided into three floors, each of which now contained half a dozen small chambers. Plaster was crumbling from the partition walls, exposing the lathes beneath. The floor was gritty with dirt.

"At least there is this to be said for the place," Richardson said as they rounded the last bend of the staircase and climbed the final flight to the second floor. "The chambers are inexpensive, and these garrets are the cheapest of all."

On the top floor, he knocked on the door at the far end of the corridor. Holdsworth heard footsteps within, and the rattle of a bolt. The door opened a few inches, and Soresby's long, anxious face peered out at them.

"Mr. Soresby, good day to you. May we come in?"

The undergraduate stepped back automatically, his expression blank with surprise, and pushed the door wide. Stooping, Holds-worth followed Richardson into the little room. Richardson closed the door behind them.

The room was about ten feet long, running along the pitch of the roof, but no more than five or six feet wide. There was no fireplace. Soresby's cap and gown hung on a nail beside the door. Because of the slope of the ceiling, it was possible to stand up only along the inner side. At the farther end was an uncurtained and unmade bed; here, near the door, was a stained deal table, on which were a few books and, on a wooden platter, the end of a loaf and a few crumbs of cheese. Attached to the wall directly above was a small shelf holding a collection of a dozen books.

As they entered, Soresby retreated towards the bed. Holdsworth stopped when he was next to the window, a dormer that stood wide open. The window faced south, towards the college, but there was little to be seen except a blank wall, part of the Master's Lodge next door. Holdsworth looked down. Unpleasant smells rose up to greet him. He was directly above the little yard where the privy and the washhouse were, and where the Carburys' servants sometimes worked in the day. No one was about.

"Mr. Soresby, I regret to say we are not here on a pleasant errand," Richardson was saying.

The undergraduate, bewildered, looked from Richardson to Holdsworth. "I don't understand, sir. Has there been an accident? Is my father—"

"No, no," Richardson interrupted. "You may make yourself easy upon that score, at least. No, this concerns the library. Before I continue, is there anything you wish to tell me? You may find it is in your interest to do so."

Richardson paused. Soresby shook his head.

"Very well then. I have to inform you that there has been a burglary. A thief entered the library some time today, probably during or just after dinner. He forced the lock of a particular cupboard and stole a valuable book."

Soresby seemed to shrivel into himself. "I'm heartily sorry—I—"

"What? You admit responsibility?"

"No, sir." The undergraduate's face lost what little color it had. "Of course not. I—I only meant to say I wish I had been there to prevent the loss. As library clerk—"

"Yes, indeed, there may be a question of a dereliction of your duties," Richardson said. "But that does not concern me at present. What concerns me is the far more serious possibility that you yourself may be the thief."

Soresby raised his hands as if to ward off a blow. He retreated from Richardson and the backs of his legs came into contact with the edge of his bed. Taken by surprise, he sat down suddenly.

"It is clear that the person responsible not only knew which cupboard to open, but also which book to steal. In other words, the thief was intimately acquainted with the library."

"I beg of you, sir, pray do not entertain such a suspicion," Soresby cried. "I would never—"

"I would be obliged if you would hear the accusation before attempting to defend yourself from it. As I was saying, after dinner Mr. Archdale had occasion to go up to the library. It was he who discovered the theft. He also discovered the implement used to force the door of the cupboard. Very properly, he brought it at once to me. I may add that he recognized it and so did I."

Richardson took the penknife from his pocket and held it out. Soresby, still seated, stared at it for a moment, then stretched out his hand as if he meant to take it. The tutor pulled his own hand away.

"You acknowledge it is your knife?"

"Of course it is, sir. I would know it anywhere—I have had it since I was a boy. It was my father's."

"Very well." Richardson threw a glance at Holdsworth. "Then I must ask you again whether you stole the book."

Soresby opened his mouth but could not speak. He shook his head violently, his ragged hair swinging from side to side.

"I regret to say that the evidence against you is so strong, Mr. Soresby, that I have no alternative but to search your room. And the necessity is as distasteful to me as it is to you, I am sure, but you will understand that in the circumstances I have no choice. If you are innocent, which is possible, though the evidence against you is black, then you will naturally wish to see your innocence established before the world." Richardson looked up at Holdsworth. "It is important to do these things according to the proper form, sir. You would oblige me infinitely if you would stand by the door and witness the search." He turned back to Soresby. "Pray stand beside Mr. Holdsworth. And, before you do, would you be so good as to turn out your pockets?"

Soresby rose unsteadily to his feet. He turned out the pockets of his coat and his breeches, one by one. "I—I had noticed I had mislaid the penknife, sir," he said. "I had thought . . ." His voice trailed away. He stood beside Holdsworth. He was trembling like a man with an ague. There was a loud crack as he pulled a finger joint.

Richardson worked his way round the little room. He was methodical, as in everything he did. He turned over the books and examined the table, even peering underneath it. Beside it on the floor was a wooden box containing Soresby's notes, and he tipped the contents on the table and sifted them with his forefinger. He searched the small press where Soresby kept his few clothes and a jumble of items, from candle ends to rusty needles.

Soresby's breathing was fast and irregular. The young man was hot, too, as if running a fever. Holdsworth felt the heat coming from his body, and also a sour smell, as if fear were expressing itself as an odor.

At last the tutor came to the bed. He stripped it down to the straw mattress. He examined the bolster and the pillow. Underneath he found dust, a pot that slopped urine when he moved it, and the skeleton of a mouse. He turned his attentions to the mattress itself, feeling and kneading it on both sides, like a physician conscientiously searching for lumps all over his patient's body.

Suddenly he looked up. "There appears to be a rectangular object lodged in the straw, Mr. Soresby. Here—where the stitching has come adrift. Would you be so good as to extract it for me?"

Soresby swallowed. He opened his mouth and closed it again. He did not move.

"Did you hear me, sir?" Richardson said sharply.

Soresby stumbled across the room and fell to his knees by the bed. Richardson stood aside, watching. The student pushed his hand into the canvas cover that contained the straw.

"Not there," Richardson said. "The other side."

Soresby's hand wriggled invisibly, changing position. Then, at last, he brought out a leather-bound quarto. Wide-eyed, he sat back on his heels and stared at it.

"Pray give it me, sir," Richardson prompted.

Barely a yard separated the two men. Still on his knees, like a supplicant, Soresby held out the book to Richardson. The tutor took it and opened it, turning to the title-page. He angled the volume so Holdsworth could see it too. *The Massacre at Paris.*

"I swear," Soresby said in a hoarse whisper, "I swear I—"

"Pray do not add perjury to your other sins, sir. Well, we shall take our leave for the moment. You will stay in your room until I send for you." The tutor turned to Holdsworth. "It distresses me that you should have had to witness such a disagreeable interview. But may I trespass further on your good nature and ask you to accompany me to the Master's Lodge?"

He gave Soresby the slightest of bows and left the room with his nose in the air, as if trying to raise it as far as possible above the stench of moral corruption in the atmosphere.

Holdsworth followed. In the doorway he turned back. Soresby was still on his knees. His face was a dirty white colour, almost gray. His eyes were wide and blank. Only his hands were moving. A finger joint cracked.

34

PHILIP WHICHCOTE DISMOUNTED from the hack and opened the gate. He led the horse into the yard, and the sound of its hooves sent a dozen doves fluttering into the air. When he released the reins, the horse walked to the trough and lowered its head over the water.

Whichcote tried the heavy door of the mill. It was locked. He had found the place easily enough. The ostlers at the livery stable had an encyclopedic knowledge of the surrounding countryside, and one of them had once worked for Mr. Smedley, the college's tenant at Whitebeach. Whichcote knew that the next hour could settle the direction of his future life. Prudence pointed one way. His instincts urged him in the opposite direction.

There were footsteps behind him.

Mulgrave appeared at the corner of the thatched cottage on one side of the yard. He marched unsteadily forward, tilting to and fro as he shifted his weight between the shorter leg and the longer. He stopped a few paces from Whichcote. The two men stared in silence at each other.

"Thought I heard hooves," the gyp said at last with the gloomy satisfaction of one who feared the worst and now at least has the comfort of knowing he was right.

"I'm come to call on Mr. Oldershaw. Where is he?"

Mulgrave spat on the cobbles, scarcely a foot away from Whichcote's boot. "He ain't at home to visitors."

"Damn your impudence," Whichcote snapped.

Suddenly furious, he drew himself up to his full height. All the worry and frustration of the last few months flooded together and funnelled into a glorious surge of rage. Without pausing for thought, he swept up his right arm and slashed the whip across Mulgrave's face.

Taken unawares, the gyp tried too late to step back from the blow, putting his weight on his bad leg. He missed his footing and fell to the ground. Whichcote cut him again with the whip, this time sending the tip curling around the angle between Mulgrave's neck and shoulder.

The gyp howled and scrambled to his feet. He had lost his hat and wig. He ran back the way he had come, staggering, but moving surprisingly fast. Whichcote stalked after him, swinging the whip, his riding boots clattering and slipping on the cobbles. His anger had found a safe target. He felt almost grateful to Mulgrave.

He rounded the end of the cottage and found himself in a neglected garden.

Mulgrave was nowhere to be seen. Perhaps he had taken refuge in the cottage, or even in the mill beyond. Whichcote caught sight of a figure by the water, barely visible beyond the unpruned fruit trees at the bottom of the garden.

A whipping, then a ducking. That would teach the knave a lesson.

He realized his mistake before he reached the trees. It was Frank himself down there, quite alone, and sitting with his back to the cottage. His coat and hat lay beside him on the grass. There was a rod in his hand and the line trailed limply into the water, shifting with the current. He did not turn as Whichcote drew nearer, though he must have heard the approaching footsteps.

Prudence, Whichcote told himself. He felt unusually calm now. He would play the long game.

"Frank!" Whichcote drew level and smiled down at him, knowing that now he must dissemble as never before. He shifted the whip to his left hand, ready to shake Frank's hand with his right. "I give you good day. I am rejoiced to see you."

Frank laid down the rod and stood up. He ignored Whichcote's outstretched hand and bowed stiffly.

"And looking so well," Whichcote went on, placing the spurned hand negligently on his hip as if that had been his intention all along. "Why, you are a positive advertisement for the beneficial effects of rural pursuits. I declare you tempt me to come and live in seclusion with you. We shall do nothing but fish and shoot and ride, and be happy the livelong day. Are you quite alone?"

Frank said nothing, but Whichcote fancied he nodded. It was difficult to be sure because the sun was low in the sky. It was behind Frank, obscuring his face and shining into Whichcote's eyes. The heavy golden light caught the ends of Frank's hair, which he was wearing loose and unpowdered for all the world as though he were a ploughboy.

"I am sorry to say I was obliged to discipline your servant as I came in," Whichcote went on. "That man Mulgrave—damn the fellow, he's old enough to know better. He was downright impudent. You should turn him out of your service, you really should."

He paused but Frank said nothing.

"Your friends are anxious for news. May I tell them you are fully restored? When will you be back among us?"

He heard sounds behind him, and turned. Mulgrave was limping down the path. The gyp stopped beside the trees, keeping a safe distance between himself and Whichcote. There was already a weal burning across his left cheek, and another cut like a red furrow around his neck, just below the jaw.

"He took a whip to me, sir," Mulgrave called. "Ain't right. I'm not his servant. And he owes me money, too."

"Hold your tongue," Frank snapped, his sense of propriety outraged by Mulgrave's daring to speak so rudely of his betters.

"You'll chastise him yourself, I hope," Whichcote said. "Good God, what is the world coming to?"

Frank turned his eyes back to Whichcote. With sudden violence, he leaped forward and seized the older man around the waist. Whichcote, taken entirely by surprise, at first made no attempt to defend himself. Frank pulled him down the slope of the bank. Whichcote struggled, and briefly succeeded in breaking Frank's hold. But Frank was younger, larger and stronger than him. He embraced Whichcote and squeezed, pinning the latter's arms to his side.

"Damn you, let me—"

Frank dragged him farther down the slope. The ground near the water was soft. Whichcote's riding boots slipped in the mud. He butted Frank's face with his forehead as viciously as he could. Frank swore and shifted his grip. He raised the older man off his feet.

"For God's sake—"

Frank pivoted, lifting his victim higher. Gathering momentum with the force of the swing, he flung Whichcote away from him. For an instant Whichcote hung in the air, limbs flailing. There was a great splash as he hit the water.

"Quack," Frank said, smiling. "Quack, quack."

Holdsworth loped swiftly out of Cambridge, climbing the long hill from the river as though the Furies were pursuing him. As he walked, two faces constantly flashed before him in the inner the-ater of his mind: one was Tobias Soresby's, white, bony and full of fear; and the other was Elinor Carbury's, turned up to him with those lovely eyes trained on him—those eyes, so unexpected and indeed ravishing in that stern, thin, heavy-browed face.

Why do we think only the dead haunt us? he wondered. For the living are just as good at it.

The town dropped away behind him. As the light began to fade, the clouds were coming in from the west and it grew noticeably cooler. Holdsworth slowed his pace. He remembered how, on his first night at Jerusalem, Richardson had taken him out into the gardens and had talked of the place as a fortress, enclosed and inviolate. But there was another way of looking at it, namely that the walls kept people in as much as they kept others out. The place was a trap, and animals caught in traps cannot escape one another. Once, in the days of his prosperity, Holdsworth had employed a journeyman who delighted in collecting rats and placing them together in a cage. The rats would fight until only one was left, bloody, victorious and often dying. It was such sport to watch them, the journeyman used to say, and he would take bets on who would be the winner.

A rider appeared a quarter of a mile away. His horse was moving at a walk, so the man was in no hurry. Slowly he and Holdsworth drew together. There was something strange about the figure slumped in the saddle. His head was down. His coat looked limp and bedraggled. He wore neither hat nor wig.

The distance between them decreased. The coat was more than bedraggled—it was wet, and so were the rest of the man's clothes. When they were no more than twenty yards apart, the rider raised his head. His eyes met Holdsworth's but slid away as the head bowed again over the horse's neck. But there had been time enough for Holdsworth to recognize him.

"Mr. Whichcote," he said. "Good evening, sir. Have you met with an accident?"

Ignoring Holdsworth, Whichcote urged the horse into a trot and passed him. Holdsworth turned to watch his retreating figure. Once he was safely past, Whichcote allowed his horse to slow to a swaying, ambling walk.

Holdsworth went on as quickly as he could, trying to ignore a blister developing on his right foot. He passed through the little village, where the dogs barked at him and the smith, smoking his evening pipe outside the forge, watched him curiously. Holdsworth turned into the track to the mill.

Mulgrave was in the yard, also smoking. He stood up with obvious reluctance when he saw Holdsworth and made only a token effort to hide his pipe. There was a mark on his left cheek, a long, angry weal, and another on his neck partly concealed by his neck-tie and collar.

"Thank God it's you, sir," the gyp said, casting his eyes piously towards heaven. "I thought for a moment you was that devil again."

"Mr. Whichcote?"

"Who else, sir? The devil incarnate."

"I passed him on the road."

"He took his riding crop to me. In this very yard. I'm as free a citizen of this country as he is, sir, and maybe I'll have the law on him for it. It's assault and battery, that's what it is. And there's the money he owes me, too, the villain, he's as good as stolen it."

"What happened? Where's Mr. Frank? Did Mr. Whichcote talk to him?"

Mulgrave wriggled, as though the questions were bullets and he was trying to avoid them. It took Holdsworth an instant to realize that the gyp was laughing silently.

"Mr. Frank gave him a ducking in the millpond."

"What?"

The silent wriggling began again. "Gave him a ducking, he did, that'll teach the devil a lesson."

"But where's Mr. Frank?" Holdsworth repeated, raising his voice.

Mulgrave jerked a thumb. "In the parlor, if you can call it that."

Before the gyp had finished speaking, Holdsworth was walking away. Mulgrave's lack of respect could wait until later. He found Frank sitting on the elbow-chair by the table in the parlor, with a dish of tea beside him. His hair was combed and lightly powdered, and he was neatly and soberly dressed. He could have attended divine service in Great St. Mary's without causing anyone to raise an eyebrow. He was so absorbed in his book, *Night Thoughts*, that he appeared not to notice Holdsworth's entry.

"Mr. Oldershaw—I am heartily sorry for the intrusion you suffered this afternoon. I hope you are not harmed?"

Frank laid the book carefully on the table and, with great condescension, rose and bowed to Holdsworth.

"I should not have left you unprotected," Holdsworth went on. "I have been racking my brains how Whichcote found out your direction—"

"I am perfectly well, sir, as you see, so it don't signify."

"Why did he come? What happened?"

Frank smiled. "Quack," he said. "Quack."

That evening it rained, not heavily but a steady drizzle that kept Elinor indoors. She sat by the window and turned over the familiar pages of *Rasselas. There is no people, rude or learned, among whom apparitions of the dead are not related and believed.* She was aware of almost constant movements in the house around her—footsteps on the stairs, doors closing, comings and goings in the hall beneath and the murmuring of servants.

At eight o'clock, she rang for Susan, ostensibly to have her bring the tea things. But while she was in the room, Elinor asked her maid about the movements below.

"It's Mr. Richardson, ma'am, he's been in and out all evening. And we've had Mr. Holdsworth and young Mr. Archdale, too, and Mepal. And now Master's sent Ben to fetch Mr. Soresby."

Time dragged on. After tea, Elinor found it necessary to go downstairs on two occasions, once to fetch a book from the dining room, and again, when the rain had stopped, to venture out for a turn in the Master's Garden while it was still light. On both occasions she heard voices behind the closed door of Dr. Carbury's book room. Though sorely tempted, she could not bring herself to sink so low as to listen at the door; and besides the servants were to and fro so there was always the risk of discovery.

Outside, she strolled up and down the gravel walks and it was surprising how often she found herself passing the book-room window. Unfortunately it was closed. When she was nearby, she heard voices, but could not distinguish what they were saying. There was one exception, however, when she heard Soresby saying, or rather shouting, "But I swear it, sir! By all that's sacred!"

As the evening drew on, the mystery deepened. Soresby left the Master's Lodge. Elinor, who happened to be in the dining room at the time, looked up and saw his lanky figure pass the window, his head bowed and his gown trailing along the ground.

The hour for supper arrived. Elinor ate alone in the dining room. There was no sign of Dr. Carbury. He was still in the Lodge. His usual practice was to sup in hall or in the combination room, but if he remained at home, he would sup with his wife. Elinor discreetly interrogated Susan and learned that her husband had not even told Ben to bring him a tray in his book room. She discounted the possibility that Dr. Carbury was feeling exceptionally unwell—for he would have made Elinor and the servants aware of it if he had been; he was not a man to suffer in silence.

His behavior was inexplicable. But she dared not disturb him to satisfy her curiosity. He had laid it down as a rule of their marriage that she never went to him. He came to her if and when it pleased him to do so.

After supper, she returned to her sitting room and had the candles lighted and the curtains drawn. She had not been there long when she heard the familiar dragging step on the stairs. Her husband entered the room, leaning on his stick. His face was gray and seemed thinner than usual. The skin hung from his jowls like folds of stained and wrinkled canvas.

"Why, there you are, sir." She rose and turned his chair towards him, so it would be easier for him to reach it. "I had almost given up hope of you."

He gave her the briefest of bows and sank down heavily in the chair.

"You have not had any supper. Are you unwell?"

He waved away the question with his hand. "Yes, I suppose I must peck at something, if only a trifle. I have sent Ben out for a mutton chop or two, and a slice of that pigeon pie we had last night, if there's any left. I cannot face anything else."

"My dear sir, you're not yourself."

He grunted. "I have received intelligence this evening that quite removed my appetite. I would not have believed it possible. Soresby of all people."

"What has happened to him?"

"It is more a case of what he has done, ma'am. I had Richardson come to me an hour or two ago—oh, he was looking very glum but you could see the glee in his eyes. It appears that Soresby has stolen a valuable book from the library."

"Stolen? Not borrowed?"

"One does not borrow a book by breaking into the cupboard where it is locked away, sneaking off with it and concealing it in one's mattress. No, there's no doubt. Soresby denies it, naturally, but the evidence against him is incontrovertible. He must have intended to sell the book, for I'm told it would fetch a few guineas in London. And God knows he must be in want of money. Sizars always are."

"But surely, with the promise of the Rosington—?"

"Ah, but that does not become vacant for more than six months. Besides, he could not expect to enter directly into the fellowship in any case. In fact he would find it hard to borrow on the strength of the offer because he has not even taken his degree yet. Still, it is strange—he should have come to me, I would have advanced him the money if necessary. I can only hypothesize that the fool had a brainstorm and was seized by a desperate impulse. And after I had given him such a mark of favor, too."

Elinor shifted in her chair so the glare of the candles was not on her face. "What will you do? Can the matter be dealt with quietly?"

Carbury shook his head. "It gives Richardson the perfect opportunity to have his revenge on me. I imagine the news is already halfway around Cambridge—he will have made sure of that. Had it rested on his word alone, it would have been easier. But unfortunately the theft was discovered by Mr. Archdale. Soresby had left a penknife at the scene, and it was Mr. Archdale himself who recognized it as Soresby's. And then who should chance to come by but Mr. Holdsworth."

"Mr. Holdsworth!"

He looked sharply at her. "I thought you saw him this afternoon. You knew he was in college."

"Yes, sir." Elinor recovered herself quickly, hoping her color had not risen. "It was merely that I had not expected that Mr. Richardson would be so indiscreet as to recruit the services of an outsider."

The doctor gave her a quick nod. "You have a point, madam. Mr. Richardson did not act wisely. Nevertheless, knowing that Mr. Holdsworth has a special knowledge of our library and a knowledge of the book trade in general, he asked for his assistance. Mr. Holdsworth was actually there when Richardson found the book in Soresby's mattress. Which means, of course, that Lady Anne must know the full history of the affair in a day or two. Oh, Dirty Dick is as cunning as a barrowload of monkeys."

"And Mr. Soresby? Will he be prosecuted?"

"No, I hope to prevent that at least. It can serve no useful purpose. Even Richardson must see the harmful effect it would have on the college as a whole."

"So you will merely send him down?"

He twisted in the chair so he could look fully at her. "I—I have not yet decided the best course of action."

Elinor stared at him. "But surely he must go? He cannot be allowed to take his degree."

Dr. Carbury said nothing. He scratched his forehead under the line of his wig with a long yellow dog's claw of a fingernail.

Ben came into the room. "The chops is below, your honor. Would you like them downstairs or up here on a tray?"

35

WHEN MORNING CHAPEL WAS OVER, the congregation streamed through the west door, eager for breakfast and, in the case of late risers, to finish dressing. Harry Archdale hung back, sheltering under the arcade. Huddled in their gowns, the fellows and undergraduates of Jerusalem flowed round him. Umbrellas bobbed over the rain-slicked cobbles of the court. Gradually the stream of the congregation diminished to a trickle.

At last the tall figure of Tobias Soresby appeared in the chapel doorway.

"Soresby? Have you a moment?"

The sizar avoided looking at Archdale. "I regret—I am pressed for time—"

"You needn't worry," Archdale said kindly. "I shan't keep you long." He hesitated, his assurance dropping away from him. "How are you?"

Soresby tried to sidle past. "Very well, thank you."

Archdale moved a pace to his left, blocking Soresby's escape. "Was it you?" he burst out.

For the first time Soresby looked directly at him. The sizar's face was pale, his eyelids were red and swollen. "No," he said. "But what does that matter now?"

"I daresay it will come right in the end," Archdale said.

Soresby shook his head. He tugged at his fingers as if trying to pull them off. A joint popped.

"I am sure it will look very different in a day or two. Upon my word it will."

"Everyone knows."

"What?"

"Everyone knows," Soresby repeated. "They're all looking at me. They're whispering about me."

"Nonsense. If I were in your shoes, I'd carry on as usual. Shall you go to Ricky's lecture this morning? Or the library?"

"Neither."

"Ah. I must go to the library at least. I wish to consult Maclaurin, and also Mr. Dow's little book on Euclid. If you change your mind, perhaps you—"

"I have borrowed the Dow, Mr. Archdale," Soresby said. "I have it in my chamber—I'll return it. I'm sorry to inconvenience you in—"

"Oh nonsense. You do not inconvenience me in the slightest. Listen, Soresby, even if it goes against you here, there must be many other means of employment for a man of your parts."

"It is easy for you to say that, Mr. Archdale."

"Yes it is, but you must listen to me even so, for it's no more than the truth. You must let me stand your friend, do you hear? I shall speak to my uncle, Sir Charles, and see if something can be done. You must not despair."

"You are too good, Mr. Archdale," Soresby said, his eyes on the ground. Another joint popped. "And you are in the right of it—I must not despair." He bowed, a quick, nervous movement like a chicken pecking. "Much obliged, Mr. Archdale, much obliged."

Mulgrave had loosened his stock so it would not chafe his neck so badly. The two weals, one on the neck and one on the cheek, had darkened in color overnight, and acquired a livid tinge. But he wore clean linen and had even shaved himself. The model of respectful sobriety, he stood before Holdsworth with his head slightly bowed.

"Obliged if I could take a day's leave of absence, sir—a bit of business that won't wait. I'd take it very kindly."

The request was less a request than a statement of intent: he would have his leave of absence, whether or not it was granted. The gyp was entirely within his rights, for Holdsworth had hired his services on Frank's behalf, and it was a contract that could be broken at any time by either party.

"It's inconvenient, but if your business won't wait, then you must attend to it. Perhaps, while you're in town, you can supply the deficiencies of the larder. We are running short of tea, you said last night, and Mr. Oldershaw expressed a sudden desire for strawberries as he was going to bed."

After Mulgrave had gone, Holdsworth sat at the breakfast table with a book in his hands but he scarcely read a word. He had woken that morning with an odd notion in his mind: yesterday, he had hardly thought of either Maria or Georgie. It had been as if his wife and his infant son had never existed. He did not know whether he should feel guilty for forgetting them or merely relieved that he had briefly escaped their shadows. But he had thought of Elinor Carbury almost constantly and at times in a way that no man should think of another man's wife; and was that not an even greater betrayal?

There were footsteps overhead, and then on the stairs. Frank passed through the parlor on his way to the pump and the privy in the yard. His feet were bare and he wore only shirt and breeches.

"Good morning, Mr. Oldershaw."

Frank grunted, but did not return the greeting. Five minutes later, he came back inside, his hair dripping. He left a trail of wet footprints on the parlor flagstones. "Where's Mulgrave?" he demanded. "I want tea and toast."

"He asked leave to go to Cambridge on private business."

"And you let him? Without consulting me? That's coming it a bit high."

What happened next took Holdsworth completely by surprise: he lost his temper. "That's because you were not there to be consulted. If you choose to stay in bed for half the morning, you can't expect the world to stop and wait your convenience."

Frank's color deepened. "You can't talk to me like that—what do you mean by it?"

"It means you're laboring under a misapprehension. I can talk to you like that. There is nothing in the world to stop me."

"You'll regret your insolence."

"Will I?"

"For a start, you'll leave my service instantly."

Holdsworth laughed. "You can't dismiss me. Her ladyship retained my services, not you."

Frank lunged forward. Holdsworth moved before the blow landed, and the fist connected with his shoulder rather than his face. Before Frank could hit him again, he seized the boy's wrist and twisted it. He spun Frank around and pushed him downwards, face first over the table.

"You don't use force with me, sir. I'm not your servant. You're not my master."

Frank struggled violently, hacking at Holdsworth's shins with his bare heels. In reply, Holdsworth jerked the boy's arm higher up his back until Frank cried out. Holdsworth shuffled his legs back, away from the flailing feet. For a moment, neither of them moved.

With one fluid movement, the ginger cat streaked into the still silence. It had been watching events from the kitchen doorway. Now, choosing to interpret them in its own way and judging its moment had come, it leaped lightly on to the table. It meowed. It nudged Frank's forehead repeatedly, demanding affection from the source that experience taught was most likely to provide it. Frank shook his head, trying to repel its advances, but the cat took the movements as caresses, primitive perhaps but worthy of encouragement. It pushed the side of its head against Frank's hair and rubbed it enthusiastically to and fro. It began to purr.

Holdsworth trembled with suppressed emotion. The laugh erupted from him in a great bellow. The cat licked Frank's ear, as if to inspire him to further exertions. Holdsworth felt the tension ooze from Frank's body and from his own too.

Frank joined in the laughter, so far as he could with his cheek pressed hard against the tabletop, producing a snuffling, snorting sound that made them both laugh all the more. Holdsworth released him and stood back.

The laughter died. The cat continued to purr, looking from one man to the other. Frank stood up slowly. He turned to face Holdsworth. He held out his hand.

"I beg your pardon, sir."

They shook hands.

Holdsworth said, "I do not think there is anything more I can do for you. I shall write to her ladyship and resign my position."

"No. I beg you not to act hastily. Do you believe I'm cured?"

"I am not perfectly convinced you were ever mad in the first place."

Frank sat down in the chair by the window. "You're talking in riddles."

"It's clear enough to me, and largely a matter of common sense. You're not a maniac."

"I am obliged to you, sir. But Dr. Jermyn would not agree."

"For all his learning, Dr. Jermyn sometimes behaves like an ass. I believe you've been liverish, and in low spirits. I believe you received a great shock, or rather a series of them. If you saw or sensed the presence of another person in the college garden that night, it was not a ghost but someone as alive as you or I. Or perhaps what you saw was a creature of your disordered fancy—born of too much laudanum, too much wine, too much unhappiness. It doesn't matter. The point is that you were predisposed to see your ghost, and that is where the real heart of this mystery lies. I'm persuaded that the solution to it will also reveal the reason why you do not wish to mix with the world, and why you do not wish to see your mother."

The ginger cat leaped on to Frank's lap. Automatically the young man began to stroke its head. The cat arched its neck and purred even more loudly than before, while its tail waved like a flag of victory.

"You see that animal?" Holdsworth said. "It interprets our actions in terms of its own wishes and fears, as is very natural. It is equally natural for us in our way to do the same. You feared to see the ghost of Mrs. Whichcote in the garden, and there she was. Dr. Jermyn looks for madmen for he has been trained to do so and he wishes to find them. Do they not provide him with his place in the world and a comfortable income? He interprets your ghost as a symptom of mental disturbance, whereas his father or grandfather would have seen it as a sign of demonic possession or some other supernatural interference in our mundane existence. We put the labels we choose on things, Mr. Oldershaw, and for our own purposes: that is the long and the short of it."

Frank moistened his lips. "And you? Is that what you do?"

"Of course."

"Then it follows you may be as wrong in your conclusions as Jermyn is in his."

"You may be right. But the difference between us is that I gather my evidence before I construct my theory, while the doctor looks for evidence that supports his theory. In all events, it seems to me that none of us can get very far unless we know what set all this in motion."

"But who can tell the causes of madness?"

"In this case, I believe you can. Leaving the question aside of whether this is truly madness or some lesser form of nervous disturbance, it is impossible for any of us to come to a rational conclusion if we do not know what happened at the meeting of the Holy Ghost Club that you attended in February, shortly before Mrs. Whichcote's death. This is the heart of it, sir, is it not? The Holy Ghost Club and the death of Mrs. Whichcote. That's why you have played host to an entire regiment of the blue devils. That's why you made matters worse with laudanum and wine and the rest of it."

Frank leaned forward and pushed the cat from his lap. He put his head in his hands. With his smooth skin and his fair disordered hair, he might have been a boy, no more than twelve, prey to some sorrow, or trapped in some misdemeanor. Holdsworth realized something so obvious that he could not understand why he had not seen it before: Frank's youth had played a part in all this. For all his airs and graces, for all his wealth and position, he was no more than eighteen. He was a desirable prize, too—a boy who would have a great fortune and a great place in the world. But still a boy. He had few defenses against older people who knew what they wanted and knew how to get it. He was easy meat for the likes of Philip Which-cote, Dr. Jermyn and even Mr. Richardson and the Carburys.

"What happened at the meeting of the Holy Ghost Club?"

Frank did not reply.

"Then let me hazard a conjecture or two."

The boy did not move but his stillness seemed to intensify.

"It seems to me that Lambourne House is a species of college and Mr. Whichcote is a species of tutor," Holdsworth went on. "And the club members are in a sense his pupils. In return for your money, he teaches you the vices of a gentleman."

Holdsworth waited, but still Frank said nothing.

"But something out of the ordinary occurred that night. Something that drove Mrs. Whichcote out of the house. Something that led to her death. I do not believe this nonsense about sleepwalking. Was she taken away? Or did she run away?"

Frank raised his head and looked at Holdsworth. He shut his eyes, as if to close out the world.

"Tell me," Holdsworth said. "I promise it will not harm you. And it may help."

"It was my doing," Frank whispered.

"Yours? How?"

"It was arranged that after the club meeting I should spend the night at Lambourne House. She . . . came to me, in my bedchamber."

A silence grew between them. The cat surveyed the room. After a moment's consideration it jumped on to Holdsworth's lap.

Frank stood up. "I have laid too many burdens on your shoulders already, Mr. Holdsworth," he said, with the vertiginously lofty dignity that only a very young man can achieve. "I apologize. I must learn to carry a little of the load myself."

"Come, sir, you can't stop now. Tell me the rest."

"I burned for her. I worshipped the very ground she trod on. I would have done anything for her. To my amazement, I found she returned my passion and—not to put too fine a point on it—on that very night she granted me the last favors."

Holdsworth stroked the cat's head. "And where was Mr. Whichcote in all this?"

"He was not in the house—he was escorting some of the club members back to their colleges. Most of them were in their cups and quite incapable of finding their way." Frank sat down again and rested his arms on the table. "But he came back, that was the trouble. He saw her coming out of my room, and then—well, God knows what happened. That devil Whichcote. I heard him shouting and her crying out. I think he beat her."

And what were you doing to prevent it?

Frank blundered on, as if Holdsworth had spoken the question aloud: "I would have stopped him if I could but he locked me in my chamber. And then it was too late. Early in the morning we were roused by Mepal banging on the door with the news of what had happened." He buried his head in his arms. "Dear God, Sylvia was so beautiful, Mr. Holdsworth, so lovely. She was all the world to me. And for her to end like that, running alone through the streets by night and drowning in a pond. Was ever anything so cruel?"

36

ADVERSITY, LIKE COMPETITION, brought out the best and the worst in Dr. Carbury. At times, he seemed almost his old, vigorous self. He bustled about the college and, as did Richardson, talked individually to most of the fellows. He announced that an extraordinary meeting of the fellowship would be held at midday tomorrow.

It would not do, he told Elinor, to let the college think he was skulking in the Master's Lodge because his protegé had been disgraced. She watched over him anxiously, as a wife should, though she scarcely knew whether her concern was more for him or for herself.

Mr. Archdale was summoned to see the Master. Elinor learned from her husband that Soresby had attended chapel as usual and had dined in hall. But the sizar sat by himself and talked to no one, and no one talked to him.

The Master's vigor stayed with him until the middle of the evening. He returned early from supper, leaning on Ben's arm, and had to be helped into bed. Elinor went to see him. He was exhausted and clearly in pain. But he would not allow her to send for a doctor or even for a nurse to sit up with him.

"No, no," he said testily, rolling his head from side to side. "I shall do very well as I am, Mrs. Carbury. Besides, if we send out for someone, the news will be around college in five minutes." He smiled grimly, wincing as he did so. "And Dirty Dick will start work on his eulogy of me. If he's not written it already."

He turned his face away and groaned. Elinor had had the apothecary make up a supply of opium pills. She took the little waxed box from her pocket, summoned Ben to help her, and persuaded her husband to take two of them. Ben raised him up and, ignoring her husband's discomfort, she forced him to take his doses. The pills at least eased the pain, which was more than the physicians had been able to do with their diagnoses and their degrees.

Dr. Carbury dozed fitfully. Elinor, Susan and Ben took it in turns to sit by the bedside. Elinor did not sleep. Throughout the night, the chimes of the college clock relentlessly announced the slow procession of quarters and hours. Day and night the chimes reminded her that she was in Jerusalem, her prison and her sanctuary.

She wondered whether she should summon another clergyman but decided against it on the grounds that it would only infuriate her husband because his true condition would then become known outside the Lodge. Also, it might make him more afraid because it would show that Elinor thought he was dying. Through the long hours, she told herself over and over again that he—and she—had grounds for hope. Her husband's constitution was enormously strong and he had survived worse crises than this one. She did not let herself think of what would happen to her if he died. She did not let herself think of John Holdsworth.

Two o'clock was striking as she left the sickroom, where Susan now sat beside the bed. Dr. Carbury was awake but comatose. He seemed free from pain. Elinor closed the door behind her and walked slowly and softly down the passage towards the door of her own room. She was tired but not sleepy. She paused by the window that lit the landing and pulled the curtain a few inches aside.

The window looked west, across the little court in front of the Lodge and over the town beyond. The rain had stopped during the afternoon. The sky had cleared. There were many stars and somewhere behind her there was a moon. The roofs, towers and spires lay before her like a sleeping herd of monsters. In their shadows clustered the lesser buildings of the townsfolk.

A movement caught her eye. There was somebody moving in the court below. She made out a dark figure making his way towards the railings that separated the court on its north side from Jerusalem Lane. The man's awkward and erratic movements reminded her of ungainly, long-legged insects like crane-flies.

In an instant, she remembered that when she and Sylvia were young at school, they had called such insects daddy-long-legs, and that Sylvia had trapped one and removed its legs, in a spirit of experiment rather than cruelty. It was true that Sylvia had never been cruel. But she had always been desperate for knowledge and hungry to experiment, and sometimes that had amounted to the same thing, for desire had always been its own vindication.

The memory of Sylvia brought with it a sour and nameless sensation, bitter as wormwood. Simultaneously, as if Sylvia herself had ignited a flare that threw a brief light on to the present, Elinor recognized the figure below as that of Mr. Soresby. He had reached the far corner of the court, where the railing met solid masonry. He hauled himself up and gingerly negotiated the spikes. For a few seconds she watched him clambering over the barrier, but suddenly he was gone, swallowed up by Jerusalem Lane.

She let the curtain fall across the window and returned to her room. Mr. Soresby had absconded. Her duty, she supposed, was to inform her husband immediately or, if that proved impossible, to send Ben with a message for Mr. Richardson. On the other hand, who would gain by it? Certainly neither the college nor Mr. Soresby. She could not blame the sizar for running away from a situation that promised him only disgrace. And who was she to make matters worse for him?

On Wednesday morning, Holdsworth woke to hear Mulgrave whistling cheerfully as he went about his work in the kitchen. It was nearly eight o'clock. He went downstairs, washed and sat in the cottage parlor, where Mulgrave brought him tea. The gyp had returned late yesterday evening. He had said nothing except that he had concluded a little business on his own behalf and that it had gone as well as could be expected.

"Is Mr. Oldershaw downstairs?" Holdsworth asked.

"Still abed, sir. Might I have a confidential word, sir?"

"What is it?"

The gyp took out a pocketbook, extracted a small newspaper cutting and laid it gently on the table. "From the *Chronicle*, sir. February last."

Holdsworth scanned the item. It recorded a verdict of accidental death on a fatality in Trumpington Street—a girl named Tabitha Skinner, fourteen years of age, who had suffered a fit as she slept and suffocated. The melancholy event had occurred on the night of Thursday, 16 February, at Mrs. Phear's house. Four months ago, Holdsworth thought, almost to the day. There was a particular pathos to the story, for the girl had been an orphan from the Magdalene Hospital in London. Mrs. Phear, the widow of a clergyman, was active in the affairs of the charity and had brought the girl to Cambridge at her own expense in the hope of apprenticing the unfortunate girl into domestic service.

He looked up. "When was Mrs. Whichcote found at Jerusalem? What date, precisely? Do you know?"

"The morning of Friday, the seventeenth of February, sir," Mulgrave said.

"Who is this Mrs. Phear? Does she come into this?"

"She once worked as the governess in the household of Mr. Whichcote's father, sir. I've seen her more than once at Lambourne House, and I believe Mr. Whichcote sometimes visits her in Trumpington Street." He waited a moment, his face impassive, but Holdsworth did not speak. "Shall I bring the rolls, sir, or will you wait until Mr. Frank joins you?"

"No—rouse him now, will you?"

The gyp limped up the stairs, dot and go one. He knocked on Frank's door. He rattled the handle. His footsteps descended, dot and go one.

"Not answering, sir. And the door's bolted."

Holdsworth went upstairs. He tried the door and called Frank's name. He raised the latch and threw his shoulder against the door. It burst open. He plunged into the room so quickly that he almost fell.

The bed was empty, the covers thrown back. There was no sign of Frank, and nowhere he could be hiding.

Mulgrave came up behind him. "At least he ain't hanged himself, sir. Not here, anyway."

"Hold your tongue," Holdsworth snapped, though a moment earlier the same thought had been in his own mind. He went across to the window, a small casement, which was immediately under the eaves and overhung with thatch. He put his head out and looked down. It was no drop at all for a man of Frank's size, not if he had managed to get through the window feet first and let himself down. There had once been a flower bed directly underneath, now full of weeds. It would have given him a soft landing.

Holdsworth withdrew his head and looked about him.

"He's took the coat and hat he wears for shooting," Mulgrave said. "And the stout shoes."

Holdsworth opened the drawers in the little chest, one by one. There was no telling what else Frank had taken, if anything. He found a purse containing a half a dozen guineas and some silver. Did Frank have other money? Or perhaps he hadn't needed money where he was going.

"So where the devil is he?" Holdsworth said.

Mulgrave glanced up at the ceiling, as if perhaps the answer lay there. "God knows," he said. After one of his carefully calculated pauses, he added, "Sir."

Early on Wednesday, 14 June, there was a hammering on the front door of Lambourne House. Augustus, who slept in a room beside the kitchen, was deep in a dream involving his long-dead father, a journeyman carpenter, and at first the hammering merged with the dream and became part of it. But then the noise transferred itself to the back door of the house and became louder. At last the sound forced Augustus reluctantly out of his dream and into the waking world.

As he stumbled out of bed, his first thought was that Mr. Whichcote would be in a fury at such a racket so early in the morning. The hammering continued even when he called out that he was making all speed he could. He struggled with the bolts on the kitchen door.

Outside in the yard were four men, none of whom he recognized. They gave him no opportunity to change his mind about admitting them. As soon as the door was open a crack, one of them had his foot over the threshold. Another pushed the door wide, took the footboy by the shoulder and moved him backward. The men pushed their way into the house.

"Bear witness, boys," said the eldest of the four, a man with a round red face and a great stomach straining against his waistcoat. "This obliging young lad asked us to step in. We have not forced an entry." He patted Augustus's head with a hand like a flap of belly pork. "Is Mr. Whichcote within?"

"Yes, sir. But he won't be stirring for—"

"Never you fear, he'll stir for us."

"But, sir, it's more than my place is worth."

The fat man laughed. "Why, your place ain't worth a brass farthing, so I wouldn't worry about that. Either you take us to your master directly or we find our own way. We're sheriff's officers, and I have a writ to serve against him. Who else is here?"

"Only me, sir."

"Other servants?"

"Cook left yesterday. So did the maid. There's old Jem, but he don't sleep in."

The fat man tramped upstairs, followed by his men. As he reached the first floor, Mr. Whichcote appeared in the doorway of his bedchamber. He was wearing only his nightshirt and his nightcap, and his delicate features were twisted with anger. "Who the devil are you?"

"Sheriff's officers, sir," the fat man said cheerfully. "I've got a writ against you here for seventy-nine pounds, eight shillings and fourpence at the suit of Mr. Mulgrave."

"Don't be a fool. He's lying. Besides—you can't come in here. You've forced an entry. I'll have you up before a magistrate."

"No, sir, you won't. This lad of yours invited us in, bless him. As all of us will swear on the Holy Bible itself if need be."

"God damn him, the little blockhead."

"All I care about is this writ, sir," the bailiff said. "And that tells me you got a debt to discharge, plus fees. You find me the money, sir, I give you a receipt, and away we go."

"Do you suppose I keep that sort of money in the house?"

"In that case I have to ask you to come along with me, sir. But there's no reason why we shouldn't do everything pleasant and easy, is there? You'll want to write a letter or two, I daresay. We shan't stop you doing that. And if you want an hour or two to make yourself ready, sir, you'll find us very obliging in that, and I'm sure you're a gentleman as knows how to show his gratitude."

Whichcote held up his hands as if attempting to make a physical barrier between himself and whatever was going to happen to him. "This is such a trifling matter," he said to the bailiff. "It could be so easily arranged. All it will take me is an hour or two."

"I am sure that will be very agreeable to all concerned, sir. Now, perhaps you'd like to dress. We ain't got all day, you know."

One of the sheriff's men waited on the landing. The bailiff ordered another in a stage whisper to wait outside Mr. Whichcote's window in case the gentleman was in a hurry to leave. He then invited Augustus to give him and his remaining colleague a tour of the house. The fat man moved from room to room like a prospective buyer. He did not seem impressed by what he saw.

"Oh, they've let things go here, my boy, haven't they? You'll be well out of it. Take my advice and look for another situation. You'll thank us one day, you know. This is only the start of it." He patted

Augustus's head in an avuncular way. "Writs are like sheep, you see. Once one of them finds its way out, all the others follow. You mark my words, we'll be serving more of them before the end of the day."

"But a gentleman like Mr. Whichcote—"

"Is a gentleman that owes money, that's all I care about, and in the eyes of the law that makes him as common as you or me. Maybe he'll be all right. Maybe he's got rents due at the end of the quarter. Maybe his creditors will come to an arrangement. But if you ask me, it all depends on whether his friends will rally to his help. That's what pulls a man through in these cases, nine times out of ten. But in the meantime it's the sponging house."

The bailiff, one of his men and the prisoner left in a closed carriage, the cost of which would also be charged to Mr. Whichcote. The other two men remained at Lambourne House to make sure, the fat man explained to Augustus, that nothing untoward happened to its contents in its master's absence. Their services would also be charged eventually to Mr. Whichcote. For another consideration, the fat man had agreed to have a letter conveyed to Mrs. Phear in Trumpington Street.

Left alone, the two sheriff's men took Augustus on another tour of the house. They kept up a running commentary on its contents, casting a critical eye over them and estimating their worth. Much depended, they condescendingly explained to Augustus, on who actually owned the house and on whether there was a mortgage on it. All being well, they assured him, the contents would raise a tidy sum, particularly the wine cellar.

They brought up a couple of bottles of wine and sat down with them at the kitchen table. They were not impressed, however, pronouncing the contents nasty thin stuff. It was a little after nine o'clock in the morning, while they were discussing whether or not they should try another bottle just to make absolutely sure, when there came a rapping on the hall door.

The officers accompanied Augustus when he answered it. The visitor was standing with his back to the door when Augustus opened it. At first the footboy took him for a tradesman, for he was plainly dressed and the dust on his lower half showed he had come a good way by foot. But when the man turned, Augustus recognized him at once.

"Where's your master?" Frank Oldershaw demanded.

37

ON THE SAME MORNING, while the college was in chapel, Dr. Milton called at the Master's Lodge. He was a dried-up little man, well past seventy, with a face like a prune and a snuff-stained waistcoat. His manner was never amiable but today it was worse than usual, partly because he had been forced to hurry his breakfast and partly because he had heard that his patient had had the temerity to call in a second opinion.

"Well, ma'am," he said to Elinor when he had seen Dr. Carbury, ordered a few ounces of blood to be taken from him, and prescribed more opium. "I do not know why you needed to send for Dr. Jermyn. He can have added nothing of value to my diagnosis. The case is as plain as the nose on my face."

"Then there is no possible room for doubt, sir?"

"None. It is a type of cancer that is beyond the reach of any physic."

"Perhaps a surgeon—?"

"No, ma'am, no. As I have already told Dr. Carbury, the location of the swelling rules out surgery entirely. The remedy would be as fatal as the disease, only swifter in action. The knife would kill him as it cut out the cancer."

Elinor turned aside. After a pause, she said quietly, "How long?"

"That is a harder question. It may be days or weeks—even months, though I doubt it. These matters are notoriously hard to calculate. So much depends on the progress of the disease and the constitution of the patient, you apprehend. I will continue to do my best, ma'am, but you should not expect miracles."

"No, sir," Elinor said. "Never that."

He looked sharply at her, suspecting irony, then took out his watch and said his other patients were awaiting him. When he had gone, Elinor stood by the window looking down over the Master's Garden and the Long Pond. She had known this day would come but had not expected it so soon. Her future had suddenly become a dark hole in the path before her; and she was sliding inexorably towards it, unable to change direction or even to delay the moment when she would fall into the pit.

There was a knock at the door and Susan came in to say that Dr. Carbury was awake and was asking for her. She found her husband in bed, propped up against the pillows. Beside the window sat a hired nurse with her knitting. The illness had aged him still further overnight and also shrivelled his face and body. His eyes, paradoxically, seemed to have grown more youthful. She had never had occasion before to pay much attention to them but now she realized they were large and lustrous, like those of a wolfhound Frank used to have in the country when he was a boy.

Dr. Carbury beckoned her towards him, nearer and nearer until her face was only inches from his. "Send the woman away," he whispered. "And have them bring me Soresby." His fingers gripped the sleeve of her dress. "It is most important, madam."

She tried to pull herself away, wondering whether Soresby had returned from his illicit excursion the previous evening. "It shall be done directly, sir."

"Soresby," he whispered. "Soresby."

They were interrupted by a knock at the chamber door. Mr. Richardson appeared; Ben followed behind him, his face fixed in an expression of mute appeal because Elinor had ordered him not to allow anyone to come up.

"Mrs. Carbury, your servant, ma'am." Richardson advanced into the room. "My dear Dr. Carbury, my gyp told me you had had Dr.

Milton this morning, and I simply could not keep away. I hope your indisposition is not serious?"

"Dr. Milton does not advise visitors," Elinor said. "He was most insistent."

"But I am hardly some chance acquaintance, ma'am." Richardson smiled, as if to take the sting from the words. "All of us in the combination room have been anxious for news and of course we are praying that it will be good news. Besides, you may remember that the fellows are due to meet at midday and this business with poor Mr. Soresby makes it particularly urgent that we should do so. If the Master is too unwell to attend, I suppose I must do my poor best to take his place for the occasion."

Carbury, who until this moment had given no sign that he had noticed his visitor, turned his head on the pillow and stared fixedly at the far wall.

"I regret to say that the Master will probably not be well enough to join you today, sir," Elinor said. "The doctor has ordered him to rest."

"Oh dear." Richardson's face became a picture of sorrow and concern. He neatly sidestepped Elinor so he could address the figure on the bed directly. "Goodbye, my dear friend, and you may be sure I shall pray for your speedy restoration to health."

The tutor bowed again to Elinor. But at the door he stopped. "By the way—have you heard the news? Mr. Soresby was not in chapel this morning. I sent over to Yarmouth Hall but his room is empty. I regret to say that he appears to have absconded. It's scarcely the act of an innocent man, is it? But I hope that no harm has come to him."

Dr. Carbury groaned. Elinor turned. Her husband had not moved: he was still staring at the far wall.

"Damn the man," he said. "Damn him. Damn, damn, damn."

The smith, up early to tend his forge, had seen Frank Oldershaw walking south through Whitebeach not long after dawn. He had wished him good morning but Frank had not replied. The sighting confirmed that Frank was almost certainly making for Cambridge.

Holdsworth walked after him. Once he reached Cambridge, he tried Jerusalem first. Mepal, standing by the gates with his little eyes bright with curiosity, told him that he had not seen Mr. Oldershaw since they took him to Barnwell all those weeks ago. He advised Holdsworth against calling at the Master's Lodge at present, explaining that Dr. Carbury was indisposed. Mr. Richardson was unavailable, for he had just begun a lecture. Holdsworth asked after Mr. Archdale, only to learn that the young gentleman was among Mr. Richardson's audience.

He walked back the way he had come and crossed the bridge. In Chesterton Lane, the gates of Lambourne House stood open. Could Frank have been so foolish as to go there? A man in a frayed brown coat was smoking a pipe on the front doorstep. He wore a red-spotted handkerchief round his neck and watched Holdsworth's approach with a detached, faintly amused air, as a man with time on his hands might watch the antics of a stray dog. The door stood open behind him. Inside the house, someone was whistling "The Girl I Left Behind Me."

Holdsworth had never seen the fellow before but there was no doubt about his identity. There were enough of the breed in London, and Holdsworth had lived in fear of finding a pair of them—they rarely worked alone—outside his own door.

"If you're looking for Mr. Whichcote, he ain't here," the man said, removing his pipe and peering into the bowl.

"Where is he, pray?"

"A pressing engagement elsewhere, that's what I'd call it." Like so many of his fellows, the sheriff's officer had developed a taste for elephantine humor, a perquisite of petty power.

"Do you mean to tell me he's been taken up for debt?" Holdsworth asked.

"Ask me no questions, I tell you no lies."

"At whose suit? How much for?"

The man tapped his nose with the pipe-stem. "Ah—I cannot quite call the name or the amount to mind."

Holdsworth sighed and felt in his pocket for a shilling. He held the little silver coin in the palm of his hand, just outside the officer's reach.

"A matter of eighty pound," the man said, his eyes on the shilling. "And fees and expenses. Suit of Mr. Mulgrave."

"Where's Mr. Whichcote now?"

The man tapped his nose again, and continued to do so until Holdsworth had placed another shilling beside the first.

"At Mr. Purser's in Wall Lane, sir."

"Mr. Purser's your master?"

The officer nodded. Holdsworth dropped the two shillings into the outstretched hand, smelling the wine on the man's breath as he did so. "Do you happen to know if a young gentleman called here to see Mr. Whichcote this morning?"

"Big fellow? Fresh-faced?"

"The very man."

The man tapped his nose again but then looked at Holdsworth's face and thought better of negotiating for more.

"He was in a devilish hurry to see Mr. Whichcote, I tell you that."

"Was that before or after he was taken up by Mr. Purser?"

"After. You've only just missed him. We sent him over to Wall Lane. Maybe he's going to lend Mr. Whichcote the ready. Mind you, he'll need deep pockets. More to come before the end of the day."

"More what?"

"More writs."

They had shown Whichcote into an apartment on the first floor near the back of the tall, thin house. The building belied its narrow frontage, straggling back from Wall Lane under a cluster of ill-assorted roofs. He sat with his elbows on the scarred table, supporting his head. Everything he was, everything he depended upon, rested on his being Philip Whichcote of Lambourne House. He had worried enough about his debts before, but in his heart he had felt he was armored against the worst consequences of owing money to other people. A gentleman lived on credit: that was entirely to be expected. For a man of his rank to be harried by Mulgrave, who was little better than a servant, was against the natural order of things.

Someone was knocking on the street door. The hammering seemed to pound in time with his headache, the one exacerbating the other. In a place like this there was necessarily a good deal of coming and going. He knew that Purser must be entertaining other guests, as he tactfully called them—the more fortunate class of debtors, those who had connections who were likely to pay their debts in the long run, one way or another, and in the meantime were in possession of sufficient resources to pay for their board and lodging at Purser's. The bailiff's charges were exorbitantly expensive but the sponging house was infinitely preferable to the debtors' prison, the only alternative.

There was a tap at his door and Purser's manservant showed in Mrs. Phear. Abandoning ceremony for once, she came straight to him and took his hands in hers. Neither of them spoke until they were alone.

"I came at once when I had your note," she said softly.

"I am ruined, ma'am."

"Whose suit? And how much?"

"Mulgrave's. Ninety pounds would see me clear of him and deal with Purser's fees too."

She frowned, calculating. "Then we shall have you out in an hour or two at most."

"If only it were that simple. They will all be at it now. God knows what the whole will amount to."

"Hundreds?"

"Thousands, probably."

Releasing his hands, she sat down beside him. "I cannot lay my hands on a sum like that. Can you raise the money, if you were given time?"

He shrugged. "As likely see a hog fly."

She stared at him, her eyebrows a little raised.

"I beg your pardon, ma'am," he said quickly, alert as ever to her moods and even in this situation amused by her genteel abhorrence of a vulgarism. "I spoke without thinking. But truly, there is no hope left."

"What about the house? Can you raise anything on that?"

"I have only a life interest. And I've already borrowed on the strength of that. If I cannot redeem the bill at Michaelmas, or failing that renegotiate it, I am entirely done for. I will lose the house."

Without the house, there would be no meetings of the Holy Ghost Club. Without the house, he would not have a roof over his head.

"Are you owed money?"

"Perhaps a hundred or two. But I have no chance of laying my hands on a penny for months, if not years. You know what these young cubs are with their gambling debts. They run them up and then, if they cannot pay, what can one do but wait?"

She left him and went to the window. He knew what she would see there: the house had eaten up half the little garden. There was a scrubby little yard, a privy and a pigsty, where one could watch the lean backs of two hogs as they rooted in the mud.

"Perhaps hogs *can* fly," she said.

"What?"

"You are wrong to abandon hope," she said calmly. "I have sufficient resources laid by to deal with Mulgrave. That will buy us a little time."

"What use is a few hours? The writs will be flying again before I get home."

She looked sternly at him. "Even a little time may be enough."

The room was stuffy and smelled of illness. At first Dr. Carbury was restless, turning this way and that as he tried to make himself comfortable. As the hours slipped by, he grew quieter. Elinor sat by his bed until she heard eleven o'clock striking, when she rose and tiptoed to the door. She waited there for a few seconds, listening to her husband's heavy breathing.

The nurse, who was knitting by the window, looked up. Elinor whispered that she would soon return. She left her husband's bedroom and almost ran downstairs. Without pausing for thought she left the Lodge by the garden door and walked slowly down the gravel walk towards the pond.

More than ever, she needed a clear head. She could no longer rely on the protection of her husband. She had known for months that he was ill, but it was only now, after Milton's visit this morning, that she was forced to accept that he was dying, and that the melancholy event could be expected within weeks, or even days.

If she was not to be utterly ruined, Lady Anne's support was more than ever essential. All her ladyship wanted was the restoration of her son to her. If Elinor could earn her gratitude by helping Frank, then truly anything might be possible.

Even John Holdsworth?

The last question set off an undesirable train of thought. Or, to be precise, not exactly undesirable in every sense, but certainly inappropriate, immoral and inconvenient. Breathing faster than usual, she reached the Long Pond at its widest point, opposite the oriental plane. It was here they had found Sylvia. After a moment's hesitation, Elinor took the path along the bank to the gate by the Frostwick Bridge. She laid her fingers on the gate's wrought-iron screen, touching it at the precise spot where Holdsworth's hand had touched hers. The metal was cold, rough and unresponsive. She snatched her hand away. She opened the gate and walked quickly over the bridge.

As far as she could tell, she had the college gardens to herself. She slipped under the shelter of the plane, which enclosed her like an enormous green tent, with its branches hanging like curtains to the ground.

It was cool and private here. No one could see her. She could think of anything she wanted. Goodbye, Sylvia; forgive me and now leave me. She hugged herself and tried to imagine what it would be like to have a man's arms around her.

Come what may, she decided, she would write to Lady Anne when she got back to the Lodge. She would tell her that Dr. Carbury was dying.

But she was not alone after all. Wheels rattled and scraped on the flagstones of the chapel arcade. Someone was talking. Keeping well back, she changed her position so she could see through a gap between the branches. At first she thought Tom Turdman was making his rounds. She realized her mistake as a man and a woman appeared, framed in one of the arches of the arcade.

It was Philip Whichcote. And on his arm was a dumpy little lady old enough to be his mother.

As Elinor watched, they walked along the façade of New Building. Behind them came a barrow piled high with portmanteaus and boxes and drawn by two servants, scarcely more than children. Elinor recognized Whichcote's footboy. The other was a tall, thin girl whose legs and arms had grown too long for her dress.

The rooms in New Building were arranged in sets served by three staircases. Whichcote went into the nearer of the staircases, accompanied by the lady. The barrow stopped and the servants set to unloading its cargo.

Whichcote was coming into residence. It was a sign, Elinor thought, a manifestation of God's displeasure with her for her adulterous desires. How could she forget Sylvia when Whichcote was here?

38

W HAT THE DEVIL do you think you're up to?" Holdsworth said.

"None of your business." Frank glared at him. "You said you
could do nothing more for me, so I'm doing it myself instead."

They were on the corner of Wall Lane and King Street. Holdsworth's irritation subsided rapidly, for Frank was so clearly safe
and more or less in his right mind.

"How did you know where to find me?" Frank said.

"I met a sheriff's man at Lambourne House when I came searching for you. Why did you run off like a thief in the night?"

Frank flushed. "I knew you'd try to stop me. But I won't be
stopped, do you hear? I've been living a nightmare all these weeks,
and I have determined to deal with it once and for all."

"I am rejoiced to hear it," Holdsworth said. "And I would not
stand in your way for the world. Have you seen Mr. Whichcote?"

"They would not let me in."

"Have you eaten this morning?"

"I've not had time."

"Nor have I. Let's remedy that now. If they won't allow you to see
Mr. Whichcote, there's nothing you can do here for the moment,
and we cannot talk in the street."

Frank allowed himself to be drawn down King Street, where the
smells through the open door of a coffee house added to the force

of Holdsworth's arguments. They went inside. It was a down-at-heel establishment frequented in the main by poorer students. No one paid much attention to the newcomers.

They ordered a substantial breakfast. While they waited, Holdsworth tried to initiate a conversation, but Frank avoided this by seizing one of the newspapers that were about the place and reading it with great concentration.

After they had eaten, however, he laid down his fork and said casually, "I'm damned if I'll skulk in the country any more."

"No more quack quack then?"

Frank laughed. "No more quack quack."

"What will you do?"

"Why, I shall go back to Jerusalem. And I shall deal with Whichcote as he deserves, one way or another. For Sylvia's sake."

Dear God, Holdsworth thought, pray do not let the young fool call him out. The romantic and quite possibly fatal trappings of a duel were just the thing to appeal to a young man in Frank's condition.

"There's no point in delaying," Frank went on. "I shall return today. Now, in fact."

"Now? Should you not at least write and—?"

"I do not think there is the slightest need to do so." He stared down his nose at Holdsworth. "I do not think I am under any obligation to consult anyone's convenience in the matter."

"I have a question for you."

Frank shook his head. "I've nothing more to tell you so you need not trouble to ask. Besides, I have told you enough already. My mother hired you to be my keeper, Mr. Holdsworth. Whatever I say will go straight back to her."

"You forget, sir. I discharged myself. And you confirmed that yourself when you told me why you walked into Cambridge without informing me of the fact. Anything we talk about will therefore be in the nature of a private conversation. If you tell me anything that you wish to remain confidential, it will be so."

Holdsworth sat back and poured himself another cup of coffee. He knew his argument was sophistical. But that, he thought, might not signify very much. This was not a matter of reason, and never had been. The only problem was that Frank was sitting tight-lipped and silent. He showed no sign of wanting to talk about anything.

"Tabitha Skinner," Holdsworth said, abandoning finesse.

"Never heard of her. Who's she?"

"A fourteen-year-old girl. She died on the same night as Mrs. Whichcote, apparently in consequence of a fit, in the house of Mrs. Phear in Trumpington Street."

Frank shook his head. "Never heard of her either."

"I cannot believe that the two deaths are not linked in some way," Holdsworth said. "The same night. The connection between Mrs. Phear and Mr. Whichcote. And the meeting of the Holy Ghost Club."

"Well, if they are I know nothing about it," Frank said, pushing back his chair. "You'll oblige me by putting this out of your mind entirely. I shall go back to college now."

"Perhaps you'd permit me to walk with you," Holdsworth suggested. "I shall have to call at the Lodge to tell Dr. Carbury that I am no longer acting for her ladyship, at least in regard to you. And I'd better advise Mr. Richardson of it too, as your tutor."

"You may accompany me," Frank announced in a lordly manner. "It would not inconvenience me in the slightest."

"Then once we have paid our shot here, we may as well be on our way."

Frank waved to the waiter. Suddenly his assurance dropped away. "I have no money on me, as it happens. That's why that blockhead at the sponging house wouldn't let me in."

Holdsworth said nothing.

"I'd ask them to send me the bill," Frank rushed on, "but they do not know me here and it might be a little tiresome. If you'd advance what's necessary, it would oblige me extremely."

Holdsworth bowed politely. Frank seesawed between needy schoolboy and imperious young gentleman. When he opened his mouth, it was hard to know which of them would speak.

On their way back to Jerusalem, Frank's irritation evaporated and he grew more and more cheerful. He looked about him as they went, peering in shop windows and surreptitiously glancing at the prettier girls they passed. "I have been so dull these last few weeks," he said as they were passing Christ's. "I had not realized how much I missed all this."

They met no one they knew on the way. Frank was travel-stained and dressed in the clothes he wore for shooting. He was not immediately recognizable, shorn of his trappings as a fellow-commoner. But all this changed once they passed the gates of Jerusalem. Mepal saw them enter and was outside his lodge in a flash.

"Mr. Oldershaw, sir." He doffed his hat and bowed as low as he was able. "A sight for sore eyes, sir, if I may be so bold."

"I'm glad to be back," Frank said with a wave that embraced the entire college and conveyed the impression that all of it belonged to him. "I want someone to go over to Whitebeach Mill. They must tell Mulgrave he must close up there and bring our belongings— mine and Mr. Holdsworth's—back to college. I shall want to see him as soon as he's here. In the meantime, where's my bedmaker?"

"Sal, sir? She's on your staircase now, sir, in Mr. Archdale's rooms."

"Send her to me. And I want a shave, too. Send for the barber as well. You'd better tell Sal I want hot water brought up. By the bye, is Mr. Richardson in the way? I should call on him first."

Mepal's eyes slid towards Holdsworth, who had played no part in the conversation but had remained to one side, a spectator. "The fellows are in the combination room, sir. College meeting."

"Oh. So Dr. Carbury will be there?"

"I regret to say the Master is unwell, sir."

"I'm sorry to hear that." Frank glanced at Holdsworth, as if for guidance. "I shall go to—" His forehead wrinkled. "Good God."

He was staring past Mepal and Holdsworth. Holdsworth turned. The court itself was empty, but there were two figures, a tall, thin girl and a smaller but equally thin boy, framed in the arched opening at the right-hand end of the chapel arcade.

Frank said, "Isn't that Whichcote's footboy?"

"Yes, sir," Mepal said. "He's attending Mr. Whichcote."

"Whichcote?" Frank spoke so loudly that the boy heard and raised his head. "Do you mean to tell me he's here in college?"

Augustus picked up a small but heavy black valise stamped with Whichcote's crest and secured with two brass locks. He staggered with it to the bedroom door.

"Not in there," Mrs. Phear said. "In the other room, the little study."

Augustus changed direction. Dorcas was already there, setting up a writing desk on the table.

The pile of baggage stood just inside the sitting-room door. Mrs. Phear was at the table. Whichcote stood on the hearthrug in front of the empty fireplace, his thumbs hooked in his waistcoat pockets.

"Words cannot express how obliged I am—" he began.

"Words need not express anything at all, my dear Philip." She lowered her voice. "Mr. Richardson made no difficulty?"

"None in the slightest. He's not a fool. He grasped the situation in an instant."

"Still, I am surprised he did not need more convincing."

"Two reasons for that, I fancy, ma'am. The first is that he was already late for a meeting in the combination room. And the second reason, the more important, is that the situation at Jerusalem is particularly delicate at present." He winced as Augustus allowed the edge of the valise to graze the corner of the table.

"The reason for the meeting?"

"On the surface, at least—there is some scandal afoot involving one of the sizars. He was caught red-handed in a theft and now he's run off. But the real news is the Master. It appears he is very ill."

Mrs. Phear's eyes slid away from the window. "Dying?"

"I believe Richardson thinks he may be. Certainly he wishes it. And if he does, there will be an election. The very last thing Richardson will want is anything else that smacks of scandal. A word or two in the right ears would quite destroy his chances. To be a head of house, the Master of Jerusalem, is the very summit of his ambitions."

There was a clatter from the study and a sharp intake of breath. When Augustus and Dorcas came out of the room Mrs. Phear beckoned them over.

"A faithful servant is pleasing in the eyes of God," Mrs. Phear announced. "A faithful servant never prattles of his master's business. He is always on the watch to find any way he may serve his master better. On the other hand, an unfaithful servant infallibly lives to regret his treachery. He will weep bitter tears. And then, after his miserable death, he will go to hell."

The children stared at the carpet. The tips of Augustus's ears turned red. Dorcas dug her nails into her pale, freckled forearms, which were already covered with scratches.

"Well, get along with you," Mrs. Phear said indulgently. "Satan soon finds work for idle hands."

In a touching display of quasi-feudal loyalty, the bedmaker showed her joy at seeing Mr. Frank by throwing her apron over her head and weeping loudly. Embarrassed, Frank fulfilled his side of the bargain by asking Holdsworth to give her half-a-crown on his behalf. When matters had been settled to everyone's satisfaction, the bedmaker departed in search of hot water and Frank made a tour of his rooms.

Holdsworth sat at the table with pen and ink and began to write a letter. He had hardly begun when Frank returned to the sitting room and stood over him, blocking the light. The young man dropped something metallic on the table, a gilt button that sparkled in the sunlight.

Holdsworth touched it with his forefinger. It was the missing button from Frank's coat in the club livery. Mr. Richardson had mentioned that it was on the dressing table when he showed Holdsworth the rooms.

"*Sans souci*," Frank said. He swallowed. "Devilish funny, ain't it?"

"Why?"

Frank did not reply but a flicker of movement passed across his features. His eyes had filled with tears. He turned aside and examined the spines of the volumes in the bookcase.

"What is it?" Holdsworth said.

"Nothing." Frank did not turn. "Nothing at all."

After a moment, Holdsworth dipped his pen in the ink and continued the letter.

"Anyway, what are you doing?" Frank said, still staring at the books.

"Writing to her ladyship to acquaint her with what's happened and inform her that you are back in residence in Jerusalem. And therefore I intend to resign my responsibilities."

Frank swung round. "No, Mr. Holdsworth, pray don't do that."

"Write to your mother?"

"No—resign. I have turned it over in my mind and—well, I spoke hastily just now. I'd much rather you stayed with me for a little while yet."

"I consider I have discharged what her ladyship hired me to do, sir."

"And so indeed you have, as far as it touches me. Still, I would take it as a favor if you would delay your departure. I might have a relapse, after all, and there's the matter of the college library and my father's books, remember. My mother will still want your advice on that."

Holdsworth looked at him without speaking. Then he shrugged. "I will make a bargain with you, sir. I will agree to stay for two or three nights, to conclude my survey of the library for her ladyship."

"Thank you, sir, I take it kindly, I do indeed, and—"

"On one condition. That you do not cause a scandal with Mr. Whichcote. If you encounter him while you are here, you must ignore him as far as possible. You must not offer him any provocation."

"But, sir, I cannot—" There was a knock on the door and Frank stopped speaking. Unexpectedly his face broke into a smile.

"Very well, sir," he murmured to Holdsworth. He raised his voice. "Come in."

The door opened, and Mr. Richardson entered. The tutor seized Frank's hand and shook it up and down. He congratulated Frank on his restoration to health. Such was his emotion, he too wiped away what appeared to be a tear from his eye.

"Well, sir, I won't pretend I'm not glad to be back," Frank said. "But pray tell me, what's Mr. Whichcote doing here? We saw his footboy as we came in and Mepal says he's staying in college."

"That's quite correct, Mr. Oldershaw."

"I wish he wasn't, sir."

"I'm afraid Mr. Whichcote's affairs are somewhat embarrassed. When he asked me for refuge, I could hardly deny him. It's not easy to turn away an old Jerusalem man in distress."

"I hear more writs are on the way," Holdsworth said.

Richardson bowed. "You're well informed, sir. But the bailiffs cannot reach him here. He will be perfectly safe as long as he does not stir from the boundaries of the college during the day, except on Sundays. He will have leisure to arrange his affairs and find the way out of his difficulties. But now let us talk of something more pleasant. I hope you will prolong your stay in Jerusalem, Mr. Holdsworth? We must not forget the library."

"Just what I've been saying, sir," Frank put in. "My mother would insist on it."

"In that case you must not refuse us, sir. By the way, did you tell Mr. Oldershaw the sad news about our library clerk, Mr. Soresby?"

Holdsworth shook his head.

"Soresby?" Frank said. "The sizar? What of him?"

"I regret to say he stands accused of stealing a book from the library," Richardson said. "Such a promising young man, too, and with the world at his feet. To compound the matter further, he has run off."

"How very tiresome," Frank said mechanically. "Oh, and by the way, sir, Mepal says the Master is indisposed. Where will Mr. Holdsworth stay? He had better not go back to the Master's Lodge."

"If I am to be here for another day or two, I'll find lodgings in the town," Holdsworth said.

"No, no," Frank said. "I am sure Mr. Richardson would not hear of it—eh, sir?"

"The college would be delighted to entertain you, Mr. Holdsworth. Leave it with me, and I shall see what can be done. We shall find you somewhere in New Building, I am sure." Richardson turned to Frank. "You will dine in hall with us, I hope, Mr. Oldershaw? That is, if you are well enough. Perhaps you would prefer to rest after your journey from Whitebeach."

"Thank you, sir, I am perfectly well," Frank said testily. "I shall dine in hall. And Mr. Holdsworth too."

Richardson smiled. "Oh yes, of course—and Mr. Holdsworth."

39

R EMEMBER," MRS. PHEAR SAID, "you must not stir outside the college walls during the day."

"Why, ma'am, I can hardly forget with those jackals waiting at the gates."

There came the sound of breaking crockery from the gyp room where Augustus and Dorcas were clearing away the tea things.

Mrs. Phear screwed up her mouth. "Dorcas," she said, not troubling to raise her voice unduly.

Her maid appeared, wiping her hands on her apron, and curtsied clumsily.

"What was broken? Who was responsible?"

"If you please, ma'am, it was a teacup, and it slipped out of my hand, ma'am, I'm terrible sorry, I—"

"You're a wicked, clumsy girl," Mrs. Phear observed without anger, as one expressing a fact. "You shall go without your dinner today. I have noticed before, an overfull stomach makes you inattentive and stupid."

"If you please, ma'am," Augustus said, from the doorway of the gyp room. "Please don't be hard on her, it was my fault, she was handing it to me, and I—"

"Be silent," Whichcote snapped.

Mrs. Phear turned back to Whichcote and said in the sweet, soft voice she reserved for him, "I shall leave you, my dear. I must have my dinner and you will soon want yours."

"You must allow me to escort you, ma'am."

"At least as far as the gates." She smiled at him. "But mind you lock your doors here. The door of the study, as well as your oak. Your future is there."

Followed by Dorcas, Mrs. Phear and Whichcote went downstairs and into the sunshine. Mrs. Phear paused on the way to admire the majestic spread of the oriental plane.

"It is truly charming," she observed. "If you have to spend a few weeks in exile, there are worse places to be."

They strolled through the arcade and across Chapel Court to the main gate. Mepal was not in his lodge but outside on the forecourt by St. Andrew's Street, engaged in conversation with two men wearing black.

Mrs. Phear laid her hand on Whichcote's arm. "Ah—your jackals, I fancy."

They shook hands. But before Mrs. Phear passed through the gateway, they heard quick, light footsteps behind them. Augustus ran up to them with a handkerchief that he held out to Mrs. Phear with a low, swift bow, like a duck tucking its head underwater.

"Found it on your chair, ma'am."

Mrs. Phear nodded to Dorcas, who stepped forward, head bowed, and took the handkerchief from Augustus. Whichcote saw the girl's sidelong glance at Augustus, and his at her. Surely Mrs. Phear's beanpole and his own grubby dwarf could not be sweethearts? The very idea struck him as so bizarre that he almost laughed out loud.

When Mrs. Phear had gone, Whichcote walked back to his rooms. He paused outside his staircase in New Building. As chance would have it, Frank was coming from the direction of the Jericho, looking across the garden as he walked. He did not see Whichcote until it was too late to avoid him.

"I am rejoiced to see you in college," Whichcote said blandly. He was alert for any possibility of violence; he would not be caught off guard again. "Dare your friends hope that this means you are entirely recovered? I do hope so."

Frank muttered something and tried to slip past him.

Whichcote moved to block him. "We shall be near neighbors. Augustus, go upstairs and wait for me outside my door." He waited until the boy was gone. "I have come into residence myself for a few days, or even a few weeks. I'm here in New Building—in G4. You must do me the honor of calling on me."

"I'll see you damned first."

"That remains to be seen. If I were to tell the authorities what you did to that girl and bring witnesses to support the accusation, it is very probable that you would be damned before me."

"What do you mean—what in God's name do you want?"

"All in good time. I am sure we shall discuss this further. You may be interested to hear that I took the precaution of bringing the archives of the Holy Ghost Club when I came into college. They are exquisitely absorbing. For example, there's your signature, all duly witnessed, in the membership book. You were pleased enough to become an Apostle, weren't you? And you did so on the very night the girl died. On the very night that all these people saw you with her, about to seize her and deflower her. Yes, just before she died. The implication must be that the one led to the other."

Frank seized Whichcote's arm. "You blackguard," he hissed. "How dare you? Is this your revenge for Sylvia? And for me giving you a ducking?"

Whichcote stared at him but said nothing. Frank was larger than he was and Whichcote already knew the young man's capacity for violence. But he also knew that power takes many forms. After a few seconds, Frank released his grip and took a step back.

Whichcote straightened the sleeve of his coat. "We shall talk later. No doubt you will want to run to your bear-leader, Holdsworth, and cry on his shoulder. You must not let me detain you. But I warn you, it won't answer. You and I will have to come to an accommodation sooner or later."

Elinor Carbury had a headache. She sat at her writing table and composed the third draft of her letter to Lady Anne Oldershaw. She hated herself for writing it. Life had made her do a great many things that encouraged her to hate herself.

There was a tap on the door, and Susan entered. She closed the door and stood with head bowed, waiting for her mistress to speak.

"What is it?" Elinor said, dipping her pen in the inkwell.

There was no reply. She glanced at her maid. There were tears running down her cheeks.

"What is it?" Elinor repeated, more sharply. "For heaven's sake—"

"Oh, ma'am, I have been so foolish." The girl cried harder. "So sinful," she gulped between sobs. "And you such a kind mistress! So generous! Oh, my heart could break."

"Do stop crying and tell me what it is," Elinor ordered.

Susan looked up. She said quietly, in her normal voice, "Oh, ma'am—I'm with child."

Elinor had a brief and unwelcome vision of white muscular thighs pumping up and down in the washhouse. "You foolish girl. Whose is it? Ben's?"

The maid nodded. "I couldn't help myself, ma'am, he was so pressing. I'm sorry to trouble you, now of all times, with the Master like he is."

"Are you sure?"

"Yes, ma'am—I've missed my courses twice and soon it'll be again."

"Has this been going on for long?"

"Since March—he persuaded me to walk out with him one night under the big tree and . . . and he took advantage of me. Soon the baby will show. You'll turn me out without a character and it'll be the poorhouse for—"

"Do stop talking," Elinor snapped. "You're making my headache worse. Can you not marry Ben and be done with it?"

There was a knock on the door downstairs.

"He'd lose his place and so would I, ma'am. And we've nothing to fall back on."

"Let me turn it over in my mind," Elinor said. "You have been a very foolish girl. But perhaps something can be retrieved."

A visitor was coming up the stairs. Ben announced Mr. Richardson. The servant's eyes widened as he saw Susan standing red-faced by the door. Mr. Richardson bowed, with a graceful flutter of his fingers. Elinor sent the servants away.

"I do not wish to disturb the Master," Richardson said when they were alone. "But I wanted to find out how my dear friend does. Is there any change?"

"No, sir. He is sleeping. The nurse is with him and has orders to call me when he wakes."

"Ah—what does the poet tell us?—'Tir'd Nature's sweet restorer, balmy Sleep!'" Richardson murmured. "I bring with me the good wishes of the entire fellowship, of course, and the assurance of our prayers. But one other reason I presumed to call again was that I had a piece of news. News that Dr. Carbury may find cheering. And so, I believe, will you, my dear madam. Mr. Oldershaw has returned to college."

"I am rejoiced to hear it. Is he paying a visit or—?"

"Oh no. He seems fully restored, and I believe he intends to come back into residence, at least until the end of term."

"I shall be sure to tell Dr. Carbury. What of Mr. Holdsworth? Since Mr. Oldershaw no longer has any need of him, I suppose he will return to London."

"Not yet. He has to complete his survey of the library, and it is not impossible that Mr. Oldershaw may have need of him again. So I have arranged for him to have a guest apartment in New Building. When he heard how things were with the Master, he did not want to disturb him—or of course you, madam."

Elinor bowed her head. "Is there news of Mr. Soresby?"

"He appears to have vanished from the face of the earth. But we have another visitor. Mr. Whichcote is in college. I hope this won't distress you."

Elinor looked up and surprised an air of calculation on the tutor's face. "Why should you suppose it might?"

"I feared the sight of him might bring painful memories of your dear friend, Mrs. Carbury. I meant nothing else."

She thanked Richardson for his consideration. She said nothing more and he rose to take his leave. After he had gone, she sat at her writing desk, pen in hand, but could not write another word. She thought about her dying husband, about John Holdsworth, almost within a stone's throw of where she sat, and about Sylvia. Elinor did not know whether she loved or hated Sylvia now. Richardson had touched a sore spot when he mentioned her. All the memories were painful.

Later, when the nurse told Elinor that her husband was awake, she went into his room. They were alone, for the nurse was downstairs. The curtains were drawn against the glare of the day. Dr. Carbury was lying on his back with the covers wrapped around him like a straitjacket. He stared at her with his huge doglike eyes.

"How are you, sir? Do you feel rested?"

He ignored the questions. "Is there news?"

"Mr. Oldershaw is returned, and Mr. Richardson says he is fully restored."

"Good. But what of Soresby?"

"Nothing, sir. I hope no harm has come to the poor young man."

"Aye, that is certainly a possibility." Carbury's head reared up from the pillows in a sudden access of energy. "Self-murder. Now I think of it, it is not at all unlikely."

"I hope it's not so."

Her husband appeared not to have heard her. His head fell back heavily on the pillows. "Soresby dead?" he muttered to himself. "Yes, very likely. Quite, quite dead. But is it too much to hope for?"

"That devil has brought the club archives with him," Frank said to Holdsworth as soon as he came back from the Jericho. "They are in his rooms, and he will blackmail me with them. Dear God, to think I esteemed him once. I thought him a man of breeding. What's to be done?"

"Nothing in haste, Mr. Oldershaw."

Frank glared at him. "That's all very well for you to say, sir, but—"

There was a knock at the door and Harry Archdale bounced into the room like a cheerful cherub.

"My dear Frank, how do you do!" He seized Frank's hand and pumped it up and down. "You're back at last, safe and sound. I give you joy of it. A happy return indeed."

Holdsworth bowed and drew back, looking for an excuse to withdraw.

"Have you heard our latest excitement?" Archdale said after the first greetings were over. "Soresby has disappeared."

"Ricky told us just now. Bit of a scrub, eh? Always cracking his knuckles, like a regular fusillade."

Archdale wrinkled his nose. "There's been hell to pay. I can't understand it myself—he was Carbury's pet. The old man had even reserved a fellowship for him."

"I thought Soresby was Ricky's man. By the way, have you been down to the stables lately? My horses have been—"

"Wait, Frank—this Soresby business—you haven't heard to the end of it. I was coming into college just now and Mepal runs up with a parcel. Somebody left it in the box last night—he didn't see who. And it turns out it's from Soresby." Archdale took a small, slim volume from his pocket. "Look here."

Frank took the book and opened it to the title-page. "Euclid? What on earth's this?"

"I am become quite the reading man since you last saw me. But that's not the point. This was inside. See here."

Archdale held out a scrap of paper, which looked as if it had been torn from a pocketbook. Holdsworth drew nearer and read the few words it contained over Frank's shoulder.

Mr. Archdale—here is the book. Mr. Dow's second paragraph on page 41 must be mastered if one is to grasp Proposition 47 (the Pythagorean Theorem). Pray do not believe this terrible lie about me. I swear I did not steal anything. T. S.

40

DINNER WAS STILL AN HOUR and a half away. Holdsworth made his excuses and left the two young gentlemen to talk among themselves. It was as well that he had agreed to stay with Frank for a day or two longer, now there was the new danger from Whichcote. Besides, what did he have in London to go back to?

In his heart, he knew there were other and more powerful reasons for him to stay, though he could barely admit some of them to himself and certainly not to Frank. The unexplained deaths of Sylvia Whichcote and Tabitha Skinner irritated him like a stone in his shoe. They were none of his business now Frank was himself again. But still they rankled. Moreover, the matter of Sylvia's ghost was unresolved. If he did not lay the poor woman to rest, his failure would pique him for the rest of his life. Would it not leave open the possibility that Maria had been right all along, and that she had indeed been visited by Georgie's ghost?

The hardest reason to admit, and the most powerful, was the living woman, not fifty yards away in the Master's Lodge, who had the power to do far worse than pique him. I am shameful, he told himself, immoral, foolish and mad. If I were a superstitious man I would say she is a witch who has put me under a curse. But in truth the fault is entirely mine.

As Holdsworth came out of Frank's staircase, he saw Mr. Which-cote's footboy slipping through the gateway with a basket over his arm. Holdsworth set off in pursuit.

Two sheriff's officers were standing outside the paved area in front of the Jerusalem gate. They recognized the boy, and called out to him, but he scuttled past and darted into St. Andrew's Street.

Holdsworth quickened his pace. The footboy turned into Petty Cury and threaded his way up to the market, where he bought fruit from one stall and cheese from another. Afterwards he drifted towards the Conduit, where there was always a little crowd. He helped himself to a strawberry. Next, he unwrapped a corner of the cheese with great care and examined it, as though looking for crumbs.

The boy was no longer alone. A tall, thin girl, drably dressed, sidled up to him. Holdsworth recognized her as the girl he had seen with the footboy in college. As if she felt his eyes on her, she looked up and stared at him. She must have said something to the boy too, for he turned in Holdsworth's direction.

Holdsworth abandoned subtlety and made his way over to them. The two children backed away.

"Pray do not alarm yourselves," Holdsworth said quickly. "I mean you no harm. You are Mr. Whichcote's boy, are you not? I have seen you at Lambourne House and just now out at Jerusalem."

"Yes, sir. Mr. Whichcote's waiting—"

"It's merely that you looked hungry and I wondered whether you would care to share a pie with me." Holdsworth gestured towards a nearby pie stall. "I should like a mouthful or two myself, but I do not have the appetite for an entire pie. And it would be a sin to waste what I cannot eat."

The boy looked at the girl. Some sort of signal passed between them.

"And perhaps your friend would like some too. Will you be so good as to choose a pie, as large as you wish, and bring it to me?"

Holdsworth held out his hand, palm upwards, and uncurled the fingers, revealing three pennies and a threepenny piece. The boy's hand swooped on the money. He and the girl went over to the pie stall and negotiated with the woman who was serving. When they came back, the boy held out the pie to him. The girl held out the two remaining pennies.

Holdsworth made no move to take either. "I wish to talk to you," he said.

The boy took a step back and then another.

"Stay," Holdsworth said, realizing he was about to lose him and that, to make matters worse, the lad might report Holdsworth's blundering attempt to talk to him to his master. "Listen to me, it is for your own good." He brought his head down to a level with the boy's and lowered his voice. "I know what happened at the Holy Ghost Club."

Alarm flared in the boy's eyes.

"Does Mr. Whichcote owe you money, sir?" the girl said suddenly.

"No. But I wager he owes this lad his wages." Holdsworth saw from her face that the shot had gone home and he pressed his advantage. "All I want is five minutes' conversation with you," he said to the boy. "And your friend may stay with you and see that you come to no harm. And while we talk, you and she may eat the pie. Can we strike a bargain on it?"

It was the pie that provided the clinching argument. Holdsworth had watched it in the boy's hands. The small, grubby fingers were fiddling at the crust. The smell was rising to his nostrils. A piece of the pie lid came away from the rest and the boy crammed it into his mouth. He glanced at the girl and mutely offered the pie to her. She too broke off a fragment of the crust.

"Come," Holdsworth said. "You will not wish to eat and talk in the middle of a crowd. Is there somewhere nearby?"

They took him to the little churchyard attached to St. Edward's, where they found a corner in the sunshine and away from the gaze of passers-by. The boy broke the pie in two and offered the larger part to the girl. They ate swiftly and with concentration. Holdsworth made no attempt to talk while they ate. He leaned against the wall of the church and thought how like they were to small animals, only partly tamed.

"Your friend will not mind moving a little aside while we talk," Holdsworth said to the boy when he had finished.

"She knows as much as I do, sir."

"About the club?"

"Indeed I do, sir." The girl's voice was more Cockney than Cambridge. "I helped them make ready and I cleared up their foulness afterwards."

"And—and we're friends, sir."

"If you say so," the girl said with a touch of scorn.

"Very well," Holdsworth said. "You know that I am Mr. Holdsworth. I am in the employment of Lady Anne Oldershaw. Let us begin at the beginning and first you shall tell me who you are."

"He's Augustus," the girl said. "I'm Dorcas."

"And are you in service too?"

"With Mrs. Phear in Trumpington Street, sir."

"I begin to understand," Holdsworth said.

The girl said nothing but her eyes lingered on his face.

"Mr. Oldershaw is a very rich young gentleman," he went on. "He has it in his power to reward you well and to find you both new situations. Do you remember that meeting at the club in February?"

Augustus nodded.

"And do you remember what happened in the pavilion? Were you there?"

Color flooded through Augustus's face.

"I see that you do. There is nothing to be afraid of—no blame attaches to you. Tell me about the young girl."

"How do we know you ain't gammoning us?" Dorcas said suddenly. "Maybe she put you up to it."

"She?" Holdsworth said.

"Madam. Maybe it's a test."

"It isn't. Augustus knows I am acting for Mr. Oldershaw and he has no love for Mr. Whichcote."

The boy nodded, but he kept his eyes on Dorcas.

"A guinea," she said. "A guinea apiece."

"What about the situation?" Augustus whispered.

"A guinea's a guinea when it's in your hand," Dorcas said. "A promise is only a promise."

"If you serve me well, you shall have both." Holdsworth took out his purse and laid two guineas on the top of the nearest headstone, where they glinted in the sun. "You shall have these in a moment or two, when we are finished here."

The children stared at the coins.

"Tell me about Tabitha Skinner," Holdsworth said.

He knew instantly, by their stunned silence and their blank faces, that the gamble had paid off.

"The girl," he prompted.

Dorcas sighed softly, as if with relief. "She come from the Magdalene, sir—you know, up in London. Same as me. But she was pretty."

"So are you," said Augustus.

"Mrs. Phear brought her?" Holdsworth said.

"Yes. That's how she does it, see? Brings them up here. She tells the Magdalene Board that she can maybe help place them in service and at least train them up while they're here." Dorcas's pinched little features contorted and became older than their years. "Very charitable lady, Mrs. Phear. The girls have to pretend they's a virgin when the young gentlemen come."

"You mean to tell me that Mrs. Phear brings these girls up from London to be servants and then prostitutes them?"

Dorcas laughed soundlessly, opening her mouth to reveal where her front two teeth had been. "Bless you, sir, the girls don't mind. Not in the general run of things. Half the time the gentlemen are too drunk to mount them, but they get paid just the same. But Tabitha was different—she really was a maid."

Holdsworth turned aside. The smell of the pie made him want to vomit. After a moment, he said, "To put it plainly, Mrs. Phear and Mr. Whichcote procured a virgin to be raped?"

"Tabitha said at least she'd lose her maidenhead to a nice clean gentleman and get a good price for it. Miracle she still had it to lose. She said maybe the young gentleman would fall in love with her and offer to marry her. And then she'd have a place of her own and drive around in a gold coach and I could come and be her lady's maid."

"I saw 'em," Augustus said. "Her and Mrs. Phear, when they come in the coach while the company was at supper. I lighted them down the garden to the pavilion."

"Did she speak to you?" Holdsworth asked. "How did she seem?"

"Didn't say nothing, sir. She was all muffled up, too. Next thing I knows, she's dead."

"Mrs. Phear's dressed as a nun," Dorcas said. She made a face.

Augustus gave a high and nervous giggle.

"Where did they go in the pavilion?" Holdsworth said.

"Little room downstairs," the boy said. "It's fitted up as a bed-chamber, all in white. I had to light a fire there earlier in the day and keep it high. It was all made ready for them, with wine and nuts and fruit and everything."

"Tell him how it happened," Dorcas said. "That's what he wants."

"They were having their supper—and Mrs. Phear comes out of the bedchamber and goes up to the house—and after she comes back, she goes into the room. They were having the toasts upstairs by then. And a few minutes later she sends me up to the master with a note. He comes down and goes in to see them. And then, in a while, Mr. Oldershaw comes running down the stairs and goes in. He was that hot for Tabitha he couldn't wait. Didn't even close the door. That's when I heard the girl's dead."

"How did she die?"

Augustus shrugged his thin shoulders. "She was all in white, and tied to the bed. Her face was funny. Her eyes were open—they bulged like marbles. Maybe she died of fright."

The boy sat down on the grass, wrapping his arms around his knees. Dorcas touched the top of his head in a gesture that was al-most maternal.

"It was just one of them nuts, boy," she said. "That's all. I told you—she couldn't move, could she, on account of being tied down. She choked herself on half a walnut. Found it in her windpipe when we laid her out."

"So then they took her back to Mrs. Phear's?" Holdsworth said.

"They put her in with me," Dorcas said. "All stiff and cold beside me. And I ain't been free of her since."

"She haunts her," Augustus whispered. "Tabitha's ghost."

"It is nothing but a bad dream," Holdsworth snapped. "And you, boy, what did you do after they found her?"

"They sent me back with her, sir. Me and master carried poor Tabitha up the garden in a chair like she was too drunk to walk. Nearly dropped her once. She was flopping about all over the place. We got her in the coach and back to Mrs. Phear's. And when me and Mr. Which-cote got back to the pavilion, all the gentlemen had gone home."

"All? What about Mr. Oldershaw?"

"Not him, sir—he was up at the house." The boy looked up and swallowed. "Mistress was with him."

"Mrs. Whichcote?"

There was a quick nod.

"Where?"

"In his chamber. Master found out and flew into a terrible passion. He locked me in the cellar for the night, nearly froze to death. I never saw her again, sir, not till she was in her coffin."

And then? The upshot of it all had been that Sylvia had run through the streets of Cambridge to seek refuge at Jerusalem College. There, somehow, she too had died. Holdsworth said, "Did you hear nothing of what passed between them that night—Mr. Older-shaw, Mr. and Mrs. Whichcote?"

"No, sir."

"He hit her," Dorcas said.

Holdsworth swung round to face her. "I don't understand you. How can you have been able to form an opinion on the matter?"

"Because I saw the lady dead, sir. I helped Mrs. Phear lay her out. He'd hit her—"

Holdsworth, remembering what Tom Turdman had told him, said before he could stop himself, "On the head?" He touched his temple. "Here?"

"Yes, sir, she'd knocked her head on something. But I didn't mean that. When we laid Mrs. Whichcote out, we washed her all over. The bruises were on the back."

Holdsworth stared at the girl, looking for signs that she was lying. She returned his gaze but any liar knew how to do that. Why would she lie? "Bruises?"

"Yes, sir. The skin weren't broken, not so you'd notice. Just looked like someone tore off her gown and beat her with a stick till she was black and blue."

The Master's illness touched them all, one way or another. Nobody knew for certain how grave it was, and Dr. Carbury had a reputation for being as strong as a horse. On the other hand, no one could rule out the possibility that on this occasion his illness might be either fatal or at least incapacitating.

Whichcote watched as most of the fellows who dined in college found one excuse or another to talk to Mr. Richardson and do the civil to him. They were jockeying for position, he thought, and much good might it do them.

Mr. Miskin, who could not yet be entirely certain of his promised living, told the tutor a good story he had heard the other day about the Vice-Chancellor, and he also recommended a man who could supply the finest eels in the Fens; all Mr. Richardson had to do was to mention Mr. Miskin's name and the thing was as good as done. Mr. Crowley asked Mr. Richardson's opinion on a difficult passage in the *Anabasis* and listened with flattering attention while he elucidated a crux in a way that threw unexpected light on Socrates' influence on Xenophon and his comrades. Mr. Dow wanted to discuss an ingenious scheme he had devised for the construction of water closets for the use of senior members of the college, employing a particularly hygienic and efficient modification that was all his own. Even Professor Trillo, who never stirred from his rooms these days, found the time to dictate a few lines to Mr. Richardson praising his latest volume of sermons and offering to lend him his notes towards a grammar of the Chaldean and Assyrian branch of Eastern Middle Syriac.

Frank Oldershaw and Harry Archdale were also there, exercising their right as fellow-commoners. Everyone wanted to shake Frank's hand, to congratulate him on his restoration to health. After dinner, Whichcote took advantage of the general movement in the combination room to approach Frank under the pretense of drawing out a chair.

"Remember your mother," he murmured. "Her ladyship's happiness is so bound up with yours."

Frank's head snapped round. Whichcote tensed, half expecting a blow. Suddenly Holdsworth was between them, at once helping Whichcote with the chair and nudging Frank towards the other table where Mr. Archdale was already sitting with some of the younger fellows.

Glancing across the table, Whichcote registered the fact that Richardson had been watching the little charade. Ah well, he thought, they would soon dance to another tune. In the meantime it was enough to remind them both, Frank and Richardson, who held the whip hand.

Whichcote did not linger over his wine. He walked back to his rooms. Augustus had returned with the fruit and cheese from the market and was occupied in unpacking his master's clothes.

"Are they there still?" Whichcote asked without preamble.

"Who, your honor?"

"The bailiff's men."

"Yes, sir. They—they tried to talk to me but I wouldn't let them."

"Good."

Whichcote left the boy to his work and went into the little study. The black valise was standing on the table. His first task was to go through the register of the Holy Ghost Club, which went back to its earliest years. Unlike the other records, which used only the apostolic names of the members, the register gave their real names as well, and the dates of their admission and departure from the club. Some of the older members were of course dead. He intended to work backward from the present, making a list of those whom he knew to be alive. Many of them would not be worth the trouble of approaching. He needed only those who had a position in the world, or great resources, or both. Then it would be simply a matter of cross-referencing these names from the register with their activities as Apostles, as recorded in other volumes of the club's archives.

Next would come the most delicate part of the business, writing the letters. It was a risky endeavor, which was why he had not tried it before, but if he prosecuted it with care, there was every chance of success. He would need to consider carefully the individual circumstances of each recipient and adjust the demands he made of them accordingly. One should make it a maxim never to ask for too much, he thought, nor for anything that the donor would not find it easy to give.

After all, one could always come back for more.

He had been working away contentedly for twenty minutes when there was a knock. He heard Augustus answering the door and the rumble of a man's voice. The footboy knocked on the study door and opened it to say that Mr. Holdsworth presented his compliments and wondered whether Mr. Whichcote was sufficiently at leisure to receive him. The foolish boy left the door ajar so Whichcote, looking up, saw his visitor standing at the outer door. For a fraction of a second their eyes met. Holdsworth was sufficiently well bred to look away and pretend that no such recognition had occurred.

"By all means," Whichcote said, rising to his feet. He restored the papers to the valise and turned the key in both locks.

In the sitting room, the two men bowed to one another.

"Are you staying in college now, sir?" Whichcote asked.

"Yes—in the apartments above this, as it happens."

"A charming view of the gardens. Quite delightful, is it not?"

Holdsworth nodded. He glanced at Augustus and begged the favor of a word in private.

When they were alone, Whichcote indicated the chair for Holdsworth. Holdsworth said he preferred to stand.

"No doubt you are come from Mr. Oldershaw," Whichcote said, smiling.

"No, sir, I am not," Holdsworth said. "Mr. Oldershaw went off with Mr. Archdale shortly after you left the combination room."

"Well—that may well make things easier. Some matters are best settled between men of mature judgement."

"Quite so," Holdsworth said. "I shall not beat about the bush, sir—I am here to tell you that you must leave Mr. Oldershaw alone. He has already had to pay too high a price for your acquaintance."

"That's plain speaking, at least. What if I were to tell you that Mr. Oldershaw owes me a considerable sum of money?"

"Then I should say you were wrong."

Whichcote smiled. "I make every allowance for the fact that you cannot know everything your charge has done. But I cannot believe that either you or her ladyship would welcome the truth about him being made public."

"You forget," Holdsworth said. "You are not in a position to make threats. A man who faces the threat of imprisonment is in a delicate situation."

Whichcote flicked his fingers as though brushing the threat away. "You allude to my temporary embarrassment, I collect—well, I don't see what business it is of yours, but you need not trouble yourself for it is only temporary. And I shall not be inconvenienced while I lodge here in college."

"No, sir. Not that. I allude to the possibility of a criminal prosecution. This college would be no refuge to you then."

41

HARRY ARCHDALE had intended to spend the hours after dinner at his books, but he had not reckoned on the unexpected reappearance of Frank. The two young men sat together at dinner and celebrated their reunion with a number of toasts. Afterwards, Frank had a fancy to go on the river and revisit old haunts.

They took a punt to Grantchester. It was warm work in the early evening sunshine. When they reached the village they quenched their thirst at the Red Lion for the better part of two hours.

Frank did not talk about his experiences since he had gone away. Harry did not like to pry. Indirectly, however, they arrived at the subject of Mr. Whichcote and the Holy Ghost Club and found themselves in perfect agreement that they wanted nothing more to do with either the man or his club.

"You know this business with Soresby?" Archdale said as Frank was punting them towards Cambridge. "Didn't you read with him last term?"

"Yes. Not for long—I found it didn't answer."

"He's been reading with me this last week or two," Harry went on. "Devilish clever."

Frank thrust the pole down. He twisted it and brought it up again. "I daresay. Still, he's a thief."

"You don't think there might be some mistake? Mind you, he ran off yesterday so I doubt there was. He wouldn't do that if he was innocent, would he?"

Frank said nothing. He concentrated on negotiating a large willow branch that had fallen into the water.

"And then there's the letter he left for me in the book. Said he didn't do it. Perhaps he didn't."

Frank squinted down at him. "What?"

"You're not listening. Perhaps he didn't steal that Marlowe play after all. So I don't know what to think."

"Do you have to think anything at all?"

"Yes—he was most obliging to me, you know. In any case, if any a man needs a friend, he does."

"A friend?"

Archdale laughed a little awkwardly. "Well, perhaps not exactly that. But someone to lend a helping hand. Like you and that man Holdsworth."

It was the first time Archdale had touched directly on Frank's madness. Neither of them spoke. The punt glided through the weed-streaked water, startling a pair of ducks.

"Ask Mulgrave," Frank said. "That's what I'd do."

"Mulgrave? Why?"

Frank paused, allowing the pole to trail behind them, making a silver streak in the green water. "That's what I do if I want something here. But perhaps Soresby can't be found. Have you thought of that?"

"What do you mean?"

"Perhaps he's drowned himself."

Soon after this, they reached the landing place and walked in silence back to college. The gyp was in Chapel Court, unloading Frank's portmanteaus and boxes from the same barrow that had carried Philip Whichcote's belongings a few hours earlier.

"Mulgrave, you know Mr. Soresby, don't you?" Archdale said without any preamble. "The sizar?"

"Yes, sir."

"Have you heard what's happened to him?"

"Mr. Mepal said something about a missing library book, sir."

"That's it. And have you also heard he's made off? Stole away in the dead of night?"

"Yes, sir." Mulgrave hoisted a box on to his shoulder and took a step towards the doorway.

"Any notion where he might be? Are his parents living?"

"I believe his mother is dead, sir, and his father works as a road-mender somewhere beyond Newcastle. But I doubt if he'd have gone there, sir. There's bad blood between them."

"Anyone else he might have gone to, anyone who might know where he is?"

Mulgrave sucked in his cheeks and shifted his grip on the box. "I suppose Mr. Soresby's uncle might have some notion of his where-abouts, sir."

"His uncle? Who's that?"

Mulgrave kept his eyes respectfully on the ground but he moved another step towards the door, staggering slightly under the weight of the box. "Why, sir, the night-soil man. Tom Turdman."

With the exception of Mrs. Carbury's maid, Susan, and the duty porter, none of the servants spent the night in college. The porter guarded the main gate throughout the night. In theory he made regular tours of the college and never went to sleep, but in practice he rarely stirred from his lodge and often slept as soundly as any-one in Jerusalem. There was one other exception—sometimes the night-soil man came early, by special arrangement with Mr. Mepal, and the porter would admit him at the main gate.

Since Augustus could not spend the night in college, Whichcote had settled that he would pass his nights at Mrs. Phear's house in Trumpington Street.

"You might as well go now," he'd said when the chapel clock was striking seven. "I shall manage very well without you for the rest of the evening—you are all fingers and thumbs. Mind you give

Mrs. Phear my best compliments and be sure to say that I wish you to make yourself useful while you are there."

Augustus walked slowly through Chapel Court, his mind groping for a possible future that did not include his being involved with Mr. Whichcote's ruin. The bailiff had advised him to look for another situation. Could he put his trust in Mr. Holdsworth? If not, how could he even start? His present position would be no recommendation to a possible employer. He doubted that Mr. Whichcote would give him a character. He was without friends, and in a town that was positively crawling with boys looking for employment, most of whom had an uncle here or brother there willing to extend a helping hand.

Lost in his thoughts, he almost collided with two undergraduates who were talking in the arcade by the porter's lodge. As he cowered back, begging the gentlemen's pardon, he recognized Frank Oldershaw and Harry Archdale.

"You, boy," Archdale said. "Do you know the town well?"

"Oh yes, sir. I was born here." In the cellar of a rat-infested building in a court off Green Street. "Every nook and cranny."

"Do you know Audrey Passage?"

"Yes, sir—off King's Lane." Desperation made him cunning. "Not easy to find."

"Will you take us there?"

"Yes, your honor. Now, your honor?"

Frank Oldershaw laid a hand on Archdale's sleeve. "This is Whichcote's footboy. I knew I'd seen his face somewhere."

Archdale blinked. "So it is."

"But I'm looking for another situation, sir," Augustus put in quickly.

Archdale murmured to Frank, "Can't harm, can it? This is something quite different."

"Please, sir," Augustus said.

Frank shrugged. "I pity anyone in Whichcote's service."

"You'll come with me, I hope?" Archdale went on, still addressing Frank. "There's music at the Black Bull on Wednesday and we might step in there afterwards if it took your fancy."

The three of them left the college and walked down Bird Bolt Lane. Augustus congratulated himself—Audrey Passage lay on the other side of Trumpington Street between King's Lane and the Black Bull Inn. He would have taken this direction for Mrs. Phear's house in any case, and she was not expecting him to arrive yet. There was a chance of a handsome tip—young gentlemen tended to be open-handed.

He led them into King's Lane and then turned off to the left. The two gentlemen already had their handkerchiefs up to their noses. They picked their way through narrow lanes, scarcely more than open corridors between buildings, until they came to Audrey Passage. It was a dark and winding alley, a cul-de-sac with a communal cesspool at the far end. The cobbles were greasy and damp, despite the dry weather. The place was haunted by ragged children and scrawny cats.

"Ask where Tom Turdman lives," Archdale ordered Augustus, his voice indistinct because of the handkerchief.

"The night-soil man, sir?"

Archdale nodded. Augustus seized one of the larger children by his ear, who pointed them to a doorway halfway down the passage. The door stood open. The child said that Tom and his family lived in a room on the top floor, at the back.

"You won't want to go up there, sir," Augustus said to Archdale. "Shall I tell the girl to bring him down for you?"

Archdale nodded and the child sped off. The three visitors waited outside. Augustus shifted restlessly from foot to foot. Undergraduates were not popular in a place like this and nor were strange boys. There was a danger they might be attacked. On the other hand, the young men were strong, especially Mr. Oldershaw, and they carried sticks.

The child reappeared and scuttled between their legs into the safety of the alley. A woman followed, negotiating the steep and narrow stairs with caution. The first thing Augustus saw of her was a cherry-red slipper with a pointed toe. Another joined it on the step. Then came the ragged hem of a dark blue dress to which age and use had lent a green patina. At length the whole woman appeared, though she kept well away from the doorway as though fearing the visitors might bring infection into her house.

"Who are you?" Archdale said, lowering his handkerchief.

"Mrs. Floyd, your honor."

"Who?"

"My husband's the night-soil man, sir. John Floyd, sir, they call him Tom Turdman. Nothing wrong, is there?"

Augustus stared at the cherry-red slippers. On the toe of each was a decoration, finely worked in silk, a geometric pattern that reminded him of the carpet in Mr. Whichcote's study at Lambourne House.

"No, not in the world," Archdale said. "I understand he has a—a connection with Mr. Soresby of Jerusalem."

Mrs. Floyd curtsied, as though honored that the gentleman should be aware of anything concerning her husband's family. "Yes, sir—Tobias is Floyd's poor dead sister's child."

"Have you seen Mr. Soresby in the last day or so? I am particularly anxious to talk to him."

The woman stared at the ground. "No, sir. He don't come here. He's a scholar, you see, up at the college."

Augustus frowned at the slippers. They reminded him of something else. He was conscious that all around them were ears and eyes, that the building was invisibly alive.

"Well, look here, my good woman," Archdale said. "Tell your husband I want to see his nephew, and—and that I wish him nothing but good. And if either of you sees him, let me know directly. A message addressed to me at Jerusalem will reach me—you may leave it with Mr. Mepal, the porter. My name's Archdale."

The woman curtsied again and the slippers vanished from view for an instant, masked by the hem of the dress. In that instant, Augustus remembered.

Frank turned and began to move away. Archdale glanced after him, shrugged and followed.

"Sir," Augustus said, with a nightmarish sense that he was about to jump off a very high cliff with his eyes closed. "Sir, sir."

The undergraduates turned back. "What is it?" Archdale said.

"The slippers, your honor, Mrs. Tom's slippers. I swear they're the same as madam's."

"Eh? What the devil do you mean? Which madam?"

"Mrs. Whichcote, sir."

On the first evening after his return to Jerusalem, Frank supped in his own rooms. He had only Holdsworth to keep him company. Archdale, whom he invited to join them, cried off, saying he had one of Mr. Crowley's lectures in the morning. They were reading selected passages from Grotius, he explained, and Mr. Crowley was not always kind if a man made a blunder while construing. Last week, someone had mistaken *merx* for *meretrix*, and half the college was still laughing at him.

"Why?" Frank had said. "What's so droll about that? They sound much the same to me."

"*Merx* signifies an item of merchandise," Archdale explained. "But *meretrix* is a loose woman."

Here Archdale blushed. Holdsworth thought of that hot evening when he had seen Mr. Archdale vanishing into the darkness of the Leys in pursuit of a whore.

So Frank's only guest was Holdsworth. Mulgrave served their supper in the keeping room. It was, Frank said drily to Holdsworth, quite like old times at Whitebeach Mill. Their table was by the window and they looked out over the garden, at the oriental plane and the Long Pond.

There was a feverish gaiety about the young man that evening. It reminded Holdsworth of the night when the two of them had sat by the millpond in the darkness and taken more wine than was altogether good for them.

When Mulgrave withdrew, leaving them to their wine and nuts, the atmosphere changed. It was still light outside, but Frank rose to his feet and made a great to-do of lighting a candle.

"Perhaps it's as well Harry couldn't join us," he said with his back to Holdsworth.

"Yes. I have something I wish to say to you alone. This threat of blackmail from Mr. Whichcote—do you wish me to try to help you? Or not."

"Oh, sir—I will be utterly confounded if you won't." Frank turned his head. The gaiety had drained away from his face, exposing something pinched and desperate underneath. "If he talks about the club, it means ruin for me. And my mother—I believe it would kill her. I will do anything you ask, sir, anything—only save me from this devil."

Holdsworth leaned back in his chair. "Mr. Oldershaw, I cannot hope to be of service to you unless you tell me everything."

"Of course—whatever you like."

"Tabitha Skinner."

There was silence. Frank looked away.

"When I asked you about her this morning in the coffee house, you said you had not heard of her, and then you were very haughty and we left."

"I beg your pardon, sir, I was unmannerly—I acted out of turn, I—"

"But this afternoon I hinted to Mr. Whichcote that he might be in danger of having a criminal charge laid against him. It was a bow at a venture but it struck home. Just as Tabitha Skinner has done with you. Young men drink and gamble and join clubs—that is reprehensible, no doubt, and their mothers will disapprove if they learn the truth. But you fear more than disapproval here, just as Mr. Whichcote does. And I am persuaded that the key to this puzzle is Tabitha Skinner."

Holdsworth waited. Frank came back to the table and poured more wine. He raised his glass and Holdsworth thought for a moment that the foolish boy was about to propose yet another toast. Instead he stared at the candle flame through the wine and said, "If I tell you what happened that night, will you promise not to tell a living soul? And also—" He broke off and swallowed the wine. "I—I know I have not acted wisely."

Holdsworth thought of his own behavior since Georgie had died. "You are not alone in that."

"Well, then, sir. When a man is made a full member of the Holy Ghost Club, it is said he becomes an Apostle and an apostolic name is bestowed on him. I was made an Apostle at the meeting in February. And there is a ceremony that is done on these occasions, a part of the proceedings that must not be omitted. We were sworn to secrecy but I shall break my oath." He looked into his empty glass, which was still in his hand. "The candidate must lie with a girl. There and then."

"So Mr. Whichcote provides a whore for the purpose?" Holdsworth said, after the silence had grown too long.

"Not exactly. The club is named for the Holy Ghost." Frank rapped the table with the spoon, as if to put a peculiar emphasis on the words "Holy Ghost." "And so . . ."

"So?"

"We are taught that when Mary bore the Infant Jesus she was—in a manner of speaking—impregnated by the Holy Ghost." He sat back and at last put down his glass. "Now do you see?"

Holdsworth shook his head.

"Mary was a young virgin, sir," Frank hissed.

"Ah."

Frank recoiled from the distaste in Holdsworth's face. "Mr. Whichcote made it seem—made it seem so entirely a matter of course. Indeed, something devoutly to be desired."

"I don't judge you," Holdsworth said. "I judge him."

Frank began to speak again, more rapidly: "A little room at the pavilion is fitted up as a bedchamber and the virgin waits there for the candidate. She is dressed all in white and tied to the bed. There was also an old woman in the room, though I did not see her properly and I believe she wore a mask. She was an ugly little thing like an old toad in a nun's wimple. I was not meant to meet her—I was before my time, you see, for I was so hot for the girl I could wait no longer. I went in and the girl was lying on the bed, just as Whichcote promised. But—but as soon as I saw her, I knew she was dead."

"How had she died? By her own hand?"

"I saw no wound on her. She was merely—merely dead. Her face was strange—terribly discolored and disfigured. Her eyes were open."

"You told no one of this?" Holdsworth said. "You realize that lays you open to a charge of misprision of felony at the very least?"

"It's worse than that, sir. Whichcote will say her death was my doing, that it was at my hand, and I forced him to help me cover it up. But I swear I never touched her, I never even saw her living face. You must believe me. I swear I did not kill her."

At suppertime, Dr. Carbury stirred. He became conscious and was sufficiently lucid to indicate that he was hungry. First, they got him on to his night-chair. Then they wiped down his stomach, as near as they could judge where the cancer was, with a decoction made from the leaves of deadly nightshade boiled in milk. They changed his nightgown and put him in his bed, propped up against the pillows. He was tired but still in remarkably good spirits, considering everything, and still hungry.

Elinor fed him with a light gruel of oatmeal and butter, and a spoonful or two of a jelly made of calves' feet flavored with lemon peel, cinnamon, mace and sugar. He asked for wine, and she allowed him half a glass. He seemed to enjoy the food, though he brought most of it up almost at once. Afterwards, he beckoned Elinor towards him, closer and closer until her face was no more than two inches from his, and she smelled the wine and the sickroom on his breath.

"Soresby?" he whispered.

"No news, sir. As soon as there is, you shall know."

Carbury patted her hand and said unexpectedly that she was a good girl. Tears pricked her eyelids.

They laid him down and in a few minutes he was asleep again. By now it was quite dark. Elinor left her husband in the care of the nurse. She went downstairs and ordered Susan to take up the sal ammoniac and quicklime to place in the doctor's night-chair to neutralize the disagreeable smells.

Susan peeped through her lashes and asked whether her mistress knew that Mr. Frank Oldershaw had returned to college.

"Yes, of course."

"Please, ma'am, Ben says Mr. Mepal said he's quite his old self again."

As Susan mentioned Ben's name, she twitched as if someone had touched her skin with the point of a pin. It gave the girl pleasure even to mention his name to a third party. Elinor shivered at the thought of what a man's touch could do. It led her quite naturally to the next question, though she already knew the answer to it.

"And Mr. Holdsworth?" she said. "Is he returned too?"

Another shiver, a tiny internal tremor, delicious and disturbing.

"Yes, ma'am, but Mr. Richardson decided it was better not to disturb you so they found him rooms in New Building. And he's not the only one, ma'am. Mr. Whichcote's there too, and the bailiffs are at the gates."

Elinor sent Susan away. The room had grown intolerably stuffy, which did nothing for her aching head. The stink from Dr. Carbury's night-chair seemed to fill the house. She went out into the garden to escape it. There was no one to stop her now: she could walk there whenever she pleased, day or night.

Her eyes gradually adjusted to the darkness. Here the air smelled clean, of earth and growing things. She drifted down the path towards the gate that led to Mr. Frostwick's bridge over the Long Pond. She had in her mind some half-formed notion that she might take a turn about the college gardens.

But before she reached the gate she stopped abruptly a few yards away from it. It was only a trick of the light but it seemed to her that there was something pale moving behind the elaborate pattern of the ironwork: something pale and formless on the bridge itself.

But it was not in the least like a person. Or mist. Or like anything at all. Merely an impression of pallor, fleeting and fluid. There was nothing unsettling or mysterious about it whatsoever. But the harder she looked the less of it she saw, until it seemed to have evaporated entirely.

Nonsense—there had been nothing there. The more she thought about it, the more she thought that the thing—the pallid patch—whatever one called it—must have been a trivial consequence of tiredness acting upon her imagination, and that there had been nothing really there on the bridge. Alternatively there was a simple physical cause, which the science of optics could explain in a flash. It was probably connected with the headache.

For some reason she wondered what John Holdsworth would say if she told him of these absurd thoughts. She shivered again. She was growing a little cold, and perhaps she should make herself eat something. She must keep up her strength, after all, for everyone knew that lack of food could give a person quite absurd fancies.

42

MRS. PHEAR MADE AUGUSTUS work for the privilege of having her roof over his head. He was up before dawn and set to cleaning shoes and scouring pots. Dorcas had her own tasks; and besides she was cross and there were dark smudges under her eyes. "That Tabitha," she muttered as they passed each other in the scullery, "she don't let me rest. Worse than the old cow herself."

Mrs. Phear sent him away in time for him to join the crowd of college servants waiting for admission on the forecourt outside Jerusalem. Early though it was, he found Mr. Whichcote already out of bed. Still in dressing gown and nightcap, he was at the table in the little study with his papers spread out before him. He swore at the boy, but absentmindedly, and set him to tidying the rooms and laying out clothes.

Slowly the college came to life. The bell rang for chapel. The footboy had just begun to brush his master's coat when Whichcote sent him out to fetch breakfast.

With a feeling of release, Augustus ran downstairs. He joined the queue of servants at the college kitchens. After chapel, everyone wanted breakfast at once, some in hall, some in their own rooms. The worst part of the waiting were the smells—hot rolls and coffee in particular—which seduced his tastebuds and set his mouth watering.

There was a tap on his shoulder. Startled, he looked up. Mulgrave was looking down at him, his mouth pursed and nose wrinkled.

"Do you know how to find Mr. Oldershaw's rooms?" he demanded in an undertone.

"Yes, sir."

"Cut along there now."

"But, sir, Mr. Whichcote's breakfast—"

"This won't take long. You won't get served for at least another ten minutes. I'll hold your place."

Augustus hesitated.

"See that?" Mulgrave pointed to the weal on his cheek. "That devil Whichcote did it to me. If you're not careful he'll do worse to you. You don't want to stay with a master like that. This is your chance, boy, so for Christ's sake take it while you can."

"There's not much time," Holdsworth said. "Listen carefully."

They were alone because Frank was still in his bedroom. Holdsworth stared down at the boy, who was standing with his head bowed and his scrawny little body trembling.

"You're in want of another situation. As I told you yesterday, Mr. Oldershaw is a very rich man. He and his family have many servants. He has promised he will find you a position. I don't know in what capacity yet but I assure you it will be vastly more satisfactory than the one you have now."

The boy raised his head. "But what do I have to do, sir?"

Holdsworth concealed his relief. "Mr. Whichcote brought certain papers into college with him. He intends to use them to cause harm. I wish to remove them before he can do so. Do you remember when I called on him yesterday after dinner?"

Augustus nodded.

"He was sitting in the little room when you opened the door to me. I think he was working on these papers then. Do you know the ones I mean?"

"Yes, sir. He keeps them in the little valise. He takes them out when he's writing his letters."

"Letters? To whom?"

"Don't know, sir."

"This valise—I believe I saw it on the table."

"It's got his crest on, sir, and two big locks. Most particular about locking up, he is, every time—the valise and the study door."

"And where does he put this valise when he is not there?"

"There's a cupboard in the window seat. They keep extra coals there in winter."

"Good. One more thing. If Mr. Whichcote forms the design of leaving college, for any reason, you must find a way to let me know." Holdsworth felt in his pocket for a coin. "Here—take this."

He held out a half-crown. Augustus moved as if to take it but then stopped when his hand was a few inches away from Holdsworth's.

"Dorcas, sir?"

"What about her?"

"Can Mr. Oldershaw find her a situation too?"

"Mr. Oldershaw is always generous to those who have rendered him a service," Holdsworth said, wondering whether this was in fact true. "I have already told him of her frankness yesterday. He will find a position for her if she wishes to leave her mistress."

He let the coin fall. Augustus caught it in mid-air.

When Augustus had gone, Holdsworth walked up and down the room. By talking to Augustus and Dorcas, he had inevitably placed himself in their power. But there was no other way to achieve what he wanted. If they exposed him, which was possible, he would become an embarrassment to Frank and to Lady Anne. He thought the Oldershaws would protect him but he could not be entirely sure. On the whole, the great ones of the world had become great and remained great partly because they resolutely placed their own interests first.

The bedroom door opened and Frank emerged.

"I heard voices—how did you fare with the lad?"

"I think you are not the only one."

"What?"

"The boy says that Whichcote is writing letters," Holdsworth said. "He has other victims. The archives of the club are full of them."

"Will the boy help us?"

"He says he will do it. But he's in want of a situation, here or in London, and so is that friend of his. Can it be arranged?"

Frank shrugged. "Cross will see to it. The boy seems obliging. I met him yesterday, you know. I saw Archdale last night and he said I might tell you about it."

"Why should there be any secret?" Holdsworth asked.

"Because it concerns Soresby. Harry has a bee in his bonnet about the man. He asked me not to mention it before."

"Why?"

"He feels sorry for him, I think. Or some such nonsense. Mulgrave tipped us the wink that Soresby is Tom Turdman's nephew. Soresby kept that very quiet, which I suppose is not to be wondered at. And nothing would satisfy Harry but that we should go and ask Tom where Soresby might be. Mepal knew where to find him and Whichcote's footboy showed us the way. It was the damnedest thing, Mr. Holdsworth—Tom wasn't there but his old wife was. And she was wearing a pair of slippers. Just as we were leaving, the boy pipes up and says they were his mistress's slippers."

Holdsworth frowned. "His mistress?"

"He meant Mrs. Whichcote."

"Then surely the boy was mistaken?"

"No. You do not understand—I recognized them too. I chanced to be with Mr. Whichcote when he bought them. The shopman said he had them from a Barbary merchant, and they were very finely made. And of a particular red with a pattern on it. Ricky had been trying to din some Euclid into me at the time and the pattern seemed to illustrate one of the propositions about congruent triangles. Whichcote made quite a joke of it and the shopman said he had not taken us for mathematical gentlemen."

"Are you sure of the identification?"

"Of course I'm sure. I have them here."

Frank went into the study. He came out with a pair of slippers in his hand and placed them on the table.

Holdsworth stared at them. "Where did Tom get them—and when? Have you talked to him?"

Frank nodded. "The boy fetched him out of an alehouse. He was a trifle boozy, but we got some sense out of him in the end. He said he'd picked them up at the back of the Master's Lodge. It was a day or two after Mrs. Whichcote died, he wasn't sure when. You recall that there is a paved walk from the garden door? One of them was half concealed beneath the hedge that borders it, and the other was nearby beside an urn."

The slippers were sturdy enough in their way but designed to be worn in the house or when strolling in a garden on a fine day. Holdsworth turned the nearer one over. The original sole was still there but it had been covered with a much heavier one, clumsily stitched to the upper. Both uppers were scuffed and stained.

"She must have run through the streets in them," Frank said. "Just before she died. Tom had a cobbler repair them."

"Why slippers? Why not something stouter, and a pair of over-shoes as well?"

"I think she was so desperate to leave that brute of a husband that she took what lay to hand—the gown, the cloak, those slippers. After that beating she'd have run stark-naked through the streets to get away from him."

"But still, is it possible there is another explanation for the slippers?" Holdsworth said, half to himself. "Why did no one else see them? Could she have left them at the Lodge after a previous visit, perhaps because they were damaged?"

"I know she was wearing them. Do you hear? I know it."

Holdsworth looked up. The boy's eyes shone unnaturally bright, as if with tears.

"When she came to me that night, at Mr. Whichcote's, I was sitting on the bed in my chamber." His voice was hoarse and scarcely louder than a whisper. "She heard the sounds of my distress, sir, and she came to me like the angel she was. I was weeping because of that poor girl, because of everything. And Sylvia drew my head against her bosom. She called me her poor love and mingled her tears with mine."

Holdsworth suppressed an unkind desire to laugh at this affecting narrative. Trust youth to turn an episode of drunken adultery into a three-volume novel and present it to you before breakfast.

"Then the button dropped off," Frank went on.

"What button?" said Holdsworth, taken by surprise.

"The one from my coat—the club livery. I was still wearing the coat. She and I bent to pick up the button at the same time. Which was when I saw those slippers on her feet. And that was when her dressing gown fell open, and, oh God—and I—"

Frank slumped forward, covered his face with his hands and wept.

Holdsworth no longer wanted to laugh. For where in God's name was the humor in a weeping boy and a drowned woman? Or, for that matter, in a pair of Barbary slippers and a gilt button bearing the motto *Sans souci*?

After breakfast, Harry Archdale paid his usual visit to the Jericho. He joined the knot of men waiting their turn at the door. Tom Turdman was wheeling his handcart on the path beside the Long Pond. Afterwards, as Harry walked back to his rooms, he met the night-soil man outside New Building. Tom stood to one side with his eyes respectfully on the ground.

He took off his hat as Harry drew level with him. "If it please your honor," he muttered in his low, thick voice.

Harry stopped.

Tom held out a grubby square of paper. "Begging your pardon, sir, you let this fall."

Harry had never seen the paper before and he had no desire to touch anything that the night-soil man had touched. Nevertheless he took it. He walked on with the note, holding it a few inches away from his body. He did not look at it until he was back in his keeping room.

He dropped the scrap of paper on the hearth and washed his hands. Afterwards, he crouched in front of the fireplace and picked up the tongs and a pipe spill. Using these implements, he unfolded the note. He was not usually so squeamish but there was something about Tom Turdman's dirty hands that would make a man break the habit of a lifetime.

There was neither salutation nor signature on the paper but he recognized Soresby's neat and clerkly hand.

If you would be so good, pray meet the bearer at one o'clock at the river end of Mill Lane. He will guide you to me.

Harry was suddenly irritated. Who did that man Soresby think he was? It was one thing for a gentleman to feel pity for an unfortunate wretch, but it was quite another for him to be summoned by a filthy billet to a squalid rendezvous with the wretch's disgusting uncle. Why, anyone might see them together. It was quite intolerable.

Elinor heard a knock at the door, footsteps in the hall and the murmur of low voices. She laid down her pen and listened. Then Ben came up with the news that Mr. Holdsworth was downstairs and sent up his name, but he did not wish to intrude, merely to ask how the Master did.

"Ask him to step up," Elinor said.

The servant left the room. She pushed her letter to Lady Anne under the blotter, darted across the room and examined herself in the mirror over the mantel. Her own dark-browed face stared back at her, stern and dreary. The gown she wore was a sober gray, fit for the wife of a man in the anteroom of death. She straightened her cap and pushed a lock of hair underneath it. It made no improvement. She still looked a fright.

Ben announced Mr. Holdsworth. The notion of him she had in her head did not quite correspond with reality, which was unsettling.

"How is Dr. Carbury?" he asked immediately. His time at the mill had left a healthy glow on his face.

"A little better, thank you, sir. You will forgive me if I do not disturb him. He is sleeping now. But I know he would take it as a favor if you would call on him when he is awake. I have told him that you and Mr. Frank are back in college."

"Would he be well enough to receive me?"

"That I cannot say. If you were to call at about two o'clock, perhaps, you should find him awake."

"I am glad to report that Mr. Frank continues to improve. I have every hope that familiar scenes and old friends will complete his cure."

"I shall be sure to mention that to Dr. Carbury—and to Lady Anne." She gestured towards her desk. "I am writing to her now."

Suddenly they ran out of things to say. The silence between them lengthened beyond the point where it was comfortable or even polite. She wished he would not look at her with such close attention, particularly when she was not at her best.

"There is one other thing, madam," Holdsworth said at last. "A matter I wished to raise with the Master himself, but I wonder whether in the circumstances I should confide in you instead. If you would permit it?"

She inclined her head, indicating her willingness to be confided in, but said nothing. The hairs on the back of her neck rose.

"The matter is very delicate."

She drew back in her chair, preparing a suitable snub in case Mr. Holdsworth intended an impertinence. Her caution seemed confirmed when he drew his own chair closer to hers and leaned towards her.

"It has to do with Mr. Whichcote," he said in a low voice. "He is staying in college to avoid the bailiffs and he has certain papers in his possession. There are many people, in Cambridge and elsewhere, who would prefer it if these papers were suppressed. One of them is Mr. Frank. And I am persuaded that the destruction of the papers would also be to the benefit of the college."

"What are they about?"

"The Holy Ghost Club, madam. Whichcote hopes to use them to retrieve his fortunes."

Elinor moistened her lips. "Blackmail?"

"Unless he is stopped."

"Are you sure? It's a grave accusation to lay at a gentleman's door."

"Gentlemen may grow desperate like the rest of us, madam. The papers are in his rooms in New Building. If we can find them and destroy them, then the difficulty is resolved."

"You intend to play the housebreaker?"

"I can see no alternative," Holdsworth said. "I know where he keeps them. But I cannot break into the room like a burglar. It would be impossible to do so without arousing attention, even when he is absent. Besides, the outer doors of those sets are made of seasoned oak near two inches thick. I would need to take a crowbar to the lock and even that might not be easy. Which is why I had hoped to apply to the Master for help."

She frowned. "Even if he were well, how he could help you? He could not be seen to condone a forced entry into a guest's rooms."

"The only way to come and go unobtrusively is with a key. I understand that Mr. Whichcote guards his own keys very carefully—when he goes out, he keeps them on his person. But Mulgrave tells me that the college Treasury contains duplicate keys for every lock in the college."

She stared at him, scarcely believing her ears. "You wish to borrow the duplicates for Mr. Whichcote's rooms?"

"If Dr. Carbury had been well enough, I would have laid the difficulty before him and asked for his assistance."

"But the very idea of—"

"I should not ask you if I could see any other way."

She did not speak. Her mind worked furiously.

Holdsworth leaned farther forward, bringing himself even closer to her. "Madam, I must move as soon as possible if I am to move at all. Would you be able to act for Dr. Carbury? Would you be able to lay your hands on the Treasury keys?"

She studied him, thinking that he was not plain-featured, after all; there was too much force and expression in his face. Part of her relished the temporary power she held over him, the power to make him wait, the power to grant or withhold a favor.

"What would you do with these papers?"

"Burn them, madam. They can do no good, only harm."

She came to her decision. "I know where he keeps the keys, sir. If we are to go into the Treasury unobserved, now is as good a time as any to do it. Susan is out on an errand. The nurse is with Dr. Carbury, and Ben will not stir unless rung for."

Elinor stood up, taking care to turn her face from the window in case her expression betrayed even a hint of what she was thinking, and left the room with more speed than dignity.

She visited her husband's bedchamber, where the patient was still sleeping, lying on his back and snoring, while the nurse knitted by the window. She found the first key in his dressing-table drawer. Afterwards, she went downstairs and fetched the other key from the book room. She almost expected Dr. Carbury to suddenly materialize at her shoulder, his face black with anger, and demand what in heaven's name she thought she was doing.

Holdsworth followed her downstairs and was waiting for her in the hall of the Master's Lodge. The door to the Treasury was set back in a deep alcove. The walls were particularly thick here; Dr. Carbury had told her that they might once have formed part of the monastic church that had once stood on the site. The door was blackened oak, bound with iron. The locks were new, installed last year and as cunningly constructed as the locksmith could make them.

Elinor handed Holdsworth the keys. He unlocked the upper lock and crouched to insert the key in the lower. She looked down at the back of his neck and the thick, lightly powdered hair. She wondered what it would be like to touch it, whether it would feel like a dog's hair, say, or more like a cat's.

The second key turned in the lock. Holdsworth twisted the handle, a heavy iron ring. The door opened inwards. A current of cold and slightly musty air flowed out into the hall. The Treasury was a small, windowless room, perhaps twelve feet square, with a flagged floor like the hall and a barrel-vaulted ceiling. The walls were lined with shelves and cupboards.

Holdsworth looked about him, pursing his lips. "What do they keep here?"

"The Founder's Cup and the best of the plate. Some of it is very valuable, I believe. There will be the deeds for college properties and probably the leases. I think rents are kept here, too, and other sums of ready money."

She made a circuit of the room, treading lightly like a thief and with her ears alert for any sounds in the house. She had not expected there to be so much in here. But she fought back the temptation to hurry for she would not give Mr. Holdsworth the satisfaction of believing her to be a poor, weak representative of her sex, easily driven to hysteria. There was enough light from the doorway for her to read most of the labels attached to the boxes. It occurred to her that she might be the first woman ever to be in this room, the first woman ever to read these labels.

She came at last to the cupboards. They were not locked. The first of them contained more boxes, but the second, to her great delight, held row upon row of hooks, and from each of these hung a bunch of keys. They were neatly labelled, too, and divided alphabetically into staircases and then numerically into rooms.

She looked back at Mr. Holdsworth. "Where are Mr. Whichcote's rooms?"

"G4," he said.

She ran her finger along the rows until she found the staircase G. She unhooked the keys for number 4. She closed the door and turned round.

Holdsworth was nearer than she expected, no more than a yard away, and staring intently at her. Automatically she held out the keys and he took them, his hand touching hers as it had at the garden gate. Despite the coolness of the air, she was suddenly far too warm.

"Madam . . ." he said.

He stopped, still staring at her, and leaving whatever he had been about to say hanging in the air, unformed, full of promise and fear. Slowly his head moved nearer hers. Inch by inch, his face drew closer. Plain-featured? Oh no, she thought, quite the reverse.

There was a knock at the hall door.

They sprang apart from one another. She reached the safety of the hall. "Quick," she hissed. "Close the door. Ben will be here directly."

For a big man, he moved quickly. He was out in a moment and had the door closed. She snatched the keys from him. She would lock up after he had gone. She glanced at her hands and apron, fearing to find tell-tale dirt or dust there. They were clean enough. What about her face, though? Was there some mark there, some clue to the treacherous desires of her heart?

Ben's footsteps were approaching in the passage.

"You called to see how the Master was," she murmured to Holdsworth. "And now you are leaving and I am come down with you to see you to the door."

Ben arrived in the hall, hesitated when he saw his mistress with Holdsworth, and then, at a nod from her, opened the door.

Mr. Richardson was on the threshold. His eyes flicked past the servant to Elinor, and then to Holdsworth standing behind her. He uncovered and bowed.

"Mrs. Carbury, your servant, ma'am. And Mr. Holdsworth too. This is indeed convenient—I find I kill two birds with one stone."

43

THERE HAD BEEN RAIN in the night and the river bank was muddy. Thirty yards ahead, Tom Turdman slouched steadily along the footpath, moving with unexpected speed. He was still wearing his working clothes and a whiff of the man lingered behind him like a bad dream.

Harry Archdale plodded after him. Tom had been waiting at the end of Mill Lane. As soon as he had seen Harry, he had moved off. Harry had followed because he did not know what else to do. Now his shoes and stockings were spattered with mud and he had made the unwelcome discovery that one of the shoes leaked. His clothes were too heavy and too smart: he had dressed with pavements in mind, not country rambles. Worst of all was the sensation that he was making himself ridiculous. But he could not turn back without making himself even more ridiculous.

He paused to take out his handkerchief and wiped the sweat from his face. When he looked up, Tom Turdman was no longer to be seen. Harry swore and set off down the path again, walking more quickly than before. Everything looked unfamiliar. He was used to seeing this stretch of country from the water, not the land.

The path came to a stile set in a thick hedge. He climbed up and peered into the field beyond. Half a dozen cows were farther along the path, at a point where the land shelved down to the water. Two of them were drinking from the river. The others, however, were lumbering in his direction.

Harry was no expert on the habits and temperaments of the bovine species. But it seemed to him that there was something particularly menacing about the way these cows were approaching, picking up speed as they did so and quite clearly taking a personal interest in him. It was also possible that one or more of them were not in fact cows but young bulls that would see him as a dangerous intruder and therefore try to trample him to death.

Prudence was undoubtedly the better part of valor. Harry was about to jump down from the stile and return the way he had come when he heard somebody say his name. Startled, he imagined for a nightmarish instant that one of the putative bulls was so ferociously intelligent that it was endowed with human speech. But then he saw Soresby standing not five yards away, down by the water in the shelter of the spreading branches of a large willow tree, with the night-soil man beside him. Lying in the water behind them was a rowing boat.

"Soresby! What the devil do you mean by this charade?"

He heard a familiar crack as the sizar tugged at his fingers. "So kind, Mr. Archdale," Soresby said in a rapid mumble. "So truly condescending. Would you be so good as to step this way, sir, and into the boat?"

It was an unexpectedly attractive offer. In front of Harry were the approaching cattle. Behind him lay a sea of mud and the certainty that if he walked back he would get even hotter and filthier than he already was. He pointed at Tom Turdman with his stick. "What about him?" Even the mud and the heat were preferable to sitting in a small boat with the night-soil man.

"My uncle's leaving us now, Mr. Archdale."

Tom Turdman nodded and bowed, making a curious twisting motion that seemed to spread from his hands to his arms and then up to his shoulders. The gesture said, as clearly as if he had spoken the words aloud, that he would be delighted beyond all measure to have the honor of drinking Mr. Archdale's health.

Harry dropped a sixpence into the waiting palm. He scrambled down to the water. Soresby crouched, an ungainly spider. With one hand he held the boat close to the bank, while he offered Harry the other. The boat rocked alarmingly as Harry clambered aboard and settled in the stern. Soresby followed him and pushed off with an oar. The cattle had stopped moving and were now eating grass.

The oars dipped and rose. Harry listened to the creaking of the rowlocks and watched the green river slipping past them. Soresby was taking them towards Grantchester. The boat transformed him: the clumsiness and the diffidence dropped away. He rowed as Mulgrave opened a bottle of wine or—and here Harry blushed—as Chloe fucked, with the unassuming assurance of someone who knows exactly what he is about.

"Well, this is a fine thing," Harry said.

His words were rougher than his tone. It was cool and agreeable to be borne along on the water and, besides, he was a man who found it hard to be irritable with anyone for very long.

"I am sorry, Mr. Archdale, I didn't know what to do—who else to turn to. And I thought perhaps—"

"There's nothing I can do. Anyway, I don't know what all the fuss is about. They haven't laid information against you."

"Not yet. But they may at any moment. I wondered whether perhaps Dr. Carbury has restrained them?"

"Jerry Carbury's not doing much of anything at present. They say he's at death's door."

Soresby leaned on his oars and the boat glided into the silence. "That's what I feared."

"You'd hoped he might stand your protector? But why should he do that even if he was well? Oh, I know he took a liking to you before but—well, the fact remains, that library book was in your room. The evidence against you looks black, very black."

"But I didn't do it. If only I could see Dr. Carbury—"

"But you can't. In any case, what could he do?"

Soresby looked up. "Mr. Archdale, may I tell you something in confidence?"

"If you must, I suppose you must," Harry said.

Soresby's mouth was working and for an instant Harry thought he might burst into tears. "Through no fault of my own," the sizar began, "I have in my possession a piece of information. It is of a delicate nature."

"There's nothing I can do about that so pray don't tell me what it is. I don't want to know."

"It's something that Dr. Carbury would not wish to have made public."

"Ah." Harry stared at him, sensing that at last there was a glimpse of a pattern in all this. "Do you mean to tell me that's why Carbury offered you the Rosington?"

"I—yes. But it was not like that, I swear—I did not make interest with him for it—I merely sought an interview and I believe he mistook my motive."

"Very likely," Harry said. "But when you went over to Carbury's camp, you burned your boats with Ricky, eh? And now Carbury's dying, Ricky won't do you any favors."

"But the information, Mr. Archdale. I simply do not know what to do. It weighs on my conscience. Is it my duty as a Christian to tell someone or should I simply let it lie? Or perhaps I should see Mr. Richardson and make a clean breast of everything?"

Archdale sighed. The fresh air was making him hungry. "This information, Soresby—is it of a sort that would damage the college if it came out?"

Soresby nodded.

"Surely that would have some weight with Ricky?"

"Perhaps not in this case."

Harry felt his bewilderment grow. Ricky identified his own interests with the college's. If Carbury died, and he became the next Master, that identification of interests would strengthen rather than diminish.

Unless there was something that Ricky thought was a greater good? Or was this not a matter of deriving benefit so much as satisfying hatred?

He stared at Soresby's pale, thin face, which was sprinkled with muddy freckles like small sultanas. The sizar's expression reminded Harry of a stray dog fearing a kicking but hoping against all hope for a pat. It was true he was an able scholar and a good teacher; if Harry were going to pursue his studies any further, then Soresby's assistance might be useful, though not irreplaceable. Over and above this, Harry felt that he had acquired without conscious volition a sort of responsibility for Soresby. It was as if he had patted the stray dog once or twice and the brute had responded by selecting him as his master throughout all eternity.

"Damnation," he said aloud.

"What's wrong, Mr. Archdale?"

Harry opened his mouth to tell the fellow to go to the devil but, as he was about to speak, he glimpsed a way that might resolve the problem, or at least transfer it. "Look here," he said. "If Carbury's too ill to see you and Ricky hates you too much, there's only one person who can be of any use. Only one person who can protect you: and that's Lady Anne Oldershaw."

"But she's in London, Mr. Archdale, and I—"

"I don't mean you should go to her directly. That wouldn't answer at all. But you could talk to her man Mr. Holdsworth. He's back in Jerusalem with Mr. Oldershaw now, did you know? You may depend upon it, Mr. Holdsworth can tell you what to do if anyone can."

"Good afternoon, Mr. Holdsworth," Elinor said.

"And how is Dr. Carbury, ma'am?"

"He is awake now, and more comfortable in himself. He has just eaten a little soup. Susan and the nurse are changing his night-gown. He asked after you when he woke. I shall ring for Ben and send him to ask whether my husband is in a fit state to receive you."

"Shall I ring the bell?" Holdsworth moved towards the rope that hung to the left of the fireplace.

"No—one moment, if you please, sir. I have been turning over that . . . that other matter we discussed." Elinor paused, and through the open window of her sitting room came the chimes of the chapel clock working its way through the quarters before striking two. "It occurred to me that you might not find it easy to—to dispose of the materials we discussed earlier."

He bowed, thinking that she was a woman of such quick perceptions it was sometimes hard to keep up with her.

"There is a brazier at the back of our little yard," she went on in a lower voice that made them conspirators. "The gardener uses it a good deal at this time of year and Ben too when there are things to be disposed of. Sometimes they leave it smoldering away all evening."

"So if something were burned after dark, say, no one would remark on it?"

"It's most unlikely it would even be noticed. At present the servants hardly stir from the house. When they retire, they are out of the way—Susan sleeps in an attic overlooking the front and Ben lodges in a cottage outside college." She frowned. "Besides, if there were any difficulty, they would do as I tell them."

"And the brazier—is it visible from the college gardens or any of the windows?"

"It's not overlooked at all. It's quite secluded."

Holdsworth had already fixed in his mind that the best time to set to work would be while Whichcote was at supper. Assuming all went well, it would be better to move the valise entirely away from New Building, for Whichcote might well suspect that Holdsworth had had a hand in its removal.

"Well, sir? Do you think it would answer?"

"In many ways, yes, ma'am. But there is a difficulty. I cannot knock at your door in the evening and demand admittance without someone noticing. And to get here, I must pass the combination room or the hall, and Mr Whichcote might well—"

"I have thought of that. I will make sure the gate over the bridge is unlocked, with the key on the ground beside the gatepost, the one nearer the oriental plane. All you would have to do is cross the bridge, open the gate and slip into the garden. If you lock the gate behind you, you will be safe from interruption."

He smiled at her, glad of the excuse. "I believe you have hit upon the perfect solution."

She smiled back, turning towards him, which showed the swan-like curve of her long neck. For an instant she seemed to him not at all like a woman whose husband lay dying a few yards away. The fact they were conspirators brought a dangerous sweetness in its train.

Before he could stop himself, he took a step towards her and raised his hand, reaching for hers. Her face changed instantly. She rose abruptly from her chair and rang for Ben.

Neither of them spoke. Holdsworth stared at an engraving on the wall. Elinor returned to her chair and picked up a book.

When Ben came, she inquired whether the Master was ready to receive Mr. Holdsworth. Shortly afterwards, the servant conducted Holdsworth along the passage to the sickroom.

Susan opened the door when Ben knocked. She had a bundle of dirty sheets in her arms. Dr. Carbury was in bed, propped up with pillows, but he waved feebly, beckoning Holdsworth towards him. His nightgown was very white and so was his nightcap, accentuating his gray skin, which hung in folds from the cheekbones as though the skull within had shrunk. His jaw was covered with greasy stubble, for he had not been shaved since being confined to bed. The nurse was tidying the bottles and pillboxes that littered the night table.

Holdsworth approached the bed. The curtains were open and he glanced out at the sunlit court below, where Mr. Miskin and Mr. Crowley were deep in conversation. People might live and die in the place but Jerusalem itself continued, blandly indifferent. He began to make the conventional inquiries but Carbury cut him short. He tugged at the sleeve of the nurse's gown.

"Go away, woman."

"But, sir—"

"Do as I say." His hand twitched on the bed, digging the horny nails into the coverlet. "You too, girl. Shut the door behind you."

Susan followed the nurse out of the room.

"They tell me young Oldershaw is back," Carbury said, forcing the words out. "Safe and sound?"

"Yes, sir. He seems himself again."

Carbury winced. "What ailed him?"

"I believe that Mr. Whichcote and the Holy Ghost Club had done him no good whatsoever. They had undermined his health and encouraged him to all sorts of folly and dissipation. And the death of Mrs. Whichcote on the very night he joined the club quite overthrew him—it was the final straw. He believed he was in some sense responsible."

"Absurd." Carbury's nails now scratched the freshly laundered sheet. "But I am heartily glad to hear he is himself again. What of Lady Anne?"

"I have written to her, naturally, and so has Mr. Frank and of course Mrs. Carbury. She should have received our letters today."

"I would not wish her ladyship to think ill of us, particularly now." Carbury's head dropped to his chest. His eyelids closed.

Holdsworth wondered whether he had fallen asleep, or into a swoon. He looked down at the invalid. "Sir, there is something else I must tell you. It concerns Mrs. Whichcote."

Carbury's head jerked up as if tugged by a string. "What? What do you mean?"

"A curious circumstance has come to light," Holdsworth said. "I am at a loss how to explain it. On the night of her death, when she was at Lambourne House, the lady was wearing a particular pair of slippers. They were distinctive in color and design. You may recall that when she was found in the Long Pond the following morning, she was wearing only a gown and torn stockings—her feet were bare."

"Well? What of it? No doubt she lost them on the way or they were washed into the culvert that drains the pond. What is this nonsense, Mr. Holdsworth? I do not see the purpose of it. I am not well, sir, not well—would you have the goodness to ring the bell?"

"One moment, if you please." An idea hovered like a ghost in a far corner of Holdsworth's mind: something forgotten? A question to ask? But as soon as he was aware of it, it was gone. There was no time now to pin it down. "Pray hear me out."

"No, sir, the bell, I say."

"Forgive me, sir. I will not be long. The night-soil man found the slippers a day or two later. They were near the garden door of the Lodge. He knew they must be Mrs. Whichcote's. He's used to finding unexpected trifles when he goes about his work, and he makes the best use of them he can. He reasoned that Mrs. Whichcote, their owner, could no longer have a use for the slippers, so he cleaned them, had them mended, for they were much torn, and presented them to his wife."

Dr. Carbury sank back against the pillows and let out a long, windy sigh. "Curious, perhaps, but nothing to be wondered at. Noctambulants cannot be judged by normal standards. The sleeping mind follows its own illogical motions. But enough, sir. I am weary."

"But I have good reason to believe that the lady was not walking in her sleep."

"Eh?" Carbury's head was drooping again. "I do wish you would not go on about it. You are fatiguing me."

"She was greatly distressed. Mr. Whichcote had beaten her savagely that night. That is what drove her to flee to Jerusalem. I cannot believe that she would throw away her slippers. Why should the thought even enter her mind? Nor is it likely that she lost them. Not on a paved path in a place she knew so well by daylight."

Dr. Carbury's forefinger scratched the coverlet and his chin sank down on his chest. In his present state, did he realize what Holdsworth was implying? The gate to Jerusalem Lane was locked. The college itself was locked and guarded. The Master's Lodge and its garden were locked within the college. The gate over the bridge was locked. A *hortus conclusus*, as Richardson had said with a touch of scholarly license on Holdsworth's first evening, within a *hortus conclusus*.

"Suppose, sir," Holdsworth went on. "Suppose that Mrs. Whichcote came running through the streets in her distress, looking for shelter here. She gained entry by the private gate to Jerusalem Lane. And then—"

A gurgle deep in Dr. Carbury's throat interrupted Holdsworth in mid-flow. The head jerked up and down. The arms flailed. The body twitched under the covers. The right arm swept to one side, colliding with the night table, which rocked, sending the tray of medicines sliding to the floor.

Holdsworth tugged the bell so hard that the rope broke. He ran to the door, opened it and called for help. Footsteps clattered on the stairs and in the hall below. Dr. Carbury groaned and lay still.

Holdsworth crossed the room to the bed. He bent over the man lying there and reached for the wrist to feel for the pulse.

Dear God, have I killed him?

44

NOTHING WAS SIMPLE in this matter of Sylvia Whichcote, Holdsworth thought, nothing was substantial. It was like mist or smoke. If you put out your hand to touch it, there was nothing there. But when your hand moved, your own action had the mysterious effect of changing the shape and appearance of whatever it was you had failed to grasp.

In one way, there was consolation in the fact that the problem was none of his. Lady Anne had employed him to act on her behalf. He would hear from her tomorrow at the latest and she would almost certainly command him to bring Frank back to London. Her interest was her son, not the death of a woman she had never met.

In the meantime, Holdsworth made a conscious effort to throw himself into other activities. He dined in college, where he sat between Mr. Dow and Mr. Crowley, and talked a little about the library and its shortcomings from the perspectives of their particular interests. But the main topic of conversation around the table was Dr. Carbury and his illness. Holdsworth, who had seen him most recently, was much in demand as an eye-witness.

"I understand from his servant that they almost despaired of his life when you were with him," Mr. Richardson said. "Were you actually in his chamber?"

"As it happens, yes—he suffered an acute spasm of pain, but fortunately it was brief."

"What brought it on?"

"I cannot say, sir," Holdsworth said. "These things are a mystery to me."

Afterwards, he visited the library and worked on his survey of its contents and condition. Holdsworth had to look to his own future—if the late bishop's collection were transferred to the college, someone would have to oversee the operation, and there was no reason why it should not be him. And why not? Had he not fulfilled his side of her ladyship's bargain and brought about Frank Oldershaw's cure?

He worked steadily throughout the afternoon and the early evening until he heard the chapel clock striking seven. He put away his notes and walked across the court to Frank's rooms. Frank himself was not at home, but Mulgrave was making everything ready for what he called a genteel little supper.

"You're setting three places," Holdsworth said, glancing at the table.

"Yes, sir. Mr. Frank asked Mr. Archdale to join you."

Holdsworth took up a newspaper and settled on the window seat. After a few minutes he heard a gentle tapping at the sitting-room door, which he had left unfastened. Mulgrave was in the gyp room and did not hear. The door swung open.

Whichcote's footboy was outside. He jumped backward as he saw Holdsworth. "Beg pardon, your honor," he mumbled. "He's to go out tonight."

Holdsworth threw down the paper and went to the door. "Mr. Whichcote?"

"Yes, sir. We're to wait till after sunset so the bailiffs can't nab him. We're to sup at Mrs. Phear's. I brought a billet from her this morning."

Holdsworth motioned the boy into the room. "And you accompany him?"

"Yes, sir, with the lantern to light him on the way back."

Holdsworth heard a faint movement behind him and turned. Mulgrave was standing in the doorway of the gyp room.

"What is it?" Holdsworth said.

"I thought I heard a knocking, sir."

"You did—as you see."

Mulgrave bowed.

Augustus stared at the carpet. "Can't stay, sir," he said. "Master sent me out for some wine."

Holdsworth accompanied Augustus to the door. On the landing outside, he said, pitching his voice so low that only the boy could hear, "Are matters otherwise unaltered? Is your master at work in the same place? And does he leave his papers in that valise?"

"Yes, sir. But for God's sake, if he finds me out I'm as good as dead. He must not know."

Augustus pulled back and jerked his head like a nervous horse. He slipped down the stairs, keeping close to the wall. Holdsworth went back inside and closed the door. Mulgrave was polishing the glasses on the table.

"You did not see the boy," Holdsworth said.

"No, sir." Mulgrave continued to polish the glass he was holding. "Mr. Whichcote's footboy." He set down the glass and limped towards the door of the gyp room.

"What's it to you?" Holdsworth asked.

Mulgrave turned. "Nothing, sir. Nothing in the world. A tolerably promising lad, I find."

"I saw Soresby today," Archdale said. "I talked to him."

Frank dropped his fork with a clatter. "The devil you did. So he's hiding with Uncle Tom Turdman?"

"Probably—I don't know. He didn't say." Harry turned to Holdsworth. "But there's something he wishes to tell you, sir. He has some information—I don't know what it is—and he's uneasy about it."

They were waiting on themselves—Mulgrave had been sent away. None of them had eaten much, though Frank and Harry Archdale had drunk a good deal.

"And is this why he's in such a difficulty now?" Holdsworth asked.

"I don't know. But it weighs heavily on him. I—I took the liberty of suggesting he confide in you, as you are in a manner of speaking a neutral observer, and—and you are here on behalf of her ladyship."

"What's that got to do with it?" Frank said.

Harry shrugged. "If anyone has the power to make things right for Soresby, to see the poor scrub is fairly treated, it's her ladyship."

"I am happy to meet him," Holdsworth said. "Where?"

"He begged me to inquire whether it would be convenient for you to call in at Mr. Turpin's Coffee House tomorrow. It is in St. John's Lane, at the Round Church end. He'll be waiting there in the morning between eleven and twelve, and he would be infinitely obliged if you could find the time to see him."

"Ha!" Frank said with a leer. "An assignation!"

Holdsworth said he would see what could be done. "Assignation," an ugly word, made him think of Elinor, not Soresby. He might see her before the evening was done.

The meal proceeded with little conversation. Frank kept glancing at the clock. Harry, who knew nothing of the proposed expedition after supper, made his excuses and withdrew, saying with a virtuous air that he hoped to do a little reading before bedtime.

They listened to his unsteady footsteps on the landing. Holdsworth laid five keys on the table. They were tied together with a piece of string.

"Should we wait, sir?" Frank said in a whisper, though there was no one to hear. "Until it's darker, I mean."

"Too dangerous. We don't know how long Whichcote will be."

"What's your plan?"

"It will be better if I go alone. But would you be so good as to walk awhile in the arcade by the chapel, as if you're taking the air? If Whichcote returns, he must come that way. You will see him coming through the main gate and you will have time to warn me. I am on the same staircase so no one will wonder to see me there."

"And then?"

"And then we shall see." Holdsworth stood up and pocketed the keys. "It partly depends on Mrs. Phear, does it not? How long she keeps him."

"Under the tree?" Elinor said as Susan cleared away the supper things.

"Beg pardon, ma'am?"

"Yesterday you told me Ben took advantage of you for the first time in March. 'Under the big tree.' Which tree?"

Susan, always rosy, became purple-faced. "Oh, ma'am—the one by the pond, the Founder's tree. He fooled me something terrible, he did, said he wanted to see my new cloak—you remember, ma'am? You'd just given it to me, and I'm so grateful, truly I am. So I slipped out in the night, he came over the wall from his lodging and he wanted to touch the cloak, and he was saying it was soft and warm like my skin, and then it was fondling and kissing and sweet words, and then—"

"Stop," Elinor commanded. "But it was night-time. How did you get out of the house?"

For an instant she surprised on the girl's face a smug, almost mocking superiority. "Oh, ma'am," Susan said, "he made me come down the back stairs and let myself out the garden door. He'd left the gate at the bridge unlocked when he was doing his rounds. And he was there waiting for me."

Elinor thought how cold the March night must have been, and how warm their desire.

"But I learned my lesson, ma'am. Next time we tried it, I had a terrible fright. I was there first, see, and someone bumped into me in the dark." She stared at Elinor with large brown eyes. "So I never went there again."

No, Elinor thought, you and Ben used the washhouse in the daytime instead. "Tell me," she said. "The person you encountered in the dark, the person who wasn't Ben. I suppose it was Mr. Frank Oldershaw?"

45

AFTER SUPPER, Mrs. Phear made tea, humming as she set to work. Whichcote sat back in his chair. The curtains were drawn across the window, and the door was shut. He listened to the humming and the chink of spoons on china and the rustle of water into the pot. For the first time in days, he felt tranquil. When all this was done, he thought, he would move to London, and perhaps winter abroad in a dry and sunny climate where money would stretch further. He had had enough of the dampness of Cambridge with its Fen fogs and its dreary, provincial inhabitants.

Mrs. Phear passed him his cup. "You look a little better now. I declare you seemed quite hag-ridden when you came to the house."

"It has not been easy, dear madam. I am like a rat in a hole. If you'd not been here to lend a helping hand I might be still in that sponging house."

She frowned at him, rejecting his gratitude. "When will you send the first letters?"

"Tomorrow, I think. To start with, I have a peer of the realm, a dean, an under-secretary at the Ministry of War and a member of the Royal Household."

"It will take time. No one likes parting with money."

"I have time," Whichcote said. "Too much time."

"Though of course it is not merely money that's the issue here. If this scandal with the girl rears its head, you will need powerful friends who feel it in their own interest to oblige you."

They stayed together for another hour, sometimes talking, sometimes sitting in a comfortable silence. Mrs. Phear took up her embroidery. At one point Whichcote was on the verge of drifting into a doze to the sound of her humming; and when he snapped awake, he was momentarily confused, believing himself a boy again in his father's house, sitting in the little parlor with Mrs. Phear and nodding over his book.

He left the house at about a quarter past eleven, with Augustus beside him to carry the lantern. Inevitably they were obliged to walk slowly because Trumpington Street was ill-paved and ill-lit. Pembroke Lane was even darker and dirtier underfoot.

"You are to return to Mrs. Phear's tonight," Whichcote said to Augustus. "I shall expect you to wait on me in the morning as soon as the gates open. I intend to make an early start of it."

They were passing the dark open space of the Leys on the right. Ahead, and on the left, was the faint glow of the lamp on the corner of the Beast Market.

All of a sudden, Whichcote sensed the presence of danger. Perhaps there had been a sound or even a movement of the air. Something alerted him but the warning came too late.

There were running footsteps behind him. The lantern was thrown to the ground, extinguishing the flame, and rolled away with a clatter. Someone seized his arm. Whichcote swung round, trying to bring his stick to bear, but his assailant twisted the wrist and forced him to drop it. His other arm was gripped and pushed up behind his back.

He shouted for help. A hand clamped over his mouth, strangling the sound. Panic rose in his throat. He gasped for air.

Thieves, damn them, but they would not find much in his purse. How many? All he had seen were indistinct silhouettes against the night sky. Two or three, possibly four.

THE ANATOMY OF GHOSTS

He struggled but it was no use. They held him tightly and dragged him into the field. In the distance he heard more footsteps, but they were running down the street, not towards him. That damned cowardly boy had abandoned him.

Did they mean to murder him?

His attackers threw him to the ground. He was face down in the mud with the taste of earth on his tongue. Someone kneeled on his back, jolting his spine. Many hands turned him this way and that. A rough and foul-tasting rag was thrust into his mouth. He gagged, fighting the urge to vomit.

It was at this point that he realized that these were no thieves. No one had said a word. They were not searching his pockets or snatching at his rings. Then what the devil did they want?

They bound his arms and legs with ropes, tightening them until he yelped at the pain. They grasped his legs and his shoulders, and swung him into the air. They marched deeper and deeper into the darkness. With every step they took, the jolting bruised his body.

Time and distance lost their meaning. He was aware of nothing but pain and fear. They stopped abruptly. A bolt scraped. A hinge squealed. They carried him a few more yards and dropped him. He landed heavily and the impact winded him. He lay on the ground, whimpering.

The door closed behind him. One bolt rattled home, followed by another. His nose pressed into cold earth. There was a smell of pigs. There was no one to hear him, no one to save him. He could not move.

Tears forced their way through his eyelids. What were they going to do? His assailants must have some purpose. They had made him as helpless as a baby in swaddling clothes.

An uncomfortable memory flooded into his mind: Tabitha Skinner, all in white, her face discolored, tied to the bed with her legs apart, and waiting for the Holy Ghost to ravish her.

Elinor Carbury's bedchamber was next to her sitting room. She pressed her face against the window, to avoid the reflections of the room behind her. Her breath misted the glass. In daylight, if she stood to the right, and craned her head, she would be able to see the wall of the service yard and, if she stood on tiptoe, a corner of the private gate to Jerusalem Lane. She saw none of these things now because it was dark.

An orange glow flickered and danced on the wall of the yard. She was almost sure of it. She could not see the source of the glow, only a faint, blurred reflection of the movement of flames.

Elinor was still dressed. Farther along the passage, Dr. Carbury lay snoring gently, wrapped in the peace that only opium could give him. There was a night nurse sitting beside him. She was a sensible, experienced woman who could be relied on to do her duty. Ben had been sent away to his lodgings. Susan was in her attic. For a few precious minutes, even hours, Elinor was as free as air.

She draped a shawl round her shoulders and went quietly downstairs. She unbolted and unlocked the garden door and went outside. She waited on the path, listening, feeling the coolness of the evening grow on her cheek. Her breath was coming more quickly than usual.

She set off along the flagged path. The entrance to the yard was just before the Jerusalem Lane gate, bounded to the north by the crumbling, windowless wall of Yarmouth Hall. She heard the flames crackling as they devoured the fuel.

The fire was brighter than Elinor had expected, shockingly vivid against the darkness. Holdsworth was standing beside the brazier. He must have heard her footsteps because he was looking in her direction. The flames changed his face, making it fiery and fluid, turning him into a devilish stranger. Suddenly she was mortally afraid.

What am I doing?

The fear vanished as quickly as it had come when he came forward and saw her.

"I didn't know who it was, madam," he said in a low voice. "I feared for a moment I was discovered."

She stood beside the brazier, holding out her hands to warm them. Scraps of paper flared brightly and crumbled almost instantly to gray ghosts of their old selves. Holdsworth poked the fire with a stick and the ghosts crumbled to powder. He dropped another handful of paper on to the embers.

"How is Dr. Carbury?" he said.

"Sleeping soundly."

"Does his health improve?"

"Between ourselves, no. I am afraid that Dr. Milton does not hold out any hope."

"I am sorry to hear it. I hope my visit this afternoon did not—"

"No, you must not trouble yourself in the least. Nothing you did or said can have made matters worse."

He did not speak. She watched him feeding the flames. The pile of papers diminished.

"I've something to tell you about the ghost," she said. "But first—did it all go well?"

"It could not have been easier. Mr. Whichcote went to sup at Mrs. Phear's. No one was about. I found the valise where the boy said it would be and left with it bundled in a cloak. While I remember, I had better give you these." He took out a bunch of keys and handed them to her. "Will it inconvenience you to return them?"

She shook her head. "What have you found?"

"There is a book, a sort of club register, that gives the real names of the members and identifies them with their apostolic *noms de guerre*. And then there are two or three other volumes, journals or minute books, I believe, recording the activities of the club and its members. Over the years, each president of the club, each Jesus Christ, has maintained both the minute books and the register. One is of no value without the other. But, taken together, it is quite clear who did what and to whom. There are also drafts of letters that Mr. Whichcote intends sending to a number of former members. They are carefully worded but their sense is quite clear. All he asks from them is their good offices and perhaps a small loan, and in return they may be quite sure that their youthful indiscretions will never return to haunt them."

"More ghosts," Elinor said. "It seems that we constantly manufacture them. We are factories of ghosts."

"These ghosts will soon lose their power."

"Have you read the material, sir?" She moved back from the brazier, and in doing so stepped nearer to him. "Surely there's not been time?"

"I saw enough. I came by Mr. Oldershaw's rooms to make sure we had the right valise and went through the contents. It's vile stuff."

Holdsworth had already torn the pages out of the books so they would be easier to burn. She crouched and took a handful of papers at random. She heard him draw in a sharp breath but he said nothing, and he did not try to stop her. She angled two or three of the sheets at the flames. Words danced before her in the shifting orange light.

"My God! Mr. Whichcote is writing to the Dean of Rosington! He dined here last term, a most agreeable man, and drank tea with me afterwards. And to Lord—"

"Pray throw them on the fire, ma'am."

She let papers flutter into the brazier. She took up another page at random.

"You should not distress yourself with this trash," Holdsworth said. "It is indelicate. And worse."

"I may be a mere woman, sir, but I am not easily shocked," she said without looking up. "This is but a record of human folly and there is nothing so out of the ordinary in that. Women are foolish creatures too."

He did not reply. He stooped and threw more papers on to the flames.

"Who is this Richenda?" she asked.

"It appears that Morton Frostwick, a fellow-commoner at Jerusalem who was the president some twenty or thirty years ago, had a servant girl of that name. Pray let us leave it there."

"Good God," Elinor said.

It was too late. She had turned over that piece of paper and found on the back a sketch, the likeness of a girl with regular, pretty features, looking over her shoulder at whoever was taking the likeness with a coyly inviting smile. Her finger toyed with a ringlet. Underneath was the single word *Richenda*.

"But this—this is so like—"

"Yes." He stretched out his hand for the paper. "You must be growing warm, ma'am—pray allow me to feed the fire."

On the other side of the brazier, the flames made Mr. Holdsworth a stranger: half-silhouette, half-fire, all mystery. *Richenda*. The girl's face and name came together in her mind with certain rumors about Morton Frostwick that had necessitated his abrupt departure from Jerusalem more than twenty years before. She recalled that there was a person still at college whom rumor (and Dr. Carbury) had associated with him. As Soresby's career showed, it was not easy for a poor and friendless sizar to defray the expenses of a University education, and in those days it had been even harder.

"I recognize the face," Elinor said, studying the sketch. "See—do you not remark the likeness?"

"Give it me, madam."

"In a moment. It might almost be Mr. Richardson's sister or daughter. But I know he has none for he told me once he was his parents' only child and of course he is not married. Is it possible that this is not a servant girl at all, or any sort of girl, but—"

"Yes," Holdsworth said. "Pray give me that paper."

"But, you see, this explains it."

"Explains what?"

"Oh—many things. And, most recently, why Mr. Richardson has been so complacent about allowing Mr. Whichcote to find refuge in college."

Holdsworth pulled another handful of papers from the valise. "This is not a pretty business, however one looks at it. I will not make it worse."

She watched him feeding the last of the papers to the flames. She glanced at the sketch. It might be necessary for her to negotiate with Mr. Richardson in the near future and he had no reason to grant her favors. Perhaps this would help tip the balance.

Holdsworth turned aside to empty the rest of the papers on to the fire. To Elinor it was as if he had reproved her, even rejected her, though God knew she had offered him nothing. He took out a pocket knife and slashed at the soft leather of the valise, chopping it into small fragments.

"I do not know what I shall do," she said in a small voice.

She stood with her head bowed and the sketch of Richenda in her hand. She tried not to think of the future. Was not the present enough for anyone?

Holdsworth put down the knife and the ruined bag. He came towards her, making hardly any noise. For a big man, he moved quietly. She did not know what she would do. She did not know what she wanted, either.

The fire was dying. The air was growing cooler as the night advanced. She shivered, though whether it was from cold, fear, desire or a mixture of all three, she could not tell.

"Let me put that paper on the fire for you, ma'am. It will be for the best."

Elinor looked at him. *What are you really asking? What am I choosing?*

He came closer. She saw his face, the skin tinted orange by the light of the dying fire, and the hand he held out towards her. She did not move. His hand closed about her upper arm.

For a long moment, nothing happened. Then she turned towards him like a door swinging slowly on its hinge. His other hand slipped behind her waist. Frowning, she raised her head. He lowered his face and kissed her full on the mouth. She knew this was not possible. This must be a shameful dream.

Her lips moved under his. There was an alien softness there, a warmth, which she had not expected, and also the prickle of stubble on his skin. Anything was possible in dreams. Her lips parted, and so did his. He tasted of smoke and wine and darkness.

She pulled away from him and dropped the sketch on the fire. Richenda, the pretty girl with the coy smile, gained a final lease of life: she glowed with bright colors; she danced in the flames; she curled gracefully; and at last she blackened and crumbled away.

"It's growing cold, madam," Holdsworth said, in a voice so low she could hardly hear what he was saying. "You must go indoors. It would not do for you to catch a chill."

It was only afterwards, as she lay in bed hugging herself and thinking of what had happened, thinking of the feel of him on her skin and the taste of him in her mouth, that she realized she had forgotten to tell John Holdsworth about the ghost.

46

PHILIP WHICHCOTE DID NOT SLEEP. As the long night hours drifted past, he lay in a paralysis of discomfort varied with stabs of cramp that became steadily more frequent and more acute.

He did not know who had attacked him, or why. Did they mean to leave him here to die? Did they mean to murder him?

The temperature dropped lower and lower. A full bladder caused him exquisite unhappiness until at last he lost control of it and there was a new element added to his misery. The bells of Cambridge chimed, muffled and distant, marking the hours of his suffering. He slipped into a trance-like state, neither waking nor sleeping.

A crack of metal roused him. Then another. The bolts were sliding back. He opened his eyes. It was growing light. There were footsteps behind him. He knew there was more than one person because he felt their hands on him and heard their breathing. A dark, coarse material was thrown over his head and pulled down over his shoulders. They lashed the material down with a strap passed around his neck.

They hauled him to his feet. But his legs gave way underneath him and he collapsed. His captors hooked their arms under his armpits, one on either side, and dragged him outside. He lost consciousness from the pain of it.

When Whichcote came to, he was again lying face down. Something was rattling and jolting his body. His limbs were no longer bound and his head was uncovered. The gag had been removed. His mouth was parched and his tongue felt swollen and alien. There was a foul smell in his nostrils and his face was moist.

Iron-shod wheels rattled on paving stones. He retched and brought out a mouthful of sour liquid. He tried to turn himself over and sit up. He called out, "Stop!" but his mouth had lost the habit of speaking and the word came out as another mouthful of thin vomit.

He heard voices and the rumble of other wheels. The cart jolted over a curbstone, swayed and came to a halt. The air was full of nagging voices, as vulgar and insistent as quarrelling magpies.

He rolled over and sat up. To his astonishment, there was a burst of cheering.

"Make way for My Lord Shit in his chariot!" a man shouted.

The cheers turned to laughter and catcalls. Whichcote looked about him. He realized that he was sitting in a handcart in front of the main entrance of Jerusalem College. The forecourt was crowded with college servants, dozens of them, men and women, waiting for Mepal to open the gates. Whichcote put his hand to his head. His wig and hat had gone. His coat was ripped and soiled.

Oh God. He was sitting in the night-soil cart in a pool of excrement before all the world.

All of a sudden the jeering diminished, though it did not die away. Tom Turdman let down the flap at the side of the cart with a great clatter, exposing Whichcote like a freak at Stourbridge Fair.

"Look at his breeches!" a woman screeched. "My Lord Shit's pissed himself!"

The crowd parted, making way for two burly men in black who were advancing towards the handcart.

"Good morning, Mr. Whichcote," said the older man, who had a large red face and a rounded belly that went before him like a great cushion. "Here we are again. I've got four writs against you, I'm afraid. Unless you've the upwards of two thousand pounds in your

pocket, I'm afraid I shall have to ask you to accompany me again to
Mr. Purser's."

Whichcote looked wildly about him, hoping against hope to find
a friendly face in the crowd. He caught sight of Mulgrave only a few
yards away, standing with a squat little man nearly as broad as
he was tall. They were both staring at Whichcote. The other man
murmured something in Mulgrave's ear. The gyp smiled and fin-
gered the red mark on his cheek.

Good God, Whichcote thought, that's where I hit the crooked
little knave. And this is his revenge.

A few paces behind Mulgrave was his own footboy near the gate,
waiting admittance to the college.

"Boy," Whichcote called, suddenly finding his voice. "Come here
this moment."

Augustus seemed not to hear.

"This instant, I say!" Whichcote called. "Quick!"

Mulgrave turned and laid his hand on Augustus's arm. Mepal
unlocked the college gate and swung it open. But no one entered the
college. They were watching Whichcote. This was the revenge of the
servants, the cruellest revenge of all.

"You come along with me, sir," said the bailiff. "We'll soon have
everything pleasant and comfortable."

The sand on the floor needed changing. The air was heavy with old
tobacco smoke. The glass on the windows was coated with pale
yellow-green grime.

A waiter wandered over, wiping his hands on a dirty apron. "Good
morning, sir."

"I am engaged to meet someone," Holdsworth said, looking round
the low-ceilinged room. The place was almost empty. "A pot of coffee
while I wait, if you please, with two cups."

He chose a table in a booth with a view of the door. While he
waited, he took a letter from his pocket. A groom in Lady Anne's
livery had arrived with it just as he was leaving college. He toyed

with the letter but did not break the seal. He knew what her lady-ship would say: that now her son was restored to himself, Holds-worth should bring him back to London immediately.

Why not? There was no longer anything for Frank to fear from Philip Whichcote. The records of the Holy Ghost Club were de-stroyed. Thanks to Mulgrave, Whichcote himself was in the spong-ing house and it was unlikely that either he or Mrs. Phear would be able to pay his debts. If Whichcote were lucky, he might find a way to flee to the continent. If not, if the worst came to the worst for him, he could anticipate only a transfer from the sponging house to a debtors' prison, where he would grow old and die. Better to be trundling a barrow of broken-backed books through the streets of London than that.

After all, what did it matter what had happened to Sylvia Which-cote? The unhappy woman was dead and nothing they could do would bring her back. But Frank Oldershaw was restored to him-self. That was something worth having. Somehow life had to con-tinue. One could not allow the dead to act as a brake on the living.

Holdsworth broke the seal on the letter. But he still did not un-fold it. He had hardly slept last night. Confused memories of Maria and Georgie had jostled in his mind with newer but in some ways equally confused memories of Elinor Carbury, particularly as she had appeared beside the brazier, lit like a devilish temptation by the flames. His own behavior, his own desires, were perfectly vile to him. He lusted after a woman whose husband lay dying. And he could not altogether rid his mind of the notion that perhaps she too had a kindness for him. She had not moved away from him at once. And had not her lips parted a little when he kissed her mouth?

The light changed. He looked up. Soresby was standing in the doorway of the coffee house. He saw Holdsworth and gave a start, as if Holdsworth were the last person he had expected to find. The sizar's face was even more gaunt than usual. He looked not only shabby and dirty but also ill. Holdsworth beckoned him over and called to the waiter to hurry with the coffee and to bring a plate of rolls as well.

"Mr. Holdsworth, words cannot express my—"

"Have something to eat and drink first," Holdsworth said. "Then you can search for the right words."

The waiter, scenting a tip, did not delay. Soresby ate four rolls and drank three cups of coffee. Holdsworth watched, remembering how, less than a month before, he himself had fallen like a ravening wolf on Mr. Cross's sherry and biscuits in St. Paul's Coffee House. It wasn't easy to act a man's part on an empty belly.

"Mr. Archdale tells me you wish to ask my opinion about what you should do," he said when Soresby had paused.

"All I ever wanted, sir," Soresby said in a rush, "was to be a scholar. Why will they not let me? And to come so near to it and to see my prospects blighted for ever through no fault of my own—"

"Is this to the point, Mr. Soresby?"

The sizar flushed. His hands were hidden under the table but he must have tugged at his fingers, for there was a familiar crack.

"I beg your pardon, sir. I—I do not know where to turn, I am beside myself. I scarcely know what I am saying."

"Mr. Archdale says you wish to speak to me. What about?"

Soresby nodded vigorously, and his ragged hair flapped on either side of his face. "You have seen my room, sir."

Holdsworth looked blankly at him. "Yes. You know I have. When I accompanied Mr. Richardson."

Soresby nodded. "Almost all the rooms in Yarmouth Hall look out over the lane. But my garret looks the other way. I wonder, is it possible that while you were there you chanced to look out of the window?"

There were three in the little party that entered G staircase in New Building. Mr. Richardson was there to represent the college. He led the way, followed by Augustus because he was still, in theory, in Mr. Whichcote's employ. Behind them came Mulgrave, who came for his own amusement. Mr. Richardson did not know that the gyp no longer had a connection with Mr. Whichcote.

On the landing, Augustus unlocked the outer door with the keys that the bailiff's man had brought from Mr. Whichcote. Once inside, Richardson stood in the middle of the sitting room and looked about him.

"Mr. Whichcote writes that he wishes you to pack his brown portmanteau. A change of linen, his blue coat and his shoes with the silver buckles." The tutor paused to consult the letter. "Also, the wine in the gyp-room cupboard and his tea caddy. Mulgrave, pack the wine and tea, the boy can do the clothes. Mr. Whichcote also requires some items from the study. I will deal with those."

Richardson took the keys, unlocked the study door and went inside. He pushed the door closed behind him. Mulgrave glanced at Augustus and winked. The weal on his cheek made his face lopsided. Augustus went into the bedroom and laid the clothes out on the bed. He wondered why Mr. Mulgrave had winked at him.

"Boy!"

He looked up at Richardson in the bedroom doorway, with Mulgrave hovering behind him.

"Do you recall your master having a small black valise? With his crest stamped on the leather?"

"Yes, your honor. It was in the study."

"It's not there now."

Augustus looked blankly at him.

"It must be somewhere," Richardson said sharply. "Your master asked most particularly for it. He wished me to take charge of it."

"Well, I don't know, sir."

The tutor bit his lip. "It is most vexing. Inexplicable, too. But he may have put it somewhere else. Under the window seat, perhaps, where the coals go. Look there."

Augustus found nothing but an empty scuttle. Afterwards the three of them searched the rooms but to no avail. Richardson spoke sharply to Augustus as they were leaving and took charge of the keys.

"Take the portmanteau to your master. At Mr. Purser's in Wall Lane."

"What shall I say about the valise, sir?"

"Eh? Nothing. You may leave that to me—tell him I shall call on him."

Richardson walked quickly away. Mulgrave had followed them downstairs. He stared after the tutor, and the weal on his face buckled as he smiled.

"Well, boy," Mulgrave said.

"Yes, sir?"

"You must be in want of a position?"

Augustus nodded. "Yes, sir. Oh yes, sir."

"I could make use of a sharp boy. If you don't mind hard work, you could be a gyp yourself one day." He took a half-guinea from his pocket and held it out in the palm of his hand. "Well? Shall we shake hands on it?"

Augustus stared at the little gold coin. "But sir—the money?"

Mulgrave smiled again, and the weal changed shape. "You do right by me, and I'll do right by you. Come—give me your hand."

On his way back from Turpin's Coffee House, Holdsworth took shelter from a heavy shower of rain in King's College Chapel. High above his head, the fan-vaulted ceiling was dusky with shadows. It seemed an ill omen indeed, that a midsummer day should be so gloomy at noon.

He was not alone, for others came and went and talked among themselves. A beggar was discreetly plying his trade among them, but he sheered away when Holdsworth scowled at him.

Rain, rain, damnable rain.

It had been raining for several days before Georgie drowned at Goat Stairs. One evening, the boy said that rain was God's tears, and that God must be sad indeed to be weeping so hard. Holdsworth had told his son that such foolish thoughts were better ignored and that rain was nothing more than the precipitated vapors of watery clouds. Georgie had laughed at him. He did not believe his father. Maria said Georgie should not play outside, for the rain had made the Bankside cobbles greasy and dangerous.

"Pooh," Holdsworth had said. "We must not mollycoddle the lad."

The chapel was full of noises—footsteps, meaningless words and unattached echoes. He walked up and down, careless of other people and brushing against those who did not get out of his way.

Had he sunk to this? Even Georgie, even Maria, had become distractions from the terrible intelligence that Soresby had brought him. He thrust clenched hands into his coat pockets, pushing at the lining. His right hand touched the corner of a folded paper, the unread letter from Lady Anne.

The letter was no longer important. Soresby's information overshadowed everything else. It lay festering in Holdsworth's mind. It was an infection. A poison. But he had it in his power to suppress it, for Soresby did not understand its full significance. Besides, the sizar was vulnerable, which made him malleable if Holdsworth chose to dismiss what he said as a malicious attempt to curry favor with a slanderous fabrication.

But would that be enough, for surely he could never suppress it from his own memory? Such a course would merely make everything worse in the long run—for him, undoubtedly, and perhaps even for Elinor. There was only one certainty about the whole black business: that whatever use he made of Soresby's information, the result would be unhappiness.

His head throbbed. It seemed to him that the light was oozing out of the chapel, leaving a gray mist behind. He was quite alone. He could not see his way. He was filled with a terrible presentiment of his eternal helplessness.

So, he thought, this is what it comes down to in the end: a man's future haunts him as well as his past.

❧ 47 ❧

T HANK YOU, SIR," Elinor said, hoping her face did not betray her feelings. "My husband is no better, but at least he is no worse. Most of the time he sleeps, or the next best thing to it. When he awakes, though, he is unquiet in his mind."

"That's not to be wondered at," Holdsworth said.

"Yes—but why should he want to see Mr. Soresby, and so urgently? It may be the opium, of course. It can encourage strange fancies, can it not?"

"No doubt that has something to do with it."

She looked sharply at him, catching in his tone something she did not quite understand. "I am glad you are come—there is something I wish to tell you."

But there was a knock on the door and Susan entered with the tea things.

"Are you sure I am not intruding, ma'am?" Holdsworth asked.

"Not at all, sir." She smiled at him and instantly felt guilty, not so much for the smile as for the quite inexcusable happiness that had prompted it. He did not return the smile, and her happiness vanished as swiftly as it had come. But the guilt remained. "Dr. Carbury's asleep," she went on in a colder voice. "I had already ordered tea for myself. It is merely a matter of setting a second cup on the tray."

Neither of them spoke until the maid had left them alone. Elinor busied herself with making the tea. Holdsworth stood up and went to the sitting-room window. It was raining steadily from a sky like smudged ink. The gardens below were sodden and forlorn. The great plane tree blotted out half the sky. She was about to break this awkward silence, to tell him about the ghost, when he turned to face her.

"I am come to say farewell," he said.

"Ah—you have heard from her ladyship. So have I." Her hand shook as she tried to insert the key into the lock of the tea caddy. "She has summoned you back to London—it was only to be expected. Her will overrides us all, does it not? When do you and Mr. Frank leave?"

"As early as we can tomorrow."

"She said she hoped you would leave today."

"We could not hire a chaise at such short notice and, besides, Mr. Oldershaw had already invited several of his intimate friends to another little supper party this evening. He was loath to put them off."

Elinor poured the tea. "He is such a hospitable young man."

"Do you have any commissions we may execute for you in town? Should you like us to take a letter to her ladyship?"

"Thank you—I shall write to her directly and send Ben to you with the letter." After what had happened last night, she could not understand the alteration in Holdsworth's manner, now so stiff and formal. "And you, sir—what will you do?"

"That must depend in part on her ladyship. She may send me back here to continue work on the library. The survey is hardly begun. Otherwise I shall stay in London and perhaps she will set me to work on the bishop's library in Golden Square."

"Then we are both condemned to live with uncertainty. It is not pleasant, is it?"

She handed him his tea. Cup in hand, he returned to stand by the window. Silence settled on the room. She had hoped her last remark would lead to some word of comfort, to the merest hint that after her husband's death there might be some other possibility than at best her becoming dependent on Lady Anne's capricious generosity. However, as so often, when Holdsworth spoke he took her completely by surprise.

"I saw Mr. Soresby this morning."

"What! Is he here?"

"No," Holdsworth said. "He is too scared to return with this charge hanging over him."

"But where is he? I must tell my husband. It will relieve his mind of—"

"No, madam. I do not think that would be wise."

"I don't understand."

"Mr. Soresby's room in college is at the top of Yarmouth Hall."

"And pray what's the significance of that?"

"Because one night last February, he felt ill and in need of fresh air. Despite the cold, he opened the window."

She said nothing.

"His room is the only one in the building that looks to the south," he went on, speaking rapidly in a hard, monotonous voice. "It's the garret above the service yard at the back of the Master's Lodge. One can even see a little of the Master's Garden from the window."

"Not at night, surely?" she said sharply. "Unless it was clear and there was a moon, of course."

He bowed, acknowledging the point. "Soresby could see nothing of any consequence, madam, but he could hear well enough. He heard footsteps and voices below in the garden."

"You say he was not well. Perhaps he had a fever. Perhaps he was imagining it."

"I do not think so. And nor, I think, did Dr. Carbury. After all, by your own admission, Dr. Carbury had already reprimanded you for walking in the garden at night."

She sat up and glared at him. "If you mean to accuse me of something, sir, pray do not beat about the bush."

"Mr. Soresby was referring to the night of Mrs. Whichcote's death," Holdsworth said. "Gradually he realized the possible significance of what he had heard. About a fortnight ago, he took his story to Dr. Carbury, who told him he must have been mistaken. And in the next breath he offered Mr. Soresby the reversion of the Rosington Fellowship."

With an enormous effort of will, Elinor set her cup down on the table without spilling any tea. "I need hardly say that if Mr. Soresby insinuates that I was outside at any time that night, it is either a terrible mistake or a gross fabrication."

"Why should he lie?"

She forced a laugh. "To gain advantage for himself. And it answered admirably, did it not? He's poor, and he sought to improve his situation. I cannot blame him for that. But I do blame him for slandering me, even by implication. And I blame my husband for believing him."

"Madam, I do not believe it was a slander. He said the first thing he heard was a howl that chilled the blood, the cry of a woman in distress. It seemed to come from near the garden door to the Lodge."

"And clanking chains, no doubt, and spectral groans. This becomes more ridiculous with every word you say."

Holdsworth moved away from the window and put down his cup on the writing table. The cup toppled over, and tea flooded across the leather top. He ignored it. She held her breath. She wondered whether he were drunk.

He sat down so suddenly beside her that the chair lurched beneath his weight. He leaned towards her. "I will tell you what I think happened: Sylvia Whichcote came here that night, fleeing from her husband's brutality. She used her own key to let herself in by your private gate from Jerusalem Lane. She came along the flagged path at the back of the house to the garden door. Of course it was locked and bolted. But your bedchamber, madam, is above it. I think she tried desperately to attract your attention—perhaps she threw earth and gravel at your window? And perhaps the cry that Soresby heard was one of terror and frustration when Mrs. Whichcote believed she had failed to rouse you. But she hadn't."

"I find that Mr. Soresby is not the only one with a lively imagination."

"What else would she have done? Having stayed at the house so often, she knew where the bedchambers were. Besides, where else could she hope to find sanctuary but with you? You were her friend."

My friend.

The words burned into Elinor's mind like acid on a metal plate. She stood up, moving so clumsily that she jolted the table with the tea things. "I had thought you had more penetration, Mr. Holdsworth."

He too rose to his feet. But he did not speak.

"I loved her and I despised her," Elinor said. "Sylvia was all impulse and sentiment and vanity. A handsome face or an ardent compliment could turn her head in a moment and fire her appetite. That's why she married Mr. Whichcote. And that's why she flung herself at Frank." She was crying now, the warm tears running silently down her cheeks. "She was such a giddy creature, always chasing after a new bauble. For all her winning ways I think she never really cared for anyone. But she always came back to me in the end. Ever since we were children. Because she knew I would not desert her. She knew me, and I knew her."

She turned away from him and wiped her eyes with her handkerchief. He said nothing. *His silence is a blunt instrument,* she thought, *and I do believe the hateful man will bludgeon me to death with it.*

"Is that all?" she said, turning back to him. "Or does the young fool claim he heard more?"

"Mr. Soresby says he heard movement below—with hindsight he believes it was the sound of a struggle. And later there were other sounds on the gravel path towards the pond. The next morning Mrs. Whichcote's body was found in the water. But Tom T—, that is to say, the night-soil man, picked up her slippers on the flagstones by the house. Not far from the garden door, as it happens."

"Her slippers? What's this?"

"You will recall that no shoes were found on or near the body. Mr. Archdale and Mr. Frank retrieved Mrs. Whichcote's slippers from Mrs. Tom on Wednesday."

"This is a farrago of nonsense. You must see that." Elinor sat down again, because otherwise she feared her legs might give way. She squeezed the damp handkerchief into a tight, hard ball. "For a start, why did neither of them mention these interesting . . . inventions and discoveries at the time?"

"Soresby is a timid and friendless young man. He assumed that some private business of Dr. Carbury's—"

"Private business! Fudge!"

"He is poor and afraid, ma'am. He dared not speak out and risk the Master's wrath. And in any case he did not know the precise significance of what he had heard. As for the night-soil man, he thought the lady could no longer have need of the slippers, and besides no one was looking for them—so why should not Mrs. Tom have the benefit of them? He is convinced that such things come his way as of right."

"I can't believe you condemn me on the basis of such flimsy evidence and from such sources."

"Of course I do not condemn you." He took a step towards her and for an instant she thought he was about to take her hands. "But the evidence cannot be wholly discounted and others may condemn you on the basis of it, even if I do not. Consider, madam—this place at night is a fortress. Your servant's window looks over the court on the other side of the Lodge, and so does Dr. Carbury's. Yours is the only one that looks over the garden. If someone came out to Mrs. Whichcote, they will say, who could it have been but you?"

"And you, sir? What do you say?"

He stared grim-faced at her. "I don't know."

"Well, sir, so now I know where I stand. You have judged me and found me wanting. But now it is your turn: so have the goodness to consider this." Her temper had slipped away from her without her noticing, and she was furiously angry. "It appears that others leave this house at night. In March my maid slipped out of the garden door on at least two occasions to meet her lover, Dr. Carbury's manservant. Their rendezvous was under the plane tree by the pond. On the first occasion, he had his way with her. On the second, she was before her time, and she met someone else at the rendezvous. Or rather he blundered into her. Frank Oldershaw."

"Good God! The ghost? But the cloak—the clasp?"

"The gardener found the cloak the morning after Sylvia died and brought it to me. No one else had a need for it, and it was quite new. Sylvia had not had it more than a day or two. In the end I gave it to my maid. The foolish girl dotes on it. And the clasp was in the form of the letter S, if you remember. My maid is called Susan, so in a way it seemed providential."

"The cloak?" Holdsworth's eyes widened. "The cloak? Madam, I have been such a fool—"

There was a sudden racket outside, footsteps running along the passageway. The door was flung open, and Susan herself was on the threshold.

"Oh, ma'am, you best come quick."

48

THE COMBINATION ROOM was a scholarly beehive, humming with speculations and subdued excitement. Everyone knew that Dr. Milton was at the Master's bedside and that the chaplain had called at the Lodge to read the Order for the Visitation of the Sick, including the Commendatory Prayer for a person on the point of departure.

Mr. Richardson presided at supper with a long and sorrowful face. Afterwards, as they sat over their wine, the tutor took the chair next to Holdsworth's. "I wish to take this opportunity to wish you Godspeed, sir. You and Mr. Frank will leave too early for me to say farewell in the morning. May I have the honor of a glass of wine with you before you go?"

Richardson accompanied the wine with civil compliments about the benefits that Holdsworth's visit had brought to both Frank and the college. Gradually he moved the conversation to Lady Anne.

"I know her ladyship will be anxious to hear how Dr. Carbury does—she takes such an interest in the affairs of the college. And it is wise that she should be forewarned, is it not? It is, I am afraid, more than possible that the prayers of Dr. Carbury's friends will not be answered and that a melancholy eventuality will soon take place—you may even carry the news of it to her yourself. In which case, her ladyship's counsel will be quite invaluable. She has the experience we need to guide our deliberations—the knowledge of the world—and a mother's profound understanding of what is best for Jerusalem—so natural, indeed, in one who is a direct descendant of our Founder."

Holdsworth said he was sure she would do everything that was fitting.

"If you have the opportunity, my dear sir," Richardson continued, "I should be greatly obliged if you would emphasize to her the importance of avoiding a lengthy interregnum in the Master's Lodge. I fear Dr. Carbury has let matters slide during his illness, and the fellowship needs a Master who knows the college, and who can be trusted to direct its affairs with decision. My friends tell me I should allow my name to go forward but I think our best plan is to rely on her ladyship's benevolence. If matters come to the crisis we fear, I am persuaded that we may depend upon her to lead us safely through our difficulties."

Holdsworth bowed, acknowledging what Richardson had said, but not committing himself either way.

"What a sad time this is for Jerusalem!" Richardson glanced piously upwards. "Of course we must not question the ways of Providence. Troubles never come singly, do they? Poor Dr. Carbury's decline is by far the hardest blow to bear. But Mr. Whichcote's misfortunes will have their effect on the college too. Why, the entire University is prattling about that scandalous scene this morning. And outside our very gates!"

"I suppose the unfortunate Mr. Soresby is also weighing on your mind, sir?" Holdsworth suggested.

"Ah! That reprobate! Well, he has gained nothing by his treachery. And if poor Dr. Carbury dies, he will have lost his only ally. *Homo proponit, sed Deus disponit.*"

"Man doesn't know God's wishes in the matter, sir," Holdsworth said. "In which case God must surely intend us to do the best we can with what we have. No charge has been laid against Mr. Soresby. I wonder if the facts concerning the theft are not entirely what they seem."

"I wish with all my heart that I could believe it," Richardson said. "But—well, sir, you were there yourself when his crime was discovered."

"Yes, but the evidence was in a manner of speaking circumstantial. I cannot help thinking that there might be other explanations. For example, perhaps the evidence was fabricated to discredit him." Holdsworth paused, staring into Richardson's face. "By a malicious servant, or some such."

Richardson looked away. "I cannot credit it. Forgive me, sir, this is nothing but wild speculation."

"But there is an element of doubt here, sir, you must admit. And it's a pity to ruin a man's career, simply for a doubt. Particularly a man like Mr. Soresby, who has no resources and so few friends. If the matter were smoothed over, if he were allowed to resume his studies, I am persuaded it would be to the advantage of everyone."

Richardson studied him. "I do not take your meaning."

"No scandal would attach to the college. The gesture would be seen as wise and merciful both within the college and by the college's friends in the greater world. Of course the Rosington Fellowship would be quite another matter—if Dr. Carbury dies and there is a new Master, then he may well prefer another candidate when the time comes. No one could blame him for that."

Richardson shook his head slowly. "I think not, Mr. Holdsworth. I do not think it would answer."

Holdsworth bent closer, bringing his mouth close to Richardson's ear. "Richenda," he murmured.

The tutor turned his head and looked at Holdsworth. He said nothing. His features were unnaturally still, drained of their usual animation.

"I am persuaded that such a merciful gesture would earn her ladyship's approbation," Holdsworth went on.

"But we do not even know where Soresby is."

"I think we should be able to lay our hands on him when we need him, sir, without too much difficulty." His lips moved silently. *Richenda*.

"Perhaps . . . in that case, perhaps we might be able to do something." Richardson leaned closer. "Tell me, sir," he murmured. "A black valise with a crest on it. Does that mean anything to you?"

Holdsworth shook his head. "Nothing at all, sir. Nothing in the world."

Holdsworth did not stay long in the combination room. He went outside, where the rain had stopped and the air was cool and clean, smelling of damp earth. In Chapel Court, he looked into the uncurtained bay window of the combination room. Everyone was at Richardson's table now and listening avidly to something the tutor was saying.

From the far side of the court came the sound of singing. Holdsworth walked towards it. The noise came from Frank's rooms. He could not make out the words but he recognized the tune from that first evening when he had walked with Mr. Richardson in the garden at Jerusalem.

> *Jerry Carbury is merry*
> *Tell his servant bring his hat*
> *For 'ere the evening is done*
> *He'll surely shoot the cat.*

There was a burst of cheering and laughter. Holdsworth hung back in the shadows of the arcade, where a solitary lamp burned above the chapel doorway. He heard footsteps and two young men emerged into the court and walked unsteadily towards the next staircase. The supper party was ending. Holdsworth waited a moment and went up to Frank's rooms. Archdale and the others had already left, and Frank was by himself, sitting by the window in his shirtsleeves and drinking brandy.

"Holdsworth, my friend," he said, stumbling over the words. "My dear, dear friend. A toast, sir. I insist."

"It is getting late, Mr. Oldershaw. The chaise will be at—"

"No, no. Charge your glass. Damn me, you're a fine fellow. Wait till we get back to London and I shall show my gratitude."

"I've found your ghost."

Frank rose to his feet. "Are you—are you gone mad?"

"No, sir. To be blunt, you stumbled into a little maidservant waiting for her lover under the tree, and she was too terrified of the consequences to tell the world what had happened. That's your ghost. That's your Sylvia."

"No, no—you're bamming me. I don't believe you. The cloak, the clasp—"

"Were Sylvia's. You were right there, at least." Holdsworth stared and stared at his own dark reflection in the windowpane by Frank's head. "They found the cloak in the garden on the morning after Mrs. Whichcote died. Mrs. Carbury gave it to her maid. There's no mystery about it, except in your mind."

Frank sat down. "But I was so sure."

"Perhaps because you felt so guilty."

"Of course—first that girl at the club, then poor Sylvia falling foul of that brute of a husband—"

"I don't mean that."

Frank poured himself more brandy and drank it off. "Well, it's all done with now, ain't it? And tomorrow we'll be in London. You know, I don't think I shall come back to the University—it don't suit me, you see, and I don't suit it."

Holdsworth had the sensation that he stood at a crossroads. Behind him was the past, and before him was a multiplicity of futures, most of them dark and unattractive. He felt tired and angry and full of regret. "On the night Sylvia died, someone heard a struggle at the back of the Master's Lodge. Her slippers were later found nearby. She was with someone. I think it was you, Mr. Oldershaw."

"What? You *are* mad. You must be."

"How else could you know which cloak she was wearing? Even the shape of the clasp on the cloak? No one else mentioned it. And of course she would have wanted you to escort her through the streets. Who better to escort her than her lover?"

Frank stared up at him. "You're a fool, Holdsworth, as well as mad. Did you know that? Don't you know I shall ruin you?"

"A witness heard a scream. Was she going to wake the college, Mr. Oldershaw, and make a scandal about her husband? And no doubt you feared what her ladyship would say. She is an indulgent mother but even her indulgence must have its limits. Perhaps you tried to hush Mrs. Whichcote and you succeeded too well. I cannot think you wanted to kill her."

"This is—this is nonsense. I cannot now recall who told me about the cloak—Dr. Carbury, perhaps, or one of the college servants. But someone did. They must have done."

At the door, Holdsworth looked back. He had nothing to lay before a magistrate but a cluster of suspicions. "You kept a cool head," he said. "You must have locked the Master's gate behind you and thrown away Sylvia's key as you fled back to Lambourne House."

Frank was staring at him, red-faced, with the empty glass in his hand. He looked a child again, and on the verge of tears. "Damn you," he said. "She said I must make Whichcote divorce her, and that I must marry her."

"Well?"

"But it was quite impossible. Her ladyship would have prevented it. And besides . . ."

"Besides what?" Holdsworth said quietly.

Frank shrugged. "She was only a woman, after all. She was older than me—she had no fortune—no connections. No, no—it would not have done. You must see that."

"So you killed her?"

"But I—I didn't mean to."

"You attacked her." Holdsworth thought what a fool he had been, for the evidence had been before him all the time. What had Dr. Jermyn called it? *Mania furibunda.* "Just as you attacked both myself and Mr. Whichcote at the mill, and Dr. Jermyn in Barnwell, and poor Mr. Cross. When a difficulty presents itself to you, you are inclined to address it with violence."

"You can prove nothing, remember that. I'll see you committed for slander, I'll—"

"You'll travel alone tomorrow, Mr. Oldershaw." Holdsworth paused in the doorway. "And remember this: you will never escape her now. Sylvia will be with you always."

Chapel Court was deserted. The night was cloudy. Few stars were visible. Holdsworth walked through the arcade and into the darkness beyond. He crossed the wet grass towards the oriental plane and the Long Pond. There had been nothing scientific about this investigation, he thought, nothing that a man could write up in a pamphlet and put before the world. It had been a matter of shadows and nuances, of things half seen, half heard and half understood.

A matter of ghosts?

It was dark under the tree. With his arms outstretched before him, Holdsworth moved slowly beneath its canopy until he came to the bank of the Long Pond, close to the spot where Sylvia Whichcote had been found in the water. He looked through the branches. Lights burned in the first-floor windows of the Master's Lodge. Colors had faded and shapes had become fluid, their outlines dissolving into the gathering night.

Maria. Georgie. A matter of ghosts.

The names formed in Holdsworth's mind. With them came the memories, together with that familiar sense of emptiness. He touched them delicately with his full attention, as the tongue probes a sore tooth to assess its condition. Something had changed during these weeks in Cambridge. Something had shifted. The beloved dead were a little farther away.

There was a flicker of movement on his extreme left, which he caught on the very edge of his vision. He turned his head quickly. The footbridge from the Master's Garden was just visible, a gray curve over the water. For a moment, he thought there was something pale at the apex of the shallow arch—a sort of lightening of the gloom rather than a shape, partly obscured by the handrail. But the more he looked, the less he saw. His eyes were playing tricks on him.

Elinor?

What was he to do? He had wronged her. He had been foolish and cruel. But he could not help rejoicing too. She was innocent. Would she listen to him if he went to her?

While he stood in the darkness, with his hands in his pockets, thinking of Elinor, he became aware of sounds elsewhere in the college. In the distance, a door opened and closed. There were running footsteps in Chapel Court.

He must go to her, he thought, as soon as he possibly could, beg her forgiveness and throw himself on her mercy.

His eyes were still fixed on the bridge. For an instant, he was sure that there was someone on it, someone moving.

Elinor? His heart pounded. Nonsense, he told himself—what would she be doing outside at this time? It must be a trick of the light, a trick of the dark. But still his heart pounded and still the possibility of her remained.

There was only one way to make sure. He walked slowly along the water's edge towards the bridge.

As he was doing so, the college bell began to ring. It sounded strange, as if farther away than usual and filtered through a fog. Holdsworth stopped to listen. The bell tolled on, muted, solemn and sombre. Doors and windows were flung open. Everyone in Jerusalem was coming to unnatural life, as if this were daytime, not night.

But not quite everyone.

A muffled bell tolled for the dead: so Dr. Carbury had gone at last. Elinor was free.

Holdsworth glanced at the bridge. The paleness in the dusk had slipped away.

Author's Note

THE EIGHTEENTH CENTURY was not a glorious period for English universities (by and large they managed things better in Scotland). At Oxford and Cambridge, individual colleges followed their idiosyncratic paths with little to guide them apart from their own statutes, which were at least two centuries out of date, as were the syllabuses that the universities prescribed for their students to study. By the standards of the 1780s, Jerusalem College might have been considered conservative, and some of its fellows perhaps a little eccentric; but they would not have been unusual in this.

Those who know modern Cambridge may notice that there are remarkable similarities between the fictional Jerusalem College and the entirely real Emmanuel College. I should like to emphasize that these resemblances extend only to its layout and aspects of its early history. I should also like to thank Dr. Sarah Bendall, Fellow of Emmanuel, and Amanda Goode, the College's Archivist, for their help. Dr. Bendall, with Professor Peter Brooke and Professor Patrick Collinson, is the author of *A History of Emmanuel College* (The Boydell Press, 1999), which gives an illuminating account of the development and organization of a medium-sized college over more than four hundred years.

The Holy Ghost Club is of course fictional. There are rumors, but no hard evidence, of the existence of hellfire clubs at the universities. By their very nature, such societies can be hard to